S0-AGE-215

# Wild Destiny

## Gina Delaney

**ZEBRA BOOKS**
**KENSINGTON PUBLISHING CORP.**

ZEBRA BOOKS

are published by

Kensington Publishing Corp.
475 Park Avenue South
New York, NY 10016

First printing: April, 1988

Printed in the United States of America

*This book is dedicated to Patricia Rae, the person who caused me to fall in love with "Australia" in the first place, and to Bobby E. Alsobrook, the person who caused me to fall in love with "love."*

## SPECIAL THANKS

I would like to express a special thank you to the following: Wilma Stubbs, of Victoria and Paul Whelan, of Queensland for giving me insight to what Australia is really like. To the Upshur County Library for all their help in getting the books I needed. To the Gilmer High School, especially to vice-principal, Don Peek, for setting up important interviews. And especially to my family, for putting up with me while my thoughts were so completely "down under."

# Chapter I

*November, 1875*

Christina stood dazed and confused as she stared at the unfamiliar surroundings. Although she had no idea where she was, she knew she did not belong there. The elaborate brass bed and the tall upholstered chairs were different from any she had ever seen, the intricately designed wallpaper and large ornate rugs far more elegant than any to which she was accustomed. No, she had never even seen this grand room before; of that much she was certain. So what was she doing there now?

In an effort to clear her muddled thoughts, she pressed her brown eyes closed and shook her head lightly. She needed to wake up a little more before she could even hope to cope with her present predicament, a predicament that was all too familiar. Obviously, she had been sleepwalking again, but where had her sleep-walking taken her this time, and how long had she been there?

Christina sighed and drew her pretty face into a tight

7

frown. Old Dr. Edison had promised her she would outgrow her sleepwalking someday, and she'd honestly thought she had; after all, it had been two years since the last occurrence. But evidently she had not outgrown it altogether. Twenty-one years old and still sleepwalking. There was no doubt in her mind. There could really be no other explanation.

Thinking back over the past few days, she wondered what exactly had triggered tonight's episode. The last time it had happened, she had been only nineteen and just getting over a fever that had swept through her family. She could remember waking in the wee hours of the morning only to discover she was over a mile away from her parents' home, inside Mrs. Sobey's shearing shed, hugging a bullock harness as if it was her last link to life. The doctor had quickly blamed the fever for that recurrence. So what had caused this one? She was not ill. But then it really did not matter what the cause was. What did matter was that it *had* happened again, and as a result, she had no idea where she was much less how to get back to wherever she was supposed to be.

As she thought more about it, she supposed the recent events in her life—the accident, followed by the loss of her fiance and her sudden decision to leave New Zealand and come to the Bathurst district to live in Australia with her brother had a lot to do with this recurrence. In the past, her sleepwalking had been linked to times of extreme duress. With all the uncertainty and change in her life recently, she must have been under a lot more stress than she had realized. Considering everything, she was surprised that she had been able to fall asleep at all with all she had to worry about. And now this!

Pressing the tips of her fingers softly against her lips, Christina tried her best to recall where she was supposed to be. She was still having a hard time bringing herself fully awake, but then she'd always been a slow one to wake up, especially from such a sound sleep.

While she stood in the middle of the dimly lit room thinking her situation over, trying to straighten it out in her mind, she noticed man's clothing strewn about the bed and across one of the chairs. A brown valise twice as large as her own had been stored under the only bed in the room, partially hidden from view by the pale blue skirt of the bedcovers. A white porcelain pitcher with delicate blue etchings sat on a polished wooden washstand with a wadded blue towel beside it. Slowly her groggy thoughts came together enough to realize that she was in a hotel room, an occupied one at that. Then it struck her and a great weight was lifted from her mind, for she was indeed supposed to be in a hotel room—just not this one. She could never afford anything as grand as this.

"Maybe I haven't strayed too far," Christina muttered quietly to herself as she headed for the door with every intention of getting back to her room as quickly as possible. She did not have to be fully awake to realize she needed to get out of there before whoever belonged to those clothes returned.

"Maybe I'll be in luck and find that my room is in this hotel," she prayed fervently and took a deep, hope-filled breath as she neared the door. She wondered what time it was, though it really did not matter. All that truly mattered was getting out of the room unnoticed.

Remembering now that her room was the last one on

the left at the far end of the hall on the second floor, Christina placed her hand firmly on the door latch. As she did, a strange, unsettling feeling crept over her. Suddenly she wondered about her own door. Would it be locked? Her heart constricted. In the past she had taken such careful precautions, even during her sleep. How she hated the thought of having to go downstairs and admit her dilemma to that haughty desk clerk so she could get back into her room. But, if it turned out her door was locked, she would have no choice.

Just as Christina had turned the brass doorknob and had almost opened the door she thought to check her pockets to see if she still had her key. But with one quick glance down to search those pockets, she was horrified to discover she had none. There was hardly even a place for a pocket because, to her mortification, all she had on at that moment were her ruffled white camisole and her bloomers! Why wasn't she at least in her sleeping gown?

Then she remembered her exhaustion from her long, tiresome trip across the Tasman Sea, and then having to carry her baggage over to the Cobb and Company coach office to prearrange her passage on to Bathurst before she dared bother with a room for the night. By the time she had done all that, she'd been far too weary to search her valise for her sleeping gown and wrapper. After she had removed her skirt, blouse, and underskirt she had quickly washed the day's dust from her face, legs, and arms, then had fallen into bed.

"What am I going to do now?" she wondered aloud, her eyes wide with the horror of her situation. She certainly could not go traipsing through the hallways dressed like this, or rather "undressed," and she could hardly stay where she was.

Feeling the color rise in her cheeks, she rubbed a hand over her face with growing frustration and stepped away from the door while she considered the problem further. What on God's green earth was she going to do now? She did not dare go out into the hallway to search for her room wearing nothing more than her underclothing!

Nervously, she crossed her arms across her scantily clad breasts and realized that she had already wandered through the hallways dressed in so little. She blushed right to the roots of her dark brown hair and covered her face with both her hands, shaking her head over the utter horror she felt.

Mortified by the mere thought of someone's having seen her, she wondered just how long she had wandered through the hotel corridors in nothing more than her personals and how *many* people might have seen her before she had found her way into this room. Growing redder still, she also wondered how many of those people would recognize her in the morning.

"Oh, Christina, you've done it now," she moaned and pressed her hands over her mouth while her wide brown eyes swept the room in search of another way out. That was when she noticed the open window. She rushed over to it in hopes she would find herself still on the second floor and prayed that there was a wide and sturdy ledge on which to crawl—high above the street and out of everyone's sight.

Though she was not sure if she had the courage to actually try such a thing, she still felt a tug of disappointment to discover that although she was indeed still on the second floor, the window faced a well-lighted street still full of people despite the late hour. And even if it hadn't been so open to public view, the

11

ledge was barely ten inches wide, was far too narrow to risk climbing out on anyway.

As she peered at the street scene below, she was relieved to remember that her own room faced this same street and in fact the very same mercantile she stared at now, though at a slightly different angle. Her room must not be far away, but even if she dared risk crawling along the narrow ledge, she had no idea which window was hers. One quick glance let her know all the windows on that floor were completely dark, and that left the very real possibility of getting herself rightfully shot by climbing into the wrong window at this hour. No, there had to be another way.

Finally, she turned away from the window to look back at the door. At least now she knew for sure she was in the right hotel and probably within sight of her own room. It had to be just down the hallway to the left. If by some stroke of luck she had left her door unlocked, she might be able to make it into her room without anyone's seeing her. She had no other choice but to make a run for it. But the idea of stepping outside into the well-lighted hallway in nothing but her camisole and bloomers was just too embarrassing. She could not do it.

Then again, the thought of this room's occupant returning to find her standing there so very nearly undressed was equally terrifying. And since the man had bothered to leave a lamp burning low, it was obvious he planned to return shortly. In fact, he could be back at any minute. What if he had a wife? What would she think? Clearly the worst.

Her heart began to hammer wildly as she considered having to face an angry wife dressed as she was. Her eyes quickly scanned the room again. She had to do something, and quickly.

With every intention of bringing the clothes back as soon as she had returned to her room and put on her own clothes, Christina rushed over to the bed and picked up some of the clothing strewn haphazardly across it. As she held up first one shirt, then another, she noticed the tantalizing outdoorsy scent that clung to each garment and wondered only briefly about the man to whom they belonged.

It was obvious he was a large man, even larger than her brother, for the shirts were all huge when she held them up against her own small frame. What would people think if she came waltzing out of a hotel room dressed in an oversized man's shirt? Not much better than what they would think if they saw her running down the hall in her scanties.

Then she thought of the valise. Maybe she would find a dressing robe or even a few ladies' garments. Dropping to her knees, Christina bent over and pulled the heavy leather case out from under the bed and tried to unlatch it, but she found the latch would not budge. In desperation, she tried to force it open.

At that moment, she heard the metal clink of a key being slipped into the lock, and before she had time to do more than look up and gasp aloud, the door swung open and a tall, broad-shouldered man stepped inside.

"What the . . ." he said in angry surprise when his eyes fell on Christina's guilty face.

"I-I . . ." she stuttered. She could not think of anything else to say as she sat helplessly on the floor and watched him spring into immediate action.

Before she managed to produce more than a sickly smile on her suddenly pale face, he had her by her wrists and jerked her painfully to her feet.

In a purely reflexive action, Christina screamed as loud as she could. But she discovered her throat was seized by her sudden fear, and her cry came out strangled. She had never seen a man so angry. Instinctively, she kicked him as hard as she could in the thigh, though her aim had actually been for a higher, more appropriate target. The force of his hard muscle against her bare toes caused her a moment of excruciating pain, but she had no time to notice it. Her attempt to disable the man had merely served to make him even angrier than he already was.

"Why you little . . ." he muttered and twisted her wrists harder. The pain from his grip became so severe it forced her forward and back down to her knees.

"Please, you're hurting me," she tried to cry out. To her dismay, the plea sounded like nothing more than a mere whimper. Yet somehow he heard her.

"Bloody right I'm hurting you," he spouted back at her, his face rigid with his mounting fury. Then with one mighty jerk, he had her back on her feet and tossed her unceremoniously across his bed, facing up. Quickly, he was atop her, a knee on either side of her hips while his hands held her wrists one on either side of her bare shoulders. His thick brown hair fell forward in a sidewards sweep across his forehead as he stared angrily down at her.

Christina struggled to free herself, but the man quickly lowered his weight on top of her, effectively pinning her to his bed, her body pressed intimately beneath his, their faces only inches apart.

Finding it almost impossible to breathe, Christina lay perfectly still, too stunned to move, too confused to

14

fight back. All she could do was stare helplessly up into a glinting pair of narrowed blue eyes and wait for his next move. The gaze that met hers was so angry, so intense, that it sent an icy shudder down her body to her toes.

She did not need any more proof that this man could do her very great harm. Although she was no weakling, he had proven his strength was far superior to her own, and even if she had been a closer match to him, he already had an obvious advantage over her.

To her chagrin, while she frantically considered her choices, or obvious lack of them, his stunning blue eyes broke from her horrified gaze and dipped down to take in the view that the straining white camisole allowed him. She saw his eyes darken with desire and then realized just *how* great a harm he could do her.

"Did you really think I would keep it here in my room?" he asked, his voice deep with the powerful emotions that clashed inside of him. His face was so close to hers that his breath felt warm and moist against her cheek. Then he leaned even closer and she was able to smell that same outdoorsy scent, a strange blend of eucalyptus and tobacco, she had noticed earlier.

"I-I don't know what you are talking about. I got in here by mistake," she said the moment she had enough breath to speak again. Aware of how badly her voice had quaked beneath the force of his penetrating gaze, she tried to swallow in an effort to steady it, but found she could not. Her fear would not let her.

"Of course you did," he replied with obvious sarcasm. "And right after you happened into this carefully locked room by mistake, you just accidentally started to go through my things."

"Not exactly," she said in a voice so weak she could

barely hear it herself. She started to panic. How could she explain it so that he would understand? Now that she had learned his door had been locked, she didn't fully understand herself. Another brave look into his glittering eyes made her realize it would not be easy to get such an angry man even to listen, but then again, she had to try. Somehow she had to make him believe her. "Please, listen to me. I had a reason for going through your things."

"I'll just bet you did," he muttered, then nodded slowly. His eyes again raked boldly first over her face, then down to where his own weight pressed against her body and caused her creamy white breasts to swell high above the ruffled edge of her camisole. He laughed sardonically as he considered the situation further.

Despite the harshness in his facial expression and the fury that glowed from his stark blue eyes, at that moment Christina realized that he was an incredibly handsome man. But he was also a tremendously strong man—and one who could hurt her if she did not do something quickly to convince him of her innocence.

"I do. I do have a reason for going through your things." She could feel her pulse pounding in her throat as she tried again to swallow.

"I can just guess what that reason might be," he quipped and produced just enough of a sarcastic smile to form long, narrow dimples in his hard, lean cheeks. "Judging by the way you are dressed, my pretty little lass, I think you originally intended to have a go at seducing me into letting you stay the night in my bed. Aye, then you would be able to search for it while I slept. Maybe you were even hoping to get me good and drunk to assure I wouldn't wake and catch you. Isn't that how your type usually does it? But then, when I didn't answer the door, you realized I was out and chose to alter your plans a bit. That's when you decided to enter my room through that window I well remember closing and not even bother to wait around to seduce me after all. Quite daring, I must say. It's a pity you are so impatient."

Christina's brown eyes grew wide with outrage as she realized what he had implied. "How dare you suggest such a thing! I am not that sort of woman!"

There was so much indignation in her dark angry eyes that it caused the man a moment of doubt. Her haughty speech indicated true propriety. Yet her dress, or rather her lack of it, and her rummaging around in his room, obviously in search of his evening's winnings and Saturday's pay docket money, clearly marked her as a thief and a harlot. He was truly amazed by her acting abilities.

"I am not a common thief!"

A smile spread slowly across his face while he studied the beauty trapped beneath him. Her long brown hair formed shimmering waves across the pillow and splashed down wildly across her lovely white shoulders. "No, I quite agree. There is nothing common about you. Nothing at all. In truth, I find you to be quite an exquisite thief. You are extremely beautiful. I wish I'd gotten back in time for your seduction scene. It just might have been worth all my winnings and the entire payroll to have a woman as beautiful and as full of fire as you try to seduce me. In fact, you might yet find yourself with some of my money. Do a good job of it and I promise to reward you handsomely."

All Christina could do was gasp with further indignation at what he had suggested. If her hands had not been pinned, she would have slapped him just as hard as she could.

"Darlin', you wouldn't have found the money in this room anyway," he went on to say as his devilish smile deepened. "I carried it straight to the desk clerk and had it placed in the hotel safe, for obvious reasons. But I will gladly go down and get part of it for a wild night of passion with a tigress like you." Then, without giving her a chance to respond to his outrageous words, he lowered his lips to hers and kissed her hungrily. His mouth pressed hard and demanding against hers, causing her teeth to bite into the soft flesh inside her lips. She wanted to cry out her pain, but the sound was lost in her throat.

Tossing her head frantically, she tried her best to tear her mouth away from his, but he held her so securely that no matter which way she turned her head, his mouth managed to follow. Then as she wondered if she should dare try to scream again for help, *if* she could ever manage to get her lips free from his, the kiss suddenly softened and his strong grip on her wrists eased. He was obviously becoming more involved in what he was doing and she realized that could be to her advantage.

Slowly, his hand slid down her silken arms to her elbows. Then he moved his fingertips lightly across the thin material of her camisole. To her amazement and utter disbelief, she felt herself starting to respond not only to his powerful kiss but also to the intimate way his hands had come between them and gently stroked the outer curve of her breasts. Despite her brain's loud cry for her to try again to escape, she could not. As he worked his strange, evil magic, icy-hot tingles spread through her, causing tiny bumps to form under her skin, and she lay immobile, allowing him to continue.

She was mortified by her own behavior. How could she let a total stranger do such things to her, a man who had accused her of being nothing more than a—a common whore? That thought was just enough to rekindle her anger and, gave her the strength to fight him, to try and save whatever was left of her virtue.

Just as his hand went to one of the tiny silken ties at the top of her camisole, she moved her own hands between them in a pretense of wanting to explore his body the same way he was now exploring hers. She willed herself not to become intrigued with the hardness of his muscles or the gentle heat of his body that seeped right through the soft material of his shirt.

While his attention was focused on untying the shiny white ribbon over her left shoulder, she turned her palms against his chest and gently massaged him. She waited only a few moments more, then shoved with all her might, tossing him over the edge of the bed and to the floor.

Without looking back to see where he had landed, she made a wild dash for the door, clutching at the drooping left side of her camisole as she ran. She could hear movement behind her and knew he had wasted no time in getting up. After fumbling frantically with the latch, then the knob, she finally managed to get the door open. But before she had made good her escape, his arm appeared around her waist and she was quickly jerked back inside.

"No, you don't. You're not going anywhere," he told her as he slammed the door shut again. His anger had returned to mingle with his passion as he stepped forward, easily trapping her against the cold, hard surface of the door. Pressing his length against her, leaving his hands free to roam, he dipped his head and took another fiery kiss. At the same moment, his hand slid up to untie the other pair of silken straps.

"So you want to play games?" he said in a low, raspy voice. Though he had pulled away enough to be able to speak, his mouth remained close enough to allow the tip of his tongue to snake out and gently tease the sensitive edge of her lower lip. He seemed to take extreme pleasure in her shivering response.

"No, you don't understand," she tried again to explain, but she found her words cut short by another devouring kiss.

Suddenly aware that he had succeeded in untying both sides of her camisole, she tried to grab the garment, but to her horror, he captured her hands and yanked them high above her head. As he took a step back, still holding her hands, the camisole dropped to her waist, giving him a full and delightful view of her heaving breasts. She tried again to free her hands to cover herself, but couldn't. He was too strong.

"You may be having second thoughts, darlin', but you are getting just what you deserve. Maybe next time you will think a little more carefully before setting out to rob a man," he said as a wicked smile spread across his face.

Aware of the hungry look in his eyes as he stared down again at the glory revealed to him, Christina tried again to wrench herself from his grasp, but he held tight. Her movements only seemed to arouse him more for he quickly explored the softness of her breasts with his mouth. She gasped in horror at the fiery sensations that shot through her body as he suckled first one breast, then

20

the other. Never had she felt anything like it, and it frightened her more.

"Please, mister, listen to me," she pleaded. Her legs were rapidly growing weak and she could not seem to breathe. Her eyes wanted to flutter shut so that her other senses could have full reign. Terrified by what was about to happen, she knew she had to get him to listen to her while she still had the strength to talk. "It's not what you think."

But he did not answer her. Instead he continued to suckle hungrily at her breasts while he transferred both her hands into one of his and allowed his other one to slide down into her bloomers and tease the soft skin across her stomach. Realizing he was totally absorbed in his own actions, she jerked her hands as hard as she could. To her relief, they came easily out of his grasp. She shoved him away and brought her knee up hard.

This time her aim had been true, and he doubled over from the pain. She grabbed the latch, twisted it until it clicked, turned the knob, then fled from the room. She was glad to find no one in the hallway as she clutched the thin material of her camisole to her breasts and ran as fast as she could toward her own room.

Relief flooded her when she finally reached her door and discovered that although it was indeed locked, it had not been pulled completely closed. A brief backward glance proved that the man was not, as of yet, in pursuit of her. Once inside her room, she wasted no time in locking the door and turned to rearrange the furniture quickly so that most of it rested firmly against the only door.

Quivering from the very real danger of what might happen next, she hurriedly dressed, then sat down on the

21

side of her bed with her parasol across her lap to wait for the assault that was surely to come.

Waiting was all she could do. She certainly could not go for help. The man might be right outside her door. And she didn't dare report him for what he had tried to do— and had very nearly accomplished. It would surely come out that she had been in his room without permission, dressed only in her undergarments, and had been caught going through his things. The facts could not get any more incriminating than that. No, she would have to face this problem alone. Her only hope was somehow to keep herself safe until the overland coach left Sydney early the following morning.

# Chapter II

Christina did not sleep again that night. The fear of the man's finding out which room was hers and trying to crash through the door was more than enough to keep her awake. But that, coupled with the very real possibility that she might sleepwalk again, removed any possibility of sleep for the night. The thought of sleepwalking again and somehow managing to move all that furniture and get out into the hall before she could wake up was especially terrifying.

As a result, she refused to lie down and paced the small area of floor around her bed several times during the night in order to keep her eyes wide open and her mind alert.

Somehow she managed to keep awake and to stay safely tucked away in her room until it was almost time for the coach to leave Sydney. Because she had left most of her baggage at the coach office the day before for it to be loaded as soon as the coach arrived, and since she already had her ticket, she had no reason to leave early. All she had to do was get the one valise she still had with her onto the coach, and that posed no problem.

The thought occurred to her that if she had been willing to spend more and travel part of the way by train, she might already be gone and none of this would have happened. After all, she had over four hundred dollars saved. Then again she might have been in a train accident by now, the way her luck was going.

After the sun finally gave light to another warm and clear day, Christina began to check her father's watch every few minutes, anxious for the time to come for her to hurry to the coach office. She wanted no opportunity for a run in with that horrible man from last night and she shivered at the thought of what those angry blue eyes must look like in the daylight.

As she kept a careful eye on her watch, she decided to wait until the very last minute to return her key to the desk downstairs, then hurry on down the street to Cobb and Company. If she timed it just right, she would be able to climb into the coach only moments before it departed. She did not dare risk having to wait around at the station. Not when that man could be just about anywhere.

When the time finally came for Christina to leave her room, she did so with extreme caution. Having moved the furniture out of the way only minutes before, she carefully secured her brown beribboned bonnet that matched her dark brown dress and would keep the road dust from her hair. Then she slowly and carefully eased the door open wide enough to let her see out into the hallway. Luckily her door opened toward his end of the hall. To her relief the only person in sight was another woman, an older woman, who stood waiting beside a large trunk, glancing impatiently toward the nearby stairway, her slippered foot tapping on the bare wood floor.

"Good day," Christina said as she stepped out into the hallway and saw the woman glance in her direction.

"Good day." The woman nodded back with a cheerful smile. "And a fine day it is. I just wish the baggage boy would hurry up here and get my trunk so I could be out there enjoying such a beautiful morning."

Just then the loud clomping of someone coming up the stairs in a not too hurried pace caught both their attention. As Christina watched the top of the stairs, she hoped with all her heart that it would be the baggage boy coming for the woman's trunk and not a tall, handsome stranger headed for the room she now stood only a few feet in front of. Not proceeding any further down the hall until she knew for sure, she held her breath and waited, so relieved she felt weak when she caught sight of the short, squatty man in his braided red uniform.

Ready now to be on her way again, Christina nodded first to the woman in a friendly gesture of passing, then to the man who had paused near the top of the stairs looking as if he could not decide which of these two women he had been sent to help. When he bent sideways to take Christina's valise from her hands as she came near, she smiled and directed him to the other woman.

She thought about hanging back with those two in hopes that she would be safer with them, but realized she had waited too long in her room to allow herself to dawdle now. Taking a deep breath, she continued on her way alone.

To her relief, the man she feared she might run into was not among those milling about the lobby. Hurriedly, she walked over to the desk and handed the clerk her key, then turned on her heel and headed out the door and to her right, her valise causing her to tilt slightly to one side as she walked.

Several men offered to help her with her load, but she was in too much of a hurry. She barely had enough time to make it to her coach before it pulled away and headed out of town. Though she kindly thanked each of the men who offered assistance, she never paused a moment in her brisk pace along the crowded walkway.

Then she saw him. He had just come out of a tobacco shop with a small package in his hands, looking very dignified in a dark blue cutaway coat with shining black Hessian boots and well-cut white breeches. Realizing her danger, she froze in the middle of the sidewalk and quickly considered what she should do next. He had not yet spotted her, but he stood directly between her and the coach office. She did not dare miss that coach. Having already sent a letter ahead to her brother detailing her plans, she knew he would worry himself sick if she did not get off when it reached Bathurst. But she also did not dare risk trying to slip by that man with any foolish hopes of going unnoticed.

The only solution was to turn around, make the block, and pray that she could walk fast enough to get to the station before her coach left. As she glanced beyond the man, she noticed that the coach stood in front of the office and already had the baggage strapped securely to the top. There near the front was her own trunk. Some of the passengers were already inside and leaning out to tell friends their final farewells. She had to hurry.

As she turned to backtrack to the corner, which was several yards behind her, the man looked up and his eyes grew wide with recognition. Christina's heart beat wildly against her breast as she hastened her steps, knowing without a doubt that he would pursue her. She had the advantage of more than half a block; maybe that would be enough. She could only pray it would be.

When she turned the corner that would put her out of his sight, she glanced back again and noticed that he had started to run, pushing anyone that got in his way aside with easy grace. At that rate, he would be upon her in a matter of minutes. She had to find a place to hide.

Gripped by fear and driven by a growing panic, she dashed into the very next door she came to, nearly tripping on her wide brown skirts, and found herself inside a small dressmaker's shop.

When the elderly woman inside looked up from her handwork to notice the frantic state of the woman who had just entered, she quickly put her work aside and asked in a concerned voice, "May I help you?"

"Yes, please, there's a man following me and I must get away from him. Do you have a back door I can use?" her voice pleaded with the woman not to ask questions. She had no time to answer any.

"Follow me," was all the dressmaker said and she hurriedly pushed aside the drapes that shielded the back room from view. Without another word, she led Christina through a room filled with brightly colored fabrics and delicate laces to a small door in the furthermost corner and lifted the heavy crossbar.

"Thank you," Christina said in earnest as she shifted her heavy valise to her other hand and ducked out into the alleyway.

A tall, bearded man busy hammering a lid onto a large wooden barrel looked up to stare curiously at her as she rushed by. "Where you headed to in such a hurry, miss?"

It was none of his business and she ran on without as

much as a backward glance that would have revealed to her the deep frown on his weatherworn face. When she reached the end of the shadowy alley and before she dared step out onto the crowded sidewalk, she leaned out to see who might be coming toward her in either direction. He was nowhere in sight.

Letting out a relieved sigh, she pulled her valise up to her chest and held it tightly as she made a valiant run for the coach. The driver was already climbing into his seat while the stationmaster stood nearby talking to him.

"Wait," she called out as soon as she was close enough to be heard. "Wait for me. I'm supposed to be on that coach."

"There she is," the stationmaster called out and his shoulders visibly relaxed. "That's her."

"I'm sorry I'm late," she said between her gasps for breath as she came to stand beside him. "I-I got lost." She decided a lie would be quicker than trying to explain the truth.

"Get on in," he said, taking her valise and tossing it up to the driver, then turned to open the door for her. "He's anxious to be off."

Not needing to be told twice, Christina lifted her brown woolen skirt high and climbed immediately into the coach. There was only one spot vacant on the two bench seats that faced each other and she wasted no time in settling into it. She offered an apologetic smile to the woman beside her when she realized that in her haste she had sat on the edge of the woman's skirt. She rose slightly from the seat to allow the woman to jerk it free. She had expected a harsh look from the woman and was relieved when all she did was smile as if to say it did not really matter.

With no further delay, the coach gave a forward lurch and they were on their way. Christina's tension abated the moment the coach was in motion. She had made it, and with every turn of the steel-banded wheels, she was getting that much farther away from the man who was probably still out there looking for her.

As she thought about him, she glanced out the window and felt her heart leap to her throat. She saw him standing only a few feet outside the alley she had just slipped out of. He was talking to the tall bearded man who had spoken to her only minutes before. When the coach passed within yards of the pair, she could see that the bearded man was directing her assailant in the direction she had taken. She felt delightfully satisfied in knowing that although the other man thought he was being helpful, he was instead doing nothing more than leading the man on a wild goose chase. But even though she had already successfully managed to elude the evil stranger, she was almost certain it would be quite some time before he realized the futility of his search. A smile formed on her lips as she settled back for the long trip ahead.

The farther away the coach got from Sydney, the more relaxed Christina became, until at last her body, weary from lack of sleep and all the worry, demanded that she close her eyes and rest. Despite the hard jolting of the coach as it bounced along the deeply rutted track, Christina fell asleep.

It was not until she heard the driver's voice shouting something that she awakened. The woman beside her pulled back the window flap to see what all the commotion might be and Christina saw that they were entering a small village. She pulled her father's watch from the pocket hidden within the folds of her skirt and flipped open the shiny case. She was more than a little surprised to discover it was after one o'clock.

"We must be stopping for lunch," the other woman surmised and let the flap back down before too much of the track's dust could enter into the small cabin and soil her lovely green dress or coat her ivory-white skin.

"It's about time," the older gentleman sitting directly across from Christina grumbled as he readjusted the cabbage tree hat that sat atop his silvered head. Dressed in tight moleskin trousers, a dull blue plaid shirt, and knee-high boots, the man looked as though he should be astride a large horse tramping through the bush, not cramped between two older women in the close confines of the tiny coach. The deep tan of his skin and the way his hazel eyes crinkled at the edges high above a full and silvery beard led her to believe he was far more comfortable in the wide outdoors.

When the coach pulled to a stop in front of a small inn, the man had visibly to grit his teeth in order to remain seated long enough to allow the five ladies to exit the coach first. But as soon as they had finally cleared the way, he was out the door and sighing with obvious pleasure as he slowly stretched himself to his full height, which was considerable, mumbling something about taking his chances with the train next time.

"Are you hungry?" the young woman who had sat to Christina's right wanted to know while she looked hesitantly toward the small inn. Christina sensed that she did not want to enter alone, and the other three women, as well, seemed intent on waiting for their fellow male passenger before going in to take a seat.

It was easy to tell by the way the older women gazed shyly up at the tall, silver-haired man then quickly away whenever he happened to glance anywhere near their direction, that they were quite taken with him. And, in a way, Christina could see why. Though he was getting on in years—she supposed he was nearly fifty—he was still a roughly handsome man. Proud and erect. And away from the cramped confines of an overland coach, she could sense that he would be a fairly good-natured man to be around.

"Yes, I'm starved." Christina answered the question with a smile. "Let's go on in and see what they have for us to eat." Although she knew they would be given an hour in which to eat and take care of personal matters, she did not care to wait any longer. The aroma drifting out to meet them had made her stomach virtually ache to be filled. Suddenly she realized that because she had not dared risk going into the hotel's dining room to have breakfast, she had actually not eaten since early the evening before. It was not like her to miss a meal, and her body was well aware of her neglect.

By the time the two women had finished eating, Christina had learned that her friendly traveling companion's name was Rose Beene and that she was also headed for Bathurst. Rose had recently lost her parents, and having never married, had accepted an invitation to come to Bathurst and help her aunt and uncle run their mercantile. Although excited by the chance to go places she had never been, she expressed her apprehension about what she might find when she got there. Christina could very well sympathize with her, for she felt very much the same as she stared off toward the precipitous Blue Mountains that still loomed ahead and wondered to

31

herself what lay beyond them.

As the afternoon of travel wore on, the two of them discovered they also had other things in common. Not only did they both like to read, they had both tried their hand at poetry and loved to write letters. Rose seemed to have adjusted to the thought of working in a store, but Christina felt herself better suited to work in a home, away from the crowds and pressures of town. But they both agreed they wanted to be useful, to do something they could be proud of. It didn't have to be anything that would dramatically change the world, but it needed to be something they felt was worthwhile.

By the time they reached the second inn, where they were to spend the night, they had become well enough acquainted that they decided to share a room and split the expenses. Although it proved to be quite fun, it was not a very prudent decision, for neither got their needed rest and both looked a little droopy-eyed when they climbed aboard the coach the following morning.

Over the next few days, they came to know each other very well, and the more they came to know, the more they liked each other. Christina was glad to have found a friend who would be close enough to her brother's place for her to visit. She knew he had neighbors, for he had mentioned that fact in his letters, but she did not know if any of them might be women close to her own age. At least now, she was sure she would have someone to spend her leisure time with, if her brother allowed her leisure time. Though he had not mentioned exactly what he would expect of her, she felt almost certain he would allow her the time to visit with Rose on occasion.

It was not until the driver announced that they were just hours away from Bathurst that the two new friends finally felt the need to be silent. Their futures were upon them, and each became deep in thought over what that future might bring. Christina put the incident at the hotel in Sydney completely out of her mind and contemplated now the main reasons she had decided to come to Australia.

Sadly, she recalled the unfortunate incidents that had led to her decision to accept her brother's offer and leave New Zealand. She felt such an emptiness knowing she would probably never have children of her own to care for. Then her anger quickly overrode the deep, hollow feeling when she remembered just how quickly John had managed to change his mind about marrying her because of it.

Only days after he had learned she would never bear children because of the accident, he had calmly broken their engagement.

Odd though it seemed, she felt no remorse over losing John—only anger. How could he have put her out of his life so quickly? It was obvious that he had never loved her, and she wondered now if she had ever truly loved him. Maybe it was all for the best. John was nice enough when he wanted to be, but that wouldn't have been enough to base a marriage on, anyway. Too bad she'd had to find out the way she did.

She frowned when she considered the deep void that weighed heavily inside of her now, and had ever since the accident. But she knew that John was not to blame for her sorrow. No, the tears she was so quick to shed these days had nothing to do with his betrayal, with his sudden decision to dissolve their engagement. The tears were for the children she would never have, for she had always cherished the thought of having children.

She was grateful for this chance to move to the Australian mainland and help take care of her brother's two young sons. At least she would be able to be around children, though not her own. Ever since Justin's wife had died, he had been at a loss about how he could care for the lads and continue to hold down his job as a stockman at the Aylesbury station, a job which was very important to him because his own place was not yet self-supporting.

For several months after his wife's death, Justin had sent the lads to stay with his wife's only sister in Parramatta, but because of an illness, she had had to send them back home within the same season. He had next tried hiring a woman to come in and take care of them during the day, but he hadn't liked the thought of leaving his sons' care to a stranger. Then, having learned of Christina and John's breakup, and with the lads' school having let out for three months, he immediately invited her to come live with him and care for the children. Not only did his letter state that he intended to provide her with room and board, he planned to pay her a small wage besides, though he could not afford to pay too much.

He had also indicated in his last letter that he needed her help in other ways, but was very vague about that. As she thought about it, she supposed he needed her emotional support to help him get over the loss of his beloved wife, Essie. Remembering how he had never been very strong emotionally, Christina was prepared to help see him through his pain. She would do what she could to help them get on with their lives.

When the coach finally pulled into Bathurst, Christina was so eager to see her brother and her future home that she reached across Rose's lap and yanked back the

34

window flap. Having heard that most of the Australian inland was either plains or desert, she had worried that he had exaggerated in his description of Bathurst in order to persuade her to accept his invitation, but now she could see that he had written her the truth.

Although the municipality itself sat in a huge, grassy clearing that stretched far into the distance, the rolling hills beyond were covered with thick patches of gum trees, satinwoods, wattle, pepper trees, and wilgas. When she finally stepped down from the coach and out onto the dirt-packed street, the gentle fragrance of bougain-villaea vines caught her attention, but it was quickly overridden by other, more noticeable smells of horses, smoke, and dust. Closing her eyes, she breathed deeply the smells that would now be a part of her life, committed them to memory, then quickly reopened her eyes to search the surrounding faces for a glimpse of her brother, whom she had not seen in almost two years.

When she finally spotted him, he was already headed in her direction, and in the time it took to raise her arms out to him, he had reached her and swung her into a giant bear hug.

"Chrissy!" He called out her childhood nickname as he swung her around and around in a circle.

Christina laughed at his antics. "Put me down," she finally insisted and was dropped to her feet with a sound jolt. How like her brother.

"Chrissy, you've put on a little weight since last we saw each other," he said with a light chuckle.

Christina frowned at that last remark and narrowed her eyes as she tried to think of a worthy retort about his beard. Rose stepped up then and interrupted them.

"Christina, I want you to meet my aunt before you

leave," Rose said proudly, and turned to draw her new friend's attention to the short, stocky woman at her side. "Aunt Jane, this is the girl I was telling you about. This is Christina Lapin."

"And I want you to meet my brother," Christina was quick to put in as she linked her arm in his, surprised that he did not seem as tall as she had remembered. She wondered if that was because she had grown another inch since she had last seen him, but then the forbidden thought crossed her mind that maybe she was comparing him to the huge, brawny man who had accosted her in Sydney just days before. Quickly she pushed that thought aside.

"This is Justin," she finally said to Rose. Then, looking up into his questioning gaze, she smiled and explained, "This is Rose Beene. We were on the coach together. She's come to Bathurst to work at her aunt and uncle's mercantile."

"You are Mrs. Makowka's niece?" he asked, his eyes sparkling as he looked down into the young woman's upturned face. He was quick to notice her thick, shiny brown hair and wondered how long it was when taken down from atop her pretty little head.

"I gather you already know my aunt?" she asked as a tiny blush rose to her cheeks.

"Sure. Everyone around here knows Mrs. Makowka and her husband, Thomas. After all, they run the largest and the cleanest mercantile around these parts," he said as he pulled down on the wide brim of his cabbage tree hat and offered the older woman a charming smile. "How are you today, Mrs. Makowka?"

"Just fine, now that I know Rose has arrived safe and sound. I worried so about her traveling alone. Why, the lass has hardly ever had reason to leave Sydney. Hurry along, Rose, Thomas is eager as he can be to see you." Then, to Justin, she explained, "Since we never could have any children of our own, we sort of latched on to Rose early on." Then to Christina, "It was nice to have met you, my dear. Please, whenever you are in town you must stop by and visit with us. Although I don't think you'll have a problem seeing our sign, Justin can show you exactly where we are located."

"I'll do that," Christina promised, but before she could extend an invitation to Rose to come out and visit with her, Justin had already begun to speak, his eyes never leaving Rose's.

"And any friend of my sister's is more than welcome to come out to my house and visit anytime that is convenient. Christina, you should invite Rose out for supper sometime after you two are completely settled in."

Christina thought his response to Rose was a little much for a man who was supposed to be grief stricken over his wife's death, but decided he was probably just trying to be nice to her new friend and make her feel welcome to the area. As soon as Rose and her aunt were out of sight, he quickly turned his full attention to finding her baggage and her trunk among the items being quickly unloaded and getting them stacked into one neat pile on the platform.

While they waited for the final valise to be lowered to the ground, he told her about his job and that he was being considered for the soon-to-be vacated station boss position.

"It's the opportunity to make the future for me and my sons all that I want it to be. Being in charge of the entire

37

place will mean better pay, and security. I want that job so bad it hurts just thinking about anyone else getting it. Have you ever wanted anything that bad, that it actually hurt when you thought about not getting it?"

"Yes," she responded sadly, reminded once again of the children she would never have. But rather than burden him with her problems, she quickly brightened. "So, what exactly are your chances of getting the job?"

"Pretty good, I think. There's another man being considered, too, but I think I may have it over him. After all, I'm the one that was chosen to act as a temporary station boss while Todd and his present station boss are away on a business trip. That's a good sign, don't you think?"

"Is Todd your boss?" she asked. Though she was sure he and Essie had mentioned the man in their letters, she could not recall exactly in what context.

"Aye, and what a boss he is," Justin said with open admiration. "He's one of the most self-confident men I've ever known and is used to getting whatever it is he wants. He's a real man. Never takes orders from nobody, except occasionally from his grandmother, Penelope Aylesbury. The woman lives somewhere in the Hawksbury district now but seems to visit out here more often than is really necessary. Even though she turned over the station and its cattle and sheep operations to Todd years ago, she still likes to keep her finger in the pie."

He frowned as he thought about the grandmother. "But I think he only does what she says out of kindheartedness, more than anything else. It's not that he's afraid of her or anything. He just likes to please the old woman for some reason, though it's hard to imagine why. She's a stern old woman, that Mrs. Aylesbury. I'm glad she's not really in charge of the place. But then, Todd's a nice enough man to work for. He lets his men know what is expected of them, and if he ever asks extra work of any of us, he always gives us extra wages. If I can just get him to make me the station boss. . . ." He paused, his brow drawn low and his voice full of strained emotion. His hands tightened into fists. "I just have to get that job. I have to be the one he chooses."

Suddenly, Christina had a strange, uneasy feeling. There was a little too much desperation in his voice, but she pushed the dark feeling aside, realizing she had probably read more into his tone than she should. She tried to reassure him that if the station owner was half as smart as Justin claimed he was, he would surely notice how qualified her brother was for the job. She hated to see her brother so deeply worried and felt instantly protective. After all, he and his sons were the only family she had left. She should do whatever she could to show her support. But still, she couldn't shake the uneasy feeling she had about the whole situation. There was something wrong, something her brother was not telling her.

## Chapter III

While Justin waited for Christina's last valise to be lowered from the rest of the baggage piled high in the open cargo pen across the upper part of the coach, his gaze drifted from the two busy workmen to his sister's pretty, but unsmiling face, then beyond. Absently, he scanned the area that lay behind her. He felt a growing impatience. Justin hated needless delays, and having to stand around and wait for the coach hands to finally get to Christina's valise was putting him on edge.

As his gaze darted across the growing number of people who had gathered around the coach office to see the new arrivals, his attention was drawn to two men standing just outside the entrance door talking casually to each other. Slowly, Justin's brow drew into a deep frown and his jaw tensed.

"Coolabah? What are you doing back so soon?" he shouted out to the taller of the two men, and managed to keep any of the concern he felt out of his voice. Then, by way of explanation to Christina, who had cut her own gaze away from the workmen to look curiously up at him,

41

Justin's frown deepened. He spoke softly so that only she could hear his words, "Coolabah was not due back in until sometime late tomorrow afternoon. Something's up."

Christina turned to see who her brother was talking about and discovered that the same burly, silver-haired man who had ridden in on the coach with her was now headed in their direction. A broad smile had stretched across his bearded face the moment he finally spotted Justin.

"I 'ad to come back and get some things for Todd," the man said and gave Justin a good-natured slap on the shoulder. The friendly gesture was delivered with such spirit that Justin shifted his weight from one leg to the other and almost stumbled sideways. "Don't worry, mate, you're still in charge around 'ere, and it looks like you will be for several days yet. The boss 'ad a little unexpected trouble of some sort in Sydney the other day, and because of it, 'e says 'e plans to stay on there at least until the end of the week. But don't ya let it worry ya none, 'e'll be back in plenty of time to meet the pay docket on Saturday."

"What sort of trouble did he have?" Justin wanted to know and searched Coolabah's expression for some indication of how serious the trouble was.

"'E wouldn't exactly say wot 'is trouble was, but I suspect it might 'ave somethin' to do with all the recent cattle duffin' that's been goin' on around 'ere lately, because 'e woke me up early that morning to tell me about this sudden change in 'is plans, and as soon as 'e had 'anded me the money to get a ticket on the next coach out, knowing 'ow I hate to take the train even part way, 'e marched directly to the police 'eadquarters to speak with

42

Capt'n 'icks. Never saw a more determined look in a man's eye."

"Captain Hicks?" Justin repeated. His face lost some of its color as his brow lowered further and his concern deepened.

"Aye, you know, the man who supervises the troopers stationed 'ere in Bathurst. You've seen 'im around 'ere before. Comes around often enough. A short, barrel-chested man who can't seem to keep 'is 'air down or 'is britches up."

"I know who Captain Hicks is," Justin snapped ill-naturedly. "I was just surprised Todd had gone to see him is all. Something really bad must have happened. Don't you have any idea what it was all about?"

"No, I don't. And I won't know anything more until I can get back there and poke my sticky beak into matters. After I ride out to the station to get the boss the things 'e sent me for, I'll be on me way right back to Sydney. I'll probably learn more about it then. And I imagine I won't be comin' back until whenever 'e does, so it looks like you'll continue to be in charge until then."

When Christina finally drew her gaze away from Coolabah, she noticed that Justin's shoulders had tensed visibly. His face took on a grim expression that hardened his jawline into granite. Christina wondered about his strange reaction and quickly reviewed everything the man had said in hopes of figuring out what might have upset her brother.

All she could come up with was that either her brother was deeply worried about his station master or was afraid for himself—afraid to be in charge for so long a time when there obviously were cattle duffers about. But that seemed ridiculous for a man who hoped to take on the job full time. She frowned and stared thoughtfully at her brother.

"Are you the brother this little lassie 'as been talkin' so much about when she was on the coach?" Coolabah went on to ask Justin, seemingly unaware of Justin's sudden tension. His gaze wandered from Justin's face to Christina's and back to Justin's, then his brow raised quizzically as he compared the two. "Why it never even occurred to me when she went on and on to 'er little friend about 'er dear brother that she could be talkin' about you."

When Justin did not respond right away, still too deeply lost in his thoughts, the tall man shrugged and stuck out a large, weathered hand toward Christina and nodded politely. "I guess you got it figured out by now that I'm Coolabah—the man whose job your brother is tryin' so 'ard to latch on to."

"Pleased to meet you," Christina said and stared curiously down at his huge hand. When she realized he fully intended to shake her hand as he would a man's, she could not help but return his smile. She raised her hand and had it quickly grasped by his.

As he thoroughly jostled her arm with his hardy handshake, she spoke again, "I understand you plan to leave here soon."

"Aye. I've finally saved enough of me wages to start up a place of me own several miles south of here. I was lucky to latch on to such a prime piece of land at such a good price. It may not be close enough to allow me to continue to work both Todd's place and me own like Justin 'ere does, but at least it's not out in the backblocks." He smiled contentedly. "It's near enough I'll be able to come

44

around and visit with all me friends if I get to feelin' lonesome."

His pale eyes sparkled with faraway thoughts. "Aye, come late January, I'll be packin' me gear and leavin' the Aylesbury station behind. I'll be takin' over me own little parcel of land and 'avin a go at raising me own cattle. I can't seem to get along well enough with sheep even to care to give them a go."

Then his smile faded. "But for now, I'm still on Todd Aylesbury's pay docket and I'd better be gettin' on out to the station and musterin' up the things 'e's sent me for. But first I'd better be securin' me passage back. I just hope I don't have to board no train to get back to Sydney on time. The bludgers terrify me. It'll be bad enough 'avin to come back part of the way on one with the boss. Nice meetin' ya, Miss Lapin."

Having said that, he gave Justin another firm slap on the shoulder, then turned on his booted heel and returned to the front of the coach office with long, easy strides.

"Nice man," Christina surmised as she returned her full attention to her brother. "Imagine a big man like that being afraid of trains. Imagine him actually admitting it the way he did. I like him."

"I guess he's nice enough," Justin said darkly as he bent over to grab one of Christina's valises with a hard jerk. While they were talking, the last of her things had finally been brought to her and set on the platform at their feet.

"What's the matter?" she asked as she glanced curiously from her brother back to where Coolabah was once again engaged in a casual conversation with the

45

coach master. The man had not done or said anything to Justin that should cause such a hostile reaction.

"Nothing," was all her brother would say as he tucked the first valise up under his left arm and bent over to yank up another. As soon as he had managed to get everything but her trunk situated in his arms where he could carry it all without dropping anything, he spun abruptly away from her. As if it was an afterthought, he turned his head back and spoke in a clipped, angry voice over his shoulder. "Stay here with the trunk while I take these things on to the carriage. I'll be right back."

Frowning almost as deeply as Justin just had, Christina sank down onto the top of her tall wooden trunk and adjusted her woolen skirts around her so that her ankles would not show beneath the dark blue material. With growing irritation at her brother's sudden and childish display of ill temper, she sat tapping her foot on the planked walkway and waited for him.

Justin certainly was quick tempered, she thought as she glanced in the direction he had gone. But why had he shown such impatience with *her?* She had not done one thing to provoke such treatment. But then, wanting to give him the benefit of a reason for his sudden moodiness, she wondered if his quick temper might be directly related to Essie's death. Justin always had been a person easily affected by his emotions, and there was no telling how much he had suffered since his wife's death.

Lifting her gaze to the pale blue sky that rose high above the gray-green countryside, Christina sighed heavily while she considered the reasons for Justin's strange behavior. She had always known that Essie was the true backbone of her family, and without her, Justin was no doubt as lost as a child.

Christina smiled sadly. Only a woman like Essie could have possessed enough patience and fortitude to tame her wild brother, to settle him enough to want a real home and a family. Their parents had tried to get Justin to settle down when they still had some influence over their son, but their efforts had had little effect on Justin's wayward heart. Even their Great Aunt Dora Chun had given it a go by getting her boss, Mr. Aylesbury, to take Justin on as a stockman, and that had succeeded to a point. At least, the job on the Aylesbury station had kept him in one place for a while, but it was not until he had fallen in love with Essie that he had finally learned responsibility and truly yearned to put down roots.

Until Essie, everyone had worried that Justin was destined to be nothing more than a roaming swagman and had expected him at any moment to shuck his job at the Aylesbury station and head for a new adventure around the next bend, living on the handouts of generous station masters and never amounting to much.

There was no doubt in Christina's mind that the changes in Justin had all been Essie's doing. The woman had managed to become his guiding light, determined to save him from his own worst enemy, himself. Through Essie's letters, though they had been few, Christina had learned how very much Justin had matured over the past few years. But even so, he had continued to lean heavily on his young wife's strength and her common-sense approach to everything.

Christina could well imagine that her brother was at a complete loss now that his wife was gone, and she silently vowed to do whatever she could to help him and his two lads through these difficult times. It would be no real sacrifice on her part, because she knew that by helping them she would also be filling a painful void in her own life. A void she so desperately needed to fill.

By the time Justin finally returned for the trunk, his mood appeared to have lifted somewhat. Though he was far from the smiling, jovial man he had been when she first stepped off the coach, at least his frown was not so deeply entrenched in his forehead and his tone of voice was far less severe.

"As soon as I get that trunk loaded," he said as she quickly stood and stepped out of his way, "we'll be off."

"How far is it to where you live?" she asked and watched him hoist the large trunk up and sling it back over his shoulder so that it rested mostly on the stouter muscles of his back.

"Just a few miles. We'll be there before you know it," Justin promised as he carried her trunk to where several carriages and wagons stood waiting to be loaded.

When Justin walked over to an exceptionally large carriage with a wide storage compartment folded down in the back, already stacked high on one side with her other baggage, Christina could not help but be impressed. As she leaned into the front and ran her hand over one of the deeply tufted black leather seats and then reached up to touch the matching leather canopy, she remarked with open awe, "This is some gig you have here."

"Aye, that it is. It comes from America."

"America?" her brown eyes widened appreciatively, for she knew that some of the finest vehicles ever made came from America. "How can you afford something like this?"

"Actually it doesn't belong to me. It belongs to Todd," Justin admitted with a weak smile. His gaze dropped to stare at the ground as if he was suddenly ashamed about

48

something or trying to hide some bit of guilt. "I'm just borrowing it for the afternoon." He looked up at her again, but then quickly away as he began to secure the baggage with wide leather straps. "I wanted my sister to ride in style."

Christina did not care for the way Justin's gaze kept falling just short of hers, and the thought suddenly occurred to her that her foolish brother might not have bothered to get his boss's permission to use this carriage. She stared at him suspiciously. "You borrowed it?"

"Aye, get in," he said as he reached inside and lifted a wide-brimmed cabbage tree hat off the back seat where he had placed it for safekeeping while he worked to secure the load. He plopped it down on his head.

He still did not look at her as they climbed up into the front seat, but Christina found it hard to believe that her brother would take such a foolish risk when he so badly wanted to be the one chosen to supervise Mr. Aylesbury's entire station. Surely he had told someone he was borrowing the carriage. Yet, she had the distinct feeling that something was bothering her brother, something very serious. Something he was afraid she would be able to read in his eyes. But she had yet to figure out just what it might be. All she could really do was wait and hope that eventually he would confide in her.

As soon as the carriage lurched into motion and they were on their way, Justin quickly changed the subject. "So, tell me, Chrissy, how have you been since the accident? You look fully recovered to me. In fact, you look beautiful. You've grown up quite a bit since I saw you last."

"I find it a little hard to believe after such a long and tiresome trip on that coach that I look anything but haggard," she responded and eyed him suspiciously. "Aren't you laying the syrup on a little too thick?"

"No, it's just that I haven't seen you in so long. It's been years, you know. You've definitely changed, and all of it for the better, I might add. You have become quite a beautiful young woman."

She looked at him again. He seemed sincere enough. "Well, thank you brother dear. And I must say, you have changed, too. Whatever possessed you to grow a beard and hide such a handsome face?"

"Most of the men around here sport a beard," he said in defense of his decision. "Besides, I have never been too partial to shaving. It's a blame nuisance. With a beard all you need to do is take a pair of scissors to it occasionally. Why? Don't you like it?"

"It'll just take a little getting used to, I guess," she responded quickly with a smile, then reached over and gave it a short tug, laughing at his immediate yelp of pain.

"Be careful, you don't know how that hurts," he said as he reached up to rub the spot she had pulled. Then, raising a brow, he added ruefully, "Or maybe you do. As I recall, you always did take fiendish delight in causing me a little pain now and then. I still owe you one for that black eye you gave me a few years back."

Christina laughed again at the memory, because it had been an accident more than anything else, and when he returned her laughter she felt relieved to know that whatever had bothered him earlier had been so quickly forgotten.

"I guess you are glad to be recovered from that horrible accident," Justin said and returned to his original question. "You have fully recovered haven't you?"

"Not quite. My leg still gets a little stiff and sore from time to time, which causes me to limp a bit, but other than that, I'm fine." Christina had already decided not to tell Justin everything the doctor had told her about her injuries.

She saw no reason for her brother to be told how, although she would regain full use of her leg and even the occasional stiffness would eventually go away, it was doubtful she would ever be fully recovered. How it was unlikely she would ever bear children because of that stupid horse. She was forever doomed to the life of an old maid. No man would ever want to marry a woman who could not produce a family—especially a man like John, who had come straight out and told her that she no longer had enough to offer him. A man with no children was a man with fewer rights to purchase extra land, and land was something that John revered, something most men revered.

Sighing inwardly at the ugly quarrel she and John had had after she'd admitted the full extent of her injuries, Christina glanced at her brother briefly. Although a smile had returned to his handsome face, there was still a deep sadness about him. No, Christina did not feel Justin should be burdened with any more misery, especially not her miseries. He had been dealt enough of his own. She would keep her troubles to herself.

"I was sure sorry to hear about that accident," Justin went on to say, bringing her thoughts back to the surface. "It scared me half to death. I hope they had enough sense to shoot that bloody horse before it ended up killing someone." He shuddered at the thought of such a large animal trying to trample his sister. "It must have been horrible."

"It was not a mountain of fun," she admitted lightly, hoping to prevent him from sliding back into his ill mood.

Justin looked over at her and smiled sympathetically. "I was also sorry to hear about your sudden breakup with John. I know how that must have hurt you. But I wouldn't be totally honest if I didn't tell you that, in a way, I'm glad it happened. I personally never cared much for the man. He was far too old for you, and he is the sort who looks out only for himself. Besides that, had you gone ahead with your plans to marry the bludger, then I wouldn't have you sitting beside me now, and I'd still be searching for someone I could trust to help me manage my house and take proper care of my sons."

Justin glanced at his sister again and tried to read her solemn expression. He was more than a little curious about the sudden breakup between her and John Coventry—almost a full year into their engagement—but knew better than to come right out and ask her what had caused it. He realized that she would tell him in time if she wanted him to know, and that all the questions in the world would not wrestle a straight answer out of her. Besides, he also knew that if he dared to pry into her life too much, she might feel every right to pry into his. He certainly did not want that—for her sake as much as his own.

"How are Alan and Edward?" she asked, aware that he now stared at her with an unfathomable expression, and feeling awkward because of it.

"Eager to meet you," he said with a laugh, as if that had been an understatement. "Essie used to read them portions of your letters, and they feel they already know you."

"I feel the same way. I can hardly wait to see if my

52

mental images in any way resemble what they really look like."

"They are fine-looking lads, I can tell you that much," Justin said, his green eyes glimmering with deep, fatherly pride. "Look a lot like their father, they do."

"Not the least bit prejudiced, are you?" she teased, delighted to see such a proud glimmer in her brother's eyes when he spoke of his sons.

"Who me? Prejudiced?" He feigned innocence. "Do you actually doubt my judgment? Well, I guess you'll just have to see for yourself, won't you?"

For the next few minutes the two of them rode along the narrow rutted track in companionable silence. Christina's attention was drawn to the thick mass of gum trees and wattle that had surrounded them only a few miles outside of Bathurst and provided the track with tiny splashes of shade along the way. Any scrub that might have grown dense beneath the tall trees had been cleared away by either the land's owner or a track worker, giving the area an almost parklike quality as they made their way up a narrow incline.

Overhead the branches of the towering gum trees, known also as eucalypti, were alive with the boisterous chatter of dozens of different birds, birds of outrageous colors, birds like no others in the world. Jade and scarlet parrots, blue and yellow lorikeets, white and pink galah, along with stark white cockatoos with bright yellow crests played a lively game of hide-and-seek in the thin branches of the towering gray-green trees above, seemingly oblivious of the curious upturned eyes below.

Christina smiled at their antics as she reached up to tuck a loose strand of her dark brown hair back into her upswept chignon. Such a show they put on. When she finally brought her gaze away from the very tops of the trees she let her eyes wander until at last they came to the rise that loomed just ahead. Suddenly she was curious to see what wonders lay on the other side. "How much further?"

"We should be there within the hour," Justin told her. "My place is on the very outskirts of the Aylesbury station. It used to be owned by one of Todd's grandfather's cousins, but the last drought hit Ben Crawford pretty hard and he had to sell some of his land in order to see his cattle through it. Poor Ben, he's always being forced to sell off part of his land. He sometimes manages to buy some of it back when times are better, but this is one parcel of land he won't find up for resale anytime soon. But then, I'm sure he already realizes that. I'm just glad Coolabah was not yet ready to start up his own place that particular summer, what with the drought and all. It was through Ben's offer to sell it to Coolabah that I first became aware it was even for sale, and at such a good price."

"And you had enough money saved to buy all forty acres?" Christina asked, impressed. Although Essie had told her a little about the purchase of their land, Christina had never known the details.

"Not all of it. Ben was asking twenty-five shillings per acre, but was willing to take only half that amount as down payment if I could come up with it within the week, and agreed to let us pay out the rest in yearly installments. It took most of the money Essie's parents had left her just to make the down payment. That's another reason I'm so eager to be the station boss. The wages will be much better than what I get now, and I will finally be able to finish paying Ben what I still owe him, as well as the people I owe in town."

"I gather you are behind on your payments to the man," she surmised with a heavy sigh.

"Just a little, but Ben's been real understanding about it. He's given me a little extra time to come up with the last of it. He understands that I've had to spend a lot of my money to put a house on the place along with a decent barn and the paddocks."

"Paddocks? You have livestock?"

"A few head of cattle, nothing to brag about yet. If I ever get the chance to expand the place, I plan to run sheep on it, too."

"Sounds as if you are looking to the future," she said with a slight nod.

"There's nothing wrong in that is there?" he wanted to know.

"No, but it does seem a little strange coming from you. As a boy, you never had any real goals in life. You were a real larrikin, you were. Yet here you are now, obviously trying hard to make something of yourself. I'm really very proud of you."

"Then I hope you'll understand that for the next few days, while I'm still acting as the temporary station boss, I won't be home very much of the time and you'll have to pretty well get settled in all by yourself. The boys will help however much they can. They're good boys, but they'll have their regular chores to do, too."

"I'm sure I'll manage just fine," she told him as she strained her neck to catch her first glimpse of the huge valley that was unfolding before her. They had just crested the top of the hill and cleared the dense growth of trees at almost the same moment, allowing her a complete and sudden view of the beauty below. As she looked down across the wide, sloping fields of olive-green grass, which were interrupted only by an occasional creek, a fenceline, or a small grove of gum trees, she could not help but exclaim aloud, "How beautiful. How far are we from your house now?" She was starting to grow impatient to get there, for his "few miles" had already taken almost two hours to cross.

"Just over the next rise," he promised her. "In fact, you can see the tops of the trees that shade my dooryard from here," he told her and pointed in the direction she should look toward.

The track curved out and back to follow the lay of the land, staying with the higher regions rather than making the effort to dip down into the valley below. Soon they were on the next ridge, with Justin's house clearly in sight, and Christina was properly impressed.

The house was larger and far nicer than she had expected. Although it was a wooden structure rather than brick, it was a full two stories tall, and as grand as any she had seen in town. Spring flowers bloomed in a small dooryard garden and several ornamental bushes grew next to the house near the front steps. She suspected Essie was responsible for those small splashes of beauty and felt a sudden tug of sadness, for she truly missed the woman she had never even had the pleasure to meet.

Looking beyond the house, Christina noticed that the barn was also far larger than she had expected, as was the coach house. And the vegetable garden and adjoining orchard were huge compared to those she had seen back home, taking up several acres all their own.

"Justin, your house is beautiful," she finally said and drew her gaze back to the house itself when they pulled into the wide drive that led to the front and then around to the side of the house. She turned to stare at him in awe and noticed that his expression had dimmed rather than brightened at her comments. She felt as if she had somehow said something wrong.

"Essie liked nice things," he finally said as he pulled the carriage to a halt in front of the house and stared up at the tall, brightly painted structure. "So, I tried to provide her with only the best."

The tears that had so quickly filled his eyes tore at Christina's heart with such a force that she immediately changed the subject. She had been about to ask whose choice it had been to paint the house such a lovely blue with white trim when most wooden houses in the outback were not painted at all. But knowing the answer might again lead to Essie, she asked instead, "Where are your sons?"

Before Justin had the chance to respond, two young boys dashed out of the house and down the planked stairs with lightning speed. Squealing with delight as they greeted their father, they then came to stand before Christina, staring anxiously at her with smaller versions of Justin's huge green eyes. Although she had never met either of them, she knew right away who was who from the descriptions in Essie's letters and immediately called them by name.

"She knows I'm Alan," the smaller of the two said with noticeable pride as he nudged the taller one in the side with his elbow.

"And she knew I was Edward," the other one responded and tilted his dark curly head as he stared questioningly up at her. "How come you know which one of us is which?"

"Oh, I know all about you two," she told them as she climbed out of the carriage, then knelt down to get a better look at their faces. Smiling first at Alan, she winked and said, "I know how much you like to go swimming and have been known to sneak onto the neighbor's land to do just that without ever letting anyone know what you were about."

Alan's green eyes grew wide as he reached up to scratch his tousled black hair. Though both boys had dark hair, Alan's was straighter and darker than Edward's and at the moment also a little longer.

Then, to Edward, she said, "And I know that you, young man, like to help with the baking when you can, especially when it's a sweetcake, but that you like to help with the eating of that sweetcake even better."

Both boys grinned, delighted that their aunt already knew so much about them, and each took one of her arms, intent on helping escort her inside and show her to her room upstairs.

"You seem to be in good hands," Justin commented as he watched the pair tugging eagerly on his sister's arms.

"It would seem that way," she responded with a laugh.

"I'll be up in a minute with your things," he called out as she was being led up the stairs and into the house, after only a brief argument over which boy should enter the narrow doorway by her side and which of them should have to follow behind.

Once inside, Christina's attention was slowly drawn away from her two escorts to the interior of the house. She was truly amazed at the quality of the furnishings. Essie had shown exceptional taste in decorating the lower floor. Although Christina had only managed a quick glimpse into the living room at her right, she was

58

impressed to note the matched parlor suite and the huge, colorful carpet. Quite elegant for what she had expected a stockman to be able to afford, even with his wife's inheritance to fall back on. And when the boys next led her to her room, she was even more delighted to find that the same good taste and high quality had been used in furnishing the upstairs.

Christina entered the bedroom with overpowering awe. She had never dreamed that a station hand was paid well enough to live in such luxury. But then she frowned when she remembered how he had claimed he still owed the man who had sold him the land and even a few of the people in town. If he had the money to afford such luxuries, he surely could have come up with the money to pay his debts. He should not have bought such luxuries when there were debts to be paid.

Sighing inwardly, she realized that, as usual, Justin had his priorities mixed up, and she knew she needed to have a little sisterly talk with him, but wondered just how to go about bringing up the subject without triggering his bad temper again.

As she plucked her tiny bonnet from her head and placed it on the embroidered bedspread that adorned the tall, plump bed that lay against the center of the far wall, she could not help but wonder how much money her brother did make. And if he was to be making even more with the new job, then he would be doing very well for himself indeed.

"Do you like it?" Alan asked eagerly as soon as she had time to look the room over completely.

"Aye, it's beautiful. Far better than anything I've been accustomed to," she answered honestly, still gazing around at the ornately carved mahogany furniture that had to have been imported from either England or America. Even the chairs were made of fine imported wood.

"It was Mother's room," he told her, as he, too, let his gaze sweep the furnishings wistfully.

"And Father's," Edward supplied quickly, but he kept his gaze trained on Christina as if he feared she would disappear if he were to look away.

"This is your father's room?" she asked, ready to protest his having given it to her. She appreciated such a gesture, but was not about to take his room from him.

"Not no more. He sleeps downstairs now in the room at the back of the house. He says sleeping up here now makes him too sad. Nobody's slept in here since. . . ." Alan's voice broke off and gave way to an uncomfortable silence. Clearly, he did not want to speak the words that confirmed his mother's death.

"You should have seen all the dust in here before me and Alan started cleaning it for you," Edward quickly interjected, not any more eager to hear the words than Alan was to say them. "It took us most of yesterday to wipe all the furniture clean, then sweep and mop the floors. Father had to help us put the clean sheets on the bed when he got home and then helped us carry the spread outside and beat all the dust out of it last night."

"You certainly did a wonderful job," Christina told them, though she had already spotted the remaining splotches of dust in the corners and under the bed. She was also aware that the floor needed a good, strong rubbing of oil and wax to bring back its original shine, but she knew that helping to take proper care of the house was one of the reasons her brother had asked her to come. A man with a job to go to and two children to care for simply did not have enough time.

"We also made tucker for you," Edward added proudly. "It's ready when you are."

"You two cook?" she asked, her brown eyes widening with astonishment. The boys were not old enough to know how to cook. Edward was the oldest, and he could hardly be six years old—but then she realized he had to be older than that if he was in school.

"Well, Father helped us prepare it on Sunday, and all we really had to do today was start a fire and warm it up. Nothing worse than cold mutton stew." He wrinkled his nose at the mere thought of it.

"Mutton stew?" she asked as she raised herself to sit on the tall edge of the bed and test its softness. She was surprised to discover it was a feather mattress. "And do you three make a good mutton stew?"

"I suppose so. It's about all Father knows how to make. That and beef stew," Alan piped in. "If Edward didn't remember how to make a sweetcake and plum duff, we'd never have nothing else."

"Can you cook?" Edward asked quickly, looking at her with such eager hope that it made Christina want to laugh.

"I can do better than mutton stew, if that's what you want to know," she laughed, and having said that, she found both boys bounding in her direction eagerly, their small arms opened wide. It was all they needed to know.

## Chapter IV

While Justin spent most of his time away from the house, working hard to prove himself a worthy station boss, Christina found she quickly fit into Edward and Alan's lives. Even before she started to unpack her things and put them away, she assumed her duties, giving the boys and the kitchen first priority. By noon the following day, she had proved to her nephews she could indeed produce something better than mutton stew, though there had been enough of the bland stew Justin had made to last them at least two more days had they wanted it to.

With the few spices Christina had been able to find in the kitchen, the fresh vegetables the boys produced from the garden, and the small slab of beef she discovered in the bottom of the cooler, she produced a succulent roasted beef with braised vegetables and baked fresh bread to soak up the sauce with. Though she was disappointed when Justin was unable to get away for lunch that day, after he had told her he would try to come home for at least half an hour, she had managed to save enough of the beef from the two ravenous boys to have again for their supper that night.

The first two days after her arrival were spent mostly unpacking, cooking, and catching up on the washing, which she discovered had been badly neglected. She had all but forgotten the embarrassing incident in Sydney and the terrifying chase that had occurred that following morning. Even the horrible accident that had changed her life now seemed far removed to her. She was busy. She was needed. She was happy.

Only at night did unbidden images of the man whose room she had invaded come back to haunt her. He had been undeniably handsome, handsome in every sense of the word, but at the same time, life-threatening. She felt lucky to have gotten away from him as easily as she had. She shuddered at the thought of ever running into him again, though she knew the chances of that were very slim. She was certain the man was not the type to let bygones be bygones and would gladly seek vengeance on her.

By the third day, Christina was able to take on the regular housecleaning with the vigor and full attention it needed. The boys helped her in the afternoons, and with no one coming around to interrupt her work, she managed to have the house in fine condition, the floors and furniture gleaming, and the carpets back to their rightful color by that weekend. She had worked hard in hopes of being able to relax a little with her brother on Saturday afternoon. He and the other station hands were supposed to be given their monthly wages and their weekly rations and—except for a few of the boundary riders—have the remainder of the afternoon for themselves.

But, because the revered Mr. Aylesbury had been late

in returning that Saturday, the rations were late to be weighed, and as a result Justin was later than he had promised in getting home.

It was nearly dark when he finally came bounding through the back door, his arms loaded with the sacks that contained his weekly portions of flour, salt, sugar, and tea, along with the small tins filled with generous amounts of baking powder, tobacco, and shot.

"I'm sorry I'm late, but Todd didn't get back until the middle of the afternoon," he quickly explained. He knew Christina had been looking forward to getting her hands on his weekly stores, especially the flour and sugar, since they were almost completely out of both. "But because Todd heard I had company, he saw to it I got a little more of each."

It still bothered Christina that her brother called his station master by his first name, though he had explained how the man himself had demanded it, and he had to do whatever pleased the station master. Still it seemed to her it would appear far more respectful for the man's employees to call him by his last name, but if that was the way the bloke wanted it, she refused to make an issue of it and tried her best to ignore it. "At least you are home now. I've seen so little of you these past few days that I was beginning to wonder if you still existed."

Justin gave a tiny, bittersweet laugh just before his green eyes took on a faraway glimmer, and Christina could tell he no longer saw her. Other visions had taken his thoughts. "You sound just like Essie used to. Always complaining that my job took too much of my time and never left enough for her."

"As well she should have complained," she said with an understanding smile and reached up to stroke the side

65

of her brother's beard gently. "I was hoping to have fresh bread for you tonight, but being so low on flour, I was unable to prepare any. You'll just have to make do with what's left of yesterday's bread."

"It's just as well, you are spoiling us with all your wonderful cooking. Mum must have taught you well for you to cook the way you do."

"And you must have learned how to eat the way you do from Father. Either that or you inherited that hollow leg Mum always complained he had. It's not good for a person to eat so much."

Justin frowned. "Now you sound like Mum herself. Nothin' but complaints."

Christina lowered her pretty eyelashes in warning, but did not offer a comment as she reached for and began to take the things Justin still held in his arms. It would do no good to point out to her brother that he had given their mum more than enough reason for honest complaint in those last years he had been home.

"Oh, and I have a surprise for you!" he said enthusiastically.

"What's that?" she asked as she placed the many sacks and tins on the countertop near the stove and reached for the proper canisters to store their contents.

"While I was talking to Todd this afternoon, Coolabah walked up and mentioned to him that you had finally come for your visit, which is why I was given more of everything. But that's not all. Todd also invited us all to have lunch over there tomorrow as his personal guests."

The high level of enthusiasm in Justin's voice let her know that this was a great honor for him, but somehow she was not duly impressed and less than eager to accept the invitation. From what she had learned of Mr. Todd

66

Aylesbury thus far, she thought she would prefer not to meet the scoundrel at all.

"I can't wait for you to meet him. He's my idea of what it means to be a success. He's got money, land, power, and more women than he even knows what to do with."

"So you've mentioned before. Sounds like a real success all right," she retorted sarcastically. He sounded like everything she truly hated in a man—cocky, overbearing, egotistical, and selfishly demanding, using his wealth and the power that went with it to acquire whatever he wanted.

Suddenly, a picture of John Coventry loomed before her, for John had been just that sort of man, only she had been too blind to see him for what he really was until after they had broken their engagement. But then again, there was one obvious difference between the two men. While Todd Aylesbury had had all his land and wealth handed down to him on a silver platter, John was still struggling to acquire the wealth and power of a landowner. It was still a distant goal for John Coventry. His *only* goal as it turned out. Christina frowned at the thought of it, then tried to push the bitter thoughts aside.

"You are really going to like Todd," Justin went on to say, though now with less enthusiasm. Then, after a moment of chewing his lower lip, he lowered his green eyes to the floor, but managed to look up at her when he finally spoke again, "Please, do me a favor and be extra nice to him."

"How nice is extra nice?" she asked suspiciously, her brow raised in question. She paused in what she was doing to look directly at him.

"You know—act interested in him. Compliment him. Do whatever you can to get on his good side. Maybe get him to take a little walk with you after we eat. Get him to show you around his place. It's really something to see."

She eyed him cautiously. "And why should I do that? What if it turns out I loathe the man? There's a very strong possibility I will. He sounds too much like John. And I certainly can't encourage a man I don't even like."

"Please? For me?"

His green eyes bore into hers, pleading with her to say yes, but she refused to be swayed and turned her shoulder to him as she slowly poured the flour into the large tin canister a little at a time so as not to spill it. "I'm sorry, but I can't make any promises like that. I'm not about to complicate my life any more than it already is."

"Please?" he asked again, stepping forward so that he could turn his huge koala eyes on her once more.

"The best I can promise you, Justin Lapin, is that I'll be as cordial as I know how and on my very best behavior, but I will not go out of my way to pamper the man nor will I ply him with compliments I don't feel."

"Oh, but once you meet him, you'll feel like it. All women do, even married ones. He's just got what it takes to turn a woman's eye. He's a handsome devil."

From what she'd heard of him so far, Christina felt "devil" was certainly the appropriate word to describe the man. And the last thing she needed was to get involved with a man like that. She'd had enough rejection and humiliation in her young life without going out and looking for more. No, if she ever did feel the need to find a man to settle down with, it would be best if she looked for a nice, hardworking widower who already had so many children that he might actually be relieved to learn she would not be able to produce more. Then her inadequacy would not matter, it might actually be viewed as a blessing.

"We'll see," was all she would say when she realized Justin was waiting for a response from her. She was still unwilling to commit herself to anything she did not want to do. Then, in an effort to change the subject, she nodded toward the door. "Better go out and tell the boys supper will be ready in about half an hour. They've been cleaning out the ashbox in the privy and the floor of your horse's stall and will need to take ample time in washing up before they eat."

"At least be thinking about it," Justin said as he headed for the door. "I need all the help I can get to sway Todd'd decision in my favor." Then he was gone, leaving her more than a little angry that he could even suggest such a thing. *Be extra nice, indeed!*

Nothing else was said about Todd Aylesbury or about the station boss job that Justin so desperately wanted until after supper when Christina had gone upstairs to make sure the boys were properly tucked into bed. Edward brought up the subject again when Christina leaned over him to see if he had washed behind his ears, already having learned the lad had quite a tendency to forget such things.

"It sure is nice to have you here," he said happily, though he frowned when she bent his ear forward for inspection. "The way Father has been lately, always worried about that job he wants, he never has time for us no more. It's nice that you do."

Christina could sense the resentment in the child's voice and sat down on the edge of his bed. "Your father has little time for anything else right now, but that's because he is so worried about getting this job. It is important to him. He feels that by getting this new job, he will be able to provide better things for you and Alan and will be able to stop working altogether and make a go of his own place a lot sooner. You can understand why that is so important to him, can't you?"

"I guess so," Edward said, with no real conviction in his voice.

"We just wish he had more time for us is all," Alan tried to explain, and Christina turned to look at the younger boy in the other bed. "He's gone so much of the time. Some days he even misses supper with us and we have to eat alone."

"That won't be forever. Once the station boss's job is finally filled, by your father or someone else, I think he will become less preoccupied with his work and he will be his cheerful old self again and have a lot more time to spend around here."

"I sure hope so. I can hardly remember him being cheerful at all," Edward said, his face drawn as he thought over what she had said. "But what if he gets the job? Won't that mean he'll be away from us even more?"

"No, I don't think so. Right now, he's spending more time working in hopes of impressing Mr. Aylesbury with his sincerity. Once the need for that is gone and he has that worry off his mind, he'll have much more time for the other things that he knows are just as important. Like you two boys."

Edward stared up at her a long moment before slowly smiling and cocking his head sideways on the pillow. "I sure wish you were our mum. Why don't you marry Father so you can be here with us always?"

"You know I can't do that. Brothers and sisters don't marry. But don't you worry. I'm going to be around for as long as you need me," she said and bent down to press a kiss to his cheek, then hugged the boy goodnight. She proceeded to Alan's bed and exchanged another kiss and a hug, realizing just how fond she had become of Justin's boys. It really was a shame that he couldn't find more time to spend with his sons. A pitiful shame. It was just one more reason not to like Todd Aylesbury, allowing Justin to be away from his family so much of the time.

"Now get to sleep, you two. We'll have to rise early to get the chores all done before it's time to leave," she said, standing to go.

"That's right. We get to eat over at Mr. Aylesbury's," Edward said, and his sullen mood suddenly lifted. "I'll bet they have chocolate cake for dessert. They always have chocolate cake. Usually three layers tall, with mounds of icing between each layer. Chocolate icing."

By the time Christina had turned the lamp in the boys' room out and was headed back down the stairs, not only had the boys' moods brightened, they had managed to whet her own appetite for chocolate cake. It had been months since she'd had a slice of anything chocolate. For the first time, she had something to look forward to on the coming day. Though she would be forced to sit through a meal with a man she already did not care for, at least there was the possibility she might be ending that meal with a huge slice of chocolate cake. She could almost taste the sweetness.

"Are they asleep?" Justin asked when he noticed his sister had stepped outside to join him on the veranda. He had taken some of his new tobacco and stuffed it into a wooden pipe in preparation for lighting it.

"Not yet, but I think they will be soon enough. They

71

put in a hard day today," she told him as she walked over to one of the posts that supported the overhanging roof and leaned her shoulder against it. "Justin, I think you should know, both of your sons are feeling a little neglected these days. Edward, especially, wishes you'd spend more time at home. I told them this preoccupation you have with your work is only temporary, that as soon as the station boss's position is decided, you would settle down and once again would have time for them. I was right in telling them that, wasn't I?"

Though darkness surrounded them, neither of them having bothered to light one of the four lanterns that hung from the rafters, Christina turned to look at her brother who at the moment was a tall, unmoving, dark form in the shadows before her. She stared in his direction while she waited for a response to her question.

Justin struck a match and lifted it to the bowl of his pipe, allowing her to see the true concern on his face as he drew heavily on his pipe. Once he had the tobacco sufficiently lit, he pulled the pipe away from his mouth and shook out the match while he spoke. "What you told them was true. Once I finally get the supervisor's job, I will have a lot more time for the boys. Not only will I be getting every Saturday afternoon off like I always do, I'll also be getting every other Sunday all to myself. Just think, I'll have whole days to work this place and do things with the boys. I won't have to try to fit everything there is for me to do around here into my evenings and Saturday afternoons."

Christina was relieved to hear that and walked over to sink tiredly into one of the tall wooden chairs that lined the wide veranda. "Have you told the boys about the possibility you could be home every other Sunday if you were to get this job?"

Justin paused with his pipe just in front of his mouth, and Christina's brown eyes focused on the faint amber glow. "No, I guess I haven't. I'll do that first thing in the morning. Maybe that will help make them understand why this job is so important to me."

Finally, Christina could see that Justin had motives other than just making extra money. It would give him more time to be with his sons, something he desperately needed. She leaned her head back to rest against the tall back of the slatted chair and smiled contentedly.

For the first time, Christina found herself honestly hoping Justin did get the station boss's job. Before, when she had thought it was only a matter of more money, it had been far less important to her, because Justin seemed to be doing well enough financially without it.

Thinking of how nice it would be for Justin to be home more, she closed her eyes and listened absently to the lively concerto of distant frogs, interrupted occasionally by the bleating of a sheep from somewhere on the Aylesbury station and the even farther-distant barking of a dog. Ignoring the slight chill in the gently stirring night air, she let her thoughts drift slowly away from the not-so-happy past and dwell for the moment on all the possibilities for the future.

How wonderful it would be for the boys to have their father around more often to teach them the things boys should know, to share in life's many discoveries. And how wonderful it would be for Justin to get to know his sons better and enjoy them while they were still young. Suddenly, the prospect of being especially nice to Mr.

Todd Aylesbury and increasing Justin's chances of getting that supervisor's job did not seem quite so distasteful to Christina.

"Now, I've already told you just how important this is for us all. I want both you boys to be on your very best behavior while we are there," Justin warned his sons as he watched them climb into the back of the wagon and settle down on the freshly swept planked bottom with their backs propped against the sides. They sat near the rear of the bed so that they could see what was ahead as well as what they had just passed.

"We will," Edward assured him for the third time as he and Alan exchanged exasperated looks. "We promise."

"Just be sure that you keep that promise," Justin told them and turned to see what might be keeping Christina. He seemed pleased when his eyes lighted on her as she was coming down the steps toward the wagon. "What a pretty dress. I like it."

"Then you approve?" she asked with a slight nod and spun slowly around so that he could view the entire outfit. She had chosen to wear her best two-piece suit of light brown wool, which she had been told echoed the warm color of her eyes. It was well fitted to accentuate her feminine curves, and the neckline was just low enough to intrigue the imagination.

"Aye, I approve, and what's more, I think Todd will approve," Justin said with a knowing smile. "Get up there. I certainly don't want to be late. I want to make the best possible impression that I can today. I'm hoping he will announce who is to get Coolabah's job sometime after lunch. Coolabah won't be leaving for several weeks yet, but I think Todd will already have made up his mind about who he wants to replace him. I don't think he's going to wait until the last minute."

"And if the man has half the sense you give him credit for, he'll be telling everyone that you are the one he has chosen," Christina tried to reassure him, accepting his proffered hand and allowing him to help her up into the wagon.

"I apologize for the wagon," Justin told her as he took the driver's seat beside her. "It's the only vehicle I have at the moment, and I was afraid to ask Todd if I could borrow his carriage. I don't want to press my luck too far right now. I'm nervous as a newborn colt as it is."

"The wagon is fine," she assured him and stifled the urge to laugh at how terribly jittery Justin really was. He *was* as nervous as a newborn colt—one with a hungry dingo lurking somewhere nearby. "Calm down. We've all three promised you we'll be on our best behavior, and Todd Aylesbury already knows what a good, hard worker you are. Everything's going to be just fine."

"I don't know. I just have this gut feeling that something awful is about to happen, something I have no way of foreseeing."

"You are looking for trouble. What could possibly go wrong?"

"Why do those sound like famous last words to me? I don't know what could be wrong. I just have a feeling there is something wrong." What he could not tell her was that the horrible foreboding he had was that Todd had somehow found out what he, Justin, had been up to.

"How far is his house?" she asked, hoping to get his mind off his worries.

"You always want to know how far everything is," Justin noted with a passive smile and turned to look at her. "Always so full of questions. That's you."

"Am I?" she asked and a dimple sank into her cheek. "Why do you suppose that is?"

"I don't know. But as far back as I can remember, you've always been a regular fountain of questions."

"The way you do carry on, dear brother. If you don't know how far the Aylesbury station is from here, why don't you simply come out and say so?"

Justin narrowed his green eyes in playful warning and without realizing it, he temporarily forgot his nervousness. "It's only about two miles."

"So close? I thought the Aylesbury station was supposed to be huge."

"It is. It spreads back for miles and miles. Coolabah once told me the place is actually seventy-two thousand acres, but it is spread out in the shape of a fat T."

"He owns seventy-two thousand acres?" Christina asked, impressed. Though she never had been exactly sure how large an acre was, she did know that most people did not own even that much.

"He owns or leases. Most of it he owns free and clear. It's been in the family for years. His Grandfather Aaron was one of the first men to explore this region. And because of that, he was able to claim the better grazing lands for himself and for his future father-in-law, Oliver Cranston. As soon as it was permissible for Australians to own their lands, they bought all they could and have continually added acreage through the years."

"And now he's the sole owner of it all?"

"Just as good as. Although his grandmother is still alive and keeps a hand in the place, she prefers to live in

76

the Hawksbury District and has pretty well given it all over to Todd. Amazing thing is, that Oliver's station, which is almost as large and carries almost as much stock, was taken over by his only son, James, who never married. Todd's mother is the man's only next of kin, so it looks like one day Todd will inherit that station as well." Justin paused for a moment. "And come to think of it, his cousin, Ben Crawford, has never married either. Todd will probably inherit that station too, though it's not nearly so large."

Justin thought about that a moment longer, then spoke in awe. "Someday Todd will own a hundred fifty thousand acres of prime grazing land and will probably have double the stock, to boot. He's already running forty-nine thousand head of sheep and thirty-four thousand head of cattle." As he did a quick bit of arithmetic, adding the amount of the Cranston stock to Todd's, then Ben Crawford's, he let out a low whistle.

"And it doesn't make you nervous to think of yourself one day having to be in charge of all that?" Christina wanted to know.

"Not at all. Although the station boss has to make a lot of decisions and keep up with everything that's going on, his job itself is really fairly easy. Being the one in charge, he can have the men who work under him do all the hard work. All he really has to worry about is keeping up with who's doing what, when, and where."

"On a place that big, that doesn't sound like a very easy job to me," Christina said and wondered if her brother truly realized what he could be getting himself in for. But then she pushed the thought aside. Surely he did. And it was obvious by his eagerness to have the job that he was not at all intimidated by the enormous

77

amount of responsibility he would be taking on. If he was not worried, then she should not be worried, either.

By the time Christina finally got her first glimpse of what Justin and the lads had constantly referred to as the "main house," she had learned much more about the Aylesbury wealth, and as a result was not terribly surprised to discover exactly how very grand it was. She had expected it would be large and made of brick. She had also expected the outbuildings to be just as large as they were, though she had not expected there to be so many. As her gaze swept the yard and the surrounding paddocks, she counted fourteen outbuildings within her sight. And it looked as if there had recently been a fifteenth, that had somehow caught fire and burned.

The barn and stable were easily recognized, for although incredibly large, their structures were typical. And not far from the main house, there was a second brick building, which she strongly suspected to be the coach house because of the way the drive curled around the side of the house and ran directly beneath the building's wide double doors. What the other eleven buildings were, she could only guess.

As she waited for Justin to circle around the wagon and assist her down from the high seat, Christina continued to assess her surroundings. She felt almost relieved that even if she should not find anything about the man himself to compliment, she could offer him an honest word of praise on his house. It was grand. It seemed even grander still as they approached the huge, elaborately carved front door.

Christina smiled and cut her eyes toward her brother to see what his reaction was when they were met at the front door by a richly-liveried black doorman. Justin seemed to be taking it all in easy stride as the older gentleman greeted the four of them cordially, then slowly escorted them into the main salon to await Todd Aylesbury's presence. It was not until the man had left, with the same unhurried gait, to announce their arrival to his boss that Christina made the comment, "I wouldn't mind having his job."

The lads thought her comment hilarious and burst out in a fit of giggles.

"Shhh," Justin said, his brow drawn low in warning. "Someone will hear you."

Both boys reached up and covered their mouths with their hands and tried to control their laughter, but one glance in each other's direction made it impossible, and they burst out in an even louder round of giggles.

Curious about her elegant surroundings, Christina managed to quiet the boys to Justin's satisfaction and was finally able to turn her attention to the expensive furniture, carpets, and the many elaborate paintings that adorned the room when she first heard the footsteps approach just outside the door.

They all turned in unison to be greeted by their host, Christina by now very curious to meet a man of such wealth and such obvious good taste. Placing a polite smile on her face, she went to stand by Justin's far side and had just turned to face the door again when the tall, lanky doorman entered, followed immediately by an even taller, broad-shouldered man, far younger than she had expected.

In that second Christina recognized him. Her smile withered and her heart slammed hard against her breast, forcing a low gasp of horror from deep inside her throat. Though she did not want to believe it, there was no mistaking the man's identity. It was impossible, but true.

The man who had just entered the room but had yet to look at her was the very same man she had had such trouble with in Sydney. She felt the blood drain from her face and race to the aid of her heart, keenly aware of the muscles that tensed in his jaw at the exact moment his gaze came to rest on her. Her legs ached with a desperate need to run for safety, but she found herself rooted to the spot. Slowly, he took his first step in her direction for *he* was in no way rooted to where he stood.

## Chapter V

"*She's* your sister?" Todd asked as he stared down at the same beauty who had caused him so much aggravation only a few days earlier. The repressed anger he had fought since that night he had caught the woman searching his room flared instantly.

"Y-you know Christina?" Justin asked, clearly confused. Todd had not been home twenty-four hours, and as far as he knew, Christina had not left the house since she had arrived. She had kept too busy with her work even to take a leisurely walk out into the yard. How could the two have met?

"I know her only too well," Todd replied in a voice cold with restrained emotion. Though his words were directed to Justin, his narrowed gaze never once left Christina's face.

Christina realized that the narrower his eyes became, the wider hers grew, until she could feel her own eyes bulging almost out of their sockets. She knew it was time to do some quick explaining, but where should she begin? Taking a deep, steadying breath, she could finally feel the color climbing back into her cheeks and was well aware that the color was now bright red.

"We met in Sydney." She began by answering the question so clearly visible on her brother's confused and concerned face.

"By mistake, I believe," Todd put in with noted sarcasm. His brow dipped meaningfully as his gaze continued to pierce her.

"Aye, by mistake," she snapped in quick response to his implied meaning. "If you would just give me a chance, I might be able to explain just how I came to be in your room."

"In his *room?*" Justin asked, horrified. His eyes also had grown wide just before he reached for the back of a chair, suddenly needing its support in order to remain standing.

"Going through my things," Todd pointed out with a firm nod, his expression giving no quarter.

Christina felt her anger rising degree by degree and used all the restraint she possessed to remain relatively calm until she could at least get the boys out of the room. "Alan, Edward, why don't you two go on outside and play for a little while. It's such a pretty day."

After the lads had shrugged their shoulders and left the room, Justin looked over at his sister with a mixed expression of disbelief and anger on his face. "Just what in the bloody hell were you doing in Todd's room going through his things?" Slowly he ran his hand over his face, as if this was all he needed. Though none of this made sense to him, he could see all his well-laid plans shriveling to nothing right before his eyes.

"Aye, what were you doing in my room?" Todd repeated the question for her, then quickly added,

"Dressed in nothing more than your skimpies." His gaze dropped to her neckline, as if he well remembered what lay beneath her clothing.

Christina let out a sharp breath of exasperation. The man was determined to make this as difficult as he possibly could. Because it happened to be her brother's opinion that was most important to her at the moment, she turned her back to Todd Aylesbury and looked up at Justin, her eyes pleading with him for understanding.

Attempting to keep the growing irritation she felt from getting the better of her, she clenched her fists at her sides and opened her mouth, but was interrupted yet again by Todd's impudent voice.

"Seem's your sister likes to enter locked rooms dressed in only her lacy chemise—in bold search of money to steal."

"I wasn't searching for money," she ground out between clenched teeth, but did not bother to turn back around to look at him. She was too close to tears now to let him see her face.

"Then what were you searching for?" she heard him ask.

"Clothes," she snapped back, then closed her eyes as it became harder to hold back her tears and to control her anger.

"You broke into this man's room to steal his clothes?" Justin asked. A deep furrow dented his brow. His grip on the chair tightened as he tried to make sense of everything that the two had said thus far.

"No," she answered, and sighed heavily. Why was it that the more she tried to explain the worse it sounded? "I didn't *exactly* break into his room and I was not going to *steal* the clothes. I was only going to borrow them."

83

Justin pressed his eyes closed and steadied himself for whatever else she had to say.

Todd's voice broke in at that moment, low and accusing. "That door was locked. If you didn't break into that room, how did you get in . . . *exactly*." He put added emphasis on the word she had chosen to use.

Knowing already how incriminating it was going to sound, she turned to look up at him, still fighting back a wild torrent of emotion, and answered truthfully. "I'm not sure. I think I came in through the window."

"What do you mean you aren't sure? You've had plenty of time to think this through and get your story straight. Did you come in through the window or not? Maybe you had a key." The thought had just occurred to him. That particular door had been forced open so many times that he never could have proven she had forced it open, and maybe she hadn't. If that was so, she might have had a partner. Or maybe more than one? Could Justin have set it up?

Now that he thought about it, Justin *had* been behaving a little oddly lately. Though Justin had always been the jittery sort, he had become more so over the past few weeks. And if this woman was working as Justin's pawn, could his own stockman have been involved in other schemes against him? Did he have anything to do with the missing cattle? Or was Justin really just as surprised about all this as he seemed?

He glanced only briefly at Justin before returning his gaze to Christina. He knew Justin was down on his luck these days, and Justin was the only one who had been told exactly where he and Coolabah planned to stay in Sydney. And Justin had also been aware that he'd planned to come back with the money to meet the monthly payroll yesterday. The poker winnings might simply have been coincidental, an added bonus for them, and thus might have had nothing to do with the attempt to rob him as he had at first assumed.

He narrowed his eyes as he tried to read the woman's thoughts. "I want to know how you came to be in my room. Did you sneak in through my window or not?"

"Maybe I did," she said in angry response, tired of trying to explain to someone determined not to listen. The truth was getting her nowhere. Maybe she should just let him believe what he wanted to believe and be done with it. "Or maybe I lied to the desk clerk and told him I was your wife and explained that I wanted to surprise you. I don't think he fully believed I was really your wife, but he felt that the sort of surprise I obviously had in mind for you would be welcome. And after I passed him a gold coin, he seemed to have absolutely no qualms about handing me the key to your room."

When that absurd explanation seemed to pacify Todd, it only enraged her more. "You *believe* that?"

"It's the closest you have come to anything that makes sense yet."

"You . . . you . . . you," she sputtered, so angry now that words failed her. Unable to defend herself against his accusations any longer, she turned on her heel and stormed out of the house. She would not stand there and allow him to talk to her like that.

"Come back here," he shouted at her and started after her.

Hearing his booted footsteps coming in her direction, she reached down to raise her long woolen skirts and began to run. Tears of rage had formed in her eyes even before she fled the house. Unable to see where she was

85

headed, she slowed down once she was outside but never considered stopping for even a minute. To her dismay, the footsteps were getting closer.

"Christina!"

Relief flooded her when she recognized Justin's voice. Finally stopping and turning to face him, she waited until he reached her before responding. "What?"

"I don't know what that was all about, but I do know you are no thief," he said as he enveloped her in his arms and held her close until her angry tears eventually played out. When he was certain she was again in control of her emotions, he spoke softly. "Let's go home. We can talk there. Go get in the wagon. I'll find the boys. They are probably in the stable looking at Todd's horses."

Christina felt a stab of guilt pierce through everything else she was already suffering. Because of her, the boys' day would be ruined. She had ruined everyone's day.

When Justin did not get a response to his suggestion, he added encouragingly, "Don't worry about lunch. We can find something to eat at home."

Taking her by the arm, Justin slowly started toward the wagon. He was curious to find out exactly what had gone on back in Sydney. There had to be a reasonable explanation. Once he knew what that was, he might be able to do something to help straighten this out. And he knew he needed to get it straightened out as quickly as possible, because Todd's anger with his little sister could very well affect the man's decision concerning the station boss's job.

"No," she finally managed to say, despite the constriction in her throat. "The boys have looked forward to this visit. I don't want to spoil things for them. Let them stay, that is, if Mr. Aylesbury will still allow it.

You stay, too. Behave as if nothing has changed as far as you are concerned. I want to be alone for a little while, anyway. Let me walk home. It will help work off some of my anger. It is only a couple of miles. It will do me good."

Despite her anger at that horrible man in there, she had to remain practical for everyone else's sake.

The twisted expression that crossed Justin's face as she stepped away from him let her know just how perplexed he was over her argument with his boss. Christina could not help but smile a little at her brother's rightful confusion. But then, he could not be any more confused than she was. If only the man had not been so stubborn. If only he had let her explain what had really happened, or at least try to.

Lifting her face to the warming rays of the sun high overhead, she let it soothe her tear-streaked face and allowed the exertion of her walk to ease the tension in her body. She wondered if the man would have believed her anyway.

The boys sat in silence beside their father as the wagon rattled down the well-worn track toward home. A frown bore deep into Justin's face. His anger had slowly subsided as the wagon jolted along, and when his anger dissolved, it left him more room to concentrate on the repercussions his hotheadedness were sure to bring—a thought that was quickly followed by a sense of deep, utter misery. Not only would that foolish display of anger he had just shown cost him that station boss's job he so desperately needed, it had probably cost him his stockman's job as well. What on earth was he to do now? Time had all but run out. They just *might* kill him.

Justin groaned aloud. He had known better than to lose control like that. He should have shown more restraint with his boss, especially when he had so much to lose. But when Todd had again openly accused his sister of being a thief and a harlot, Justin had been unable to keep his mouth closed. He knew his sister far too well, and fully believed that no matter what Christina had done or how and why she had come to be in Todd's hotel room, she was neither a thief nor a harlot. But Todd had stubbornly refused to listen to reason and had kept repeating the facts as he saw them. Then the man had actually hinted that he thought big brother might have had something to do with little sister's getting into his room.

Justin shook his head as he remembered the rage he had shown after that. Of all his crimes, leading his sister into something like that would never be one of them. He might be willing to ask her to be extra nice to Todd for his sake, and might have tried to use her to get Todd out of the way when he needed her to, but he would never ask her to seduce a man in order to get what he wanted. How could Todd have thought such a thing? Christina was family. He'd have to be pretty desperate to involve his sister that deeply. But then again, his situation was becoming increasingly more desperate by the day.

As Justin drew the wagon to a halt in front of the house, he glanced across the paddock toward the slight rise that prevented him from seeing Todd's house. When he had not passed Christina along the track, he realized she must have taken a shorter route home through the paddocks. But she was not anywhere in sight. Still agonizing over what had happened at Todd's and what effect it could have on his future, but at the same time growing concerned for his sister's welfare, Justin called out her name. To his surprise the response came from inside the house.

"How'd you get home so quickly?" he asked as he stepped inside the front door to find her standing at the bottom of the stairs with one foot trailing behind her and resting on the first step, as if she had just come down.

"Walking was not taking care of my anger. I ran most of the way," she stated simply. Her eyebrows were wet, as was her hairline, and her dark mane of hair had been pushed back away from her forehead. It was obvious she had just washed her face in an effort to remove all trace of her tears, but there was still a slight puffiness about her eyes.

Edward and Alan exchanged curious glances but said nothing as they headed for the stairs, their hands already working with the buttons of their best shirts.

Justin waited until he heard their door close before speaking again. His voice did not reveal any of the different emotions that still tumbled inside of him as he gently placed his wide cabbage tree hat on the peg near the door. "I really think I need to know just what happened at that hotel back in Sydney. I know you are not a thief, and I believe you when you say you were after his clothes, but what I can't fathom at this moment is why."

A tiny smile tugged at Christina's mouth when she thought about how it must seem to Justin. She had admitted to being in the man's room, and to borrowing his clothes, of all things. It sounded even more absurd than it was.

"Let's go into the kitchen where we won't be overheard," she said, gesturing overhead to where the boys were.

Once they were in the kitchen and she had carefully closed the door, Christina started at the beginning, trying to remain as calm as her brother now seemed.

Justin listened without interrupting. Knowing from experience the amazing things Christina could accomplish when she walked in her sleep, he did not doubt a word of her story. Had he realized sooner that it had been her sleepwalking that was involved, he might have been able to explain it to Todd. As incredible as her story might sound, he might yet be able to get Todd to listen to it. Especially if he waited until Todd had had time to cool down a little. But did he have time for that?

"Justin, do you think Mr. Aylesbury will let what happened in Sydney affect his decision about who he wants for his station boss?" Christina wanted to know, worried now that she might have caused her brother serious problems. "I'd hate to think I was the cause of your not getting that promotion you so want."

"No, don't worry about that," Justin said with a reassuring shrug just before he rose from the chair he had taken and turned to face the door. "Guess I'd better get out there and get a little work done now that I have a little unexpected time."

Eager as he was to get everything straightened out, Justin knew it would be best to wait until morning to approach Todd again. Putting on a convincing smile, he headed out the door. He had no intention of burdening Christina with details of the argument he and Todd had had after she'd left and now wanted time to be alone and think. Other problems needed his full attention at the moment, especially since it was obvious Todd would not be appointing him station boss in time. He realized he had

90

better come up with a backup plan of some sort. One that would save his neck but at the same time not involve too many risks.

Christina placed the heavy iron lid over the steaming pot. It was just a matter of letting the food cook a little longer to soften the vegetables, and supper would be ready. With that task out of the way, she turned to folding the clothes she had just brought in from outside and placed in a pile on the worktable near the back door.

Though Sunday was not a day to be doing household chores, she had decided that this particular Sunday was an exception. It was a perfect day to get things done. The incident that morning had left her tense and full of anger that still needed to be burned off, and she was getting those chores done with amazing speed.

"Can I help?" she heard Edward ask as she snapped a towel by the corners to get as many of the wrinkles out as possible. She looked up to discover her older nephew standing just a few feet away. She smiled warmly, for Edward showed a real eagerness to help in any way he could, a trait that was not always present in a boy so young.

"That would be nice," she assured him and handed him a shirt to fold. She was pleased and a little surprised to discover he already knew how to fold so the creases fell in line with the seams.

As she reached for a pair of Alan's trousers and shook them, Christina sensed that Edward wanted to talk to her about something, but was reluctant. Maybe he did not know how to bring up the subject. After a few moments of silent work, Christina decided to get things started for him. "I guess you are a little curious about what happened this morning. Probably wondering why I came home alone the way I did."

Edward nodded, glanced briefly up at her, then back down at the clothes he was folding. "When Alan and I came out of the barn, we could hear Father shouting at Mr. Aylesbury, then we saw you walking away, already far along the track."

Christina paused in her work. "Your father was shouting at Mr. Aylesbury?"

Justin had mentioned nothing about having had an argument with his boss after she had left. She had assumed he had come on home without staying for lunch because he was so curious to hear what she had to say in her own defense. It had never occurred to her that Justin would have been foolish enough to have words with the man when he had so much at stake. Earlier, when he had told her not to worry about the misunderstanding, she had assumed everything was still all right between Justin and his boss. Now she wondered.

A fine blending of pride and concern washed over her when she thought more about it. For a man as selfish as Justin to have taken up for his sister at a time like this was truly a noble thing.

"We couldn't hear what Father was saying to him, but we could tell he was angry. Next thing we knew, he came outside and told us to get in the wagon." Edward shrugged and turned to her in anticipation of an explanation.

Christina was still too stunned to speak. It was still a little much for her to believe. Justin had defended her at the risk of his losing his job. Then it occurred to her that maybe he had already lost his job. If he had been unwilling to tell her about the argument, then he would have been just as unwilling to tell her about having been fired. She realized it would be just like that arrogant boss of his to fire Justin on the spot. And for something Justin had nothing to do with!

"Edward, I think Justin and Mr. Aylesbury just had a difference of opinion is all. It probably wasn't anything serious. I'm certain by tomorrow they will have forgotten all about it." She hated to lie to the child, but then again, she did not want the lad to worry about things he couldn't be expected to understand. There was no point upsetting him any worse than he already was.

It was not until after an early supper that Christina found the courage she needed to do something about the problem she had created for her brother. Swallowing her pride, knowing it was up to her to try to talk some sense into that horrible man, she told Justin she was going for a short walk before it turned dark and asked him to see that the boys came in from their play within the hour. She did not bother to tell him that her walk would lead her directly to Todd Aylesbury's door.

The sun hung low over the distant treetops when she finally came within sight of the Aylesbury house. When she saw just how close to setting the sun was, Christina realized she would be forced to return in the dark. Having no lantern with her, she considered using that as an excuse to turn back. If she hurried, she could be back at Justin's before it got too dark. But she pushed that thought aside and remained determined to see her task through. She would worry about the dark when the time came to return home. For now she had enough to worry about. Justin's livelihood was far too important.

All too soon, she stood in front of the elaborately handcarved door, her hand poised over the worn brass door knocker, trying to quiet the anxiety that raced wildly through her body. Her heart pounded so loudly and with such force she could actually feel its heavy throb beneath her breast.

"Courage, Christina," she said quietly, then gritted her teeth and rapped on the door sharply.

When her knock did not bring anyone to the door, she tried again, then stepped over to the tall, narrow window beside it and peered inside. The window was open and the curtains drawn back, allowing a breeze inside and enabling her to see into the long, narrow corridor that divided the house.

The only thing that prevented her crawling through the window was a very thin layer of wire mesh that covered the entire opening, which could be easily torn away. Knowing no one would leave his house so unsecured, she was certain the man was home. But why had he not answered her knock?

"Hello?" she called out before her hand went to the doorknob.

Though there was no response to her call, she could hear noises from inside the house. That left her certain he was in there, just stubborn and purposely ignoring her. He had obviously instructed his doorman to ignore her, too.

Tentatively, she opened the door and took a few steps inside, keeping her attention tuned to the noises still coming from just down the corridor, determined as ever to have a word with the man. Concentrating on the door from which the noises came, she jumped with a start when she heard the front door slam shut behind her. But when she whirled to face Todd Aylesbury, he was not there. No one was. Then she realized the door must have blown shut, or else the man had rigged a sturdy spring to the door frame to keep the door from being accidentally left open.

With her nerves now shattered, Christina pressed her hand to her breastbone in a protective gesture and called out again, her voice not quite as strong as before.

"Hello? Mr. Aylesbury?"

Still there was no response. Again her attention was drawn to the noise coming from the open door at the far end of the corridor.

"Mr. Aylesbury, please, I realize you are angry with me, but I need to talk with you. Calmly. I want to try again to explain," she said, heading for the door, certain that was where she would find the man who was so obviously trying to ignore her.

"You might as well answer me. I know you can hear me." More than a hint of the irritation she felt had crept into her voice as she approached the door. "And you are going to listen to what I have to say whether you care to or not."

Prepared to do verbal battle with the man, she clenched her fists and stepped bravely into the room, surprised when she did not find anyone there. There was a large multidrawer desk in the center of the room facing a wide window with a huge black leather chair behind and several other empty black leather chairs scattered about the room.

Black pipe tobacco still smoldered in a metal ashbowl, indicating that it had not been very long since the room had been occupied. Then, glancing down, she noticed a large dog lying on the floor with a ragged paper box on the floor beside it. That was where the noise had come from.

Christina felt her legs grow weak and wobbly, but she was not sure if her reaction was from relief or disappointment. Shaking her head as she realized her search had not yet ended, she turned and headed out of the room, still determined to find Todd Aylesbury and make him listen to her.

When she stepped out into the hall and glanced in the other direction, she found Todd Aylesbury. He stood inside the back doorway with his hands firmly planted on his lean, narrow hips, staring accusingly at her. Having taken off his frock coat and opened his shirt at the neck, he looked ready to do battle.

Right behind him, half hidden by his broad shoulder, was a woman about the same age as Christina, also staring at her with wide, accusing eyes.

"Up to your old tricks are you?" Todd said in a low, menacing voice, his angry blue gaze bearing right into her very soul. Unable to move her eyes away from his, she could sense that his muscles were tense, his body prepared to spring into action.

# Chapter VI

"Don't tell me," Todd said, raising his hand in a gesture meant to prevent her from uttering her next word. "You just want to borrow some of my clothes."

Christina could not have spoken if she wanted to. Though she desperately needed air to think, she could not breathe for a long, helpless moment. Still her brain gasped for the words to explain what she was doing in his house, knowing already that he would not believe her any more this time than he had the last.

"I-I was looking for you," she finally managed to say, impressed that she had indeed spoken. She was aware that the woman with him had stepped forward and made a big production out of latching on to his arm and pressing her cheek against his shoulder. It was a clear statement of ownership, and for a moment Christina felt the urge to laugh at the lunacy behind such behavior. If the woman felt she was any threat to whatever relationship she had with Todd Aylesbury, she could not possibly get any further from reality.

"You were looking for me," Todd repeated flatly,

nodding in a way that revealed he in no way believed a word of it. "If that was what you were really up to, why didn't I hear you call out my name? It really would have been very easy for you to have simply called out for me so I would know you were here."

"I did. Before I ever entered this house, I called out."

"We were just a few feet outside the house," he mentioned quickly, and the pert nod from the woman at his side let her know he spoke the truth. "Why didn't we hear you?"

"I don't know. Maybe your attention was drawn elsewhere," she said pointedly, cutting her gaze to the pretty young woman and then back. "But I did call out."

Todd let out an impatient breath and tried to shift his weight, but the woman clung to him so tightly he was unable to. He frowned with annoyance. "Let's say I believe you on that point. Let's say you did indeed call out for me and I simply did not hear you. The next question is, since you obviously heard no response beckoning you to come on in, why did you take it upon yourself to enter my house?"

Finally he managed to shake his arm free from the woman at his side and crossed both his arms in front of his chest as he stared at Christina with defiance. Insolently, he shifted his weight to one leg and waited for her response.

"I heard noises coming from inside the house. It sounded like someone shuffling papers. I thought you were in here ignoring me, but making just enough noise so that I would know it," she told him, her voice rising in anger. She crossed her arms defiantly. The two faced each other like two angry bulls for a long moment before she finished what she had to say. "I came on inside, hoping to persuade you to put aside your anger long enough to give me a chance to explain about the incident at the hotel."

The other woman's gray-green eyes widened considerably at that remark and she responded by grabbing for Todd's arm again, her curious gaze going to his solemn expression as if hoping to read something there. Her voluptuous chest heaved when she then turned her eyes to Christina and narrowed them.

Christina wondered exactly what sinister little thought had just passed through the woman's mind. It was obvious that whatever it was had not pleased her in the slightest. Ironically, Christina hoped the foolish woman had thought the worst. Let her suffer from whatever evil her stupid little brain could produce. "But as it turned out, when I finally found the source of all the noise I kept hearing, it was your dog making it and not you."

The woman continued to grow perceptibly angrier with every word Christina said, until she could no longer remain silent. With her tiny nostrils flared and her shining head of black curls tossed back, she spoke in an angry rush. "Even if it had been Todd in there making the noise you claim you heard, you still had no right to enter his house without first obtaining his permission. Even if he had been in here purposely ignoring you, that would be his right. Just who are you?"

"Let me introduce you," Todd quickly interjected and the first sign of a smile tugged at the outer corners of his lips. He was clearly amused by this woman's elaborate show of temper. "Vella Stone, meet Christina Lapin. Christina is Justin's little sister."

"Justin's sister?" Her pretty brow knitted into an

immediate frown. "And is that what that business concerning the hotel was about? She's been using her feminine charms, or what little she has of them, in hopes of convincing you to choose Justin over William? Is that it? She's out to do what she can to see that Justin becomes your new station boss?"

Rather than deny her accusation, Todd simply smiled and waited for Christina to defend herself. How dearly she would have loved to reach up and slap that insipid smile right off his face. A nice red mark across his lean cheek would have looked very good to her about now.

"I have no such intentions." Christina's voice came out remarkably calm. "Justin can get that job on his own merits. Even a man as close-minded and hopelessly stubborn as Mr. Aylesbury seems to be cannot help but see what a good, hard worker Justin is. Justin doesn't need any outside help from me."

"I don't wish to disillusion you, my dear, but your brother can't hold a candle to a man like William," Vella said with a smile that did not quite reach her dark, gray-green eyes. "*My* brother not only has more experience, he is older and far more capable of handling the men. And Todd already knows that. Justin will just have to be satisfied with the job he has now."

So that was it. This woman's brother was the other man being considered for the station boss's job. Justin had mentioned there was one man in direct competition with him, and Vella Stone's instant dislike of her made even more sense now. It was not just jealousy. She saw Christina as a threat to her brother. And glancing over the woman's fancy green dress with its shamefully low neckline that revealed far more than a modest amount of womanly flesh, Christina could not help but wonder if

100

this pretty Miss Stone might actually be guilty of doing the very thing she seemed so quick to accuse her of. And, if that was indeed the case, it was more than obvious that Miss Stone was enjoying the task.

"Vella, I told you just a few minutes ago that I haven't made up my mind which man I prefer for the job—William or Justin. They both have their good points, but then again they both have a few bad points to consider, too," Todd put in.

"Aye, Justin has quite a few bad points for you to consider," Vella was quick to add, her eyes narrowing as if daring Christina to say anything in his defense.

"So does William," Todd said tiredly, as if he had been over and over it with her and had finally taken about all he could of the subject. "Now, as I recall, you were just about to leave. I'll get your shawl for you and see you to your carriage." He lowered his eyebrows with a clear warning and said to Christina, "You stay right there. I'll be back in a few minutes. Don't you move a step."

Christina was well aware of the daggers Vella Stone's eyes cast in her direction while she waited for Todd to step inside the room Christina had just come out of and lift a white knitted shawl from the back of a chair. Nothing else was said between the two women. Nothing else had to be said. They were sending clear enough messages to each other with their eyes. Messages even Todd could not miss.

Once Todd led Vella outside and finally out of her sight, Christina felt a little foolish standing alone in the middle of the hallway and decided she did not care if he had ordered her not to move. She had no intention of simply standing there and waiting for him to return. But finding her legs were very weak at the moment, she knew she would not go very far, and she chose to return to the closest room and wait. The large golden-haired dog pricked up his ears when he heard her enter and glanced at her only momentarily when she sat down in the first chair she came to, then returned his attention to what was left of his box.

She expected to wait for quite some time, sure that Vella would delay her parting for as long as possible. But it was just a few minutes later that she heard Todd's determined footsteps coming back down the hallway. Gripping the arms of the leather chair she had chosen, she stared instantly out the only window in the room, which was huge, and prepared herself for the worst.

"So tell me. Was Vella right?" he asked as he entered the room.

She had expected his first comment to be about her having dared to move, and it took her a moment to comprehend what he had actually said.

"What?"

"Was Vella right about you?" he asked again. By now he had moved across the room and come to stand just a few feet in front of her with his back to the window. His shadow, created by the fading rays of the late afternoon sun that slanted through the window, fell across her skirt. "Have you come in your brother's behalf? Have you come here to see what you can do about his chances of getting Coolabah's job?"

"Aye, in a way I have," she conceded, and immediately stood to be on a more even level with him, but found that in doing so, she had placed herself only inches away from him. Her heart jumped as she quickly moved away.

"And how far are you willing to go to do that?" he asked in a mellowed voice while he stepped out of the fading sunlight and into the shadows of the room, directly toward her.

Finding his movement in her direction threatening, she backed further away, only to find that he had every intention of following her. For every backward step she took, he reciprocated with a forward movement of his own. He stalked her, much as a wild dingo would its intended prey. His blue eyes dipped hungrily downward more than once to take in her feminine curves while he closed the distance between them.

"I'm not willing to go that far, I assure you," she stated in a cool, controlled voice. But despite her appearance of calm and determination, her body was responding rebelliously to his continuous approach. It was as if a part of her wanted him to catch her, just to find out what might happen, to see how she could handle it, but that was not only ridiculous, it was dangerous. She continued to back away. "Maybe you should call your little friend back if that is the sort of persuasion you are looking for, because I have no such intention."

Trying not to lose herself in the glimmering blue depths of his eyes as he drew closer, she pulled her gaze from his and looked down, only to become just as distracted by the nearness of his strong, muscular body clad in a partially open silk dinner shirt and close-fitting trousers. The lingering scent of the outdoors mixed with the rich smell of pipe tobacco was next to catch her attention.

"Too bad. I have a feeling you could be very convincing if you tried," he offered with a meaningful raising of his brow, and he continued to move toward her, his eyes still on hers.

Soon he had literally backed her against a wall, and he

smiled victoriously when she finally realized she was trapped. He stood just inches away from her, and although their bodies were not quite touching, she could feel the heat that radiated from him.

"You said you had something to say to me." His voice grew low and husky. "I'm now willing to hear whatever it is you have to say."

As distracted by him as she was, she still managed to remember what she wanted to say, or at least most of it. "I came here to ask you not to fire Justin."

"I didn't intend to," Todd told her as he lifted his right hand to run a fingertip lightly over her cheek. The action sent shivers streaming down Christina's spine and caused tiny bumps of anticipation to rise along her skin.

"I wasn't sure," she said, pressing herself harder against the cold surface of the wall in an attempt to put even a quarter of an inch more distance between them. "Edward told me how he had heard you and Justin arguing after I left, and I was afraid you would use that as an excuse to take some of your anger out on him, when it all should be directed at me. I'm the one you found in your room. Not him."

"That's true. After Justin left here, I realized he had been taken completely by surprise when he learned that you had been in my hotel room. No, all Justin is guilty of is an overabundance of loyalty to his sister and coming foolishly to your defense. Obviously, he thinks highly of you. He doesn't believe you are capable of being a thief and became absolutely furious with me when I told him how you had intended to seduce me."

"I never intended such a thing!"

"Oh, come now. You were in my room, dressed in a chemise so thin that I was able to make out every tempting curve of your body. Your beautiful hair had been let down and made to curve enticingly around your soft shoulders. No woman enters a man's room looking like that unless she plans to seduce him." His eyes darkened with the memory of that night.

"I wasn't even awake!"

"That's interesting, because you certainly fought like someone who was wide awake." He bent down so that his breath fell softly against her ear.

Again tiny bumps rose just beneath the surface of her skin and delicate waves of tingling sensation drifted through her body.

"Don't worry, dear—although I admit that I originally went to the authorities there in Sydney and told them about the incident, hoping they would be able to help me find you, I don't intend to go to them again," he went on to say. "So you don't have to keep lying to me about what you did."

"I'm not lying. And I *was* asleep. At least when I first entered your room I was. That's why I don't remember how I got in there. All I know is that I went to bed in my own room, but somehow woke up standing in the middle of your room. Ask Justin. I've walked in my sleep for as long as either of us can remember. Although I haven't done it in years, that night, for some reason, I got up from my bed and found my way into your room. And if your door was locked like you said, all I can assume is that I came in through the window."

Todd brought his face to within an inch of hers and gazed deeply into the dark depths of her shining brown eyes. "Do you honestly want me to believe you crawled the ledge from your room to mine in your sleep?"

"I've done far stranger things in my sleep," she said in

105

a strangled voice. With his lips so close to hers, her heart hammered furiously in her chest and her throat tightened until she could barely swallow, much less speak clearly. When his gaze left hers to linger momentarily on her lips, she could no longer breathe. All she could do was stand mutely before him, her eyes fixed on his slightly parted mouth, anticipating his next move.

Todd gave no indication of whether he believed her or if he even cared if what she had just told him was the truth. He gazed at her full and tempting lips only a moment longer before giving in to his innermost impulse. Slowly, he brought his mouth against hers and kissed her gently.

Outraged, Christina tried to push him away. She was unable to move him out of her way. Her eyes flashed with furious indignation as she brought her hand against the side of his face with a force that shocked both of them. "How dare you!"

Todd gripped her firmly by the shoulders and brought his lips down on hers again, this time kissing her more forcefully.

Christina again fought to free herself, but found it more difficult. He had too secure a hold on her this time. Finally she gave up her futile struggle against so powerful a man and allowed him his kiss, thinking he would tire of it quickly.

A strange warmth flooded her senses, making her feel a bit light-headed, but she was not about to give in to the strange sensation. She was determined to ignore totally any feeling he stirred within her and waited for the kiss to end.

But when he did not stop kissing her, she felt the strange warmth settle into her most intimate of places.

Christina quickly panicked and brought her hands up to his chest to try once again to push him away. The effort made him tighten his hold, bringing her body closer against his. She was startled to feel her breasts flattened against the hard plane of his chest and she was mortified that he would be so bold with her. Drawing on a strength she was no longer sure she even had, she finally pushed him away and stared up at him, her eyes dark with passion.

Still unsatisfied with her reaction, though it was a definite step in the right direction, Todd pulled her into another passionate embrace and kissed her again. With her body molded to his, he put all he had into the next kiss, and for the first time, sensed her body relaxing as she finally relented and allowed herself a brief moment of pleasure.

Even though Christina had sensed the danger that lurked inside this man, she had foolishly thought the kiss would not affect her. Kissing John never had. But this man's kiss was somehow different from anything she had ever experienced, and the moment her hands moved up to his neck, she knew she was in trouble.

An unfamiliar hunger grew inside her, an awakening that was so strong it rendered her helpless. A warm and gentle tide surged through her veins, washing her with more strange sensations, powerful beyond belief, urging her to give in and weakening her desire to escape, building her need to explore these sensations further.

Her very proper upbringing firmly dictated that she make another attempt to free herself before it was too late. But her body rebelled against the idea, willing her not to pull away, but to lean against him instead, to learn more about the strange and magical pleasure she had found in his kiss.

Even when his hands moved down her spine until they came to rest on the soft curve of her hips, she was unable to move away from him. His lips were maddeningly sweet, alarmingly hungry, and as the kiss slowly deepened, fire coursed through her, spreading a heat so sensual, so all-consuming, that it melted any last shred of resistance. He had cast his spell over her and she was lost to this wondrous magic.

The frantic thudding of her heart became louder, drowning out everything else, as his hands moved from the gentle curve of her hips slowly up toward her breast. Although she was terrified of the intense power he had over her and could still clearly sense the immediate danger she was in, she could not find the willpower to stop him. Whatever his intentions were, she could not fight him. She was too unfamiliar with the passions that had so suddenly overcome her even to know how to combat them, and she was becoming less and less sure they should be controlled.

Todd moaned deep within his throat when he realized he finally had gotten the response from her that he wanted. He could sense that she was still hesitant, but when he brought his hand up to cup the underside of her breast and discovered her only reaction was to gasp for air, he knew she was his. He burned with a desire to take her quickly, but knew he must go slow. Gently, he played with first one firm mound, then the other, through the soft material of her dress, pleased that she now did nothing to stop him. His heart clamored with such overwhelming urgency that he did not at first hear the loud pounding at his front door.

Even when the sharp noise penetrated the thick fog of

passion that had enveloped him, Todd chose to ignore whoever had chosen to call at such an inopportune moment and did not break away from Christina. But when he realized it was Justin's voice calling him, he knew he had better not ignore it for long and he forced himself to pull away. It was not until he had stepped away from her that he realized the room had grown almost completely dark. Knowing that would not look right in Justin's eyes, for the man clearly revered his sister, he moved to the nearest lamp and struck a match.

He heard the front door slam shut and knew that Justin had wasted little time in entering the house and would expect him to be in his office. Todd had barely managed to get the lamp lit and the flame adjusted before Justin appeared in the doorway.

Christina had not moved other than to reach up and smooth several strands of hair back into place, and Justin did not immediately notice her as he burst into the room.

"Todd, you've got to help me. Christina went for a walk earlier this afternoon and never made it back—" his voice broke off when his gaze came to rest on his sister, her lips still full and reddened from having just been so thoroughly kissed and her hair mussed just enough to be noticeable. Her brown eyes were wide with untold horrors. "Just what in the hell is going on here?" he demanded as he came to stand protectively between the two of them and then turned to face Todd.

"Nothing much," Todd answered nonchalantly and shrugged his shoulders as if he had no idea why Justin would even suspect anything had been going on.

For some reason, the casual tone in Todd's response stung Christina's pride, for it had been quite a lot to her, more than she fully understood yet, but she wisely chose

109

to remain quiet.

"We were just doing something your sister strongly felt needed to be done," Todd went on to say as he leaned against the side of his desk.

Christina's eyes widened and she opened her mouth with every intention of protesting that remark, but he did not give her time to speak before he continued. "She felt we needed to discuss a few things. She came over here very determined to explain what happened in Sydney and why. And I'm very pleased that she did."

"So she told you about the sleepwalking?" Justin asked, and his shoulders visibly relaxed.

"Aye, she explained everything I wanted to know and to my complete satisfaction," Todd said with a slow smile as his gaze met hers across the room. "I think we are destined to become very good friends after tonight. As it turns out, your sister and I actually have several things in common—one in particular."

Christina bristled at such an obvious insinuation, but Justin could not have seemed more pleased by Todd's remark. "Then I'll just leave you two to finish your discussion. I do want you two to become the very best of friends."

"No!" Christina responded quickly. Then, seeing her brother's surprise, she lowered her voice and explained, "It's dark outside now, and you know how afraid I am to be out alone after dark. I'd appreciate it if you would let me ride back with you. Mr. Aylesbury and I were through talking, anyway." She blushed when she noticed Todd's quick nod of agreement.

"Aye, we were through talking, all right." He placed just enough emphasis on the word "talking" to let her know what thoughts had occurred to him, and followed it

110

with a knowing smile.

"We'll have to ride double," Justin told her. "I'm on horseback."

"It's better than walking back in the dark." She stepped toward her brother to show how eager she was to leave with him.

"I'll take her back," Todd volunteered eagerly. "I'll have William or Sam hitch up the gig and drive her back myself."

"No, I couldn't allow you to do that," she responded quickly. "We've put you out too much already today." Not wanting to be left alone with him again for fear of what might happen between them, she hurried to add, "Justin's horse can easily carry the two of us." Grasping Justin by the arm, she started to pull him toward the door, her heart hammering frantically when he at first resisted her. "Come along, Justin, let's be on our way. I've taken quite enough of Mr. Aylesbury's time already."

She never was so glad to be on top of a horse than when she climbed up onto Justin's, even though Justin's saddle was not at all made for riding sidesaddle and caused her injured leg to ache high near the hip. Anything was better than letting Todd take her home. Having discovered just how very dangerous Todd Aylesbury really was, she felt an almost desperate need to get away from him. And an even more desperate need to *stay* away from him.

But Todd was not about to let that happen. The following morning he stopped by Justin's house while out on his regular boundary inspection. Justin had just left and both boys were out in the barn checking the chooks for eggs. Christina was all alone in the kitchen when suddenly Todd appeared through the back door, without bothering to knock or announce his arrival.

Although he did not stay long, nor did he mention why he had stopped by, he left Christina weak-kneed from the encounter and unable to take her thoughts off him for the rest of the day.

Ashamed, she relived the incident of the evening before again and again throughout the day. She knew without a doubt that if Justin had not come when he had, she would have lost every last shred of decency she had, and to a man who not only terrified her, but made her so angry with his arrogant manner that she could not be in the same room with him without feeling the urge to slap him.

Todd returned the following morning, again unannounced, flirting openly with her, staying right on her heels, and this time touching her briefly on the arm. But when she expected him to try to kiss her again and had her defenses ready, he politely excused himself, leaving her relieved and disappointed at the same time.

It soon became clear that Todd Aylesbury was in steady pursuit of her. She could not understand why, since the man could have his pick of women. He was undeniably handsome and overtly wealthy. The perfect catch for anyone who cared for that type of man.

Finally, Todd appeared at her door early one afternoon to announce that they were going out on a picnic the following day.

"I'm sorry, but I have no intention of going on a picnic with you," she said firmly, knowing it would be the worst mistake she could make.

"Aye, you do," he stated matter-of-factly. "I'll be by for you around noon," he added as if he had every right in the world to do so.

"No, I don't, and I won't. I don't know you well enough to go out alone with you. Furthermore I don't feel like having anyone call on me just yet, and especially not you." She decided to be open about the antagonism she felt toward him, but grew frustrated when it did not seem to phase him in the least. The man was far too arrogant to realize he had been turned down. It was probably a first for him.

Stepping outside, knowing it was far safer to stay outside with him, she continued. "I want you to know I'm not the little fool you take me to be. I am clearly aware that you are just out to conquer the new lass in the area. You see me as a challenge that has yet to be met, and to tell you the truth, I resent it. If it wasn't for my brother, I'd order you off this veranda and Justin's property right now and tell you never to return."

Her mention of her brother brought Justin's image to her mind. If only she could push that desperate look of his out of her thoughts. She realized then she had better not aggravate Todd Aylesbury more than she already had, at least not until that station boss's position was decided.

"You'll feel more like going out by the time I come by for you tomorrow at noon," Todd said with a confident smile as he followed her into the yard. It was as if he had not heard a thing she had said.

"No, please, I really don't want to go," she said, taking the antagonism out of her voice and making an honest effort to plead with him. "I don't feel like going out with anyone just yet."

"Then maybe we should dine here instead. The boys will be over at my place again tomorrow helping Sam bottle-feed those two new colts. That would leave us all

113

the privacy we could want."

"What? Why would you want . . . ?"

Anticipating the question, Todd chose to demonstrate rather than answer. In one lithe movement, he pulled her immediately into his arms and brought his lips down to cover hers before she could voice the protest he knew was coming.

## Chapter VII

Todd's lips had descended on hers with such sudden-
ness and with such a maddening intensity, that Christina
was at first too stunned to think of fighting back. By the
time it finally struck her that she should stop him, her
senses had already fallen prey to the unexplainable
lunacy of passion, and, as before, her usual self-control
and staid common sense were snatched out of her grasp
and once again placed into the hands of this madman.

In the back of her mind, she sensed that she was
rapidly becoming Todd Aylesbury's pawn, something her
brain struggled to overcome, but her heart no longer
seemed to care about. All that seemed to matter at that
moment was that she was once again overwhelmed by
those warm, tantalizing sensations only Todd Aylesbury
aroused in her.

Rather than fight him off, her body cried out to give in
to the unusual pleasure he brought her, to explore the
feelings that had so suddenly been brought to life within
her, and to worry about the consequences later.

The kiss deepened, and Christina fell further and

further under his masterful spell. She felt her legs grow increasingly weak, and she had to lean against him or crumble to her knees. She felt his body against hers, and suddenly it seemed right for her to lift her arms and encircle his neck, enabling her to move even closer to him. A sensual fog drifted over her and all that existed for her inside the warm mist at that moment was Todd's kiss, Todd's caress, and the wild hammering of her heart.

Suddenly, without warning, Todd's hands were beneath her blouse, warm and searching. Another alarm sounded within her head, warning her that this was not just a kiss and demanding she break free of his grasp before it was too late. It warned her he was well on his way to seducing her, and so far she had not put up much of a struggle.

This time she heeded her inner warnings and somehow found the strength to escape from such splendid, all-encompassing pleasure. She ran immediately into the house, before he could have a chance to try to reclaim her. Terrified he would follow, she slammed the door behind her, then fled up the stairs and into her room where once again she slammed the door behind her.

Her heart was in such a wild state of panic that all she could hear was its erratic pounding. It was several deep, trembling breaths later that she calmed down enough to listen for Todd's footsteps in the hallway outside her door. To her relief, she heard none nor any other noises inside the house. Todd had not bothered to follow her after all. Then it occurred to her that he had not considered her worth pursuing, and that thought hurt more than it should have.

Carefully, so as not to be seen, she parted the lace curtains barely an inch with her fingertip and peered out onto the area below. She could see Todd's horse still tethered to a post near the barn, but she did not see Todd anywhere close by. She heard a horse approach in the distance and then heard voices—male voices.

Pulling the curtain back further and stepping to one side, Christina saw Todd walking in long, determined strides across the yard, toward the side of the house, in the opposite direction from his horse.

Justin came into her view within seconds, and she watched curiously as Todd approached her brother, not giving him time to get off his horse. The two had a very heated exchange of words. Justin glanced up at her room more than once while the two men spoke. He climbed down from his horse, patted Todd on the shoulder reassuringly, and headed for the house, taking his wide-brimmed hat off and dusting it hard against his thigh as he walked.

The last thing Christina noticed before she stepped away from the window was Todd returning to his horse, still visibly angry as he mounted the animal in one easy movement, then turned the tall black beast toward the main track.

Fearing the worst, Christina hurried over to the rocking chair beside her bed and sat down. By the time she had arranged her skirts to appear as if she had settled in at her leisure, she heard her brother's steady footsteps in the hallway as he came toward her room. She gripped the wooden arms of the rocker and tried to keep a calm expression, but at the same time steeled herself for what was to come. The louder the steady clamor of his boots grew, the harder her heart pounded, and the harder it became to appear calm.

She was determined to explain to Justin once and for

all that she would gladly do anything else he asked of her, help him in any other way possible, but that she wanted nothing further to do with Todd Aylesbury. Justin's roguishly handsome boss was far too dangerous a man for her to be around. The man had powers she did not understand. Powers over her heart. Powers over her self-control. And possibly powers over her very soul. She wondered if the man was in cahoots with the devil himself, having such powers.

"Before you say anything you might regret," she said as soon as he had opened her door and stepped inside her room, "I think you should know that Todd kissed me and without reason."

"And you could not put up with a simple little kiss?" Justin asked and came to stand before her. He raked his hands through his dark brown hair, which took out the dent his hat had left, then immediately started to pace the room. "You could not put up with one little kiss for my sake? Not even one?"

"It was not a *little* kiss."

"So it was a big kiss. So what? It's not like you haven't been kissed before. Didn't John ever kiss you?"

"It's not the same," she said quietly, feeling every fiber of her being grow taut with anger as she put the rocker into rapid motion. The muscles in her cheeks flexed with the overwhelming emotion that had come from merely talking about it. "Believe me, Justin. It is not at all the same. John had far more respect for me than to—" she broke off, unable to state verbally all the shameful things Todd Aylesbury had done to her. She was not even sure there were words adequate to reveal the way his kiss had made her feel.

There especially were no words that could relay the

118

humiliation she felt now that she realized how close he had come to making her give up every last shred of her morality. Twice now. And for what? A few moments of pleasure? Now that Todd was gone and reason had returned, Christina could view the whole situation more logically, though she still did not understand what it was that had come over her. What had made pulling away from him so difficult?

"More respect than to what?" Justin wanted to know. "Kiss you without first asking your permission? So he stole his kiss. So what? A kiss is a kiss. Most women would give their right eye to have Todd Aylesbury steal a kiss from them. So why make such a big production out of one stolen kiss?" He stared at her a moment, waiting for her response.

When she did not answer, he clenched his fists and continued his tirade. "Tell me, Christina. Tell me why you couldn't put up with one little kiss. Christina, for God's sake, please. No, for *my* sake. Please. I need for you to be nice to him. You have got to try to get along with him." Angrily, he turned his back on her.

"Why, Justin? Why is it so important that I be nice to Todd Aylesbury? Why should I try to get along with a man I cannot stand to be around? I'm not the one who needs to make a good impression on him. You are. So what good will it do you for me to be nice to him? He's not going to care if I was nice to him or not when it comes time to make the decision on who gets to be his station boss. He'll make the decision based on who is the best man for the job. Or does this actually have to do with more than your getting that job? I'm starting to feel that there is something you are not telling me. You are too eager for me to try to get more influence over Todd. What is it?

Justin, what are you keeping from me?"

"Not a bloody damn thing," he shouted and whirled to face her. "I don't have anything to hide from you or Todd Aylesbury. I just thought you might try to be a little more supportive of me. But no, not my little do-gooder of a sister. You can't even put up with a man who obviously likes you, likes you enough to want to kiss you. Not even to help me out. Damn you, Christina. It's not as if I'm asking for the world." Having said that, and having become too angry to say any more, he stormed out of the room and down the stairs.

Christina stared after him, too stunned to call him back, not sure she even wanted to. It was suddenly very obvious to her that Justin had not really changed very much after all. He had never really grown up, despite his marriage and fatherhood. He was exactly like he had been when they were children—obstinate and self-centered. Well, that was just too bad, because this was one time she was not going to give into his childish behavior. This was one time she would stick up for her own rights.

Christina first heard the front door slam shut, causing her to grip the polished arms of the chair harder, then the sound of Justin's horse as he rode off toward Todd's house—no doubt to apologize for her, and that made her angrier still.

It was hours before the boys returned, and by then Christina had worked off much of her anger, enough to be able to sit quietly and listen to the boys' tales of having helped one of Todd's groomsmen feed the two colts that had been born prematurely. The mare had never developed the milk she needed to feed her twins, and as a result the colts had to be fed from oversized baby bottles. And the two animals had had to be given a bottle almost

120

hourly during the first weeks, but the boys had not minded, in fact they had been delighted.

When they had entered the house through the kitchen, tired and smelling of soured milk and wet hay, they were bursting with such youthful excitement that Christina thought they would never calm down enough to eat their supper. Not certain Justin would come home in time for supper with the children, remembering that when he was a child he would purposely miss a meal or two to get sympathy, Christina served the boys when the regular mealtime came. As she'd expected, it was hours after the boys had been put to bed and she had just settled into the downy softness of her own bed when she heard Justin come trudging through the back door, making enough noise to wake the dead, but strangely enough, not Edward and Alan.

Though she could easily tell by the way her brother slammed things around downstairs that he was still angry, her own anger had completely subsided and she was ready to try to talk with him again. When she heard him coming up the stairs half an hour later, she met him in the hallway and waited until he had noticed her before she spoke.

"Justin, what is going on between you and Todd? Please tell me. I do want to help, but you are hiding something from me. What is the problem between you two?" Her voice revealed the honest concern she felt for her brother.

"Nothing," he muttered, his face drawn into such a childish frown that his lips almost disappeared into the dark thickness of his beard. "I've got everything under control."

"Are you sure?"

"Right now, you are my biggest problem. Todd likes you, likes you a lot, and all you can do is treat him as if he has a disease or something. You've been awful to him. Ignoring him. Refusing to let him call on you. There's absolutely no cause for any of that. Ever since he learned you weren't the thief he thought you were, he's been nothing but nice to you. Why can't you simply let him call on you for a while? What could it hurt?"

He came forward and placed his hands on her shoulders in a gentle, loving gesture. "Look, Chrissy, I'm not asking you to marry the man, just be nice to him for a while. Let him kiss you if he wants. I don't see how that can hurt you in any way. Hell, you'd probably find out you like it if you'd just give yourself half a chance. You'd probably find out you like *him*, too."

"You know as well as I do what that sort of man expects from a woman," she snapped and pulled her shoulders free from his grasp. "And it certainly is more than a kiss."

"Not from a decent woman like yourself," he reasoned after a moment's pause. It had stunned him that his sister could be so blunt about such matters, but not so stunned that it distracted him from what he had to say. "From a woman like you, all he would expect is a little social companionship and occasionally a friendly kiss or two as a way of showing genuine affection. But that's all."

Well remembering the man's fiery kiss and roving hands, she fixed her gaze on her brother's pitiful expression and said, "I really don't think you know that man very well."

Justin stared at her for a long moment, his jaw working furiously, then said in another burst of anger, "Oh, hell, do whatever you want. Forget I asked you to do anything

122

at all for me."

He turned on his heel again and stomped back down the stairs. She could hear him banging cabinet doors in search of something, and she could easily guess what. As was his habit whenever things did not go his way, Justin was looking for a bottle of whiskey to give him a brief moment of comfort. She shook her head as she turned back to her room and gently closed the door.

Christina went directly back to bed, but found sleep evasive that night. Thoughts of what she had almost allowed Todd to do shamed her, and thoughts of what Justin had had the gall to ask her to do threw anger on top of her shame. Far too much anger to allow her to fall asleep, though sleep was what she wanted most. Sweet, oblivious sleep.

It was nearly dawn when Christina finally fell asleep. By the time she awoke late the next morning and got dressed, Justin and the two boys had already left for the Aylesbury station. Though she felt a little guilty that the boys had gone off without a good breakfast, inwardly she breathed a sigh of relief. She was not ready for another confrontation with her brother, and did not want to have their next confrontation in front of the boys. It would be best to wait until Justin had had more time to calm down, and for when they were alone.

Finding the kitchen in total disarray from the boys' having made their own breakfasts, Christina decided to forego her own morning meal and started her day by cleaning up the mess. By late morning, she had the house in order and had started on the laundry outside. Bent over one of the huge, steaming wooden tubs, she heard the clattering of a carriage as it rattled along the tract. She glanced up to see who might be passing by and was surprised that the vehicle turned into Justin's drive.

As it neared the fence that divided the dooryard from the paddock, Christina lifted the white linen apron that protected her blue muslin dress from the unavoidable splashes of dirty laundry water. Slowly she wiped her hands on a corner of the apron, then reached up to find the curls that had gathered at her hairline and smoothed them back with her fingertips while she stepped away from the laundry tub. While she stared at the carriage, she pressed her cool hands against her cheeks to take away the flush of color in them.

Letting the apron fall back down over her skirt, she bent and quickly brushed it smooth again, then smiled to greet the unexpected arrival, eager to meet another of her brother's friends. But the smile quickly withered into a cautious frown when she realized just which of her brother's friends was in the carriage. It was Todd Aylesbury, and as the carriage drew closer, she could see a huge wickerwork basket at his side.

"Sorry, I'm a little early," he said as he gave her one of his most dazzling, heart-stopping smiles and reached up to tip his wide-brimmed hat politely.

"Early for what?"

"Our picnic," he responded lightly, but his pale blue eyes had narrowed slightly. "Remember? I told you yesterday that I intended to come by for you around noon to take you on a picnic. I know it is not quite noon, but I was eager to see you, so I decided to come on over a little early in hopes you too might have gotten ready."

"As you can see, I'm not at all ready. And I don't intend to get ready. I told you as clearly as I know how that I do not want to go on a picnic with you."

"Aye, I remember something like that. But I thought

124

maybe something might have happened between then and now to help change your mind."

Though he continued to smile that dazzling smile of his, she sensed by the way his lips had tightened around that smile that he was starting to get angry with her again. Everything in her wanted to rebel against him, to cause him to be angrier still, but then she thought of Justin. As long as she did not know exactly how serious her brother's problem was concerning Todd, she knew it would not be wise to antagonize the man any more than she had to. Until she knew more, she needed to be careful about what she said and did to Todd Aylesbury.

Forming a halfway convincing smile over tightly gritted teeth, she finally said what she knew he expected to hear. "Although I do have a lot of chores to get done around here and really should stick to my decision not to go with you, I will concede to a *short* picnic. Just give me enough time to change dresses and get a parasol."

"You look just fine in that dress," he argued and eyed her suspiciously. "And I don't see why you need a parasol. As you can see, my gig is covered and provides plenty of shade from the sun."

"But the spot you chose for our picnic may not be so shaded. I'll be right back," she insisted and turned away from him, already reaching around behind her to untie the sashes of her apron. She paused long enough at the small wall mirror near the stairway to repair her hair into its simple twist at her nape. While she searched for her blue parasol, she tried to reason with herself that she was not going against her principles. After all, she *was* hungry. She had skipped breakfast and that was something she did not ordinarily do. Her stomach was already feeling weak from lack of food, or was it from anxiety?

Determined to find a good reason for her actions, she remained adamant that she really needed a good meal. With hunger as an excuse, although she was still very angry at the way he had gotten the upper hand with her, she viewed her acquiescence as sensible, and under the circumstances, really not that great a sacrifice. She could bear his company for an hour or two, if the food was filling, and as long as she kept herself away from him.

When Christina walked back outside, she found Todd standing beside the carriage. She wanted to protest his hand on her elbow, but knew that it was an expected courtesy. Wisely, she held her tongue and tried simply to ignore the tingling sensations that his touch, no matter how simple, seemed to create inside her.

Todd walked around the rear of the carriage to get to his side, and Christina realized that the wicker basket had been strategically placed so that she would have to sit close to him. Hurriedly she repositioned it so that it was between them. Todd paused a moment when he noticed what she had done, but did not say anything as he swung himself onto the seat and took up the reins.

Except for Todd's explaining where they were headed and telling her why he had chosen to cut across a paddock rather than take the main track, the ride to a nearby pond was made in silence. Christina could sense the anger in him when he climbed down to open a gate that they had to pass through to reach the pond.

His usually easy strides were stiff and his movements stilted as he worked to open the gate, then returned to close it. He clearly did not like having his authority questioned, even though he had eventually gotten his way on the matter, and was probably miffed over the fact that she had rearranged the basket to her own advantage

126

and not his. But she thought to herself that he could not be any angrier at her than she was at him for having manipulated her, and she took devilish delight in the fact that she had upset his well-ordered life.

When they reached their destination, which was almost within sight of Justin's house, Todd climbed down quickly. He hurried around the rear of the carriage to assist her before she could get out of the carriage, which he had obviously known she would try to do.

Still feeling satisfied that she had already made him miserable to some degree, she gracefully held out her hand.

But Todd had a different form of assistance in mind and instead of taking her by her hand, he reached up and grasped her securely around the waist and lifted her out. His eyes met hers, as if daring her to protest as he brought her body gently down against his.

Christina was appalled at such bold behavior, yet savored the oddly tantalizing sensations that rippled through her when she felt her soft body slide gently down his hard, muscular form. Afraid he might be able to feel her heart pounding furiously against her chest and knowing he would read far too much into it, she quickly pulled away, yet strangely enough offered him no brash reprimand for what he had done.

"This spot is lovely," she said, trying to start a conversation. "Is this on your land or Justin's?"

Todd cleared his throat before answering her question. "This is my land. When we passed through that gate back there, we came onto my land."

Christina gazed around at the small pond that had formed in a deep, flat area of a narrow stream which ran like a wrinkled ribbon through the large, grassy paddock.

Small dollops of shade were provided at one end of the pond by a stand of towering gum trees, and that was where Todd chose to spread the thick piecework quilt he had brought.

The tranquility of the countryside did wonders for the anger that had been building inside of Christina from the very moment Todd had ridden up into Justin's yard uninvited and she had realized his intentions. She found it difficult to remain so angry when the colorful flowers sprinkled across the pastures and along the hillsides were in such abundance and the sky was such a perfect shade of opal.

The springtime breeze was warm and gentle as it whispered through the tall, jade-green grass that surrounded them, calling out to her to forget her hostility for the moment and simply enjoy the beauty that could only be found in Australia.

Huge butterflies with painted-parchment wings flitted about everywhere, happy with the sunshine and such a wide space to play. Even the colorful birds that had taken refuge in the spindly trees overhead seemed intent on encouraging her mood as they squawked and chattered enthusiastically to one another.

By the time Christina and Todd had settled onto the thick, colorful quilt, Christina had all but forgotten her animosity and was pleased he had also decided to make every effort to be congenial.

"I hope you like smoked ham," he said lightly when he set the huge basket before her. It was the lady's task to unpack the basket and to lay out the contents.

"Ham?" she asked with delighted surprise as she lifted the top of the basket to peer inside, then swung the lid back out of her way, letting it dangle on its hinges. She could not help but show her pleasure at the delicious contents before her. In a country where usually mutton and sometimes beef were the meats most commonly eaten, it was quite a treat to be offered smoked ham. And better yet was the huge wedge of chocolate cake he had brought for their dessert.

By the time she had placed the many treats she found within easy reach and they had helped themselves, most of the hostility she felt toward Todd Aylesbury had dwindled to nothing. They both ate ravenously and talked little, though what they did say was amicable, almost friendly. And for a little while, Christina enjoyed the moment, however brief it might be.

However, after they had finished eating, and Todd had stretched out across one end of the quilt, relaxing comfortably on his side, she realized she was actually having a good time, a very good time, in the company of this dangerously attractive man. She had never thought it would happen, and for the first time she wondered if a friendship between the two of them might indeed be possible. It would certainly make Justin happy.

Leaning comfortably against the side of a fallen log that lay next to the quilt, Christina let her gaze wander for a long, leisurely moment, then moved it slowly back to Todd. She was startled to discover he had moved closer to her. She had not heard him stir at all, yet he now lay in the middle of the quilt only a few feet away from her.

Alarmed by the way he stared at her, she tucked her skirts closer about her and tried to think of something to say to distract his thoughts from the direction they had obviously taken. She had seen that same look on his face on at least two other occasions—both times barely moments before he kissed her.

# Chapter VIII

Panic gripped her as she tried to think of what to say to prevent Todd from coming any closer, without causing any animosity. Her insides churned wildly when nothing occurred to her. To her utter confusion, the words simply were not there.

"You are so beautiful," Todd said as he moved closer still, bringing himself up beside her. His eyes continued to devour hers as he spoke. "Maybe too beautiful." Then, with no further hesitation, he gently pulled her trembling body into his arms, and as she fully expected him to do, he kissed her.

The kiss was just as powerful as she remembered, so all-consuming that Christina was soon aware of nothing but the bewildering chaos he created inside her. A force too strong and too frightening to be reckoned with, and she tried to push him away but found his hold on her too strong. Aware of the danger she was in, and not at all ready to cope with it, she tried again to utter a protest, only to find it lost in her constricted throat. Her only hope was to break away so she pushed harder.

To her amazement, she broke his hold easily and quickly scooted away from him. Her brown eyes were wide with the fear that he would make another move toward her and she would have to fight him off again. In a voice charged with emotion, she said, "Todd, I think you'd better take me home now. Right now." She steadied herself as she waited for his response.

She was amazed when he did not grab her again or try to force another kiss on her. Instead, he simply nodded his head and began to toss the leftovers back into the basket. His jaw remained rigid, his expression grim, as he flopped the lid on the basket and tested it to make sure it was closed. Then he pushed the basket to one side while she hurriedly stood and moved away from the quilt.

As soon as her feet had cleared the material, he snatched the quilt up and over one arm, not bothering to shake the grass from it or even to fold it. Then he picked up the basket, causing the jars and bowls to clink sharply together, and headed for the carriage.

As Christina followed him, she wondered about his odd behavior. He threw the basket and quilt into the back with no concern for either, then turned his back to them. If she had not known better, she would have sworn that Todd had somehow been left just as shaken by that encounter as she had. But then, Todd was used to such encounters. Justin had told her what a rake he was with the ladies. Then she realized it was simply anger that caused him to act so peculiarly. It was probably rare that his female companions refused the advances the way she did. That thought was oddly satisfying.

Again there was silence on the way home. When they reached Justin's house, she wasted no time in climbing down unassisted, hoping to avoid his touch. She was not sure she could handle even a gentle hand at her elbow at the moment, especially Todd Aylesbury's hand.

By the time Todd walked around to her side of the carriage, she was already well on her way to the house. Still no words passed between them. None seemed appropriate. A simple good-bye would have to do, if she could just get to the door before he caught up with her.

She heard him closing the distance between them as she reached the front steps and she did not pause a step, not ready to allow him to get any closer—even when she spoke her final good-bye. Nor did she wait for his response. Instead, she opened the door the moment she reached it and quickly closed it behind her. But before she breathed her first sigh of relief, she heard the doorknob click and turned in time to see the door swing wide open.

Despite the door's having been closed abruptly in his face, he had followed her. That look was back in his eyes when he kicked the door closed again with his boot, then continued toward her. This time, however, there was something more in his expression that frightened her so completely that she glanced around for something with which to defend herself. When she found nothing, she immediately began to back away from him. "Todd, I did not invite you inside this house and I suggest you leave right now or I'll be forced to tell Justin about this."

Unfazed, Todd steadily stalked her, and she backed herself against a wall. She tried to duck to the side before he reached out for her. But the move came too late.

"Christina, I will tolerate only so much," he said as he pinned her against the wall, his hand gripping her soft shoulder. "And you are about to reach the very outermost limit of my tolerance."

"*Your* tolerance? What about mine? Let me tell you something, Mr. Aylesbury—"

"No, let me tell you something, Miss Lapin," he interrupted. "No, better yet. Actions speak louder than words."

Christina's next words were never spoken.

His kiss was wondrously tender, yet just as powerful as ever. He let go of her shoulders and lifted his hands to cup her face so that she could not pull her lips away from his. But it had been unnecessary, for all the fight had suddenly gone out of Christina. That same strange warmth she had felt before when he kissed her had invaded her again. It spread through her and left her feeling light-headed and physically weak. What was this power Todd Aylesbury had in his kiss? Why did it leave her too dazed to fight him? Again she caught herself leaning into him, pressing her body against his.

Todd's hands slowly released her face as he became confident she would not try to pull away, and he slowly slid his arms around her, holding her tightly against him. The kiss grew gradually more demanding, the pressure of his mouth more insistent. His tongue teased the outer edges of her lips until she parted them willingly. Never had he tasted such sweetness. Never had she felt such fire.

Christina's insides had become a molten mass that had set her entire being aflame, yet an icy little shiver ran along her spine whenever his tongue brushed against the more sensitive areas of her mouth. The contrast of the tiny shivers against the burning heat of her newly awakened passion caused her skin to prickle and come alive.

While the kiss continued to work its magic, Todd

cupped underneath her breast ever so gently through the soft muslin material of her dress, exhilarated at feeling her heartbeat beneath his fingertips. When she showed no resistance, he began to undo the buttons that ran along the back of her dress. When he had undone the third button she realized what was happening. Her body tensed and she leaned back against the wall in an attempt to stop him from going any further.

Todd quickly brought his hand away from the buttons and placed it back at her waist and concentrated again on the simple act of kissing her. Slowly he felt her relax again, and soon he was able to bring her away from the wall and back into his embrace.

Christina's fear of his trying to undress her quickly passed. She was too consumed by the passion that he had brought to life within her. As her body absorbed the pleasure of his passionate embrace and the wonderful feel of his mouth on hers, she became less and less opposed to the danger he posed. And by the time his hand had returned to the buttons, she had all but forgotten her fear, or that there was any reason to protest.

As she felt the material slacken and his hand gently stroke the sensitive skin along her back and shoulders, she began to ache with something so new, so different, that she trembled inside. When his hand moved beneath the muslin bodice to caress the outer edges of her breasts through the thin material of her camisole, the ache deepened into a furious fit of desire.

Christina now returned his kiss with a passion she did not know she possessed, pressing her body hard against his, wanting to get closer to him but not knowing exactly how.

Unable to suppress his desire any longer, Todd eased his fingers beneath the material of her camisole in an almost effortless movement, then slowly began working his way to the nearest straining peak.

Christina gasped aloud at the intense response that shot through her when Todd's hand came into contact with the hardened tip of her breast. Her brain finally realized the danger and screamed out its warning, almost too late. Her body was still eager to continue, to lose itself in the wondrous feelings that had so suddenly claimed her, but the one last shred of her sanity prevailed and she finally pushed herself away. Confused and angry, she could hardly speak.

"Get out of here and leave me alone." Tears burned in her eyes as she fought the sudden rush of shame that flooded through her.

Todd's face hardened with anger, his eyes still dark from his own desire, as he stepped away from her. "Christina, if I leave here now, I want you to know that I won't be back. You will have to come to me."

"Don't hold your breath," she replied, and crossed her arms protectively around her loose clothing.

He stared at her a moment longer, as if trying to decide what his next move should be, then turned and walked out of the house without so much as a glance back at her.

Christina stood motionless, too stunned to move. As she heard his carriage clattering away, she pressed her lips together into a tight line. For some reason, she did not feel the relief she had expected as she listened to his carriage move farther and farther from the house. That bothered her. After all, she was not in love with the man, and even if she was, she had nothing to offer him.

Even if she fell in love with him, and it suddenly

occurred to her that she might be dangerously close to doing just that, she could never hope for a real future with a man like Todd Aylesbury. There were too many things working against it.

First of all, Todd was not the type to offer a true and honest commitment to anyone but himself. He was like John in that respect. And secondly, because of the accident, she could not bear him children, sons to carry on the proud Aylesbury name. And if he made her the same offer John had, to be his mistress instead of his wife, because of her barrenness, she would be unable to bear it—least of all, from Todd.

Confused and suddenly overcome by an inexplicable misery instead of relief at having stopped him, Christina finally gave in to the tears that had silently gathered in her eyes and wept bitterly, until she was sure she could weep no more.


Christina cried a lot those next few weeks and could not understand why. Todd had given her what she thought she wanted most, his absence. Yet it made her miserable beyond reason, and she had no one she could talk to about it.

Many times she thought of Rose and wished she could talk to her, thinking that her friend might have some insight into the strange sadness that had overcome her. But a trip to Bathurst was out of the question.

When Christina had promised her friend that she would visit her often, she had not known it was a full two-hour ride from Justin's house to Bathurst. Too far to consider going on her own, and Justin was too busy trying to impress Todd. And as angry as he now was with her after learning of the latest blowup between them, she doubted he would have taken her anyway.

For the first few days after that disastrous scene, Justin had refused to talk to her at all. And for a week after that, he remained distant, obstinately ignoring his sister's presence and only speaking to her when it was absolutely necessary.

It was perfectly clear by the way he had pouted continuously those first few days that her brother thought she had done something terribly wrong. No doubt, he felt she had done it to spite him, when in all actuality, she had done it in spite *of* him. Oddly enough, Justin had been the main reason she had gone on the picnic in the first place.

But as the days went by and Justin's anger finally mellowed, the two were on speaking terms again. But Justin was hardly ever home to talk to anyway, and Christina worried about him.

She worried about the time and effort Justin was putting into his work. It was clearly affecting his health. She knew he was not getting enough sleep, because she was also finding sleep almost impossible and could hear him moving about the house at all hours of the night, sometimes leaving to take long rides in the night. Dark circles formed beneath his now constantly bloodshot eyes, giving his face a sunken appearance. And when he learned that Coolabah intended to stay on an extra month, at least until the end of February, he did not sleep at all for two nights.

As the days passed, Christina expected Todd to come back into her life. But as more days went by and he still hadn't returned she realized he had meant what he'd said. He would not be back.

Though she tried not to think about him, she caught herself looking in the direction of his house whenever she was outside. She knew she could not see even the trees that surrounded his homestead from the shallow valley where Justin's house was, but she looked just the same.

Gradually, it occurred to her that she actually missed him—missed Todd Aylesbury. Despite all that had happened between them, or maybe because of it, she missed him dreadfully—his devilish smile, the long, narrow dimples that formed along his lean cheeks, and especially the way he looked at her—a look so deep, so provocative that just thinking about it could send tiny shivers down her spine.

And the more she thought of him, the more she found herself slipping into long moments of ridiculous fantasies—of looking up to find that he had come riding into the yard on his sleek black horse, determination in his eyes, with every intention of stealing her away. It was the sort of thing fairy tales were made of, and she knew it would never happen. Still, she could not help daydreaming about it. In some perverse way, such bittersweet thoughts helped her get through the long, lonely days of summer.

Christina had never known it was possible to miss anyone as much as she missed Todd. Or that her feelings could change so much toward anyone. She wanted him back, to look at him, to talk to him. But his grim words returned again and again to haunt her. "If I leave here now, I'll never be back."

It became more and more difficult to keep thoughts of him out of her mind, even when she worked hard. It was as if a demon possessed her. She, who had been nervous as a cat whenever she was with him, was now miserable to the point of tears simply because she did not have him around to annoy her anymore.

Clearly, she was no longer in control of her own emotions, hadn't been since the day she'd met him. On several occasions, she considered going to him, to ask that they try to be friends. For Justin's sake. For the boys' sake. But then again, she feared they could never be friends. There was too much physical awareness between them.

There were really only two choices: to stay apart and remain undeclared enemies, or to become lovers. Though she hated the idea of his forever hating her, of never seeing him again, she was terrified by the thought of becoming his lover. She knew once she allowed herself to fall in love with Todd, she would love him forever. Love a man whose life she could never fulfill. It was a relationship doomed to end in heartache.

Finally, one hot and lonely January afternoon, Christina walked listlessly through the house in search of something to do. She had to get her thoughts off her misery, but she had already cleaned the house, and the laundry was on the line drying. For a little while, her thoughts had slipped away from Todd and had focused on her chores, but they had been quick to return to him.

It was too early to prepare supper. The boys had gone to Todd's house to help with bundling the grass from a newly mown pasture and to feed the twin colts they had come to think of as their pets. She was all alone, with nothing to do.

As she moved from the living room to the kitchen, in hopes of finding something she might have missed to do, Christina wondered what Todd was doing at that moment. Did he ever think of her? Probably not. He surely had his hands full with his huge cattle and sheep station—and with Miss Vella Stone. Just the thought of that woman's bold, flirtatious nature made Christina want to scream.

She tried to push the painful thoughts away as she walked into the kitchen, then stopped suddenly. Her hand flew to her mouth to prevent a scream from escaping her lips. Everything inside of her froze, except for her heart, which raced blindly, out of control. There he was, standing just inside the door, his hat tossed on a nearby worktable, staring at her.

"I thought you were never coming back," she said, unable to keep the anger from her voice. Although she was glad to see him, she had been too preoccupied with her misery to realize he had entered the house, and it had startled her.

"I lied," he said simply, and shrugged his shoulders.

"Oh, you did?" She had gotten over her sudden fright and a smile tugged at the edges of her mouth. Warmth washed over her gently and completely as she stared at him, so glad to see him again, aware of how incredibly handsome he looked in his dark blue shirt with its double row of buttons and his fitted black trousers. His hair was tousled from the breeze and he reached up to comb his fingers through the thickest part to smooth it.

"I was just about to make myself a spot of tea. Would you care for any?" she asked, knowing very well she had lied, for she had not thought of tea until that very moment.

"Coffee would be better," he said, and although he did not actually smile, still too wary for that, a look of pure contentment settled over his face. "But if tea is what you have, I'll settle for tea."

Christina could not believe he was being quite so congenial. It would have been more like him to demand she prepare coffee, if that was what he truly wanted. "Coffee is as easy to prepare as tea. I'll make coffee."

They stared at each other awkwardly a moment longer before Todd spoke again, gesturing with his hand. "Mind if I sit down?"

"No, of course not, go right ahead," she responded, indicating that he could have his choice of chairs, for there were three in the room.

Christina's head spun wildly as she moved to the counter to measure the coffee. She felt as giddy as a schoolgirl and twice as clumsy, fumbling first with the canister lid, then with the scoop. She could hardly believe he was there and was terrified he might leave.

"The place looks nice," Todd said once he was seated and had taken notice of the highly polished floors and the gleaming wooden tables and cabinets. Everything was so clean, so orderly, he thought. So unlike when Justin had been totally in charge. More like it had been when Essie had still been alive. "You have made a big difference around here."

He wondered if she knew how great an understatement that really was as he watched her busily grind the coffee.

"Thank you," she answered and lifted an eyebrow as she considered his words, not stopping what she was doing. He was not behaving like the pushy, domineering man she had come to know. It was as if he had set out to change her opinion of him, and for that reason alone, she felt a little guilty. As she bent to start a fire in the stove, she glanced over at him and was delighted to find that he was watching her. It caused such a flutter inside of her

142

that she almost dropped the match. "It's not hard to make a place look nice when you have such nice things to work with."

Todd narrowed his eyes just a little as he glanced around at his surroundings. True, Justin managed to live very well for a man on such standard wages, especially now that Essie's inheritance was gone.

"It will be a while," Christina admitted, breaking his thoughts, while she brought a small fire to life by adding several pieces of dried kindling. "With the boys away, there was no need to cook lunch, so I let the fire go out."

"That's all right. I'm in no hurry to go anywhere."

After placing the coffee pot on the stove, Christina walked hesitantly across the room and sat down beside him. Again an awkward silence fell between them. Christina tried to think of something to say that would not cause any tension between them, but everything that occurred to her seemed ridiculous.

"Certainly has been hot these past couple of weeks," he finally said, and the silence was broken.

"Stifling," she agreed with a firm nod.

"And yesterday, there was hardly a breeze stirring," he noted further.

"Hardly a breeze," she repeated, again with a firm nod.

"I was sure glad to feel that breeze return today. For the men's sake."

Then they again fell into a silence that was only occasionally broken by more comments on the weather and about the work Justin's two boys were doing.

"Fine lads, those two," Todd commented as he accepted the steaming cup from her. "Hearts of gold. If I ever have sons, I hope they are as good in heart."

His mention of having sons cut through her like a

knife, making her aware again of the void deep inside her. He did *indeed* hope to have sons one day. Something he could never have with her.

"Aye, they are a lot of help to me, too," she agreed, and fought the heaviness that had so quickly settled over her.

Although they continued with their tiny bursts of small talk while they leisurely sipped their coffee, it was after they had finished and Christina had taken the cups and placed them in the sink that Todd finally brought up the subject he obviously had wanted to talk about all along.

"So, tell me, are you going to the Anniversary Day Ball next Tuesday?"

Christina's heart leaped with anticipation. "Aye, Justin has convinced me I should go. He says that it really isn't as uppity as it sounds, that all it really is is a huge supper where everyone brings something good to share, and a dance. He says they have it every twenty-sixth of January as a way of celebrating the day Arthur Phillip raised the old Union Jack at Sydney Cove." She knew she was rattling on and on needlessly, for she had already answered the question; but she could not seem to help herself. She was nervous over the prospect that Todd might ask her to go with him. "He says I'd be a fool to miss it."

"It really is a lot of fun. You'll get to meet all your new neighbors for miles around," he said with a confirming nod. "They have another ball at one of the Cobb warehouses in Bathurst, which is far more prestigious to go to, but not nearly the fun this one is."

"That's what Justin said. He said that everyone he knows goes to this one." And that had been what had convinced her to go. She had seen it as an opportunity to see Todd again at last. And now it seemed he was about to ask her to attend it with him. Her heart fluttered with excitement.

"Well, then, it looks like I'll see you there. You will set aside at least one dance for me, won't you?"

Christina tried not to show her disappointment as she fingered the soft material of her muslin dress. "I'm sure I'll be able to manage at least one dance for you."

"Good, I'll see you then," he said, and quickly rose from his chair. "Maybe we can sit together during supper."

"I suppose that will be all right with Justin," she said, though she knew it would absolutely delight her brother. By joining them at the supper, he would have the opportunity to continue to get on Todd's friendly side. Along with Coolabah's last-minute decision to stay on that extra month had come another month's delay in Todd's having to make his final decision on who should take over the job. But the decision would have to be made by mid-February. Unless Coolabah changed his mind again and stayed on yet another month. She hated to think of the effect that would have on Justin.

"Oh, by the way," Todd said, interrupting her thoughts. "I met a girl in town who said she knows you and asked me to tell you hello the next time I saw you, and she also wanted me to ask you why you haven't been in to see her yet."

"Rose?" she asked with an eager lift of her brows. How she wished she could see her friend again. She hoped to see her at the Anniversary Day Ball. Since all the businesses closed down for the day, Rose would certainly be free to go, but would she be going to this ball or the prestigious one held at the Cobb warehouse?

"Aye, that was her name. Rose. Pretty lass. She said to tell you that if you could not get away from your work long enough to come to Bathurst for a visit, you could at least send a letter to her."

"But how would I get it to her? Justin never goes into town."

"Aye, he does, too. He has to go in every now and again for me, after supplies or to post an important letter. But as it turns out, I'm headed there myself tomorrow. I can stop by here on my way to pick up your letter and take it to her for you. Or maybe you'd like to ride into town with me?"

The thought of being alone with Todd for the two-hour trip into Bathurst excited her and terrified her at the same time. And although she was thrilled at the idea of going, she also hated to feel she was shirking her duties by spending an entire work day on a frivolous trip to Bathurst, especially when there was every probability she would be seeing Rose at the supper dance that very next Tuesday. "How long will you be gone?"

"Depends on if you go with me or not. If you agree to go, I'll probably be gone most of the day because I would go in the gig, which takes longer than on horseback, and I would want to treat you to lunch while we were there, and you would, of course, want to visit with your friend for a while, and you might even want to do some shopping."

It was tempting. Oh, how very tempting. "But would I be home in time to start supper for Justin and the boys?" she wanted to know.

"If you wanted to be," he said with a shrug. The only clue to his feeling on the matter was in the way his pale blue eyes had started to sparkle. "Just let me know now

146

which it is to be, so I'll know whether to come in the gig or on horseback."

"Come in the gig," she said with a smile.


Christina had not known whether Justin would be angry with her for having made plans to take a day from her work without first having asked him or whether he would actually be relieved to learn she would be spending that day with Todd. But she had certainly not expected him to be so delighted about it, and so thoroughly lifted of his bad mood, that he would give her so much money to shop with.

Even if prices were as high as he had claimed they were, he had surely given her more than enough to purchase herself the new dress for the Anniversary Day Ball, maybe even enough to buy a pair of new boots to go with it. She just hoped the shops in Bathurst would have something appropriate. Now that she knew she would at least be sitting with Todd Aylesbury, she wanted to be absolutely certain she looked her best.

Todd arrived precisely at seven, as he had promised, and seemed a little surprised to find her already dressed in a lovely peacock-blue twill and ready to leave. Evidently he was used to being made to wait, and that made her wonder if she should have been a little late so as not to seem so eager. She decided that if they made arrangements to do something together again, she would try to be as fashionably late as she could.

"I'm glad we are managing to get away so quickly. I'd like to get there before the sun gets too high and the heat becomes unbearable—especially with all this dust," he said, indicating the billowing clouds that stirred to life beneath each wheel as the carriage jolted out onto the main track.

Though the vehicle was new and had been furnished with a splendid set of springs, and though the frame itself was made of the stoutest iron and the most modern fantailed axles, the ride over such a narrow, rutted track was never smooth. But as long as the horse kept up its brisk pace, they had a slight breeze in their faces and managed to stay ahead of the dust. Christina could imagine how much worse it was going to be to have to make the same trip in Justin's wagon on the twenty-sixth. How she wished Todd would ask her to ride with him, though she knew she wished it for more reasons than just her comfort.

# Chapter IX

Todd pulled the carriage to a halt directly in front of the Makowka Mercantile. He assisted Christina down and had handed her handbag to her. Then he tethered his horse to one of the posts provided at the edge of the wide-planked walkway that passed in front of the store and along one side.

"This town sure is growing," Todd said as he looped the reins through the iron ring and gave them a sharp tug to make certain they would not slip. He nodded toward a fresh-lumber skeletal frame that would one day be a very large three-story building at the end of the street. "I can remember when there was just a few scattered buildings and the cattle yards. That was back when the Government House was the largest building in town and the only structure soundly built."

Christina looked around at the small town and wondered what it must have been like then. Although it was not as small as she had first expected, it was not nearly as large as Sydney. Suddenly reminded of the incident at the Sydney hotel, she blushed and turned away from him for a moment. "I hope Rose will be at work today."

"No reason for her not to be," Todd said with a shrug as he turned back to face her. "Why don't you go on in and find out. I've got business to attend to, but it won't take too long. I'll meet you back here in time for lunch."

When Christina entered the large wooden building, the first thing she noticed was how crowded it was. Not with customers necessarily, for there were only a few, but with tables piled high with goods. A few shelves stood against the far wall near a counter and that was where the food stores lay. The rest of the room was filled to capacity with table after table of regular merchandise, with barely enough room between them for customers to turn around.

Noticing how thick bolts of material lay on the same tables with metal pots and wooden picture frames, Christina wondered why the goods had not been better organized for display. She looked from table to table, thinking that the only sign that anyone had bothered to organize the merchandise at all was the fact that the household items were kept separate from the work goods.

"Christina!"

She heard her name before she located her friend among the people milling about the room. Turning in the direction from where she had heard her name called, she finally saw Rose hurriedly working her way toward her through the jumbled maze of tables.

"Rose!" she cried out as the girl came eagerly into her arms for a warm embrace. "I was hoping you would be here."

"And I was hoping you would finally find the time to come into town and visit me. You have come to visit,

150

haven't you? Or did you come in to shop?"

"Both, really. I want to find a pretty dress to wear for the Anniversary Day Ball next week, but I also want to visit with you. How have you been? You look wonderful." It was the truth. Dressed in a tailored waist with an accordion-pleated skirt, her dark hair piled high in a rich display of curls instead of pulled back into a simple twist like her own hair, Rose looked beautiful.

"And you look tired," Rose said bluntly and reached out to tuck back a wayward strand of Christina's hair. "You must have had quite a long ride."

"Two hours," Christina admitted. "That's why I haven't been in to see you. I had no idea Justin's place was so far from town."

"Two hours isn't far compared to many," Rose informed her. "Some people have to ride for days to get here, especially if they are coming from the backblocks and bringing with them a wagonload of goods to sell or a goodly mob of cattle or sheep to auction away. That's one reason Mr. Haught is building that fancy new hotel right down the street. Although I'd guess there's at least forty or fifty hotels, there are still not enough places for everyone to stay. Especially not enough places decent enough for when the wives come along."

"Well, two hours was plenty long for me," Christina assured her.

"Care for a wet towel and the use of a comb and a mirror?" Rose asked and gestured toward the only door other than the one Christina had entered through. The door was positioned at the very back of the large room and stood wide open.

"I would love it," she answered gratefully. "As I guess you can see, I'm covered with dust."

"Then follow me," Rose said and led her through the maze of tables and into a small room at the back where they found Rose's Aunt Jane working busily at a desk.

"Christina!" Mrs. Makowka said when she looked up and saw the two enter. "My niece was wondering when you'd ever be in to see her." Though she did not bother to get up from the desk, the woman smiled warmly and placed her pen back into its holder. "She was getting so lonesome for you that she has tried more than once to talk her uncle into taking her out there to find you."

"That would have been nice," Christina told her and turned to look at Rose. "I'd love for you and your uncle to come for a visit."

"I'd come on my own if I knew how to get there," Rose muttered. "Maybe you could draw a map for me before you leave."

"Not me. I'd be hard pressed to find my way back on my own. I've only traveled the track once each way, and I am afraid I did not pay too much attention to the landmarks on either trip."

"Then you came into town with your brother?" Rose asked eagerly and her chest rose with a deep breath of anticipation. "Will he be coming here?"

Christina could not help but smile at her friend's sudden enthusiasm. It was obvious that Rose was quite taken with her handsome brother. "No, I came in with a neighbor. Todd Aylesbury."

Rose's eyebrows arched considerably. "Todd Aylesbury, is it? Now there's a perfect catch if ever there was one. Rich as they come, and handsome, to boot."

"I'm not trying to catch him. We are merely friends, and at times barely that." Though she wanted to sound firm about her relationship with Todd, she could not help

152

but offer a silly grin at the way Rose nodded with one brow raised skeptically. It was obvious Rose had come to know her too well in the days they were together on the coach.

"Wait until some of the sticky beaks around here get ahold of this information. My best friend, Christina Lapin, and Todd Aylesbury. Tongues are going to wag."

"There's no reason for them to. We really are just friends." For some reason, Christina found it impossible to continue to look into Rose's knowing face.

"No, Christina, I can see there's more to it than that. Has he kissed you?"

"Rose!" she said pleadingly.

"Well? Has he?" Rose asked, undaunted by the plea, and then bobbed her head happily as if she had it all figured out. "He has, hasn't he?"

"Rose, I think you ask too many questions," Mrs. Makowka inserted, in an effort to alleviate some of Christina's embarrassment.

"I just want to know if he's kissed her," Rose said in her own defense. "I'd tell her if a man as handsome as Todd Aylesbury had kissed me."

"How's a man ever going to get the chance to kiss you when you won't put aside enough time to allow anyone to even pay a call on you?" Mrs. Makowka asked pointedly.

"None of the men who have asked to call on me have been worth spending time on," Rose quickly protested. "I'd rather spend my time sewing or knitting, doing something useful." She paused a moment to bat her eyes coquettishly before adding, "But if a man as handsome as Todd Aylesbury asked to pay a call on me, I'd be sure to find the time."

"And would you let him kiss you?" Christina asked,

truly interested in what her friend's answer would be.

"I'd play coy, I think, but you can bet your best pantaloons I'd let him kiss me," Rose said with a huge grin.

"Rose!" her aunt admonished with a horrified look that eventually melted into a grudging smile. "I guess I would, too, if I was as young as you and unmarried."

Christina smiled. She did not feel quite so guilty about having allowed Todd Aylesbury to kiss her now, though she knew he had intended far more than a mere kiss.

"So has he kissed you?" Rose persisted as she reached for a dry towel and dipped it into a large pitcher of water that sat on a small table near the only window in the room.

"Maybe he has," Christina finally conceded, and could feel the blood rising to her face at having admitted even that much.

"What a thing to blush about!" Rose teased, then lifted her right hand to her breast and pressed it firmly to her heart, sighing heavily. "I'll bet it was a grand kiss. I'll bet Todd Aylesbury knows how to kiss a woman so that she'll have no doubt that she's been kissed," she said with a soft sigh and a terse nod, obviously having accepted Christina's evasive answer as a firm yes. "Oh, aye. I'll bet he's a *fine* kisser, that one."

"May we change the subject?" Christina asked and felt as if her foolish grin would become a permanent part of her face if she did not try to get it under control right away. "Where's that comb you offered me?"

"Here you go," Rose said and slipped her own comb out of a pocket hidden within the pleats of her skirt. As she watched Christina work to repair her hair in front of the mirror that hung near the door, she asked, "So is

Todd taking you to the Anniversary Day Ball?"

"No, he is not," Christina said, not adding that she secretly wished that he was. "I'm going with Justin and his two sons."

Through the reflection in the mirror, she saw that Rose's eyes brightened again at the mention of Justin, and Christina began to wonder if Justin might not find himself just as interested in Rose if given the chance. It might even lift his spirits to know a girl as pretty as Rose was interested in him. "Who are you going with?"

"My aunt and uncle," Rose responded quickly.

"No one has asked to take you?"

"No one that I'd care to go with," Rose answered with a half smile.

"Then why don't you go with us?" Christina asked. Her brown eyes sparkled with delight at being a matchmaker. "It won't be much out of the way to come on into town, and I'm sure Justin wouldn't mind. He'd love for me to have another opportunity to visit with you. I think he feels a little guilty that I have to spend all my time cooped up in his house cleaning, washing, and taking care of the family."

"I'd love it," Rose said enthusiastically, but then with a note of caution added, "but you'd better make absolutely certain it is all right with Justin. His lady might not care to have me riding along."

"His lady?" Christina asked, then when she realized what Rose had meant, she laughed. "Justin doesn't have a lady friend at the moment. He's too busy with his work these days."

That must have been just what Rose had hoped to hear. "Well, if you are sure I won't be any trouble."

"Then it's settled. We'll be by for you sometime

Tuesday afternoon. Where do you live?"

"In a house on the next street. Come, I'll show you. We can stop and look for your dress while we are out. I can assure you that we have nothing appropriate here," she told her. Then she asked her aunt, "It is all right if I leave for a little while, isn't it?"

Rising from the desk, Mrs. Makowka smiled indulgently. "Aye, of course, you two go and have a good time. I'll help Ruby watch the front until Thomas gets back from his meeting."

"Maybe we can stop and have lunch at Mrs. Biles's," Rose suggested as she reached for her handbag and patted the contents. "My treat."

"That won't be necessary," Christina told her and realized the foolish grin had returned to her face. "Todd's promised to return for me in time to escort me to lunch."

"And I certainly wouldn't want to impose on that," Rose said with a knowing laugh. "We should hurry, then, so that we'll be back in plenty of time. It's after nine-thirty now."

Although shopping in Bathurst left a lot to be desired, for there were not a lot of dress shops to choose from and the dresses inside the shops were not the finest by any means, Rose did manage to help Christina find a pretty ruffled and flounced gown of pale yellow foulard with a fitted bodice trimmed in white lace, and thin, puffed sleeves edged with bright yellow ribbon. To suit the hotter weather of summer, the sleeves were short, coming only a few inches down past the shoulders, and the widely curved neckline was cut modestly low.

Instead of new boots, Rose decided Christina should purchase a pair of pale yellow slippers, which Christina quickly pointed out she would have absolutely no use for other than to wear with this one dress. But it was useless to argue with Rose, who was determined that Christina should look her very best for the event, in case Todd Aylesbury should ask her to dance. In the end, Christina left the dressmaker's with both the lovely new dress, for it had needed very few alterations, and the slippers.

Rather than hear what Rose would make of the situation, Christina decided not to tell her that Todd had already asked her to save at least one dance for him. She thought that if she were to mention to Rose how he had also suggested she eat with him at the ball, Rose would probably insist they stay to pick out a wedding dress for her. If there was one thing that could be honestly said about Rose Beene, it was that she had to be the most enthusiastic person Christina knew.

"Wait until we get back to my aunt's mercantile and I show you the lovely hair ribbons we received just last week. I think a bright yellow one would look perfect with that dress. How do you plan to do your hair?"

Christina looked at Rose curiously, then away. "I haven't really thought about it."

"So, think about it now. Personally, I think it would be beautiful brought back high on your head and allowed to flow down your back in long ringlets. Or even arranged in tiny curls, like mine is today. But you really do need to make something special of it for the ball."

"I've got too much hair to try to arrange it into curls like that," Christina insisted, though she had never tried too hard to make such a display herself.

"Nonsense," Rose told her. "Your hair is not any thicker than mine, I assure you. Come. If we still have time before Todd comes for you, I'll show you how to dress it."

Rose was a master with a hairbrush and a comb. Using only a handful of hairpins and a satiny ribbon, she made a masterpiece of Christina's hair by bringing it up in sections and draping wide, looping curls around her head.

"Now that you've watched me, do you think you can do the same thing?" Rose wanted to know as she tucked the final hairpin into place and jiggled it slightly to be sure it would hold.

"Never in a hundred years," Christina answered honestly, staring in amazement at her own hair.

"Sure you can. All it takes is practice, and you have plenty of time to practice between now and the ball."

Christina still doubted it. Although Rose had made it seem easy enough by working so quickly, Christina knew it would be no simple task. "I wish you would come out and stay the night before at our house so that you could help me get ready. I'd love for my hair to look like this for the ball."

"And it will, if I can persuade your Todd to make out a good enough map to get me there," Rose said excitedly. "I'd love to come out there the night before. We could spend that entire morning helping each other get ready. It'll be fun. And Justin wouldn't have to go out of his way to come get me."

"But how would you get out there?"

"One of Uncle Thomas's horses. I can ride Digger out there on Monday, and when we leave for the ball, we can tie him to the back of Justin's wagon. That way I can come on home with my aunt and uncle as I had already planned to. All I'd have to do is untie Digger from Justin's wagon and tie him onto theirs."

Christina stared curiously at Rose. "You can ride a horse? Alone?"

"Aye, as good as most men," Rose informed her proudly. "And it's none of that silly side-saddle riding for me. I've got one of those split skirts that lets me ride astride, the way a horse is supposed to be ridden."

Christina's brown eyes widened, but she did not doubt a word of what her friend said. If Rose claimed she could ride a horse astride as good as most men, then she could. Christina could hardly wait to see it for herself and planned to keep a close watch for Rose on Monday afternoon.

By the time Todd strode into the mercantile, Christina and Rose had already convinced her uncle to let her borrow the horse on Monday—if she could get a decent enough map drawn for her. Eagerly, they had returned to the front of the store and were waiting with pencil and paper in hand.

Though Todd found it hard to take his eyes off Christina's astoundingly beautiful head of curls, he gladly obliged them by drawing a detailed map that easily met with Rose's uncle's approval. Seeing how happy that had made Christina, he decided to invite Rose to have lunch with them. Whatever made Christina this happy made him happy.

"No, I couldn't possibly," Rose answered quickly, almost too quickly. "I've been away from the store too long already today, and I'll be away from it all day next Monday. I'd feel better if I stayed here now and helped all that I can."

Nobody seemed truly disappointed at Rose's decision, and after Christina went back into the room to get her packages and her handbag, she and Todd left the mercantile, both feeling Rose's curious gaze at their backs.


"Oh, I think you two make a handsome couple," Rose said as she busily worked the tiny strip of yellow satin into the curls piled high on top of Christina's head. Though she spoke the best she could around a mouthful of hairpins, her words were muffled and could barely be understood. "And I think he'd make you a wonderful husband."

"Rose, will you quit trying to marry me off to the man?" Christina admonished good-naturedly. "I've told you, we are just friends. Nothing more."

"But he's kissed you," Rose reminded her and smiled a tight-lipped smile so not to drop the last two pins that were still held between her lips.

"I never said that," Christina reminded her.

"You never had to." Rose laughed and the pins clattered to the floor. "But that doesn't change the fact that he kissed you. And it's my guess that he's kissed you more than once."

Christina's mouth opened to deny Rose's accusation, but she could not lie to her friend. Instead she said, "You are only guessing."

"And you are not telling," Rose surmised, then laughed again. "You don't have to tell me anything, Christina. I'll simply ask Todd when I see him this afternoon."

"Don't you dare," Christina gasped and turned away from the mirror to stare into Rose's face.

"Never dare a person like me," Rose warned her with a voice light and melodious as she knelt to retrieve the pins from the floor. "I'm the sort who just might take that dare."

Christina did not doubt that for a minute and decided the time had come to change the subject—again. How did they keep getting back onto the topic of Todd Aylesbury anyway?

"Are you about finished with my hair?" she asked.

"Almost," Rose said as she tilted her head and studied the mass of curls at an angle.

"You'd better hurry. You still have your own hair to do, and I still have to press your skirt for you."

"Plenty of time," Rose insisted, though she did not dare look at the clock. "Plenty of time."

As Christina had feared, the two were late coming down from her room, but to her amazement, Justin did not complain at the thirty-minute delay, though both boys mentioned it.

"Actually I was a little upset at first, but now that I see the two of you, I know it was worth every minute we're late," Justin said gallantly. "Just think of the green eye every man will be giving me when I walk in with the two loveliest women in all of the Bathurst District."

Rose actually blushed, and Christina could barely believe her eyes.

"Why don't you four go on and get into the wagon," Christina said as she turned away from them. "I just have to go to the kitchen and get our basket, then I'll be right out."

Justin extended his arm for Rose and bent slightly to her. "May I have the pleasure of escorting you to the wagon?"

Christina had to stay long enough to watch while the two walked arm in arm through the front door before she turned to go into the kitchen. Rose was absolutely beautiful in the jade-green dress she had chosen to wear, and Justin was clearly aware of the fact. It was so good to see her brother happy again. Lately his mood had taken on an aura close to despair, and until today there had seemed no hope he would ever smile again.

As she entered the kitchen, Christina caught herself smiling, too. Her heart sang with untold joys as she swung the basket up onto her arm and headed back through the hallway toward the front door. She knew that today was going to be very special, not only for Rose, but also for herself. When she climbed into the wagon and settled in beside Rose, she felt so full of hope and excitement that she could hardly contain it.

Although two people could sit comfortably on the bench seat of Justin's wagon, three was a close fit. Yet Christina noticed that neither Justin nor Rose seemed to mind. They were too interested in whatever they were saying to notice how crowded they were. Or, maybe they did notice, but approved. Christina's smile deepened, for she was almost certain that was it. Justin and Rose definitely liked each other and were delighted they had to sit so close together.

Though Rose and Christina wore hats with thin veils to keep the dust from settling on their faces and necks, by the time they reached the huge barn where the supper and dance was being held, they were both glad Christina had thought to bring a cool, wet towel with her. Before they left the wagon, each wiped away the dust and then helped the other make whatever repairs were needed to their hair. They wanted to be sure they looked their best before entering the main barn.

Though there were probably fifty carriages and wagons

already there when they arrived, Christina realized none of them belonged to Todd. She was disappointed. She was eager to see him, especially after he had been so nice to her during their trip to Bathurst, but she knew the absence of his carriage did not mean he was not coming. She had to be patient.

"Are you two ready yet?" Justin asked as he came back from having spoken with a friend to escort them both inside. "I don't see how you expect to improve on perfection, anyway."

Christina rolled her eyes heavenward, but said nothing about the silvery words her brother kept coming up with. "I think we are as ready as we are ever going to be," she said as she glanced into the back of the wagon only to find that the boys had already climbed down and were standing impatiently beside the wagon.

"Don't forget the basket," Edward said, more in an effort to hurry her than to remind her. She had already taken more time than he thought necessary brushing the wrinkles from her skirt. "I'll carry it if you want me to. I know where to take it."

Looking to Rose with a smile, Christina commented, "Isn't it nice to be surrounded by such helpful men."

Edward straightened proudly.

"Thank you, Edward," she said as she lifted the basket from the inside of the wagon and handed it to him. "I'll go with you, though, so that I will know what to do with my things next year.

"Come on, Alan, you can come with us," she then suggested, knowing that would leave Justin and Rose alone for awhile. She glanced only briefly at her brother, and said, "I'll come find you two after I've seen to the food."

Following Edward through the crowded barn was not as easy as Christina had anticipated, and she almost lost sight of the boy and her basket on more than one occasion. By the time she had finally caught up with him, he already had the linen napkin off the top and was lifting things out and placing them on one of the huge tables.

"Let me help you," she said as she took hold of the plum pie he had lifted out and laid beside the green beans. "I think they are putting the desserts together on that table over there, and the meats are going on that table over there," she said as she indicated the appropriate tables. "We might as well do it their way."

Edward nodded and lifted the huge stoneware bowl with the sliced roast beef and headed for the meat table.

Once they had the basket emptied, except for the linen napkin that she had used for a cover, she carried it over to place it with the other empty baskets. She was glad she had her own napkin in it to identify the basket later, because there were several similar ones.

As she turned around, she caught her first glimpse of Todd near the main door and her heart soared. He had to be the most handsome man there, and was obviously popular, because several people surrounded him. Then when she recognized one of the people, the one he now spoke to, her heart changed directions immediately and sank into the darkest depths of her soul.

She wondered if Vella Stone had come with Todd, or had she simply seen him enter and approached him before he could get inside? Either way, it was clear the woman had his full attention at the moment, and by the way she kept inching closer to him, it was also clear she intended to stay as near as she possibly could to him.

"Can Alan and I go outside and play with Cody and

Brandon Sutter?" she heard Edward ask her. "We'll stay away from the horses and wagons and won't go near the paddocks."

"I don't know. Maybe you should find your father and ask him," she told the boy as she reluctantly drew her gaze away from Todd. "I see him already seated at one of the tables on the other side. You'd better go ask him if it is all right."

Edward stood on tiptoe trying to peer over the crowd to find where his father was. Finally he grabbed Alan by the arm and headed off in the direction Christina had indicated. Christina watched him until he had disappeared from her sight, then returned her attention to Todd and Vella.

They were now talking with another couple, and Vella had linked her arm into Todd's. Christina's face tightened, and it suddenly felt as if hot, boiling acid had spilled into her bloodstream.

"Hello, ma'am, pleased to meet you," Christina heard a voice say, and she frowned when she had to look away from Todd again to see who had spoken and if he had spoken to her.

"I beg your pardon?" she asked, for she had not really heard what the young man had said. She was only aware that he had spoken and that he was now staring intently at her.

"I said hello to you ma'am," he said, in an accent that was clearly American and probably Texan, as he reached up to take his wide-brimmed, high-crowned hat off his head and greeted her properly. "My name's Jake Akard. Might I be so bold as to ask for your name?"

Though Christina's thoughts were still more on Todd at the moment, she did not want to seem impolite. "My name is Christina Lapin."

"Is that Miss Lapin or Mrs. Lapin?" he went on to ask.

"Miss Lapin. I'm not married," she told him, letting her gaze leave his long enough to locate where Todd and Vella had moved to, then back. This man was certainly attractive, and he seemed friendly enough but he was not Todd, and that was who she wanted to be with.

"Good, I'm glad of that. Then it won't be out of line for me to ask you to save one of your dances for me, will it? Maybe even two, that is if'n you don't mind dancing with the likes of me," he said, and a wide smile spread across his face, stretching his mustache full width. Although Christina was aware it was a nice smile, still it was not Todd's smile.

"What's that?" she asked, still half distracted by what was going on between Todd and Vella. "A dance, aye of course. I'd be pleased to dance with you after a while, but for now I have to find my brother. I seem to have lost him. You will excuse me, Mr. . . ." She paused for she had already forgotten his name.

"Akard," he supplied for her, settling his tall hat back on his head. "Of course, you run on along. I'll catch up with you once the music starts."

By now, she was well aware that Todd and Vella had moved on across the room and were standing very close to Justin and Rose. Rather than be so bold as to approach Todd alone, especially with that woman at his side, she decided to rejoin her brother and hope that Todd would notice her and want to approach her instead.

"There you are," Rose said, quickly standing once she saw Christina working her way through the crowd toward them. While Rose waved to be sure Christina saw her, Justin stood, too, and smiled when Rose immediately linked her arm through his.

"Sorry it took so long, but I was stopped by some strange gentleman who wanted to ask me to dance," she told them and did her very best to pretend she did not know that Todd and Vella stood only a few yards away, talking with three men in freshly washed cotton shirts and dark blue denim pants.

"A strange man asked you to dance?" Rose asked excitedly. "How strange was he?"

Christina frowned, then laughed. "Strange enough to suit you, I imagine. He sounded like he might be from Texas."

"Tall? Handsome?" Rose prodded further.

"Aye to both. Would you like for me to introduce you to him? His name was Jake somebody."

They both had sensed the sudden tension in Justin at her remark.

"No, I already know quite a few 'somebodies' from Texas," Rose responded lightly, then added, "Besides, I've already promised Justin the first two dances and my uncle the third and fourth. I think I'll just leave the rest of my dances open and see what happens."

Justin seemed pleased with her answer and relaxed again, letting his eye wander around the room as if trying to see who might have noticed that such a beautiful woman had her arm linked through his. That was when he noticed Todd, and smiled, then noticed Vella and let his smile drop.

"Todd, over here," he said, and waved to his boss.

Christina felt her stomach twist into a tight knot as she turned to pretend she had just been made aware of Todd's presence.

"Hello," Todd said as he made his way around a small

group of women huddled together, talking. "I've been trying to get over to talk to you ever since I entered and saw you over here."

As he came to stand beside Justin, Christina became aware that he was not obliging Vella in any way, in fact, he was practically dragging her behind him. The only reason she still had his arm at all was because she had latched on of her own accord and refused to let go. And when the woman's gray-green eyes came to rest on Christina, her hold tightened even more.

"I no sooner walked through the door when Vella here came up to greet me, then Mack and Kelly Patrick wanted to say hello, and then half a dozen more. I swear I never realized I had so many friends," Todd went on to explain as he stuck his hand out to greet Justin. He frowned when he was unable to reach out very far because of Vella's tight hold. But he smiled apologetically at Justin, who was forced to stretch his hand out a little further for them to make contact. "Glad I got here. Thought I wasn't going to get here in time for the first dance. The belly-band broke on my harness and I had to have Sam repair it before we could leave. But it looks like I made it, after all."

"I'm glad you did," Vella said sweetly and pressed her cheek against Todd's shoulder. "I've been keeping my eye out for you."

Christina felt somewhat relieved knowing that Vella had been there waiting and had not come with Todd.

"I'd be so unhappy if you had not been able to join me," Vella went on to say, her cheek still pressed to Todd's shoulder.

Rose looked as if she was about to become ill. Her eyes rolled from Vella to Christina. Curling her pretty mouth

168

with disgust, Rose batted her own dark eyes, imitating Vella. Christina grinned at her friend's antics and had to look away to keep from laughing. When she returned her gaze to Vella, who was still chattering away, she noticed that Todd had also caught what Rose had done and was unsuccessfully struggling to keep from grinning about it himself.

"Oh, goody! They are starting to warm up," Vella said excitedly as she tried to stand on tiptoe to see where the strains of music were coming from. "Come on, Todd. Let's get closer to the dance floor."

Although he seemed reluctant, he looked first to Justin, as if to send him a silent message, then to Christina, and shrugged helplessly. "I think I promised her the first dance." Then as Vella began to lead him away, he looked back over his shoulder and added, "But I'll be back before it's time to eat. Save me a place."

# *Chapter X*

"Would you like to dance?" Justin asked Rose as soon as it was evident that the musicians had quit warming up and had begun to play a real song.

Rose looked hesitantly at Christina with a concerned frown. "I don't know. I'd hate to leave your sister here all alone."

"Don't worry about me," Christina put in quickly and smiled reassuringly at her friend. "My new Texas friend is probably already on his way over to make certain I keep that agreement to dance with him. And you did promise my brother the first two dances."

She noticed that Justin's face tensed again at the mention of the man she had met quite by accident. She wondered what he had against Texans.

"If you are sure you will be all right," Rose said, clearly eager to go but at the same time still hesitant.

"I'll be just fine," Christina said, trying to keep a smile on her face until they had turned away and headed for the dance area. But as soon as she was sure they were far enough into the crowd so they could not see her, she let the smile drop. Never had she felt such misery than she did at that moment, knowing that somewhere on that dance floor Todd held Vella in his arms.

Returning to the table where Justin's hat lay and beside Rose's drawstring bag, she sat down and waited for someone to return. She hoped that *someone* would be Todd, but she knew better than to hold her breath while she waited, because Vella was not going to let him go after just one dance. Jealousy churned inside her while she tried not to think about the two of them, but no matter how hard she tried, it was *all* she could think about.

After a few lively songs, Justin returned to find her lost in her misery. "What's the matter, Chrissy?"

Startled from the deep state of sadness that had engulfed her, she looked up as he pulled a chair out and sat beside her.

"Nothing is the matter. Where's Rose?"

"Dancing with her uncle. Then she's going to stop by to say hello to her aunt before coming back over here." He watched her a moment longer, then asked, "Would you like to dance with me while I'm waiting for her to come back?"

Christina smiled. "That's sweet, but no. Besides, you wouldn't want to be gone when she returns."

Justin's eyes widened as if he had no idea what she meant, but he did not deny anything. "She's very pretty."

"Aye, she is," Christina agreed and smiled knowingly at her brother. So he was smitten by her, after all.

"But she won't be back here for a while. I'll still be able to get a dance in and be back before she is," he suggested. "And then I want you to see if you can find a way to get in between Todd and Vella. I don't like the way she keeps

172

after him."

Neither did Christina, but she was not about to admit that to her brother. "Still afraid she will influence Todd's decision in favor of her brother?"

"Do you always have to be so suspicious?" he asked as he rubbed his hand across the smooth surface of the table in a self-conscious manner. "Just try to get him away from her. She's not helping my situation any. See if you can get Todd to dance with you, then keep him with you."

"There you are. I hope you haven't forgotten you promised me a dance," they heard a deep voice say.

Christina looked up hoping to find Todd, although she knew it had not been his voice. When she saw the tall young man she had talked with earlier smiling down at her, hat in hand again, she felt a little disappointed, but smiled back at him.

"You did promise me a dance," he reminded her, and when she did not respond immediately, he added, "So how about it? That's real toe tappin' music they're playin'. Will you dance with me?"

Although she wanted to stay and offer Justin a piece of her mind for telling her what to do again, she realized Jake's invitation would offer a good chance for her to see how close Todd and Vella were dancing and just how much Todd was enjoying it. "Why certainly I'll dance with you. I've always been a woman of my word."

Standing and accepting his proffered arm, Christina ignored Justin's frown and allowed the tall man to lead her toward the music. But when they reached the dance floor and Todd and Vella were nowhere to be found, she was disappointed again and acutely apprehensive at not knowing where they had gone. Forcing a smile to her lips, she lifted her arms to Jake Akard and allowed him to sweep her across the crowded dance floor to a lively tune she had never heard before.

When the song ended and Christina had pulled herself free of Jake's grasp, she smiled, still a little breathless, and thanked him.

"Can't we dance at least one more?" he asked, his face crestfallen. "That song was half over by the time we worked through all that crowd. That couldn't really count as a whole dance."

Not wanting to disappoint him, nor to return to the table, where she would be intruding on Rose and Justin, she nodded and smiled. "I guess we could dance at least one more." But knowing that to dance more than two in succession with the same man was the same as announcing an interest in him, she quickly added, "And after that I really should get back to my brother and my friends."

"That's not fair," another man Christina had never seen before said with a frown as the music started. "You can't dance every dance with Jake. You got to give the rest of us a fair chance, too."

Christina glanced at the young man in surprise. He looked as if he was probably younger than she, but he was clearly eager to dance with her. "I've already promised this dance to Jake, but I'll dance the next one with you. How's that?"

"Grand!" the young man said, and a smile burst across his face. "I'll be waiting."

"I was afraid of that," Jake said good-naturedly. "That's why I wanted to get my dances early on. I knew you were going to be swamped with askers once they got a good look at you."

And swamped she was. She danced nonstop, until finally there was a short intermission and she was at last able to return to the table, where all she found was Justin's hat and Rose's bag. For the first time, she realized she had forgotten to leave her own bag and had danced with it dangling from her arm. Shaking her head, she approached the empty seats. She wondered where Rose and Justin had gone, because she had not seen them on the dance floor more than twice the whole time she had been out there.

Pointedly excusing herself from the young man who had escorted her back to her table, Christina sat down to rest. She pulled her handbag from her arm, slipped her fan out, and began to work it vigorously. Although she knew the sun was probably down by now, it was still very warm inside the barn and the fan offered her a nice, cool breeze. She closed her eyes to enjoy the feel of it against her heated skin.

"Are these seats taken?" she heard someone ask and opened her eyes to see if the words had been spoken to her.

When she realized the man was a stranger to her, as was the woman beside him, she looked to the chairs they motioned to and blinked. "I'm not sure."

She did a quick count of the unoccupied chairs around her and of the people she knew for certain would be seated at the table. There would be five, if Todd had not been persuaded to change his mind about where he wanted to eat by now. Then she wondered if Vella intended to join them. If so, that would make six chairs she would need to save. There were only seven available. Delighted at the thought of there being no chair left for Vella, she answered, "No, I only need to keep five of these empty. There's plenty of room for the two of you. Please, sit down."

"Thank you," the man said with a friendly smile just before he placed his hat on the table as a way of claiming the chair. "My name's Willie Butler, this is my wife, Elizabeth."

"Pleased to meet you, I'm Christina Lapin, and the ones soon to join us will be my brother Justin, his two sons, and two of our friends, Rose Beene and Todd Aylesbury."

"Todd?" the man asked, obviously acquainted with him. "Good, I'll have someone to talk to." Then, as if he might have insulted her in some way, he added, "Someone I know."

"Well, I'm not all that certain he still plans to eat with us," Christina started to explain, then noticed that Todd was making his way through the crowd toward her. Whatever she had planned to say next left her. All she could think of at the moment was that Todd was headed toward her and he was alone at last. She felt her heart race as she waited.

"Hello Willie, hello Lizzie. I hear congratulations are in order for the two of you," Todd said with a friendly smile as he offered his hand to Willie, then doubled up his fist and socked the man playfully in the shoulder.

The petite woman at Willie's side blushed profusely, but her embarrassment did not lessen her smile any.

"News travels quick around here," Willie laughed. "I only found out last Friday. Who told you?"

"I've been talking to Lizzie's parents outside. Old Caleb is proud as a peacock over the thought of having a grandchild. And I was given the definite impression he hopes the first one will be a boy. Already has a horse

176

picked out for him."

Christina felt a twinge of envy at the way the woman virtually glowed with maternal pride as her eyes shyly looked up into her husband's for a loving moment. What passed between them was a feeling she would never know.

"I'll bet you are just as excited about it as old Caleb; I imagine more," Todd went on to say. "I know I'd be on top of the clouds if it was me."

The pain crushed Christina with such force she had to look away from the three of them. She pretended to search for something inside her handbag, though there was only a handkerchief and a comb inside of it. Like any man, Todd wanted children, but unlike most women, she could never be the one to provide him with them. Even if their relationship did advance to the point of their wanting to marry, she would never be able to. Never had she felt such a feeling of despair. The future could never be theirs. But she hated to think that his future might center around Vella Stone.

"I hope you don't think me rude, but I've been trying my best to find this lady alone long enough to ask her to dance with me," Todd said, indicating Christina by holding out his hand to her. "Come on, Christina. You did say you would dance at least one dance with me."

"Did I?" she asked quietly. It hurt to speak.

"Don't start playing games with me," he warned her. "You know you did, and I want to be sure I get that dance. If I don't grab hold of you right now, someone else will, and I may never get another chance to dance with you."

It was true. She had promised to dance with him. Even though she could never hope to share a lifetime with the man, she could at least share a dance with him. Sinking into her own self-pity, she decided that at least she would have the memory of his kiss and the memory of one dance to hold on to in the long, lonely years to come.

"I know the music hasn't started yet, but I don't want to miss any of it. Let's go on up there. I want to be ready," Todd said as he took her hand and placed it on his arm, then covered it firmly with his own. Then, to Willie as they turned to leave, he winked and said, "Can't chance a lady as pretty as this one getting away from me now, can I?"

Christina's pulses raced wildly from the excitement his touch brought her as they wove through the throng of people milling about. She felt light-headed and giddy. Warmth spread through her. It was odd the way his touch always affected her, even a touch so gentle and expected as that.

"Looks like they are getting ready to start playing again," Todd said as they neared the dance area. The six musicians had returned to their seats and had taken their instruments in hand. The fiddler plucked idly at one string.

Christina could hardly wait to be swept away into Todd's arms and watched the musicians with growing anticipation. The men exchanged a few words, nodded and laughed at something the guitar player had said, then lifted their instruments into position and began to play. To her delight, it was "Waltzing Matilda." She knew the song well and knew she would be able to dance to it, if she could just keep her thoughts on what she was doing and not on the fact that she was finally in Todd's arms again.

Todd pulled her toward him and gathered her hand into his and placed his other hand at the back of her waist. At first he kept his body away from hers, but as the dance area became more and more crowded, he brought her closer to him. In the beginning, she had been awkward in her movements, more out of self-consciousness than anything else, but soon she relaxed enough to pay less attention to what she did with her feet and more attention to the feel of Todd's manly arms holding her close. Her motions became fluid and blended easily with his as he smoothly led her around the dance floor. It was as if they were one.

Floating with ease, she was so thrilled at the feel of his breath against her cheek and of his body when it came into contact with hers again and again, that she could not imagine ever being happier. Her senses were filled with him as she breathed deeply the delicate scent of pipe tobacco, which mingled pleasantly with the natural scent she had come to know. Her skin tingled at every place where they touched and her heart soared ever higher.

The untamed emotions that spun around inside of her at twice the pace of the music made her feel slightly weak, yet strongly vibrant. Part of her wished the dance could last forever as she lost herself in the wondrous swirl of emotions. But another part of her made her very aware that the dance would end shortly and she would need to be in control of her heart and her breath when it did.

But the desire to savor the delicious moment to its fullest was too strong. Closing her eyes, she drifted with the warm fog of sensations that caressed her while the lively flow of the music and the feel of him next to her seduced her, plunging her deeper and deeper into a gentle oblivion. When the music stopped, she was so lost to the wondrous feelings that she was reluctant to move away, and he made no move to release her.

"Better break it off, you two." She heard her brother's singsong voice drift through to her thoughts. "People are going to talk."

"Look who has the nerve to say such a thing," Todd said as he suddenly pulled away from Christina and stood at her side. "I imagine they are already talking plenty over the fact that you and Rose have danced so many dances together. If you don't watch out, they are going to consider you two a couple, and her aunt and uncle will expect you to pay call on her."

"Suits me," Justin said boldly and looked to see what Rose might have thought of Todd's statement. But she barely had time to reassure him with a brief smile before the next song started and they had to either dance or get off the dance floor.

"Another dance," Todd said quickly and took Christina into his arms before she could protest or agree, though she had no intention of turning down a second dance.

But she knew she'd better say no to a third dance because her brother was right. People would start to talk, and because of her personal circumstances, that would neither be fair to Todd nor to herself.

It was shortly after they had returned to the table that someone on the far side of the building started banging on a piece of metal to get everyone's attention. As soon as a hush had fallen over the crowd inside the huge barn, a man's voice shouted out that they were ready for everyone to come up, serve their plates, and fill their cups.

Vella appeared out of nowhere when Todd rose from his chair. "Mind if I walk with you?" she asked, looking up at him through her lowered lashes.

Todd stepped around her and held out his hand for Christina. "Of course, we don't mind. You're quite welcome to walk with us, but I'm afraid there are no extra seats at this table, so I can't offer to have you join us."

Christina felt a deep surge of satisfaction as she watched Vella glance around at the chairs. Every one was either still occupied by those not in a hurry to eat or had a hat or a handbag sitting in front of it to save the spot for whoever had just left it. Even Edward and Alan had left their hats to mark their places.

Vella's eyes narrowed perceptibly, but she made no remark other than to thank him, then she quickly moved to take his right arm before Christina could. But he sidestepped her and turned so that his arm came up under Christina's. "I certainly am hungry, what about you two ladies?"

Although Vella was not pleased, she stayed at his side until they reached the tables, where he finally broke away from Christina so she could fill her plate. As soon as he had freed his arm, Vella stepped in between them and made a ridiculous production of getting Todd's opinion on which foods she should choose. But when the time came to leave the food tables, she had no choice but to go elsewhere to sit.

Christina smiled at the impudent little pout that had pulled at Vella's face when she realized she was not going to be dining with Todd. And by the time they had returned to their seats, Christina was surprised to find she was ravenously hungry, when just a few minutes before, the mention of food had not fazed her in the slightest.

"It all looked so good," Todd said as he set his heaping plate and his cup on the table in front of him. "I wish I

181

could have gotten more of it on my plate."

"I don't see how you could. I think you did pretty well there," Christina responded with a nod toward his plate, which was piled so high with such a wide selection of food that she did not understand how it kept from falling off and onto the floor.

"So did I," Justin said as he and Rose came up behind them, his own plate piled high, but not a match for Todd's.

During dinner, the conversation among the men at the table turned to the new railway that was nearing completion and how that would help them get their stock to market faster than having to take them overland. Then the conversation turned to the outbreak of cattle duffing that was going on.

"My station has been hit twice," Todd said with a deep frown and cut his gaze to Justin, as if to catch his reaction, then away.

Christina sensed Justin's wariness over the subject and turned to watch him out of the corner of her eye while Todd continued to tell Willie Butler and the other two men at the table about how the cattle duffers operated as if they had a way of getting inside information. Both times he had been duffed, he and several of his men had been away on business, which had left not enough men to keep an eye on the entire place.

"I think whoever is behind it is someone we all know. Maybe even one of our neighbors. When Ben Crawford's cattle were taken, it was while he and two of his men were at my place helping with my branding, which obviously left his own place shorthanded. And it seems to me they knew enough about Ben to know which pastures he would let go unwatched while shorthanded for the one day."

"I was thinking along those same lines," Willie said solemnly. "That's why I was reluctant to come to this thing today, afraid that while I was away and so many of my men were too, that they might pick my place to rob. In fact, I was worried enough to have my cattle mustered up into the paddocks closest to my house and hired my little brother and one of his friends to keep an eye on them."

"Well, if I ever get my hands on the blokes who took my cattle, I'm going to wring their ever loving necks," Henry Lawson said angrily from the next table, ignoring his wife's attempts to calm him. "I can't afford no loss like that."

"You know what I think?" Robert Mitchell put in, having to lean over his wife's plate in order to be a part of the conversation from his end of the neighboring table. "I think it's a few of those bleeding heart farmers who want the government to take some of our land away from us so they can have it for their own use."

Christina continued to watch Justin through this exchange and realized he was being uncharacteristically quiet, paying more attention to rearranging the food on his plate than to what was being said. Then suddenly he looked off into the distance as if he sensed something, and turned pale. His shoulders became rigid. She followed his gaze and noticed a sinister-looking man who had just entered the front door and stood to one side. Now that almost everyone was seated and eating, their view across the barn was unhampered.

The man stepped further inside and scanned the occupants of the room until his eyes came to rest on

Justin's startled gaze. No one else at the table seemed aware of the man or of the way he had singled Justin out, other than Christina. Even Rose had not noticed.

Justin watched, his fork held in midair as the man motioned toward the door with a barely noticeable jerk of his head. Then he slipped back outside and was gone.

Christina wanted to ask him who the man was, but before she could, he put his fork down and pushed his still more than half-filled plate aside. "Edward and Alan still haven't come inside to eat. I think I'd better go out there and find them. If they wait too much longer, there won't be anything left and they will complain all the way home."

"I'll go with you," Christina quickly volunteered and lowered her fork to her plate.

"No, that won't be necessary," he said firmly. "I can find them. You stay here and finish your meal."

Rose noticed the odd look on Christina's face as Justin stood from his chair and walked away. "He'll be able to find them," she assured her. "I doubt they've wandered too far away from the lights."

Christina did not voice her suspicions to Rose because she was not really certain what they were, but she kept her eye on the front doors until Justin finally reappeared, his clothes rumpled and his expression grim.

"Oh, my, I wonder what those boys were up to," Rose said to Christina as she watched Justin walk around the tables, then toward them.

"No telling," Christina replied, letting her gaze return to the door to see if the other man intended to follow. She saw no sign of either the man or the boys. "I think I'd better go see what the problem is."

Rising quickly, she hurried to meet Justin out of

earshot of the table. Keeping her voice low, she asked, "Justin, who was that man?"

Justin glowered at her. "None of your business. It is something I'll have to handle alone. Quit sticking your beak in where it doesn't belong."

Christina was too stunned and too hurt by his low, angry outburst to make a reply, but followed as he walked to the table and tapped Todd on the shoulder. She was dismayed to hear what he had to say, especially without having mentioned it to her first.

"Todd, I have to leave. Will you see Christina and the boys home for me?"

Todd quickly stood and looked from Justin's grim expression to Christina's angry one. "Is there something I can help you with?"

"Just see Chrissy and the boys home."

"Why can't you see us home?" Christina demanded to know, though she was not upset at being abandoned into Todd's company. She was worried about Justin.

"I just can't," Justin told her, then walked past them to where Rose sat staring curiously up at the three of them. "I'm sorry I have to leave so suddenly, but it just can't be helped. Something has come up that I have to attend to tonight. But if you don't mind, I'd like to call on you this weekend. There's a new traveling show at the Victoria, if you'd care to see it with me."

Rose looked perplexed, as if she didn't know whether to be upset or excited. "I'd love to go with you. What time?"

Justin's expression turned blank. "I don't know. I don't know what time those sorts of things begin. Does six o'clock sound about right?"

"Sounds perfect," she told him and smiled sweetly.

"Good. I'll see you then," he said and made an effort to return her smile, though it barely reached his eyes before quickly fading. "I've got to go now."

Before Christina could reach out to stop him, he was on his way out, never looking back to see what their reactions were or if any of them would try to follow him.

## Chapter XI

Ten minutes after Justin's mysterious decision to leave, Todd pushed his plate aside and excused himself to go outside. He told Christina he would check on the boys to make sure no harm had come to them.

Shortly, both boys, followed by at least nine others, came tromping through the front doors and headed straight for the food tables, helping themselves to what was left of the feast. Once they had their plates filled, mainly with different desserts and sweetbreads, Edward led Alan over to where Christina sat with her attention divided between them and the front door, where she had last seen Todd.

Raking her fingers through Edward's unkempt curls in an effort to tame them, and turning her nose away from the rank odor of the two youngsters, she asked them both, "Where have you been?"

"Out playing bushranger," Edward told her. "Me and Alan here were a part of the Riley gang, along with Rebel and Cole, and Cody and Brandon were members of the secret detectives, them and a bunch of other boys."

"Didn't your father find you and tell you it was time to come in and eat?"

"No, Mr. Aylesbury and Mr. Coolabah did. Mr. Aylesbury said if we didn't hurry and get our plates there wouldn't be anything left for us to eat at all. Good thing he came out when he did, too. They already had Rebel and Cole captured, and there wasn't any way for us to slip in and rescue them. It was just a matter of time till they had us, too."

Christina frowned, wondering why Justin had not at least stayed long enough to find the boys and send them inside. What had come up that was so important?

Finally Todd returned, but before he made his way back over to where she sat, Vella popped out of a small group of women and stopped him by placing her hand on his arm.

Christina wondered what the woman's reaction was going to be when she found out Todd was going to have to take her and the boys home. Leaning back in her chair, Christina kept her eyes well trained on Vella's smiling face in hopes of witnessing Vella's reaction to the news. She had no doubt that Vella would hint that Todd should take her home and he would have no choice but to tell her why he could not.

Vella continued to laugh and bat her overlarge gray-green eyes at Todd, leaning slightly forward to favor him with an opportunity to glance down her shamefully low-necked gown. Christina smiled. To Todd's credit, he kept his eyes on the woman's animated face and away from her bulging neckline.

Finally, it happened. Vella's smile dropped as if her cheeks had suddenly been turned to lead, and her eyes narrowed, but she did not show any of the outward anger

Christina had expected. Christina decided it was only the woman's stubbornness that enabled her to hide the emotion so well. She wished Vella would look in her direction so she could offer her a friendly smile. Just thinking about how that would gall her made Christina want to laugh, and if she had not pressed her fingertips to her lips at that precise moment, she might have done just that.

"You certainly look pleased about something," Edward remarked as he shoveled in another huge bite of chocolate pie. "You must have got ahold of some of this pie."

"Something sweeter than that," Christina said and smiled with pure contentment.

"Sweeter than this chocolate pie?" Edward asked, and frowned. Turning to Alan, he grumbled, "See, I told you we should have come on in to eat when they made that first call. We missed out on all the best desserts."

Alan did not take the complaint too seriously as he too continued to shove large pieces of the same pie into his mouth. He was happy enough with what desserts had been left.

Soon, the music started again, but to Christina's delight, and somewhat to her surprise, Todd did not turn and go with Vella to the dance area. Instead, he bowed politely to her and came back to sit at the table.

"It's getting late," he said as he watched the boys fill their mouths so full that their cheeks bulged. "As soon as these two get finished eating, I think we should be going. It will take a little longer to travel in the dark, and I've got a long, hard day ahead of me tomorrow. I've already arranged for Sam to ride back with Coolabah, so there will be enough room in the gig for the boys to

189

lie down in the rear seat if they want."

"I'm sorry we are putting you out like this," she said sincerely. "I don't know what got into Justin or why he left, but it is nice of you to be willing to see us home."

"I don't mind," he told her. "In fact, I'd much rather have a beautiful woman like you riding at my side than Sam, especially when he's had as much to drink as I suspect he's had. And the boys are never any problem. Are you, boys?"

They shook their hands adamantly, their mouths too full to speak. Todd laughed and handed Alan his cup of tea, suggesting he try to wash some of the food down before he choked.

Soon they were on their way home, Todd and Christina in the front seat and the boys in the back. As expected, both boys fell asleep almost immediately. Alan sagged against the side of the carriage and Edward slumped over Alan, neither bothered by the continuous jolting caused by the rutted track or by the loud clattering of the carriage.

There was enough moonlight in the cloudless night sky for them to see the silvery silhouettes of the tall trees and scrubby brush that lay beyond the small islands of light that the two carriage lanterns created. The air was cool and pleasant, full of the delicate scent of the eucalyptus and freshly mowed hay, and Christina was intensely aware of her surroundings.

At first the night felt invigorating to Christina, full of something special, but lulled by the continuous motion of the carriage and the contented feeling that had washed over her, soon she, too, was fighting off sleep.

Todd noticed Christina's nodding head. Since the back of the seat was not high enough for her to lean her head against it, he slid closer to her and put his arm around her. He pulled her gently toward him and allowed her to rest her head against his shoulder. Too tired and far too sleepy to find reason to object, Christina fell asleep in the warm circle of his arm.

Holding her close, Todd enjoyed the peaceful moment to its fullest, feeling as if he was in possession of a precious angel, a special angel he wished he somehow could make his own. He watched the faint shadows dance across her sweet face tilted comfortably against his arm, wondering if any man would ever conquer her heart, and if that man could possibly be he.

All too soon, Justin's house appeared in the distance, the shape of it dark against the grayness of the night. As the carriage stopped just a few feet away from the veranda, Christina awoke, still groggy with sleep. She sat up and blinked in confusion while Todd climbed down, turned, and offered his hand to help her down.

"Careful," he warned as she eased herself to the edge of the seat and accepted his hand.

Still very sleepy, she slipped when she thrust her foot out for the tiny iron step attached to the side of the carriage. Before she fell and hurt herself, Todd caught her by the waist, instantly pulling her to him. As he eased her to the ground, he felt her body slide slowly against his and filled his nostrils with the gentle scent of lilacs that clung to her hair. Everything about her was arousing. Before he realized it, he had brought his lips down on hers in a maddening moment of need.

At first she tried to resist, confused by his sudden show of passion, but as the languid feeling of warmth he always created in her began to spread through her, any thought of pulling away left her. Overpowered by her own needs, she brought her hands around his shoulders and pulled him closer, returning his kiss with a passion she could no longer deny. When his mouth suddenly broke free of hers and began to trail gentle kisses down the gentle slope of her neck, she moaned quietly into the night. Her skin came alive from the sensations his warm lips created. Her heart went wild, beating with such force that she was certain even Todd could hear it.

The longer his lips touched the tender flesh of her neck, the more she wanted his touch. She tilted her head back to give him easier access. Her thoughts blended into the fury of her passion and she found she anxiously waited for him to take the kiss further, so that she could at last explore the feelings she had never truly explored before.

Just as Todd's hungry mouth returned to hers and his hands came forward to the front of her rib cage, the boys finally stirred, and the sound brought Christina crashing back to reality. She could not let the boys witness such a display of wanton passion. Quickly she jerked herself free and brought a trembling hand up to make sure her hair did not show any signs of what had just happened.

"We home?" Alan asked as he pushed Edward off him and sat up, staring groggily in the direction of the house.

Edward blinked hard, then rubbed his eyes with the backs of his hands and leaned against the opposite side of the carriage, sagging comfortably back to sleep.

"Aye, you are home, lads," Todd assured them. "Are you awake enough to walk? Or would you like for me to carry you?"

"I can walk," Alan assured him, though his words were interrupted by a loud yawn that cast doubts as to whether he was truly awake or not.

"What about you, Edward? You going to be able to walk?"

There was no response from Edward, no movement at all other than the slight twitch of his lightly freckled nose.

Smiling to Christina, he waited until Alan had climbed down out of the way, then reached inside and lifted the older boy into his arms.

"Had a rough day, have you?" he said quietly as he situated the boy in his arms and held him close against his chest.

Following a stumbly Alan toward the house, he waited until Christina had opened the door, then followed Alan up the stairs and into the boys' room. Christina stayed downstairs to light several lamps and took the opportunity to check her image in the mirror. To her dismay, her hair was tousled and her cheek creased where she had lain it against Todd's shirt. She felt warm and embarrassed because he had allowed her to lean against his shoulder for such a long time.

"Both of them are sound asleep," Todd said as he descended the stairs, smiling to himself. "But then, I don't think Edward ever woke up. That boy could sleep through a raging dust storm."

Christina agreed. The boy was impossible to wake up in the mornings, even after a good night's sleep. He was much like her in that respect.

"Well, like I told you earlier, I have a long, hard day ahead of me tomorrow. And I haven't even had Gomer pack my things yet," he said as he stood in front of her.

"Pack?" Christina asked with a worried expression.

"Aye. I'm going to be gone for at least a week. Hasn't Justin told you? I've still got business in Sydney that I need to attend to. I'll be catching the afternoon coach," he explained with a frown. "I'll certainly be glad when they get that railway completed. It'll cut days off my traveling time."

"A week?" she repeated quietly.

"Maybe longer, but I hope not." He could sense that she did not want him to go, and that made him feel good, gave him his first real ray of hope. Tonight he had finally realized how much she meant to him. Even the thought of her missing him made the trip worthwhile, though he would have given anything not to have to go.

Watching her dance with all those men had eaten away at him until he had burned with jealousy, making him aware of how much he wanted her. Not just for now, not just for a while, but this time he knew he wanted her forever. Christina was different from any woman he'd ever known. She had far more spirit and more true beauty than any woman should.

While he was away, he would try to devise a plan to make her want him, too. Maybe just his being away would help. Maybe, just maybe, she would miss him. It was the best hope he had at the moment.

"How often do you have to go to Sydney?"

"Every few months. That's where I market my cattle and the wool from my sheep. I make more profit if I overland it myself and sell it there than to auction it in Bathurst."

Christina could not understand the sudden heaviness she felt inside, especially since she barely saw much of him during the week anyway, and until recently had seen nothing of him at all. But still she knew she was going to miss him. Miss him dreadfully.

After a few attempts at awkward conversation between

them, Todd finally headed for the door. He wanted to kiss her good-bye, but decided not to press his luck. He had made his decision to take it slow and easy with her. He had to try his best to do that or risk frightening her away again. "I'll stop by to see you on my way back."

Christina wanted to tell him that she'd be waiting, counting the days, but all that came out as she followed him to the door was, "That would be nice."

"See you then," he said, and paused in the doorway to turn back and look at her. How beautiful she was. Too beautiful. His firm resolve to leave without kissing her melted. He had to at least touch her again to make it through the next week.

When he bent forward and pressed his lips to hers, Christina braced herself for the onslaught and was stunned when he just as quickly pulled his lips away. The kiss had been short and extremely tender, but had left her weak and wanting.

"Take care of yourself," she said as she watched him cross the yard and climb back into his carriage. She waited until he had driven onto the main track before slowly closing the door. Suddenly a week seemed a lifetime.

Justin came in hours after Christina had fallen asleep. Although he made enough noise to wake her, she did not get out of bed to go see about him. She was too sad to want to do anything but go back to sleep. The less she thought about Todd's week away, the better.

The following morning, Justin, pale and slightly red-eyed, staggered into the kitchen with his hand pressed to his temple and one eye fluttered half shut. Christina realized he must have had quite a bit to drink the night before. Too much. She wondered when he had gotten so drunk, because he had left the ball sober.

"Todd is leaving for Sydney today," she said as a way of starting up a conversation. She wanted to talk about the strange man who had appeared at the ball and lured her brother outside, but she decided to start with a totally different topic of conversation and bend it to suit her. "Is he going to put you in charge again while he is gone?"

"No, Coolabah isn't going with him this time. Although he usually goes on these business trips, Todd did not want him along with him," Justin told her, his voice so low and so hoarse that she almost did not hear him.

"He's going alone?"

"Aye," he answered. He rubbed his temple lightly with his fingertips, then paused with a grimace frozen on his face and added bitterly, "Well, not exactly alone. I hear tell how Miss Vella Stone has plans of traveling to Sydney this afternoon, too. What she won't do to try to trap that man! I used to think all she wanted was to be sure William got that job, but now I think she really wants to become the mistress of Todd's station. She's out to lay her hooks into that man all right."

Christina forgot all about wanting to question Justin about the stranger at the ball as she felt something cold and threatening spread through her. When Justin got up to leave the room, Christina's thoughts centered on Vella and Todd, traveling together to Sydney. No wonder he did not want Coolabah along for this trip. She shuddered when she thought of what all Vella might accomplish, then slowly began to get angry. Todd had certainly been careful not to mention to her that Vella was going. But

196

then again, what right did she have to such secrets? And what reason did she have to feel so crestfallen?

Justin was gone before Christina had asked her brother about the man who had lured him away from the ball. And, to her mounting frustration, it was almost bedtime before she had another opportunity to speak with her brother alone. Only moments after the two of them had settled into their favorite chairs outside on the veranda, Christina had decided not to let this second opportunity pass. "Justin, who was that man who wanted you to follow him outside last night at the ball? I don't remember ever having been introduced to him."

Justin seemed surprised by the question. "What man?"

"The one who stepped just inside the doors while we were eating and signaled for you to join him outside," she clarified for him, though she suspected he knew very well what man.

"Oh, him? He's just an old friend," he stated evasively. "He wanted me to help him with a problem he and another friend of his were having."

"Then why did you leave so abruptly right after that?"

Justin looked at her a long moment before answering. "Because he and his friend wanted me to join them in a few drinks, and I knew you would not want me drinking around you and Rose." He ran his tongue over his lower lip, then half smiled as he added, "As it turned out, I had a few too many. And believe me, I've been paying for that mistake all day. My head still feels like it wants to burst wide open. In fact, I think I'll go on to bed and see if lying down might ease some of the pain." He reached up to massage his temples. "I'll see you in the morning."

Christina frowned as she watched Justin push himself

up out of the chair and go inside. Though she had no real reason to doubt that the man had been nothing more than another of his drinking mates, she had the distinct feeling Justin was keeping something from her.

With Todd away and both Justin and the boys working late hours, the next few days passed painfully slowly for Christina. She did not remember ever experiencing such a dismal mood before. She was unable to think of anything but what might be happening in Sydney between Vella and Todd. When Jake Akard stopped by that Friday afternoon, only two days after Todd had left, it was such a relief to have someone take her mind off her worries that she greeted him eagerly, opening the door wide to welcome him inside.

"What brings you out this way?" she asked before she bent to gather her darning and set it aside so he could have the most comfortable chair in the living room.

"To be honest, you do," he said, taking his hat off and looking around for a place to set it. Finally he dropped it onto the small table beside the chair and waited until she had taken her seat before sitting in the chair she had offered him. "I've been thinkin' about you ever since the ball. After all, you were the prettiest gal there."

Christina smiled at the way the words seemed to roll lazily from his mouth. She wanted to hear more of his deep Texas drawl, but did not particularly want to hear any more of his compliments, so she led the conversation in another direction. "Where do you work that allows you a free afternoon to do with whatever you want?"

"I don't know if I should tell you. I don't know of any delicate way of puttin' it for a lady."

"Now you've gotten my curiosity up. You have to tell me."

He rubbed his face as he thought about it, then finally looked her in the eye and stated simply, "I breed horses. Racehorses."

"Racehorses?"

"Yep, I got a small place over near the racecourse where I breed and train horses for use by the mounted police and also for racing," he told her, and when she did not speak again, he grinned sheepishly. "Well a man's got to do somethin' to make a livin'. And I must be doing that somethin' right, because I'm makin' plenty of money doing it. They all sure seemed satisfied." Suddenly his dark blue eyes widened as what he had said occurred to him and he quickly added, "The buyers. The men who buy my horses sure seemed satisfied."

Christina wanted to laugh but kept a straight expression. "I'm sure they are well satisfied. Tell me. Would you care for a spot of tea?"

"Oh, yes, ma'am. I sure would. That is, if it won't put you to no trouble."

"No trouble at all," she assured him. "I'll be just a minute."

"Can I come with you? I'd probably feel more comfortable in the kitchen, anyway. These fancy chairs of yours scare me to death. I'm always so afraid I'm going to bust up such dainty furniture."

"Certainly," she said, again wanting to chuckle at such blatant honesty. "Follow me. I may even have a teacake or two to go with that tea."

When Justin and the boys came home early, they found Christina and Jake still in the kitchen talking about a large explosion at the ironworks in Bathurst. Though

199

they had both finished their tea long ago, Jake had asked to stay and keep her company while she prepared supper, but had firmly declined her invitation to stay and eat. While she worked, he had kept her entertained with stories of Texas and with the latest news from town.

"What's *he* doing here?" Justin demanded accusingly as he stepped inside and confronted the two of them. Edward and Alan followed, their eyes wide with their youthful curiosity.

"He just stopped by for a friendly visit," Christina told him, frowning at the harshness of his voice.

"I'll just bet," Justin said, and turned to look at Jake with open contempt. "And who gave you permission to call on my sister like this?"

Jake stood and looked at Christina, then at Justin, but before he could answer, Christina answered for him.

"I did," she lied, but so angry at her brother for his behavior that it really did not bother her. "I told him he could stop by whenever he wanted. We're friends. Good friends."

Justin's green eyes narrowed as if he wanted to say something more to her, but instead he turned and stalked out of the same door he had just come in.

"How long till we eat?" Edward asked, still frowning at how angry his father and his aunt had become with each other.

"Not long. You two go on outside and wash up. You both smell like stockyard animals."

As soon as the boys had left the room, Christina apologized to Jake for her brother's strange behavior.

"That's all right. I understand how he probably feels. If I had a sister as pretty as you to look after, I'd probably react just the same way," he assured her and reached out his hand to stroke her cheek gently with his fingertip. "I hope you meant what you told him, though. That I can stop by to see you whenever I want, because I've been wanting all afternoon to ask you to come go to the racecourse with me tomorrow. It's a lot of fun. I'd come get you in the morning and have you back before it even gets dark. You would be able to see some of my horses in action. They are beautiful animals."

Christina's first thought was to say no, but when her next thought was of the lonely afternoons she had already suffered and the fact that Todd was not lonely at all, she decided she would go. "What should I wear?"

"Clothes would be fittin'," he grinned, then looked apologetic for his remark and added, "I'm no expert in what ladies should wear. Wear whatever is comfortable. You're going to look pretty in whatever you choose."

"I appreciate your confidence," she told him. "I'm certain I'll find something appropriate to wear."

"Be by for you then around nine o'clock. First race is at eleven."

He looked as if he wanted to kiss her but was afraid of what her reaction would be. Not wanting him to suffer any humiliation, and also not wanting to be kissed by him, she raised her hand out for him and let him squeeze it gently.

Justin went into a rage when later he learned of her plans to go with Jake to the racecourse. "Word of this is sure to get back to Todd. He'll be furious."

"What right has he got to be furious?" she wanted to know. "He's in Sydney with Vella Stone right now. So what right has he got to say who I can and cannot see? He certainly has no claim on me. As for you, just because you are my brother doesn't give you any right to tell me who I should allow to call on me."

"You just don't get it, do you? Todd likes you a lot. He's told me that much. And because he likes you so much, that gives you an advantage. An advantage no *man* can ever have. That advantage gives you a good way of influencing him for me."

"Oh, we are back to that, are we? Your next words are going to remind me that you have asked me to be extra nice to him. To help win him over for you. Well, I've been nice to him. And I'll continue to be nice to him. I happen to like him. But I don't see why that should keep me from being friends with Jake Akard. Jake is a nice man and I've never been to a horse race. I'm curious to see what one is like."

"Then I'll take you."

"No, Jake will. I've already told him I would go with him tomorrow and go with him I shall!" Refusing to discuss the matter any further, she went to her room and did not come out again that night.

When Christina climbed into Jake's carriage and settled onto the cool leather seats that next morning it was almost as much to spite Justin as it was because she wanted to see a horse race. He had argued that she would be leaving the boys alone, since they were not going to Todd's to work that day. She had argued back that they had been alone before and managed nicely. She reminded him how he had left them at the house alone the day he had picked her up in Bathurst. Justin then argued that they would have nothing to eat, and she had retaliated by reminding him that he could make mutton stew if the beef they had left over from supper was not good enough for them.

The more he tried to argue her out of it, the more

202

determined she became to go. It was not as if she shirked her duties every day. After all, this was only her third trip into Bathurst in the two and a half months she had been there.

Horse racing was just as exciting as she had expected it to be. Although she did not place any wagers, for Jake had warned her that a very disreputable crowd of people frequented the wager area, she still selected certain horses to win and cheered them on. Usually she found that Jake had bred and trained the ones she chose, and that made her cheer all the more.

When she arrived back home late that afternoon, Justin was angrier than he had been when she left, despite her having asked Jake to bring her home a little early so she could help with supper. It was only because the boys were present that they did not argue over her having gone at all.

Later, though, when the boys were in bed, Justin made sure he found her alone and told her again just how angry he really was and demanded she tell Jake to stay away from her. "Tell him, or I will."

"I will not. And neither will you. I have not done anything wrong and neither has Jake. And if I want to spend some of my time in his company, I will. He's a nice man and I like him." Though she knew she did not like him in the same way she liked Todd, he was indeed a very nice man and he made her laugh. With Todd away, she needed someone who could make her temporarily forget her misery, forget that Todd was not alone in Sydney, and especially, forget how very, very much she missed him.

# Chapter XII

By the following Wednesday, Christina began to feel guilty over how much time Jake wanted to spend with her. She felt she was leading Jake on, because she was in no way romantically interested in him and it was becoming more and more obvious that he was very, very romantically interested in her.

Though he had yet to kiss her, she feared it was just a matter of time before he tried, and she hated the thought of having to reject him. It would not be fair to let him kiss her when she had no intentions of being anything but friends with him. She liked being around him. She liked laughing with him. But she did not love him and knew she never would. It became clearer and clearer to her that if she did indeed love anyone, it was Todd. It was also obvious that she needed to explain her feelings to Jake before things got any further out of hand.

That afternoon, while on a ride through the countryside in his carriage, she explained how very much she liked him and how much she wanted the two of them to be friends, close friends.

"And we are," he assured her quickly and let his mustache spread with a wide smile.

"But that's *all* I want us to be. And that's all we ever will be."

The disappointment on his face made her want to reach out and comfort him in some way. She had hurt him, and she had not wanted to.

"Why, Christina? Why is that all you want us to be?" He pulled the carriage to a halt at the side of the track so that he could give their discussion his full attention.

"Because I've got more problems than I can handle right now and I can't possibly consider a serious relationship with anyone," she said, staring lamely down at her folded hands, but then looked over at him before she continued. "I don't want to complicate my life with a relationship I can't cope with. And I don't want to let you go on thinking there's a chance I will change my mind. I won't. I don't want to get involved. But I sure could use a good friend about now."

Jake looked at her for a long moment before speaking. "You've got one. It's not what I'd hoped for, but friendship is better than no relationship with you at all." He tried to smile, but the effort was futile as he snapped the reins and set the horses into quick motion again.

"I hope you understand," she said, still wishing she could ease whatever he was feeling for her news had clearly not set well with him.

"I think I understand more than you realize," he said sadly. "And I should have seen it coming."

"I am sorry."

"Don't be. I'm grateful that you are so honest and that you at least like me enough to want me for a friend."

"I do," she smiled, and felt some of the tension ease

between them. "I enjoy your friendship. I enjoy it a lot."

After that, the awkwardness Jake had shown around her slowly disappeared. There was no reluctant pause when it came time for him to say good-bye, because kissing her was no longer an option to consider. When he helped her down from his carriage and walked her to the veranda, though the sun had dipped behind the distant trees creating a cool shadow of privacy across the area, all he did was reach out and stroke her cheek lightly with his fingertip. It was a caring gesture, but nothing more.

"See ya the next time I'm out this way," he said with a smile, but Christina could sense it would be quite a while before he came that way again.

"Be sure that you do," she said and returned his smile before turning away and going inside. As she closed the door behind her she felt sad that she had hurt him, but extremely relieved to know that telling him her true feelings was now behind her. She had told him exactly how she felt and had still kept his friendship.

"Where are the boys?" she asked Justin when she walked into the kitchen and found him sitting at one of her worktables with a tall glass cupped in his hands. Beside him sat a half-empty bottle of Irish whiskey and a narrow cork.

"Gone on up to bed. They had a hard day," he told her. His voice was cold and he refused to look up at her.

"I see they liked the lamb chops well enough," she said of the meal she had left behind for them. She ignored his foul mood and his drinking again as she gathered the dirty dishes and placed them in the sink.

"Somebody came by to see you while you were gone," he said solemnly, never looking up from the amber liquid in his glass. "He was more than a little upset to learn you were out gallivanting around with someone else."

Christina felt the blood drain from her face and she almost dropped the plates she held in her hands. She had been anticipating Todd's return, but had not expected it to be for a day or two yet. She had known all along he would find out about Jake, and had intended to tell him herself and explain how the two of them were just friends. Nothing more. She had planned to explain it as best she could without admitting to him that he was one of the main reasons she had allowed Jake to come calling in the first place. How she had hoped Jake's company would help her get over the terrible loneliness she had suffered from the very moment he had left. And to help her occupy her mind with something other than the fact that Vella Stone had gone with him. No, she refused to let him know of the torment she had gone through in his behalf, for he had far too much to be arrogant about as it was.

"What did Todd say?" she asked, leaning heavily against the wooden counter.

"Plenty! What would you expect him to say?" Justin took another drink from his glass. "He was mad as hell when he left here."

"He had no right to be."

"No right? He comes by here to see you and finds out you've gone for a ride with another man and you say he has no right to be angry?"

"No, he doesn't. It's not as if we are a couple, you know. Because we aren't."

"You could be," he quickly pointed out.

"But we aren't. In all honesty, the only reason we are even friends, at all is because of you."

"Oh, sure. Now you are going to make it seem as if you

have made great sacrifices for me. Don't waste your breath. If you truly cared about me, you never would have gone out with Jake in the first place, and you damn sure never would have done anything to make Todd angry."

"How can you be so selfish?" she asked, her voice choked with emotion, and her eyes burning with angry tears.

"Me, selfish? How can *you* be so bloody selfish? All you ever think about is yourself. Never a thought for anyone else."

"That's not true." The tears had filled her eyes until she could barely see and threatened to spill down her flushed cheeks.

"The hell it isn't. All you've ever cared about is yourself. Never a thought to how you could help me."

"Justin, you don't mean that."

"The hell I don't. Get out of my sight. I can't stand even to look at you."

"Oh, I'll get out of your sight, all right, but not until I have my say! I'm tired of the way you keep trying to use me to get to Todd Aylesbury. If *you* want to cozy up to him, fine. But I'm not about to cozy up to that man. To tell you the truth, I'd rather cozy up to a snake!"

Christina turned and ran as fast as she could for the stairs, stumbling as she tried to take them two at a time in her long, heavy skirts. Never had she been so angry with her brother. Never had his words hurt her so deeply. As she slammed the door and flung herself onto the bed, her face buried into the pillow, she wondered if she would ever forgive him for the way he had treated her. This time, she doubted it, and for the first time, she considered leaving. Only the thought of how much the boys had come to depend on her prevented her from packing her valise right at that moment.

But by morning, Christina had forgiven her brother for his emotional outburst the night before. She knew he was apt to say more than he meant to whenever he had had too much to drink, and he had obviously had far too much to drink last night. Christina even considered going to Todd and explaining about Jake, but decided against it. She did not know how to approach him with the subject without sounding vain, nor did she understand why he felt he had the right to be so angry in the first place. She had never committed herself to Todd—couldn't, even if she wanted to. If anyone had a right to be angry, it was she.

But as the day wore on, she remembered his tantalizing kisses and how easily she responded to them. Just thinking about it sent her blood racing hot trails through her. She also remembered how nice he had been to her the last few times they had been together. He had made an honest effort to get along with her for the first time, and she had been thrilled.

Finally, she convinced herself that she should indeed go to him, speak with him about Jake, explain it to him. She did not want him angry with her over something as trivial as Jake Akard's calling on her while he was away.

Not wasting any more time after having finally come to a decision, and determined now to stick to it, Christina went up to her room. Once she had changed into a lime-green princess-style sheath dress, she hurriedly brushed her hair, allowing it to fall gently to her shoulders. She remembered how Todd had once claimed to find that very enticing. Still hurrying, she went downstairs, searched for her handbag, then headed out the door, knowing she would have to walk, since Justin and the boys had taken the only two horses.

As she stepped out onto the veranda, her handbag dangling from her wrist as she closed the door behind her, Christina found herself suddenly face to face with a scowling Todd Aylesbury.

Without saying a word, he indicated she should turn around and go back inside. When she did not move, he marched past her into the house and turned to look at her expectantly. Gingerly, Christina followed. She had never seen him look so angry. He stood quietly in the center of the room. His blazing eyes raked over her with such a thoroughness that it sent hot chills coursing through her, prickling the hair on her neck.

Todd, too, had dressed for the occasion, looking every bit as handsome in his dark blue cutaway coat and close-fitted white breeches as she remembered him. While she looked at him, she felt a ridiculous urge to run to him and embrace him, but knew it would be far safer if she fled in the opposite direction instead. As it turned out, she could not move in either direction. She was suddenly frozen to the spot and without a single thought of what to say.

"I want to know what you were up to while I was away," Todd said, making a noticeable effort to keep his voice level and controlled. His blue eyes were unwavering.

"Do you want to know everything I might have done or are you just after the details that concern Jake Akard?" she asked impudently. She was so upset by his behavior that she was eager to strike out at him.

Angered by her words, he moved toward her and

211

grabbed her shoulders. But when he tried to pull her to him, she wrenched herself free and stepped back out of reach. "Don't you touch me again!"

"I want to know what you were doing with Jake Akard while I was away," he said, curling his hands into rock-hard fists at his sides.

"I imagine about the same thing you were doing with Vella Stone in Sydney," she retorted, delighted at her quick wit but terrified by the rage it brought to Todd's eyes. Just what *had* he and Vella done in Sydney? she wondered as her stomach knotted.

"I had nothing to do with Vella's decision to go to Sydney. I didn't know anything about her plans until I got to the coach office that next afternoon and found her already there, purchasing her ticket."

"Oh, I'm supposed to believe it was purely a coincidence that the two of you decided to go to Sydney at the same time, and on the same coach no less. What else would you like for me to believe?"

"Quit trying to put this all off on me. I came here to find out what went on between you and Jake Akard," he said. His teeth were clenched together with such force that the muscles in his jaws twitched.

"And what right have you to know?" she asked.

"More right than you realize," he shot back at her and made another grab for her, only to be eluded again.

"No, you have no right. Absolutely none." Her intentions to try to explain her relationship with Jake dried on her tongue. "You don't now, and never will own me, Todd Aylesbury. No man ever will!"

"I don't doubt it. Not the way your heart is trapped beneath such a thick bed of ice. But that doesn't answer my question, does it? What were you doing with Jake

212

Akard while I was away? I want to know how serious it is between the two of you."

"I don't care what you want to know. You have no business asking me anything of a personal nature. No more than I have to ask what you and Vella did while the two of you were together in Sydney. But knowing you, and knowing Vella, I can well imagine."

He stared at her for a long moment. The muscles in his cheeks worked furiously as he thought about what had been said. "I guess there's really nothing more for me here."

"I guess not," she retorted quickly and crossed her arms in defiance.

Todd continued to stare at her, then turned to leave. It was her broken sob that stopped him short of the door.

Turning back, he found her cool and angry facade broken. She was hurting inside just as much as he was. Relief flooded him as he rushed back to her and took her into his arms. Tenderly he kissed her tears away, then kissed her trembling lips.

Each kiss deepened until he felt her finally giving in to his touch. Though Todd wanted more than life itself to stay, to take her to realms she had never dreamed possible, to show her just how much he loved her, this time he was the one who pulled away.

"Christina, I want you more than I have ever wanted any woman, but I won't let it be like this—in your brother's house, with you so unsure of your feelings. No. That's not how I want it to be for us. I-I have to go."

Before she could find the words to respond to *his* surprising words, he was gone, leaving her more confused than ever over what she felt. Eventually, she sorted it out enough to know she still felt ashamed for her wanton behavior, enough shame to override her undeniable desire for the man, and she chastised herself for falling so easily into his arms yet again. Had she no pride? Had she so little self-control?

By the time Justin and the boys returned from work, she was fuming. She had not resisted his kiss in spite of her anger toward him. But she was also confused that he had left her when she had been so willing. Had it been a noble gesture on his part? That seemed hardly likely. Or had he suddenly found he had lost interest in the conquest? That the spoils would undoubtedly not be worth the effort? Had his week with Vella altered whatever desire he had for her that much?

She was so confused by it all that she had a hard time listening to Justin's usual complaints as he washed his hands and face before supper. She was only vaguely aware that he had muttered something about Todd's grandmother coming for a visit. His tone of voice finally made her listen as he made it very clear that he was not at all fond of the woman or of the fact that she was coming for a visit, especially at this time when Todd had to make a decision about the station boss's job.

"But what is worse, is that his great-grandmother Aylesbury is coming along for this trip, as well as her nephew, Deen Crawford, who is also Todd's seafaring grandfather on his mother's side of the family," he grumbled. He cupped his hands and dipped them into the pannikin of water and splashed the cool liquid against his face.

"I don't see why you are so upset," she commented as she reached for the towel and handed it to him.

"It's bad enough his grandmother is coming. When that old woman tells Todd to jump, Todd asks her how

214

high," he muttered disgustedly as he unfolded the towel and pressed it to his wet face. "She'll be trying to run the place while she's there, meddling in everybody's business, and trying to make all of Todd's decisions for him. And the way William Stone was cooing up to her the last time she was down, she'll have Todd wanting to make him the station boss. You just wait. She'll have Todd convinced William is the best man for the job just because he's older and always has a compliment for her. She won't even consider that I've been there the longest."

"But why would she have a say in it at all?" Christina tried to reason with him.

"Because, although she handed over the working of the station to Todd years ago so she could move back to the Hawksbury District where her family came from, she's still the legal owner and likes to keep her finger in the pie. You just wait. She'll be making Todd's decisions for him while she's here. Hell, one reason Todd has never gone and got himself married is because he's never found a woman good enough to meet up with the old woman's expectations. Why he feels he has to please her is beyond me. And I'll bet that great-grandmother is just as bad. What rotten timing. What bloody rotten timing."

While Justin went to change his shirt before supper, Christina thought over everything her brother had said. She was glad she would not have to meet either of the formidable Mrs. Aylesburys and hoped that Justin was wrong about the grandmother's trying to interfere with Todd's decision. Justin had worked too hard and for too long to have the decision made by someone who had just come by for a brief visit. Or at least she hoped it would prove to be a brief visit, for Justin's sake.

When Justin left for work the next morning, he was so downcast over Todd's family's arriving that afternoon that he barely touched his breakfast. He went as far as to practice with Christina how he would greet each of them, so he would not make any mistakes. Christina's heart went out to her brother as he rode off toward the Aylesbury station, his brow furrowed under his hat and his jaw firmly set, determined to make a good impression on the lot of them, even if it killed him.

The boys stayed home with Christina. There was not much for small boys to do at the Aylesbury station that day, especially now that the twin colts were older. But there was plenty to do at their own station. The two of them worked hard helping her tend the garden that morning, then after lunch cleaned the stalls in the barn, and fed and watered the horse. It was late afternoon before the three of them decided to take a break and slip off to go swimming, at Alan's suggestion.

To Christina's dismay, the pond was the same pond where she and Todd had gone for that ill-fated picnic. She was deluged with memories that stirred her blood, but she was not sure why she should be affected so deeply by images of that disastrous day, and tried her best not to think about it at all. Instead, she tried to concentrate on watching the boys as they played in the water.

The three of them had just come in from their swim and changed back into dry clothes and had barely enough time for the boys to go out into the barn again when Justin came home. A scowl was so firmly implanted on his face that he looked as if he might never smile again.

"What is the matter with you?" Christina asked. She looked up from the stove where she had just added two

216

sticks of firewood and saw the dark expression on her brother's face when he entered.

"We've been invited to have dinner at Todd's tomorrow evening. With his entire family. He wants us all there."

"I thought you liked to be invited to eat at Todd's house. I thought you considered it an honor."

"Not with his grandmother and his great-grandmother there. I won't know what to say to them. Every time I try to say anything, especially to his grandmother, I seem to come up with something stupid. I'd rather just steer clear of both those women while they are there."

"Well then, it seems to me all you have to do is tell Todd we can't come. Just because he asked us doesn't mean we absolutely have to go," she suggested with a reassuring smile.

"We have to go this time. I've already told Todd we'd be there," he told her as he sank into a chair and studied his muddy boots as if the answer to his problem lay there. "We've got no choice."

"Then we'll go and make the best of it," she said, and tried to keep her own apprehension out of her voice. Though she had to be honest with herself and realize she liked the idea of seeing Todd again, she was no more delighted with the prospect of having to eat with his family than her brother was.

No surprise to Christina, Edward and Alan were happy about going to Todd's again and even happier when they learned that Todd's grandmother was visiting. They could hardly wait and started getting ready to go hours before it was necessary.

On Saturday, Justin arrived home early and began

getting ready for the dinner right away. Of all days to be late, he was determined that this was not to be one of them.

He was pleased with Christina's dress of deep blue watered silk. It had a draped, unornamented neckline revealing a modest glimpse of her swelling breasts above her corset. A tight waist accented her feminine shape, and the flounced underskirt fell in graceful folds to the floor with a matching frilled overskirt pulled back and draped over a false bustle. It was her most fashionable frock and one she hoped would impress both Todd's grandmother and his great-grandmother. She even put on her mother's intricately designed golden locket, which hung from a black velvet ribbon and nestled in the delicate hollow of her throat.

The boys also wore their best shirts and breeches and had shined and oiled their boots. Their hair was still a little wet at the tips from a thorough shampooing and their faces were freshly scrubbed. Christina could not remember having seen them so clean and neat, and couldn't help but wonder how long they would stay that way.

Before leaving the house, Christina drew on a pair of elbow-length white gloves and slipped a white silk drawstring handbag onto her wrist. She was so nervous her stomach was in knots. She did not want to make any mistakes in front of the women who seemed so important in Todd's life but felt almost certain that she would. She hoped to make the very best first impression possible on the two such obviously opinionated women.

When they arrived at the Aylesbury station a few minutes early, they were surprised that Todd met them at the front door. As he escorted them all into the main salon, he explained that Gomer was busy seeing to his guests' needs. "Both Grandmum and Great-grandmum are still upstairs getting ready and my grandfather has run off and is outside somewhere."

"Can we go outside, too?" Edward asked eagerly. "We haven't been over here in nearly a week. We want to see how Bucky and Lucky are getting along."

"They are getting along just fine. You can go see the colts after we eat," Todd assured them. "For now, why don't you both try to stay in the house. Grandmum is looking forward to seeing you two again and would be disappointed if you weren't here when she came down."

The boys frowned at each other, but made no further argument. Instead their eyes lighted on a chess set that had been left out and they hurried over to gather up the shiny, handcarved pieces.

Todd's eyes left the boys and locked with Christina's for a moment, then he let his gaze travel downward to sweep possessively over her body. Slowly, he smiled. "As usual, you are beautiful, Christina."

Christina felt a strong urge to bolt from the room, knowing he remembered as clearly as she did how he had leisurely stroked the curves of her body. And she knew he also remembered how easily she had let him do it. Embarrassed and ashamed that she had allowed him such intimacy, she looked away. Finally she thanked him for his compliment, but she was saved from further conversation with him by a sharp rapping at the front door.

"Excuse me," Todd said politely, then left the room to answer the door. Moments later, he returned with a tall, dark-eyed, dark-haired man at his side. Although it was obvious Justin already knew the man, she did not, and the handsome, elderly man was quickly introduced to her as James Cranston.

"Uncle James is my grandmother's brother and was a very close friend of my parents', especially of my mother's in the years right after Father was killed and she was so lost. He was always there for her whenever she needed him. And he's also a very dear friend of mine," Todd explained as James reached forward and gently squeezed Christina's hand. Tiny crinkles developed at the corners of the man's shining black eyes as Todd continued. "But I don't get to see very much of him these days. He's too busy with his own station."

"And how far away is your place?" Christina asked the smiling man, already having decided she liked him.

"Not very far, actually," he admitted as he stared admiringly at her face. "You'd think I'd be able to get by for a visit more often, or that Todd could break away to visit with me more than he does. But there just don't seem to be enough hours in the day." The smile on James's face faded when he thought of the real reason he rarely found the time to visit with his grand-nephew. It pained him to be reminded of how very much the lad resembled his dear mother. They had the same thick, dark, almost unruly hair, and eyes so blue they seemed unreal. And though Jessica had been dead for so many years now, having been killed in the same aboriginal uprising that had killed Todd's grandfather, Aaron, he still loved her, loved her so deeply and so completely that he had never married and probably never would. No one could ever replace Jessica in his heart.

"Then you are just here for the afternoon?" Christina

asked, wondering why his face had taken on such a distant and forlorn expression.

"Oh, aye. I'm just here for the afternoon. I'll want to be back before bedtime. I'm rather set in my ways. I have to have my own bed to sleep in."

"You always have been set in your ways, James," they heard a feminine voice call out from just inside the hallway. As everyone turned to see who had spoken, a slender woman who looked to be in her late sixties or early seventies entered the room and moved quickly to greet James with a warm embrace.

Christina knew by the way Justin stiffened at her side that this woman, beautiful and tall despite her age, was Todd's grandmother.

"You look wonderful, Grandmum," Todd said with a huge grin and stepped forward to greet her with a big hug. Once he had released her, he put his left arm around her shoulders and brought her forward to stand in front of Christina. "I want you to meet someone. This is Christina Lapin, Justin's sister. Christina, this is my Grandmum, Penelope Aylesbury."

Christina felt a ridiculous urge to curtsey but instead greeted Penelope Aylesbury with a gracious smile.

"So you are Dora Chun's great-niece," Penelope said fondly to Christina, then spoke to Todd. "My, my, she is just as beautiful as you said she was." When she pulled away from her grandson to get a closer look, her emerald-green eyes offered nothing but honest praise. "Aaron would be pleased."

Christina looked curiously from the regal woman with her fashionable dress and her lovely silver-streaked dark brown hair to Todd, who quickly explained, "Aaron was my grandfather, and your great-aunt's station master."

221

"And a finer friend I'll never have," James put in with a fond smile.

An older woman entered the room at that moment, cleared her throat, and waited until everyone had turned to face her before adding, "And a finer son a woman could never hope for."

"Millicent," James said as he stepped forward to kiss her lightly on her withered cheek, then moved back to stare admiringly at her. "You look as spry as ever."

Millicent accepted the compliment gracefully. "Thank you, James. I feel pretty spry."

"Come over here Grandmum Millie," Todd said. The slender woman had snow-white hair that had been combed away from her face and caught in a bun at the back. She walked easily toward him. Though the woman clearly had to be in her nineties, her back was amazingly straight and her brown eyes surprisingly alert.

"Grandmum Millie, I want you to meet some friends of mine. I don't believe you've ever met Justin Lapin. He started to work for me only months after your last visit; and I know you have never met his sister, Christina."

"So you are Christina," Millicent said with an approving nod, almost ignoring Justin altogether. "You were right, Todd. She is lovely."

Christina accepted the compliment and returned it, then cut her gaze to Todd. She wondered exactly what he had told these two women. They were looking at her as if they were sizing her up to be a part of the family, and that worried her. But Millicent's next comment put her at ease. "The way Todd has spoken of you and your brother, you'd think he felt you were his own brother and sister. And the boys, too. As if they were his own. And just where are these boys you've told me so much about?"

222

"Right over there," Todd said and quickly led her away from Christina and Justin, to the corner where Edward and Alan sat playing with the handcarved chess pieces. Penelope had already found her way to them and now knelt on the floor beside their chairs, listening intently to whatever comment either of them had to make about the shiny wooden pieces in their hands.

# Chapter XIII

Christina was aware of how accurate Justin's assessment had been of Penelope Aylesbury. The woman had immediately, but quietly, taken charge, telling Gomer when to go find Deen and telling the housekeeper when to serve the meal. And while they were at the table, she seemed to direct everyone's conversation, as well, though Deen and James did most of the actual talking, especially Deen, with his many tales of the unusual adventures he'd had on his whaling ships.

Deen, as Christina learned during the course of the meal, was the only son of Millicent's most adventurous brother, Buck Crawford. He had gotten the creamy mocha color of his skin and his thick, unruly black hair with its heavy sprinklings of silver from his aboriginal mother, Girraween, Buck's only wife. But his thin nose and his strong features were from the Crawfords. Christina thought that he, like everyone else in this family, was extremely handsome in his own roguish sort of way, and she could easily see why Todd should be every bit as handsome as he was.

Though she was surprised to learn that Deen was half-native, it made little difference in the way she felt about him or in the way he was treated by those around him. He was friendly and clearly as much a part of this family as any of the others.

It was not until they retired to the main salon for a final cup of spiced tea that Christina gave any thought to Todd's grandfather's being half-native. Then Todd's mother, Jessica, was one-fourth native in blood, and Todd in turn was one-eighth native, though he bore no traces of his ancestry. The thought intrigued her.

For the next thirty minutes, Deen continued with his slightly embellished tales of yesteryear. The boys listened eagerly, leaning forward to catch every word. James and Penelope listened, too, with distant expressions most of the time, as if they were reliving their own private memories. Occasionally one of them would think of something to add to the conversation, and Deen would accept their comments graciously, eagerly, for there were things even he had forgotten, details that made the stories that much more real again.

Millicent seemed content to sit and listen to everyone else until her eyes grew heavy with memories. When she finally spoke, she interrupted Deen's story about her son Aaron's noble efforts to take medical aid to the goldfields back in the eighteen fifties. She told how, at that same time, *his* only son, Eric, who was Todd's father and her grandson, had pretended to be a bushranger, when in fact he was working with a secret detective force to capture a corrupt judge, a Judge Rodney Livingston. He had brought him to justice and in the process saved many a Bathurst man from losing his land. The irony of the whole situation was that, in the end, the Aylesburys and

James Cranston, who had also been involved with the secret detectives at the time, had ended up with much of the judge's true holdings after he was convicted and all his land was put up for auction.

"I would love to chat and to listen to more of this, but I'm feeling a little tired at the moment," Millicent said, finishing her story, with a gentle smile that never seemed very far from her withered, yet still beautiful face. "If all of you would excuse me, I really think I should be on my way to bed."

"So early?" Edward asked with a confused frown and stared out a nearby window at the pale blue sky, as if to point out that it was not even dark yet.

"I'm afraid so. The long ride, first by train and then the rest of it by coach, wore me out. I fear I'm just not as young as I used to be."

"None of us are," Deen put in with an understanding smile and rose from his seat. "Allow me to escort you upstairs."

Christina watched the two of them as they walked arm in arm toward the doorway and wondered how Justin could have been so wrong about Todd's great-grandmother. Though she had still not finished forming an opinion of the grandmother, she found she liked the great-grandmother and had liked her instantly.

"Have a good night's rest," she called out to the woman.

Millicent turned and again smiled. "I'm sure I will, thank you. I do hope I get to see you again before we have to leave. I really do." Then she turned around and let Deen take her arm again.

As soon as the two of them had disappeared into the hallway, Penelope's green eyes went to the same window

Edward had just peered out of, then back to the boys, who were clearly not happy to see Deen go. "How would you two lads like to go outside with me to the barn to see how Bucky and Lucky are doing?"

Having been so completely intrigued by Deen's stories that they had forgotten all about the twin colts, they looked at each other, startled that they could have let something so important slip their minds, then quickly jumped to their feet.

"You might even discover that I've brought you a surprise all the way from Hawksbury," she said, which added further incentive.

"A surprise?" Alan asked, his eyes wide. "What is it?"

"If I told you, it would spoil the surprise. You'll just have to come with me and see for yourself." Then, without further word, she rose from her seat and headed for the hallway, both boys at her heels.

Out of curiosity, Christina and James followed the three through the dooryard and into the barn, exchanging questioning glances. Todd had come outside with them, but about halfway across the back yard he turned back, obviously having forgotten to do something.

When Christina and James arrived inside the barn, only moments behind the others, they discovered the boys already on their knees, one on either side of a wiggling mass of brown fur and a lolling pink tongue. The lanky, long-legged puppy seemed extremely delighted finally to have company.

"Oh, Grandmum," they cried out. "Thank you!"

"But boys, Mrs. Aylesbury is not your . . ." Christina started to correct them, but was halted by Penelope's next words.

"That's all right," she assured her. "These two are

probably the closest I'll ever come to having great-grandchildren." Then she sighed heavily. "If only Eric and Jessica could have had more children before Eric was killed. Then maybe I'd have had a better chance of having more grandchildren of my own. I've just about given up on Todd's ever taking a wife."

Christina felt a twinge of pain but chose to ignore it.

James also looked pained as he turned away and headed back through the huge double doors to the outside.

"Poor James," Penelope said with a sad shake of her head. "Such a kindhearted man to find himself with no children, much less any hope for grandchildren."

"Why did he never marry?" Christina dared to ask. "He's such a handsome man, even now. You'd think there would have been plenty of women who would want to marry a man like him."

"I can only guess at that one, because you are right. There were plenty of women who would have loved for him to as much as notice them, but James is a strange one. He never gave any of them much thought. It's my guess that he was once in love with someone who did not return that love, so much in love with her that he could never be happy with anyone else. But he won't admit it to me or anyone else. If there ever was such a love in his life, the secret will go with that man to his grave."

Christina looked back toward the door James had gone through. She felt a sudden wave of sadness so severe she had to reach for a stall gate to remain on her feet, for she realized she was headed for a similar fate. She was very close to falling in love with Todd Aylesbury, despite the fact that she knew she could never fulfill his needs as a wife, even if he should find a reason to ask her to marry him. But even *that* was unlikely, for Todd did not want a

228

wife. Dismal as it was to consider, she knew that her future would never be what she wanted. Love would forever be something to cause her pain, never fulfillment.

"What should we call him?" Edward asked, not realizing he was interrupting her painful thoughts. He shrieked with laughter as the puppy stretched to lick his lightly freckled cheeks.

"Let's call him Bunyip," Alan decided happily, tugging at the puppy's hind legs in hopes of interesting the animal in his own cheeks.

"We can't call him Bunyip," Edward said with an impatient frown. "Mr. Aylesbury's dog is named Bunyip. You know that. We have to give our puppy a different name."

"I like Bunyip," Alan insisted.

"Al-an," Edward said in exasperation. "We are not going to name him Bunyip! It would confuse things too much to give them both the same name."

"But Bunyip is a good name." Alan refused to give up, then turned to Christina for support. "Don't you think Bunyip is a good name for a dog?"

Seeing Edward's point of view, Christina nodded to Alan that Bunyip was indeed a good name. "Maybe for Mr. Aylesbury's dog, but I don't know if it would be for this one. The way he keeps yelping at everything, I'd be more inclined to call him Little Yabber."

Alan thought about that a moment, then his eyes lit up as if the sudden idea had been his own. "Edward, let's name him Little Yabber. Listen to him. He can't keep his mouth shut for even a minute."

Before Christina and Penelope turned to leave the two boys to their new pet, Coolabah came into the barn and was asked his opinion of the name Little Yabber. The tall, burly man stood quietly a moment listening to the puppy's constant yelping, smiled broadly, and agreed the name was very appropriate. The decision was final. The dog's name was to be Little Yabber, and Christina only hoped the animal would not live up to his name for very long.

When the two women went outside, a cool evening breeze tugged lightly at their skirts and played with the loose tendrils of their hair. After such a warm day, the coolness was welcome, and they both turned their faces toward it.

"My, but it is getting late," Christina said in an attempt to make conversation, finding the silence made her feel awkward and even a little stupid.

"I hope you aren't planning to leave," Penelope quickly put in. She turned her head sharply to look at Christina.

"No, Mrs. Aylesbury. I was just surprised to notice how late it was getting."

"Please, don't call me Mrs. Aylesbury. I want you to call me Penelope. I want us to be friends."

Christina smiled as they continued away from the barn and into the yard. Justin would love to hear that she and Penelope Aylesbury just might become friends.

The sun had already dipped behind the tallest trees, letting them know that soon it would be dark, because darkness always came quickly in Australia. Spotting James standing near the paddock fence as he stared out at the lively horses mustered there, they paused momentarily and invited him to join them on the veranda. James and Penelope walked arm in arm, with Christina by their side. As they settled onto the high-backed bench

230

seats near the back door and made themselves comfortable, Todd and Justin came from inside.

Christina was immediately aware of how stricken her brother looked. He walked past her without so much as a word and stood restlessly near the steps. Todd had a stern expression on his face that made his usually pale blue eyes appear darker, almost menacing. Clearly something had passed between the two while they were alone in the house. Did it have to do with Todd's decision about his station boss? Had he announced that William Stone would be getting the job, after all, and not Justin? Was that what was wrong between Todd and Justin? She had clearly sensed something was wrong all evening. Curiously, she glanced at Penelope. Did she have anything to do with the decision? Though she had begun to like the woman, she was reluctant to form a firm opinion of her even now.

Moments later, Justin announced he was ready to go, his voice tight, his manner brusque.

"So soon?" Penelope asked.

"Aye, I've got a lot of work to do tomorrow. I need to get on to bed. Where are the boys?"

"In the barn enjoying their new puppy," Christina answered. Her puzzled gaze continued to alternate between Justin and Todd.

"A puppy? Is that what the surprise was?" Turning to face the barn, Justin called out their names and waited until they had appeared in the wide doorway. "Come on, boys, it's time to go home."

"Not yet," Edward complained as he hurried toward the house, his eyes wide with the hope that he could convince his father to stay a while longer.

"Not yet," Alan echoed from right behind his brother,

running twice as hard to keep up with Edward's longer strides.

"Why can't we stay just a little longer?" Edward wanted to know, his face crestfallen.

"I need to get home," Justin said sternly.

"You can let them stay a little while longer, can't you?" Todd said, more as a statement than a question, taking a step in Justin's direction. "I'll bring them home in a little while. Grandmum gets to see so little of them."

Justin opened his mouth to voice his opinion, but when Todd took another step in his direction, he snapped it shut. He turned to leave, with no thought of asking Christina if she intended to stay or go. Flicking the reins hard as he climbed into his wagon, he left them all behind.

Todd watched silently as the thick trail of dust from Justin's wagon drifted quickly to the north. Christina was speechless, too surprised at having been left so abruptly to speak. Penelope's voice broke the silence.

"So how is Little Yabber? Do you think he will like it at your house or do you think he should stay here where he would have Bunyip for company?"

"Our house," came the unanimous answer.

"We've already decided where we are going to make his bed. Out in the barn near the tack room. We are going to make a cutting dog out of him, so that when Father gets all that cattle he says we are going to have one day, Little Yabber can help out and earn his keep," Edward added.

Todd stiffened and turned away.

Christina only half listened, her thoughts mostly on what had happened inside to upset her brother. She felt guilty for not demanding to leave with him. He probably needed someone to talk to, especially if Todd indeed had told him he would not be getting the job. He had wanted it so much. She feared he would go home and drink himself sick. She really should have gone with him. But her next thought was that maybe he actually preferred being alone. If he broke down and cried, he would not want her to see his tears. She was confused over what she should have done to help him and what she should do now.

"Can we bring Little Yabber out into the yard?" Edward asked eagerly, his eyes going to Todd who stood silently staring out into the distance.

The boy's words startled Todd out of his deep thoughts. "Hmm? Oh, sure. Go get him. I'll bet he'd love to romp around the yard a little. He's been cooped up in that barn all afternoon to keep him out from under foot."

The boys scurried off toward the barn, running as fast as their legs would carry them.

Todd smiled at their enthusiasm as he walked over to one of the three lanterns that hung from the overhead beams and raised the glass globe. His mood visibly lifted. "I guess I'd better light these things. It's starting to get dark out here."

No one responded to his words, and they watched while he struck a match along the side of the lantern. The only sounds that could be heard while he carefully adjusted the flame were the excited yelpings of the puppy coming from the barn; the deep, throaty croakings of distant frogs; the gentle rustling of a light breeze through the trees; and the shrill chirping of the night insects getting ready for yet another of their lively concertos.

"There now, we can at least see one another," Todd said as soon as he had lit the third lantern. For a moment, he looked out over the darkened land, then walked to

233

where his grandmother rested on one of the many bench seats and sat down beside her.

The boys came bursting out of the barn, bending and calling to Little Yabber, trying to lead the puppy where they wanted him to go. James laughed at their growing frustration when the puppy appeared to have ideas of its own about where it wanted to be.

"Did you remember to take your medicine?" Todd asked his grandmother, lifting his arm and placing it casually behind her.

"I'll take it later," she assured him and patted his leg with her weathered hand while she watched the boys try to interest the puppy in a small stick. "Besides, just having you, James, Christina, and the boys around is the best medicine in the world for me."

Todd looked at his grandmother with such open affection that Christina smiled and temporarily forgot about her concern for her brother. After all, Justin was a grown man. He could take care of himself.

"I guess you are right," Todd agreed and leaned forward to press a warm kiss on his grandmother's cheek. "You look much better. But you are still to take your medicine before you go to bed. Don't you agree, James?"

James nodded. "Never take chances with your health. Your husband and your father-in-law, and even Jessica, spent too many years fighting sickness for you to allow your health to go ignored." His expression turned suddenly sad, as if something he had just said had triggered an unhappy thought.

"I'll take my medicine. I promise," she assured them both. "But I feel just fine. In fact, I feel wonderful."

"And you look even better," Todd said lightly, and brought his hand down from the back of the seat and laid

234

it on her shoulder.

It was true. The faintly gray pallor on her face when she had arrived was completely gone. Bright touches of pink tinged her weathered cheeks again. There was that old familiar sparkle back in her green eyes. Todd had worried about her when he first saw her, and was very relieved she was doing so much better, and even more delighted that Christina and his dear grandmother were getting along so well.

Deen reappeared through the back door and joined Christina on a bench seat. "Did I miss anything?"

"Have you ever?" Todd teased, only to receive a sharp slap on his leg from his grandmother. "And if you did miss anything, would you ever admit it?" She popped him again.

Deen chuckled at the way Penelope kept coming to his defense, and at the playful pout that turned Todd's lips down each time that she did.

"Is Mum resting well?" Penelope asked after one last reproachful look at her grandson. Though Millicent Aylesbury was actually Aaron's mother, she had always called her Mum. It had seemed natural with a woman that kind and loving.

"Aye, I helped her find her gown and her wrapper and waited around until I was sure she did not need anything else. When last I saw her, she was ready for bed with the covers already turned down, and had already said her prayers and had spoken a few words to Uncle Matthew." Deen blinked back the sudden moisture in his eyes. It was so touching that his aunt and uncle had been so close that even his death had not separated the two.

"Who's that?" James interrupted, staring off toward the main gate. In the dusky light they could see the dark

235

shape of a carriage as it clattered its way onto the narrow drive leading to Todd's house.

"I don't know," Todd replied as he stood and stared at the approaching vehicle. But as it grew closer, they all heard a low groan clear his throat. "It's Vella Stone. I wonder what she wants."

"You mean you don't know?" Penelope asked innocently.

Christina wondered if Penelope knew Vella Stone and was aware that she had spent a week with Todd in Sydney. Christina's blood turned cold. Did his grandmother also know how clearly the young woman was out to get her hooks into Todd whatever way she could?

James stood and joined Todd on the steps as the carriage slowed and stopped just a few feet away.

"Hello, Todd," Vella said in a cheery voice as she climbed down from the carriage and waited for him to come forward and greet her.

"What are you doing out alone this late?" Todd asked as he grudgingly went to greet her.

"I need to see William about something. Is he here?"

"No, I thought he was at your place," Todd answered. "He said something about having to talk with you about a family matter and rode out of here early this afternoon."

Vella frowned. "I haven't been home most of the day." Then her gaze roamed past Todd to the others, until it finally came to light on Christina. She narrowed her eyes briefly, then looked back to where Penelope sat with her back rigid. "Todd, I see you have company. Hello, Mrs. Aylesbury. I'm so pleased to see you have come for another visit. Todd so loves for you to come." As she spoke of Todd, she slipped her arm around his and pressed herself close to him.

Christina noticed the sudden tension in Penelope's face.

"I'm also glad I decided to come. I miss Todd so when I'm away, and you know how I like to keep an eye on the boy," Penelope said graciously, maybe too graciously.

Christina was almost certain there was a hidden meaning under those words, as she was aware that Penelope seemed none too pleased at this latest arrival. She felt a twinge of satisfaction. If she and Todd's grandmother had nothing else in common, they both disliked Vella Stone considerably.

"And Todd misses you," Vella assured her, smiling at Penelope one last time before turning her shoulder away from the veranda, giving Todd her full attention.

Penelope's lips pressed into a thin line as she watched the shameless way Vella flirted with Todd. But she said nothing, possibly because she, like Christina, was straining to hear whatever was being said between the two.

James, who still stood beside Todd, slowly moved away from the pair and returned to the veranda. Penelope scowled at him as if he had committed a traitorous act.

"What's she saying to him?" she wanted to know as soon as her brother came close enough to be spoken to without either Vella or Todd overhearing them.

"She says she's worried for her brother," he informed her.

"I worry for her brother, too," Penelope muttered. "I worry for any man who has to put up with a sister like that."

Christina wanted to laugh and had to curl her hands into tight fists to control the urge. Hoping to appear as if she was not listening to either Penelope and James or to

237

Todd and Vella, she looked out into the side yard where the boys and their new puppy were playing tug of war with a ragged piece of rope. How she wished Vella could have overheard Penelope's comment.

"Has he invited her to stay?" Penelope asked.

"Hadn't yet," James said, his dark eyes twinkling as he exchanged knowing glances with Deen. Clearly the two men were amused by the entire situation.

"But he will," Penelope finished their thoughts for them. "And even if he doesn't, she'll stay anyway. I've come to know her too well. And Todd's so blasted polite, he'll let her."

Whether by invitation or inclination, Christina was not sure, but Vella did stay, never letting go of Todd's arm. Even when Todd suggested they join the others on the veranda, she did not let go of him, instead she pulled him down onto a vacant bench seat beside her.

Penelope managed a smile, though not a very convincing one, while everyone discussed the weather and the fact that the farms further inland had not been as lucky getting rain this season as they had. A drought and the heat were causing their neighbors more problems than usual this year, and Todd mentioned feeling a little guilty that his streams and ponds were still full.

Although Vella showed little concern with the discussion, she was delighted that she was sitting with Todd and made sure everyone noticed it. When she wasn't gazing with adoration into his eyes, she was squeezing his arm and looking around to see if everyone was watching.

"My, but it's getting late," Penelope finally said, though she had no watch to go by. She made a large production of a sleepy yawn before looking at Todd.

"Maybe you should muster up the boys and their new pup. It's about time you saw them home, don't you think?"

"You have to take them home?" Vella asked, her eyes narrowing.

"Justin had to leave early. I promised him I'd see the boys and Christina home," Todd explained and tried to pull his arm free of her grasp so he could get up. But she held on to him.

"It's such a nice night for a ride. Why don't I go along with you? That way you won't have to ride back alone," Vella offered in a silky voice.

"But I thought you wanted to wait here for your brother," Todd put in, looking a little perturbed that she had so quickly forgotten her reason for being there.

"I can always speak with him when we get back," she insisted. "That is, if he's even returned by then."

Christina's and Penelope's eyes met with mutual irritation.

"Why don't you stay here and talk with me?" Penelope suggested. "We haven't had a chance for any girl talk. Besides, that carriage will be too crowded if all of you go. I know from my own painful experience how uncomfortable it is to seat three in the front of Todd's carriage."

"I wouldn't want to keep you up," Vella replied quickly. "And I see no reason why three should have to sit up front anyway, not when three can sit much more comfortably in the back."

Deen and James exchanged amused glances again. It was clear Vella thought she would be one of the two to sit up front.

"Well, come on if you are going," Todd said finally as

he jerked his arm free. "I need to go get the box for the puppy, then I'll bring the carriage around."

Everyone stood on or near the back steps while Todd went into the barn and then followed his groomsman to the coach house to help him hitch the horse to the carriage. Conversation lagged while everyone anticipated Todd's return, wondering who would end up on the front seat with Todd. Odd patches of silence loomed, making them that much more aware of the growing anticipation. Even garrulous Deen seemed to be at a temporary loss for words.

# GET FREE GIFT

## MAIL IN THE COUPON BELOW TODAY

To get your Free **ZEBRA HISTORICAL ROMANCE** fill out the coupon below and send it in today. As soon as we receive the coupon, we'll send your first month's books to preview Free for 10 days along with your **FREE NOVEL**.

---

# BOOK CERTIFICATE

## ———— FREE ————

## ZEBRA HOME SUBSCRIPTION SERVICE, INC.

**YES!** Please start my subscription to Zebra Historical Romances and send me my free Zebra Novel along with my first month's Romances. I understand that I may preview these four new Zebra Historical Romances Free for 10 days. If I'm not satisfied with them I may return the four books within 10 days and owe nothing. Otherwise I will pay just $3.50 each; a total of **$14.00** (a $15.80 value—I save $1.80). Then each month I will receive the 4 newest titles as soon as they come off the press for the same 10 day Free preview and low price. I may return any shipment and I may cancel this arrangement at any time. There is no minimum number of books to buy and there are no shipping, handling or postage charges. Regardless of what I do, the **FREE** book is mine to keep.

Name _____
                              (Please Print)

Address _____ Apt. # _____

City _____ State _____ Zip _____

Telephone ( ) _____

Signature _____
                    (if under 18, parent or guardian must sign)

Terms and offer subject to change without notice.

Get a Free
Zebra
Historical
Romance

*a $3.95
value*

**ZEBRA HOME SUBSCRIPTION SERVICES, INC.**
**P.O. BOX 5214**
**120 BRIGHTON ROAD**
**CLIFTON, NEW JERSEY 07015-5214**

## Chapter XIV

The silence had grown almost deafening by the time everyone heard the sound of the carriage as it moved forward inside the coach house. From the faint light of an oil lantern that had been lit inside the building, they could see first the shadow, then the gig itself as it came through the door.

"There now, that didn't take too long," Deen observed as he rocked back and forth from his toes to the sturdy heels of his boots. His eyes caught James's as the women stepped off the wooden steps and into the darkened yard.

James shrugged, then returned his attention to the action he anticipated at any moment.

Neither man left the steps, having a better vantage point from the slight height, which neither wished to give up. The two of them stood holding back their amused grins as the carriage slowly pulled to a halt in front of the women.

Todd climbed down to help the boys with their puppy. "Come on, Little Yabber. Back in you go until we can get you to your new home." He spoke in a soothing voice the whole time he lowered the wiggling little animal into the wooden box, holding the pup away from his face to avoid the darting pink tongue, then quickly clamped the lid down and secured it.

To the puppy's pitiful cries, he added, "This is for your own protection, little fella. We certainly don't want you jumping out of the carriage and getting caught up in the wheels. Be quiet, now. You won't have to be in there very long. We'll let you out the moment we get there."

Edward and Alan immediately started to argue over which of them should be the one to hold the box in his lap. But neither boy had a lap large enough to hold the box, so Todd suggested they place the box on the floor between them. He explained that two pairs of eyes watching the box to make sure the puppy stayed put would be far better than one.

Once Todd had the boys and the box settled in the back of the carriage, he turned to Vella, smiled, and gallantly held out his hand. "Come, my dear, you are next."

Vella clearly expected to be led to the step to climb into the front seat, and her shoulders stiffened when she was led to the tiny step for the back seat where the boys and their noisy puppy were.

"Don't you think Christina should sit back here? What if the lads were to misbehave and need supervising?"

"Those two?" Todd asked incredulously as he lifted her hand and pulled it toward the back seat to help her inside. "Never."

Vella pulled back and opened her mouth to protest again, but Todd smiled sweetly and added, "Besides, I'm eager to see how well *you* handle children."

Vella's shoulders slumped in defeat, because to refuse

to ride in the back now would be the same as declaring she could not handle children. Eyeing the two boys cautiously, she held her head high and allowed Todd to help her inside. "I'm sure the boys and I will get along just fine. For some reason, children seem to love me."

Edward and Alan looked at each other curiously and arched their brows with disbelief, then raised their hands to suppress the grins that followed. They said nothing while Vella busily settled in beside them, taking extra pains to see that her skirt was neatly arranged around her.

Deen had to turn away and clear his throat to keep from choking on the laughter he could barely contain. James kept his face deadpan, though his throat constricted with the intensity of his efforts. The only other indication that he found the situation just as humorous as Deen did was in the glimmering depths of his black eyes.

"Your turn," Todd said to Christina and held his hand out to her.

Fighting an urge to look at Vella and see what her expression was, Christina lowered her eyes to the leather seat as she accepted Todd's hand. As always, his touch caused tiny prickling sensations to flutter through her.

"Thank you," she said politely, her dimples deepening as she smiled at him.

"My pleasure," he told her, and she saw by his smile that it really was. He was very pleased with the way things had turned out, pleased as a strutting peacock. She wondered if he was so openly pleased because he had seated Vella in the back despite her objections, or if his pleasure stemmed from having both of them along. Not only could he enjoy her company on the way to Justin's house, but he would have Vella all to himself on the way back. Her stomach tightened at the thought of that return trip.

Conversation during the short ride home was minimal. The boys fought valiantly to keep each other awake, but by the time they arrived home, the two were slumped together, sound asleep. And whenever Christina dared to look back to check on them, Vella's gray-green eyes pierced her with a look that was meant to send her running.

"I hope you had a good time," Todd said after he had brought the carriage to a halt in front of Justin's house and had come around to help Christina down. "I certainly did, and I know Grandmum did, too."

"I had a lovely time," she answered honestly. "I'm just sorry Justin ran off the way he did, leaving you to bring us home."

"Very rude indeed," they heard Vella mutter, but neither of them acknowledged that they had heard her.

"I didn't mind. As long as it meant you and the lads could stay a little longer, I was all for it," he told her, his blue eyes twinkling with something more than amusement. Then he turned to look into the back seat at the small jumble of arms and legs that needed to be separated before he could ever hope to get them out. "And speaking of the lads, it looks like they're asleep again. Hard day, I suppose."

He leaned forward and jiggled them both by their shoulders. "You're home, lads."

Todd got a grumbling response from the two and even a slight movement, but the sudden yelping of the new puppy brought them wide awake.

"Come on, Alan, let's go make Little Yabber a bed in

the barn," Edward said, coming surprisingly alert. Instantly, the two boys were down and waiting impatiently for Todd to lower the puppy to them. Then they were gone.

"I know Grandmum will want you to come visit her again while she is here," Todd said, having returned his attention to Christina as soon as the boys and their new prize had disappeared into the barn.

"Todd, darling, aren't you going to help me down?" Vella called out to him, not caring that she had interrupted him.

"You'd better go help her," Christina said and tried not to sound as irritated as she felt.

Todd looked at her a moment longer, then turned to go to Vella's aid.

Christina stepped up into the veranda and watched while Todd and Vella rode away under a beautiful starry sky. She tried to ignore the pain that gripped her when she saw Vella quickly scoot across the seat toward Todd and snuggle close, but the intensity of it was too severe. It felt like someone was trying to squeeze the very breath out of her. And when tears formed in the outer corners of her eyes as the pain clutching her heart only seemed to worsen, she suddenly realized what the severe, burning misery meant.

She was jealous! There was no denying it. Though she'd never been jealous a day in her life and didn't know the symptoms of jealousy, she felt almost certain she had named her illness. But knowing what was wrong with her did not stop the pain from eating its way through to the very core of her soul. As she turned to go inside, she wondered what, if anything, she could do to make the hurt go away.

Once inside, she called Justin's name. There was no answer and the house was dark. Not a lamp was lit. Feeling for the nearest table and for the matches she knew were kept there in a small ceramic box, she called Justin's name again. It worried her when he still did not answer. Either he was too drunk, or he was not at home, and neither possibility sat well with Christina.

A quick search of his room and then the rest of the house proved he was not home, and she was almost certain he had not been there since they'd left together early that afternoon. Where could he have gone? Suddenly she felt a cold, prickling sense of apprehension, and again she wondered what had happened between Todd and her brother. If Vella were not so prone to eavesdropping, she would have asked Todd, but as it was, she hadn't a clue.

Though Christina had intended to stay awake and ask Justin for a few answers to her many questions, she was sound asleep whenever he finally slipped in, and it had to have been after midnight or she would have heard him. However, he was clearly in no mood to speak to her the next morning as he hurriedly got ready to go to work.

"Can't you at least tell me why you left Todd's house in such a huff yesterday?" she asked, watching him pull on his work boots. He did not usually leave his boots in the kitchen near the door and she strongly suspected he had done so last night so he would make less noise when he came in. "Has he made his decision and chosen the other man? Or was it something else?"

"You ask questions that are none of your business," he told her.

"None of my business? You left me and your sons behind for someone else to bring home and you feel that knowing why is none of my business?" Her anger brought her voice a full octave higher.

"That's right. It's none of your business," he snapped, then took a deep breath, held it a moment before releasing it, and added, "It's nothing you need to worry about. It doesn't concern you. If I thought that it did, I'd tell you. It's just that I don't want to talk about it. It's something I'll have to work out on my own. And I do have a right to my privacy."

That was true, and she knew she should not be angry at him for having secrets from her. But she was.

"And I am your sister. You can confide in me. Whatever it is, I'm on your side. And I think knowing would help me to rest easier. I was so upset when I went to bed last night, that I walked in my sleep again. I found myself downstairs this morning in the pantry. It frightens me that I'm sleepwalking again."

"Maybe we should chain you to your bed."

"Very funny. Please, Justin, tell me what is wrong. I want to help you."

He looked at her for a moment, then his mouth drew into a half smile. "I've got to go. I can't be late for work."

When Justin rode out without giving her a clue to his trouble, Christina was beside herself with anger and growing irritation over her brother's reluctance to confide in her. That coupled with the extreme jealousy she still felt because of Todd and Vella made it impossible for her to concentrate on her work. She had to do several of her daily tasks a second time in order to have them done right.

Worrying about her brother and Todd, and wishing

desperately she had someone to talk to, she thought of Rose. She needed to see her friend—to talk to her. And she felt it would do Justin good to see her again, too. Although he had been in town on at least two occasions that she knew of, he had not bothered to stop by and see Rose either time. He had even canceled their plans to see the traveling show at the Victoria without giving Rose or Christina a plausible reason. And if Rose knew of his trips into town, which was very likely, Christina felt certain she was hurting, too, and also in need of someone to talk to. The solution was to invite Rose for a visit. They could talk out their miseries until they had purged their aching hearts. Then they could find a way to make each other laugh again. Maybe a visit from Rose would help Justin's mood, too.

Having made the decision, Christina sat down at the writing desk in the hallway and penned a formal invitation to Rose. Then she called the boys out of the barn, asking them to take the letter to Todd. She knew he would either take it to Rose himself the next time he went into Bathurst or would see that it reached her the next time he had to send one of his workmen in for supplies or to carry a message of his own.

"Be sure Todd gets this letter for Rose and I'll reward you by making a fat raisin pie for supper," she told them, knowing that the best incentive for these two was to offer them something sweet. And it worked, because they were off like a shot to saddle their horse.

But when the boys arrived at the Aylesbury station, Penelope told them that Todd was out riding boundary and was not expected back until much later.

"Wouldn't you know it," Edward said with open disappointment as he gave the dirt in the yard a swift kick. "There goes our raisin pie."

"What do you mean by that?" Penelope asked, kneeling before the boys to find out why they were so disappointed.

"Aunt Christina was going to make us a raisin pie if we got this letter to Mr. Aylesbury in a big hurry," he said as he pulled the folded letter out of his pocket and showed it to Penelope. "She wanted him to take it to a friend of hers in Bathurst."

Penelope took the folded piece of paper out of Edward's hand and glanced curiously at it. But when she read the contents, she had such a great idea, she could not keep from smiling. "Tell you what, lads. You leave this note with me and I'll see that he gets it as soon as he gets in. And to make up for the loss of the raisin pie, you can come inside and have some of the chocolate cake I helped Todd's housekeeper make just a little while ago."

The boys' eyes lit with excitement at the mere mention of chocolate cake, and Edward had no second thoughts about letting her keep the note. Only minutes after they had gone inside to have their cake, Todd rode up, having finished riding the boundaries earlier than he had planned.

"I have a note for you," Penelope said as she hurried outside to greet her grandson, not wanting the boys to be aware of his return.

"Oh? Who's it from?" Todd climbed down from his horse and let Sam, his favorite groomsman and a longtime friend of the family, lead the horse away. He walked to where his grandmother stood.

"Christina," she replied with a merry smile.

"Christina?" He reached immediately for the note and read the message inside, then looked curiously but happily at his grandmother. "Did you read this?"

"I admit that I did."

His smile stretched across his face. "I'll be. It says she misses me dreadfully and that I must come visit her just as soon as I can." He felt overwhelmed with this sudden turn of events and wondered if jealousy had had anything to do with the change in her attitude. Was she so jealous over Vella's constant flirting that she'd decided to stop putting him off? He could only hope.

"That's what it says all right," Penelope said with a nod and called to Sam not to unsaddle the horse. "And you must go. Right away."

"I need to change first," he told her and glanced down at his work clothes. They were not really dirty, just not the clothes in which he would choose to go calling on Christina.

"She said to come as soon as you can," Penelope reminded him, not wanting to chance his seeing the boys. They might offer him the one little detail she was purposely omitting. The note was not written to him.

"I at least need to wash up. I've been out all morning," he told her adamantly.

"Use the basin by the well pump. I'll bring you a towel," Penelope said, then quickly disappeared into the house, returning with a towel, a fresh shirt, and a comb.

Within a few minutes, Todd was on his way, the note tucked safely away in his chest pocket. As her grandson rode quickly to go to Christina, Penelope glanced heavenward, as if to ask for forgiveness in her tiny omission of fact and possibly a little cooperation in seeing that her plan worked.

Though she had not actually lied to her grandson, she had led him to believe the letter was written to him. But she tried to assuage her guilty conscience by blaming Christina for not addressing the letter to her friend. And the more Penelope thought of that manipulative Vella Stone draped over her grandson's arm, the less guilt she actually felt for what she had done. Such a situation called for drastic measures, and anything she could do to bring Todd and Christina together before Vella could succeed in entrapping him was for everyone's good.

When Christina opened the door to see Todd standing just inches away smiling down at her, she was surprised. Quickly she brushed some of the wrinkles from her pale blue skirt, then glanced around for the boys.

"Did the boys find you and give you my note?" she asked curiously, aware of the strange grin on his face but not knowing what exactly to make of it.

"They left it with Grandmum and she gave it to me," he told her, then stepped inside, though not yet invited. "I realized the urgency of the letter and left right away."

Christina's brows rose with uncertainty when she turned to follow him inside. He stood so close to her that their bodies almost touched and her heart began to hammer wildly within her breast. That glimmer she had seen in his eyes before, and knew only too well to be extremely wary of, was back. Then his smile deepened. Though he had been charming and almost likable for several weeks now, it was clear the old Todd was back. Swallowing hard, she wondered exactly where the new Todd had gone.

"I appreciate it, but I didn't mean for you to make a special trip just for me," she said and took a tentative step backward, aware that his gaze had dipped to observe her lips as she spoke. What on earth was the matter with him?

"Didn't you?" He leaned forward in hopes of sampling the sweetness he knew lingered on those lips, but she whirled away from him before he could.

"No, I meant for it to be at your convenience," she tried to explain. Her blood surged frantically when he approached her again. She looked around for a place to retreat to so that she would not be backed against a wall again.

"You told me you missed me desperately and asked that I come visit as soon as I can," he reminded her and reached out to grab her by her arms so that he could pull her into his embrace. "So I left immediately."

Christina's brown eyes widened with surprise and alarm when she realized what had happened. But before she could explain, his mouth was on hers, and for the moment all she could concentrate on were the wondrous sensations that swiftly flooded her.

"Christina, you don't know how surprised and how pleased I was to receive your note," he said hoarsely when he drew away from her lips to gaze into her eyes and to gauge her reaction to his kiss.

"But—but—" she stammered, aware of what she needed to say yet finding the words stuck to her tongue.

"I thought I'd never win you over. Whatever made you change your mind about me? About us?" He bent to kiss her cheek, then her ear, then the corner of her mouth. Delicious little shivers developed along her spine.

"I haven't," she finally said. When his brow wrinkled in confusion, she went on to explain. "That note was not written to you. It was for Rose. I just wanted you to take it to her the next time you went to Bathurst or sent one of your men in. I thought I had explained that to the boys when I told them to take it to you."

Todd's face hardened. "They left it with Grandmum, and obviously she did not understand. Or maybe she did." His eyes narrowed as he thought about it.

Slowly he pulled away, and Christina was not at all sure that was what she wanted him to do. Suddenly she felt cold, despite the warmth of the summer day. "I'm sorry for the confusion. All I meant to do was get Rose out for a visit."

Todd stepped back and patted his chest pocket. His face remained expressionless, but the muscles in his neck tensed. "And I'll see to it she gets the note. This afternoon. I'll send a rider in with it and have him wait for her reply."

"You don't have to go to any special trouble. After all, it's Sunday. It can wait until you have to send someone in for something else."

"No trouble. No trouble at all," he said quietly.

By his suddenly distant expression Christina knew his thoughts were so wrapped up in the blunder he had made that he was barely able to pay attention to what was being said.

"I'm sorry," she started again to apologize.

"Don't be. It was just a misunderstanding. I'll get this note on its way."

Christina had a strong urge to call him back when he turned and walked swiftly away. Though the note had not been written to him, it had brought him to her and had caused him to kiss her with such maddening intensity that her heart continued to race out of control at the mere thought of it. She almost wished she had kept her

253

mouth shut and let him believe the note *had* been written to him. But now it was too late.

Days went by and Christina did not see Todd. Though she kept hoping he would pop in as he had so many times in the past, he stayed away. She wondered if it was because he was embarrassed by the mistake he had made or if it was because his family kept him busy. Either would be understandable, but she feared that the real reason was because he was spending any and all the spare time he had with Vella Stone. Christina's jealousy grew until it plagued her almost constantly.

Even when Justin continuously explained how busy Todd was at the ranch keeping an exceptionally lively bunch of kangaroos from breaking down his fences, she still worried that her brother was keeping the truth from her. Because her brother wanted to promote her feelings for Todd, she knew he would not want to tell her about Vella even if Todd was seeing her. But even if it was not Vella who kept him away, she saw no reason to be happy. She was too lonely, and was becoming almost as moody as Justin. She wished more than ever that Rose would find a way to come for a visit, for both their sakes.

Rose's reply, which she received on Sunday, had been very vague. She had said she would do what she could to get away, but had made no promises and offered no possible dates for a visit. By the end of the week, Christina had given up on Rose's coming altogether and had realized she would have to get through her misery all by herself.

But the sound of a carriage coming into the yard late

that following Friday renewed her hope that Rose had indeed come. She ran out of the house the moment she had heard the noise. To her surprise, the visitor was not Rose, but Todd's grandmother.

"Good day," Penelope said as she waited for her driver to help her down from Todd's carriage.

"Good day," Christina responded with a note of surprise. "What brings you here?"

"I wanted to come see how the boys and their puppy are getting along," Penelope said with a bright smile as she stepped to the ground and bent slightly to brush the wrinkles from her skirt. "Mum and Deen left yesterday to go back to her farm in the Hawksbury district, and I found myself at loose ends, with no one to talk to. That housekeeper of Todd's keeps a still tongue. Nothing like your great-aunt was. Now there was a woman who almost always had something to say."

"They've gone back without you?" Christina asked, a little surprised.

"Aye, Millicent doesn't like to be away from home for very long and Deen has plans to visit his son's family in Sydney before heading back out to sea."

Remembering how Deen had fondly mentioned, in several of his stories, his son, Derrick, who was Todd's mother's half-brother, Christina nodded that she understood why he would be so eager to go. He did not get many chances to visit on the mainland. "But why didn't you go back with them?"

"I'm not about to go back home just yet," Penelope told her, suddenly serious. But then she smiled and lightened her tone. "I have no real reason to. My father's health has improved this last year, though not enough for

255

him to actually travel with me, and I do have an overseer who I trust to take care of everything there while I'm away. Besides, I don't get to see enough of Todd these days."

Christina could certainly sympathize with her on that. Neither did she.

"So, where are the boys?" Penelope asked as she scanned the yard.

"In the barn, I imagine. With their puppy. I'll call them."

"No, don't. Let me slip in without their knowing. I do so love to watch them play."

"I'll make tea, then," Christina offered as she watched Penelope walk quietly toward the barn. She felt a strange surge of hope in knowing that Penelope had made a trip to visit them. Was it a gesture of friendship, or was she so bored that she had to find some way to occupy her time?

When Penelope returned and joined Christina on the veranda, the woman was all smiles, eager to tell Christina of some of the antics she had witnessed between the boys and their puppy. Christina knew then that the woman was not there simply to stave off boredom. She was genuinely fond of Justin's boys.

"I wish Todd would see to it in his heart to marry and have children of his own," she said wistfully as she watched Christina pour the tea. "Before he's too old to enjoy the joys of fatherhood."

Christina's hand started to tremble. Penelope dearly wanted great-grandchildren. How she herself would have loved to be the one to provide them for her. But Christina knew that it was impossible.

"But Todd's a stubborn one," Penelope went on to say, giving particular attention to the way Christina had reacted to her words. "He's too preoccupied with the station to give romance much thought. What I wouldn't give for a granddaughter-in-law. But it would take an awfully clever woman to take Todd's attention away from his work."

Tea splashed over the edge of the cup and onto the tray. "How clumsy of me," Christina muttered as she dabbed at the hot amber liquid with the corner of a napkin.

Penelope fell silent and watched with pleased interest while Christina tried to regain her composure, babbling on and on her apologies for the spilled tea, but only making a larger mess in her attempts to blot it away.

Finally, when Christina poured tea into Penelope's cup, she handed it to her and abruptly changed the topic of conversation to one she could better handle—the boys and their new puppy. And the puppy had done enough in the short time he had been there to keep the conversation going for hours, if necessary.

When Penelope had finished her tea and had made her first indication that it was time to leave, she said what was uppermost on her mind. "Before I go, I want you to promise you will come to dinner again tomorrow night. Of course the invitation includes Justin and the boys, too."

Christina's heart soared. She would see Todd again at last, and have the chance to find out what was really keeping him so busy these days.

"Same time as last week," Penelope continued as she rose from her seat and brushed her skirt. "Do you think you can come?"

"As far as I know, Justin has no plans," Christina answered, unable to contain her excitement.

"Well, even if your brother does already have plans, that's no reason for you and the boys not to come. Just to be sure, I'll send the carriage for you tomorrow afternoon. Be ready."

After the driver helped Penelope into the carriage, she offered Christina a conspiratorial wink and a knowing smile. Her green eyes sparkled merrily as she said, "And wear something pretty."

It was the first indication that Penelope had shown of having any matchmaking ideas for the two of them, and it startled Christina. Though she liked the idea of Penelope's siding with her, she knew she had to find some way of letting Penelope know she was looking in the wrong direction if she was hoping to find Todd a wife who could give him the children he wanted and the great-grandchildren she wanted. She would watch for the opportunity Saturday night.

As it turned out, Justin did claim to have plans for that next evening, though he was very evasive about what they might be. Christina questioned him about his sudden plans but he would not tell her exactly what they were. Secretly, she hoped that the plans might have to do with Rose.

When the carriage arrived for them ten minutes late, Justin was still in his work clothes, sitting idly on the veranda. He seemed pleased to see them go, looking almost relieved when the carriage took off, leaving him behind. It occurred to her then that Justin and Todd still might not be back on good terms, and that Justin might have no plans at all other than to avoid Todd. She made up her mind to do what she could to rectify things between her brother and his boss before the night was over. She did not like seeing her brother look so downhearted.

Christina's first opportunity to speak to Todd in Justin's behalf came right after supper. Penelope and the boys went to the barn to see the twin colts, leaving Christina sitting on one of the bench seats and Todd leaning against the banister.

They had spoken very little during the meal, letting Penelope and the boys do most of the talking. But now that they were alone, Todd seemed eager to speak with her.

"I want to apologize about the other day," Todd said as he moved away from the banister and joined her on the bench seat. He rubbed his hands over the taut denim material of his pants in a self-conscious movement. "I should have known better than to believe you had sent for me."

Christina was delighted that he had decided to sit beside her, but felt awkward about the way his apology had been worded. She wanted to say something to put them both at ease, but could not think of the right words. Her insides twisted until she was a mass of knots. "It was just one of those things."

She was tempted to tell him how very much she had enjoyed the outcome of that mistake, and unconsciously ran her tongue over her parted lips while she considered the consequences.

"I should have come by to apologize sooner, but I've had my hands full around here."

"I imagine so, what with your family in for a visit on top of your usual duties." Again she wondered if Vella had occupied some of that time.

Todd sat in silence for a moment, then casually reached for her hand and held it. Christina thought she might burst with the joy that resulted from his simple gesture. Then suddenly he let her hand go and interlocked his hands together in his lap.

"Tell me something, Christina. How well do you know your brother?"

Christina could feel his gaze on her and looked questioningly from her abandoned hand to his face. "Well enough. Why do you ask?"

"Just wondering how much you knew about him."

Before she could question him about Justin, the very subject she had wanted to talk with him about, Penelope and the boys came rushing back, breathless from running the last distance in a race.

"You should see how Bucky and Lucky are growing," Edward said, having been first to recover his breath.

"Aye, and you should see how much they eat now," Alan put in, also having recovered from the race.

Penelope made her way to one of the bench seats and added nothing to the conversation as she eased herself down and tilted her head back to take in long, much needed breaths.

"Grandmum, you are going to overdo if you are not careful," Todd cautioned her with a stern frown.

Penelope nodded her agreement and smiled a broad, open-mouthed smile in order to continue to breathe heavily, but still did not speak.

Todd shook his head and laughed. "You won't do. Grandmum. You simply won't do."

Christina wanted to hear what Penelope had to say for herself on the matter, but her mind was too preoccupied with the questions she still wanted to ask Todd.

Questions she was more determined than ever to learn the answers to. She wanted to know exactly what he knew about her brother's problems—his extreme moodiness—and whether Todd himself had anything to do with them. The way he had just questioned her, she felt certain he knew something, and she was determined to find out just what it was. But she would wait until they were alone again before she asked. She did not want to discuss it in front of Penelope or the boys.

# Chapter XV

To Christina's dismay, either Penelope or one of the boys was always within hearing distance after that, leaving her no opportunity to ask Todd any of the questions that continued to plague her.

But the subject of the station boss's job did come up, and she was relieved to learn that whatever the trouble was between Todd and Justin, he had not dropped Justin from consideration. He told his grandmother he was still undecided, but that the choice had indeed come down to either William or Justin.

Christina found his frowning after having told Penelope that very unsettling. It was as if he were having second thoughts about choosing either one of them.

"When does Coolabah leave?" Penelope asked as she leaned back in the chair she had chosen deep in the shadows of the veranda. Her gaze followed the tall, silver-haired man as he strode from the coach house to the stable side of the barn, leading a tall gray and white horse. It was Coolabah's sudden appearance that had brought up the subject of the station boss in the first place.

"He will be leaving in a couple of weeks, unless he meets with further delays," Todd told her. "I can hardly believe his cattle were duffed before he even took possession of them. He was delayed one day in picking them up. *One day*. And they were stolen right out of the stockyards in Bathurst that night. It is as if someone knew they were going to be left there that extra day. Taking that many cattle had to be planned."

"It does seem that way," Penelope agreed.

"Something has got to be done about all this cattle stealing. If the detective police can't do something to find out who's behind it, and soon, we owners are going to have to band together and see if we can't find out ourselves. As angry as Coolabah is right now, I think he'd gladly muster up some of his friends who used to work with him when he was on the detective force to lead us."

"Do you suppose the thieves are bushrangers?" Penelope asked.

"In this day? In this area? I doubt it. No, I think it is someone who actually lives around here. Someone with connections to a ring of bandits where the brands are altered and the cattle hidden somewhere until those alterations heal. Then the cattle are driven out of here under that new brand. There have to be at least two of them. Maybe even three or four, judging by how many cattle they get away with each time they strike. It's never one or two. They usually take ten to twenty."

Christina listened, at first impatiently because it was not the subject uppermost in her mind. But she soon found herself listening with interest. It did sound as if someone local was in on it. Someone who kept a keen eye out for unattended cattle.

Suddenly, she had a horrible sinking feeling that

Justin knew who the cattle thieves were and was being made to keep quiet. That would account for his foul, almost jittery mood, and for the fact that he had grown so self-conscious when Todd and his friends had talked of the cattle duffing at the Anniversary Ball. And maybe Todd had come to the same conclusion and had tried to get that information out of Justin last Saturday—and the fact that Justin would not tell him was what the ruckus between the two of them had been about. Justin was probably too afraid of what the thieves would do to him if he told.

It was all starting to make sense to her. And if the cattle thieves were aware that Justin knew of their identity, they would certainly want to be sure he kept quiet about it, which accounted for the man at the dance's calling him outside and roughing him up. Of course. The man had not been a drinking mate at all. He had wanted to make sure Justin kept quiet.

At first, Christina considered confronting Justin with what she had finally figured out. But when she realized the extreme danger Justin must be in because he knew too much, she felt her insides tighten. He would only make things worse for himself if he told her anything and those men happened somehow to find out. And there was every possibility Justin would be the one to give himself away. Though her brother was very talented at being evasive, he had never been very good at lying under extreme pressure. She suspected those men would be very adept at putting just enough pressure on Justin to make him tell them the truth. And that just might cost Justin his life.

No, she needed to know more about the situation before she mentioned anything to Justin. Her next thought was to try to find out who that man was who had called him outside at the Anniversary Ball. Until she found out who he was and learned how deeply involved Justin was with them, she would keep her suspicions entirely to herself. For Justin's sake.

Christina was occupied with these thoughts for the remainder of the evening, and the more she considered the bits and pieces of information she now had, the more it all fit together. Though she was terrified by the danger her brother was in, she was deeply relieved to know what was wrong with him. Identifying the problem meant finally being in a position to help in some way.

Later that night, when Todd volunteered to drive her and the boys back home, her mind was still busy connecting the clues and finding that the pieces all fit together perfectly. She was so busy working it out in her mind that she practically ignored Todd, only hearing half of what he said.

By the time they reached Justin's house, Todd had grown very impatient with her obvious neglect and had come to the conclusion it was intentional. Then, when she climbed down from the carriage on her own, ignoring his attempt to help her, he could not hold back his anger any longer. The moment the boys had disappeared into the barn to go tell Little Yabber goodnight, he caught up with Christina before she reached the veranda steps.

"What is it with you? I've tried my best to be the man you seem to want me to be. I've stayed on my best behavior; I even let that business about Jake Akard drop. I've done everything I can imagine to please you, yet still you ignore me. Look, Christina, there's only so much good inside of anybody. What is it you want from me?"

Christina paused in front of the steps and turned to

look at him, confused by his sudden outburst. "I don't want anything from you. And I haven't asked anything from you."

"Not in so many words, but you made your demands of me pretty damn clear in other ways," he replied, exasperated, and reached up to run his hand through his thick brown hair. "And I am sick and tired of these silly games of yours. I've tried my best to please you. I've been far more considerate than I care to be, bending for you more than I have for any woman. I've done my best to play the game your way, but it is still not enough for you, is it?"

"What game are you talking about? I don't know where you came up with this idea I am playing any sort of game with you," she said, tossing her head back and staring at him with open defiance. How dare he even insinuate such a thing? "I don't know where you got the idea I am playing anything at *all* with you, because I'm not."

"Oh, but you are," he said with a terse nod, his blue eyes glinting. "And I am not playing those games anymore. I'm tired of all this light-footing around, trying to do what I can to please you. From now on, I'll be doing things my way. From now on we will be playing by my rules. I just want you to know that."

Though Christina was not at all sure what he was talking about or what had triggered his sudden outburst, she knew enough from his demanding tone and the insolent way he looked at her to be angry in return—very angry. "Todd, I don't know what game you think we are playing, and I'm not sure I care to know, but I can very well assure you that I am not now, have not in the past, and will not in the future be playing any sort of games

267

with you."

"Be forewarned, Christina, I am now in full pursuit of you. I won't let any more of your games hold me back any longer. I've reached the limit of my tolerance."

Having stated his intentions, and to prove he meant every word he said, he reached out, pulled her roughly to him, and kissed her hard.

Though the kiss did not last long, nor did he try to get more intimate with her, it left her so enraged and at the same time so light-headed that she could barely speak. "Get out of here, Todd Aylesbury. Get out of my sight right now."

"For now, that is exactly what I intend to do. I can't accomplish very much with the boys around and Justin due back at any minute. But, know this, Christina. I'll be back when the time is right and I'll finish then what I've started with you. And when I come back we'll be playing strictly by my rules."

"Oh, no we won't," she said and stepped away from him. His anger was so extreme that she feared what he might say or do next, but she was not about to let him leave without having the last word. "Because if you do come back here with intentions of playing these games you keep talking about, you'll find yourself playing alone. I have no intentions of being a partner to any of your games."

"You'll play," he said with a firm nod of his head. Without further comment, he turned on his heel and headed back to his carriage. Then, as he gathered the reins in his hands, he turned to look at her. His expression was so cold and menacing that it sent shivers down her spine, but he said nothing else.

Christina's anger told her to turn her back to him,

march into the house, and slam the door while he was still within earshot. But her pride told her to stand tall and pretend none of what he had said or done had affected her in the least. Blinking back her tears, she waited until the carriage was on the track and almost out of sight before turning and running blindly for her room.

For days after Todd's sudden outburst, Christina was especially cautious when she was left alone, afraid Todd would appear from nowhere and make good his threat. As angry as he had been that night, she was not sure what he might do to her and was terrified to find out. She already knew her weaknesses where he was concerned and was well aware of his overpowering strength. Even though she intended to fight a valiant battle should the time ever come, she felt certain he would emerge the victor.

Too afraid of guns to arm herself against him, and knowing she would never be able to shoot him anyway, she chose to keep a club of some sort handy at all times. Whenever she was outside while the boys were at the Aylesbury station doing odd chores and Justin was working, she kept her laundry paddle always within reach. When she was inside washing the dishes or cleaning, she kept the meat hammer at her side. She knew she probably would not be able to stop him even with such weapons, but she hoped at least to put up a good enough fight to remind him for days after that he had done battle against her.

But by Wednesday, four days had passed and she had neither seen nor heard from him. She wondered if perhaps his threat had been just a lot of words. Had he simply been letting off steam? There was every possibility that once he'd had time to cool down, he had come to his senses and seen how he had falsely accused her of game playing. But if that were true she was angered that he did not have the decency to come and apologize to her for his uncalled-for behavior.

Meanwhile, the thought of Justin's being in danger for knowing too much about the cattle duffing was never far from her mind. Though she had not had the opportunity to try to find out who the man was who had called Justin outside at the Anniversary Ball, she was still determined to discover what she could about him. She intended to gather that information herself, and, once she had it all pieced together, to confront Justin with what she knew and hope the cattle duffers did not think he had voluntarily told her anything. She was still very afraid of what they might do if they thought he had betrayed them in any way. But she had to know.

And once she did know more about it, then together maybe they could figure out a way to bring those cattle duffers to justice without putting either of themselves in any more danger. But until she knew who they were and exactly what they could safely do about the situation, she did not want to put Justin on the spot. She would not let him know she was even suspicious.

On Thursday, because the boys did not have any odd chores to do at the Aylesbury station, they stayed home to get some of their own chores done. Christina was pleased to have their company again. But with so much on her mind, she soon found they were too distracting. By the time Penelope rode into the yard in Todd's carriage, requesting that the boys go with her into town to help with her packages, since no man from the station was available to go with her, Christina willingly gave her permission for them to go.

She considered going with them so she could try to look for the man she had seen at the ball. She had to start somewhere, and Bathurst was the most likely place. But realizing Penelope would be at her side the entire time, which would not allow her to ask any questions of anyone without arousing the woman's suspicions, she decided against it.

For now, she would have to continue trying to pick up clues by talking with Justin, and hope to make a trip into town in the near future—alone. Then maybe she could find Jake Akard and see if he might be able to help her. She remembered how many townspeople he had seemed to know at the races that day, and if this man was a town person, maybe her description of him would earn her the man's name. Although she had not noticed any distinguishing features about the man, she had noticed one thing odd that might help Jake identify him. He had worn one glove. A tight black leather glove on his left hand. That seemed odd enough to be noticed by others.

"I'll have them home before dark," Penelope assured her, breaking into Christina's rambling thoughts as the boys quickly scrambled up into the carriage. "And I'll warn you right now they will probably have a few treats that will spoil their appetites for supper."

"I don't doubt it," Christina responded with a knowing nod. "I'll keep that in mind and not go to the trouble of preparing a large meal."

"Maybe you'd like to come too, then you wouldn't have to cook at all. We could all eat before we come home."

"I'd still have Justin to feed. Besides, I've already

heated my laundry water. I really should go ahead and get that chore out of the way. I've put it off long enough. Maybe next time I'll be able to go."

Penelope turned her attention to the two bright-eyed little boys on the front seat beside her. "At least I have you two to keep me company and help carry whatever I end up purchasing." Then she picked up the reins from her lap and flicked them lightly, turning to wave goodbye to Christina just before the carriage moved forward. "I'll try to get back in time for us to have a nice chat before I have to leave."

Then, after directing the horse to make an awkward turn in the middle of the yard, Penelope had the carriage headed onto the main track, dust trailing lightly behind.

Christina sighed heavily as she spun back around to face the pile of laundry beside the two huge wooden tubs. Though they sat in the shade of a large, drooping gum tree, there would be little comfort from the day's heat. But then again, the sooner she got started with the task, the sooner she would be finished. Then she could be inside or sitting on the veranda doing some of her lighter chores during the hottest hours of the day.

Soon she had her elbow-length sleeves pushed up as high as they would go and was hard at work over the steaming tubs, swirling the clothes around in the scalding wash water with the long wooden paddle. But the day grew hotter than usual, and as she worked to rinse the clothes and hang them out to dry, she began to feel almost faint from the unbearable heat. Sweat rolled off her in steady streams. She thought of the pond where the boys usually went to swim and of how exquisite it would be to plunge headlong into that cool body of water on such a miserably hot day.

By the time she finished draping the last of the clothing over the clothesline, she was soaked with perspiration. Her hair had come loose and was plastered to her skin. When she looked up into the bleached white sky and felt the searing heat on her face, she thought she'd never felt the sun give off such intense heat. She felt sticky, and the thought of a nice sponge bath did not suffice. What she wanted to do was submerge herself in cool water. The idea of going for a swim became far too tempting to ignore.

Hurriedly, she went into the house and gathered clean clothes and two clean towels. Almost as an afterthought, she picked up a bar of scented soap.

She thought of walking, since the boys usually walked and the distance was not terribly far, but with the heat and her being physically drained, she was not sure she was up to the walk. Unsure of how to go about hitching the wagon, but remembering Justin's lesson on saddling a horse, she took the time to saddle the boys' horse and rode to the pond.

With each step the horse took, her anticipation grew. She could hardly wait to plunge into the water's coolness. When she finally arrived at the site, she took just enough time to tether the horse to the low limb of a black satinwood, then ran directly to the most secluded spot along the water's edge, not bothering to take her clean clothes or the towels with her. She was too eager to feel the water on her. She would return for the towels, clothing, and the soap after she had swum for a while.

Delaying no further than to take a quick glance around to be sure no one was nearby, she stripped herself of everything but her camisole and bloomers, tossing her perspiration-soaked clothing to the ground with little concern about where it landed. Then, as she stepped closer to the water's edge, she spotted the rope attached to an overhanging tree limb that she had seen the boys use to swing out over the pond and drop into the deepest part of the water. Laughing aloud, she reached for it and held tight.

Suddenly, she was a child again. She backed up to get a running start, gripped the rope with both hands, and swung far out across the pond, then let go at the strategic moment that would let her drop with agile grace into the cool water.

Such sweet, sweet ecstasy. Although the water was at first a shock against her heated skin, it was exactly what she had looked forward to, and she stayed under the surface for as long as she could. Breathless, she burst through the surface with a pleased gasp. Eventually, though, she became used to the cooler temperature and began to move about freely, enjoying the gentle pressure of the water against her skin as she dove down again and again.

After several minutes of such child's play, she decided to relax and float below the sun-warmed surface. She allowed her thoughts to drift into a pleasant daydream, a daydream in which she floated in the clouds. And for the next few minutes she did not have a care in the world. She put aside her worries about Justin's safety and Todd's latest display of anger and simply enjoyed her moment in the clouds, unaware of anything but the sensations that surrounded her and her childhood fantasy of being lighter than air.

With her ears submerged just below the water's surface, she did not immediately notice the soft thudlike sounds of something hard striking the earth. She was too

274

happy with her peaceful thoughts to care. Even when she heard the muffled whinny of a horse, she simply attributed the sound to her own horse and never once opened her eyes. She did not want to break the wondrous trance. She did not have many moments like this.

The loud splash near her ear brought her from her daydreams with a loud startled gasp. Her eyes flew open as she stood in the water. By the time she saw Todd standing near the water's edge, another small rock in hand, and realized he was between her and her clothing, it was too late to make a run for it. Her heart beat wildly as she tried to figure a way out of her predicament. But there was no reward for her efforts. She was trapped.

As she stood submerged in the water to her chin, her gaze went helplessly to her clothing lying on the ground beside him. Her clean clothes were in the swag attached to the saddle of her horse behind him. Then she spotted his horse tethered to the same tree as her own, and finally her eyes rested on Todd, who stood smiling at her, his weight shifted insolently to one leg.

"Good day for a swim, isn't it?" he asked casually as he tossed the rock lightly into the air and caught it as it came down. Then he tossed it into the air again, only in her direction this time. When it landed only inches from her, causing a loud plopping splash beside her, she gasped again.

Her first thought was to order him away from there immediately, but she realized that would do little good, since they happened to be on his land. If anything, he could order her out of his pond. She shuddered beneath the water and hoped he would not think of that.

"I say. Good day for a swim, isn't it?" He repeated his question, making his voice louder, although there was not that much distance between them.

"What are you doing here?"

He ignored her question, tilted his head to one side, and smiled affectionately. "Does look cool and inviting," he said with a firm nod and his hands went to the buttons on his shirt.

"Don't you dare!"

"Dare what? Take a swim in my own pond?" he asked lightly before he stepped back and tossed his shirt over a low-hanging tree limb.

Though intrigued by the sight of his muscular chest, Christina turned her back to him. "Don't you dare come into this pond with me!"

"You can't mean to have this entire pond to yourself. How selfish can you be?"

Christina's heart pounded ferociously as she tried to think of a way out of her dilemma. "Todd, I mean it. If you come into this water I'll scream. I'll scream so loud it will bring every man on your station running to my aid."

"Go ahead and scream if it will make you feel better, but I don't think anyone will hear you. We are too far from my house and although your brother's house is probably close enough, I don't believe there is anyone home at the moment. Or at least there wasn't just a few minutes ago when I was there."

She wanted to glance back at him and see how far along he was in undressing, but at the same time she was too embarrassed. Instead she kept a keen ear and listened for the first indication that he had entered the water. Then, whenever she was certain he was well into the water, she would make for the opposite shore. Though she would have to let him see her in her underclothing again, she knew that her best chance was to make a run for her horse.

It never occurred to her that he would use the same rope she had used and drop immediately at her side. The action took her so much by surprise that she was unable to move in time to get away from him. Within seconds he had her within his grasp.

"Let go of me!" she said angrily as she tried to wrench her arm free from his grip.

"Don't want to," he stated frankly, and using only one hand, pulled her easily through the water and held her firmly against him.

In a purely defensive reaction, she lifted her hand out of the water and tried to strike him across the face, but he had anticipated the move and brought his other hand up to catch her by the wrist.

"I warned you I'd be back to do things my way. Isn't this much more fun than doing them your way?" he asked and laughed when she did nothing more to answer his question than to glare at him.

A plan of escape eluded Christina. He had her too firmly within his grasp to break free on her own, and the shoulder-depth of the water prevented her from bringing her knee up and doing enough damage to distract him. But then again, what could he do to her in the water? He could not very well wrestle her to the ground. He would drown trying.

"What's the matter? Aren't you pleased to see me?" he asked while he moved his arms quickly to surround her and locked her in place by firmly grasping his own wrists behind her back. His pale blue eyes sparkled with pure delight when she did not answer.

"After all, it's been five days. I'd think you'd want to show a little more enthusiasm than this," he went on to say. His long, narrow dimples deepened as he watched her grow angrier.

Finding that familiar dangerous look back in his eyes, Christina looked away from him in a last desperate attempt to collect her thoughts and figure out some way to free herself. That was when her gaze dipped to the strong, wet, glistening shoulders protruding out of the water. Her brown eyes widened at the thought that he probably was naked. He might not have left his underclothing on, as she had. Quickly she glanced to the shore hoping that his underclothing would not be among the clothes she would see there.

To her horror, she saw that his white underdrawers lay across the branch right beside his breeches, his shirt, and his stockings. When she returned her wide-eyed gaze to his face, she found his smile had deepened even more.

"Something bothering you, Christina? Care to talk about it?"

Her eyes lowered to the water's surface, almost as if they had a will of their own. To her relief, the movement of the water prevented her from seeing little more than a large golden blur. She was unable to distinguish anything but the color, which was the same as his sun-bronzed shoulders, but that was enough to cause her to blush.

Afraid to meet his knowing gaze, she stared helplessly at the dark hair plastered against the part of his chest that she could see. She watched as a droplet of water dropped from his chin onto the muscular swell of his chest, then ran a provocative trail through the dark wet hair and into the pond.

Realizing now that he was completely naked beneath

278

the water's surface and that he had her pressed against his body, she became greatly alarmed, for she was nearly as naked as he was. The thin material of her camisole and bloomers mattered very little. The wet fabric was transparent against her skin, and if he lifted her out of the water, he would see everything. How she hoped and prayed he would not think of doing that, for she had no doubt he would help himself to an eyeful.

## Chapter XVI

Todd's hands were behind her, holding her firmly against him, and Christina was aware that the pressure she felt in front of her could only come from one other source. Her eyes widened in alarm and her heart raced frantically with fear. She tried to keep in mind that there was little he could accomplish while they were in the water, as long as she had the strength to fight him. But she also knew that he was strong and could easily carry her to shore and do whatever he pleased. She had no weapon to fend him off, and he had such an exasperating way of capturing her by the wrists that it made her hands useless. And with nothing more than her undergarments to take off, he was well ahead of the game he seemed so intent on winning.

"You look a little frightened," he commented. His gaze searched her worried expression with just the slightest show of concern, then dipped lower to stare into the water with interest. "You are trembling. Are you cold? Well then, maybe we should get you out of this water."

"Todd, don't!" she squealed as he bent down and

scooped her instantly into his arms. She was horrified of what he would see through her translucent underclothing, if he had not already seen it, and what that sight would encourage him to do. She was especially frightened because she knew he needed so little encouragement, anyway.

"But you are trembling," he insisted. "You need to get out of the water and into the sunshine."

"No, I don't!" She struggled again, trying to make him drop her when she realized he had already started for the shore with her in his arms.

"You'll thank me once you feel the nice warm grass beneath you and the sun's gentle warmth on your skin," he assured her and fought to keep hold of his squirming catch.

"Todd, let me go!" She continued to kick and twist in an effort to make him drop her.

"When the time comes," he promised. His gaze lowered again from her stricken face to see the treasures so thinly veiled as they ascended from the water. Even with her arms crossed protectively over her breasts, he was able to see enough of her luscious body to be reminded how exquisite she really was. The image of how tempting she had looked in his hotel room, bare to the waist as she fought to escape him, flashed before his mind, making him that much more eager to get her to shore.

"Todd, don't!" She wiggled from his grasp, but found, although she did manage to slip around in his arms and make things more difficult for him, that he held her tight.

"My what a tigress you are," he laughed appreciatively as he stepped onto the shore. His eyes sparkled with pure delight at seeing her struggle despite his obvious advantage over her. He admired her spirit and her determination, and although he knew he would not take her unless she was willing, he was looking forward to trying. "A real tigress."

Tigress? She had one option—to bite him. Bending her head, she went for the tender flesh at the side of his neck and sank her teeth in as hard as she could. He dropped her with a resounding thud onto the grass just a few feet away from the water's edge.

"Why you little . . ." he said as he reached for the place where she had left her mark.

Instead of the burst of total outrage she had expected when he peered at his fingertips and noticed traces of blood, Todd started to laugh. Rich, deep, golden laughter. Overcome to the point where he could not stop, he dropped to the ground beside her, caught her by her shoulders as she tried to escape again, and continued to laugh. "Woman, you never cease to amaze me."

She stared at him perplexed, then looked first to the hand that pressed one shoulder against the grass-covered ground, then to the hand that held the other shoulder, and made her choice. She bent her head to try again.

"Oh, no, you don't," he said and moved his hand away before she could to it any harm. Although she had succeeded in freeing her shoulder, he immediately grabbed her chin, his fingers well away from her mouth, and held her firm.

As he held her prisoner, he rested almost casually on his elbow at her side. His eyes roamed freely over her body while she tried to free her shoulder and her chin. She kicked at him, but she could not bend at the waist far enough to meet her target. Even so, he moved his lower torso away from her a few extra inches.

Finally Christina gave up the struggle. Until she could come up with another way to get an advantage, she was captured. Then, as she lay there defeated, staring up into his wide, incredibly blue eyes, she suddenly realized she did not want to escape. There was no intense anger in his expression. No threatening glint to his eye. Only a glimmer of adoration, and something more. Something that stirred her blood and made her wonder why she had feared him in the first place.

As his gaze left hers to sweep slowly over her near-naked body, he smiled gently. "Christina, you are the most beautifuil and most alluring woman I've ever laid eyes on."

She glanced down to see what had captured his attention and saw the straining peaks of her breasts clearly visible through the wet fabric. She was surprised that she was not at all embarrassed to have him see her this way. Instead she felt proud that he appeared so pleased with what he saw. She sensed her body relax as he brought his gaze back up to meet hers once again. Her trembling stopped.

Slowly, he released his hold on her shoulder and chin, and at the same time came forward, lowering his face to hers. She was too mesmerized by the thought of his lips once again touching hers to move. She was bound by his spell.

His kiss was so warm and tender that it sent an instant flood of joy and womanly desire coursing through her. The sudden rush of her emotions was so acute and so all-consuming, it was almost painful. It was the most intense feeling she had ever known.

As Christina's body absorbed the pleasures that came from his kiss, he moved closer until his gleaming, wet body came to rest more on top of her than beside her, warming her outside as much as inside. His kiss deepened, becoming deliciously demanding. His tongue dipped and teased the outer edges of her lips until she parted them willingly and let him again sample the intimate areas of her mouth.

His hand moved to the garment that covered her breasts and struggled with the wet ties until he finally had them undone. He peeled the soaked garment to her waist, then moved his warm, searching hand to first cup, then cover her straining breast.

While his kiss continued to work its strange magic on her, his fingers played lightly with the sensitive peak, until Christina found herself gasping aloud with pleasure. No thought of pulling away came to her. Instead she found herself arching her back, eager to lose herself in the sensations he created. When he peeled away her bloomers and touched her intimately, her brain finally sounded its alarm and she tried to push him away.

When he saw her horror-filled expression, he frowned. His eyes were so dark with desire that they appeared almost black. "Christina, don't stop me now. I need you."

"What you need you can get from your other women admirers," she said as she rolled out from under him and grasped for her wet garments. She was so mortified by what had almost happened that she broke into tears.

"That's true enough. I can. But I don't want anyone else. I want you. And not just for now. Not just for a moment of pleasure. I want you forever. What I really want most is for you to be my wife."

"That's impossible," she cried out and stood, clutching the wet garments to herself. Christina tried not to stare at his naked body when he moved toward her, but she could not help catching a glimpse of his magnificent form. She had never seen a naked man before and was amazed at how truly beautiful his body was.

"Why? Why is it so impossible?" he asked and continued toward her, but before he reached her, she ran.

"Because we don't love each other, for one thing!" she cried out over her shoulder as she ran as fast as she could for her horse. "And because . . . because . . ." She could not say it. She could not admit her barrenness, could not admit that she was an incomplete woman, and sobbed uncontrollably as she jerked her clothing from the swag on the saddle and quickly singled out her underskirt.

"You'll grow to love me," he said as he caught up with her. Though he wanted more than anything to grab her and stop her from dressing, to make her listen to him, he did nothing. "You'll grow to love me as much as I already love you. I know you will. There's already something special between us."

"How can you say you love me? You don't even know me. All I am to you is forbidden fruit. Can't you see that? And since you haven't been able to taste that fruit by any other means, you have decided to marry me." She never stopped putting her clothes on.

"You are wrong. I know what I feel," he said, his voice revealing his anger.

"It's not love," she insisted, looking up from her task to glare at him, only to find his nakedness too distracting. She looked away again but not before she had seen the cold and determined expression on his face.

"Christina," he said, in a slow and deliberate voice, "I

286

suggest you go have a long talk with your brother before you say anything more. I have a feeling he will help change your mind on this matter. I want you more than I have ever wanted any woman, and I fully intend to have you. And since you have made it perfectly clear that you are the kind of woman who has to be married before you can give of yourself freely, I'm more than willing to honor that and marry you. And, once we are indeed married and you are legally my wife, I will proceed to make you love me as much as I already love you."

"I can't marry you," she told him simply, pleadingly. Having finally gotten into her clothes, she decided against going back for the dirty clothes or her boots, which were piled near the water's edge, and moved to untie her horse's reins. Her hands trembled from the emotions that tore at her heart as she worked with the stubborn leather straps.

"You *can* marry me, and you will. Talk with your brother. Hear what he has to say. I'll be by for your answer tomorrow morning."

Without another word, he turned and walked away.

Christina was in such a state of turmoil as she rode away from the pond that she knew she could not return to the house and wait for Justin to come in from work. Remembering where he and his station boss were working on a downed fenceline that afternoon, she turned her horse in that direction and prodded the animal into a quick gallop.

Never having ridden astride before that day, she hung on to the saddle horn for dear life. It was impossible to keep her bare feet in the stirrups and her posterior planted to the seat. But she was too eager to find Justin and hear what he had to say to slow the animal down.

"Christina? What are you doing here?" Justin asked, openly surprised to look up from his work and find his sister riding across the field, already nearly upon them, on horseback no less. So unlikely was the sight, his first thought was that the heat had finally got to him.

Coolabah stopped what he was doing to stare at her, too. His gaze dipped only briefly to the show of leg that was provided by a skirt that had not been made for riding astride and had hiked up to her knees. But being the gentleman he was, he quickly looked away.

"Justin, I have to talk to you," she said as she swung her leg over the front of the saddle in a very unladylike manner, then dropped to the ground. The force caused her previously injured knee to throb.

"Sure, what is it?" he asked and set the wire cutters aside.

She cut her gaze toward Coolabah, who had resumed his work but was clearly close enough to hear every word, and stated, "I need to talk to you in private."

Noticing the seriousness in her voice and realizing that she had come to him with her feet bare and her hair wet and matted with grass, he grabbed her by her arm and escorted her far away from the area of downed fence, out into the grassy field.

Christina took several deep breaths to steady her shattered nerves as she tried to decide where to begin. There were too many important questions to know which to ask first.

"Christina? What happened?" Justin held her by her arms and stared into her pale face with open concern.

"Todd," she said in a whimper.

Justin took a deep breath and held it while he waited to hear more.

"Todd asked me to marry him and when I said no, he told me I'd better come and have a long talk with you. He sounded as if you would have something to say that would change my mind. He seemed certain of it. Why would he think you would try to change my mind over something like that?"

When Justin did not answer and instead turned away, her fear grew more intense. "Why, Justin? Why does he think you would try to convince me to marry him? Even though I don't want to."

Justin closed his eyes. When he opened them again and turned to look at Christina, she could see traces of tears. "Justin? What is it?"

"Christina, I'm in trouble," he began. "I've gotten myself involved in something I wanted no part of. It started when I had to help three other men duff some of Todd's cattle—by setting a fire to one of his outbuildings."

"What?" Her hands flew to her mouth and her eyes widened with disbelief. "Why?"

"A diversion. But helping them to steal the cattle is not all of it. I also forged a document of sale on Todd's personal stationery, and once the cattle reached their destination, I was the one who went there to make the sale, pretending to be representing Todd."

"Why?"

"Because I was in debt to one of the other men involved. I had lost a lot of money to him in a card game. Money I didn't even have. It was either do that one favor for him or sell most of what I own in order to raise the money I needed to pay him back. And I can't sell my land if I don't own it outright, and until I make that final payment to Ben, I don't have full title to the land. I really had no choice but to help them."

"And Todd found out?" she asked, looking ahead in his story.

"Not about that. You see, after I got the money from the sale of the cattle, I felt so terrible for what I had done I went into the nearest tavern and got drunk. Then somehow I got into another card game and gambled away all the money."

"All of it?"

The tears of shame that had filled Justin's eyes finally spilled onto his cheeks when he nodded. "Aye, Chrissy, all of it. Two of the men paid me a visit the next morning and demanded that money and threatened to kill me if I did not pay up. They gave me one month to get it. That's when they told me to expect a visit from them. Meanwhile, I've had to keep them satisfied by giving them bits of information about when and where cattle would be left unattended in the area."

Christina was too horrified to comment as he paused to swallow back his bitter emotions.

"Chrissy, when the time limit started to get close and I did not have the money and could see there was no other way to get that much money in time, I panicked. I tried to steal it from Todd's safe and got caught. It was that same night after you first met him and I realized he had no intention of coming through with his decision about the station boss's job in time to help me." He looked up into the bleached white sky and squinted against the sun. "That's one of the reasons I wanted you to be nice to him and get him away from the house. So I could give that safe a go while he was with you."

He dropped his head suddenly and faced the ground.

"If only he had decided about the job that night, I wouldn't have had to try to steal from him at all. The bonus would have been enough to buy me some more time. But when he did not make the announcement and I could see he had no plans to do so in the near future, I had to do it."

Christina stared at him lamely, her brow knitted. She found it all so hard to believe. "If all that is true, why were you never arrested?"

"Because Todd made a bargain with me instead. He told me that if I'd help him get you, he'd see that no one found out I had tried to rob his safe. He would then lend me the money I need to pay off what he thinks is a gambling debt. All of it."

"The man at the anniversary dance was one of those men, wasn't he?"

"Aye, and one of the other men was waiting outside. Those two are actually the only two I've ever had to deal with. There's another man involved, but I've never met him. But I think I know who he is."

"Who?"

"William Stone."

"Vella's brother?"

"Aye. I'm not sure why, but I just have this gut feeling it is William. Those men knew too much about the operations of Todd's station, where Todd would be and when, and exactly how I could help. Things William would know. The two men I worked with kept referring to this third man as their boss and told me the night at the dance that the boss had sent them to inform me that my time was way past being up. They wanted their money. I explained to them how I'd made a business deal with

Todd for the money and asked that they give me a little more time to fulfill my part of the bargain. They finally agreed, only this time they threatened not only to kill me if I didn't come through, but to burn down my house, too, which would leave you and the boys homeless. And they'll do it, too."

"How much do you owe them? I have a little money set aside."

"Eight thousand."

"Eight thousand?" Suddenly her measly four hundred did not seem quite as substantial as it once had.

"And there's only one way for me to get that money and save my hide—and keep you and my sons from being left homeless," he added, his eyes pleading with her to understand. "You have to marry Todd. The sooner the better."

Christina's eyes widened at the thought of what her brother had led her into, then narrowed as she considered it further. "No. I want to have a talk with those men. I want to try to make arrangements to settle this in some other way."

"They are past talking," Justin said. His face tensed at the thought of what the outcome of such a meeting would be.

"Maybe not. Maybe if I promised to give them my four hundred and also promised to help you save the money and pay them as quickly as possible, maybe they will give you more time."

Justin looked at her as if she had lost her mind. "Believe me. They are beyond wanting to bargain. In fact, if I don't produce that money pretty damn soon, they are going to give up on me and do exactly what they threatened to do, Christina. They *will* kill me."

"Have they killed anyone yet?"

Justin frowned. "Not that I can be sure of, but that doesn't mean they haven't, and that certainly doesn't mean they won't."

"At least let me talk with them. Set up a meeting."

"Believe me, you don't want to meet them. I won't let you."

"Justin, do you have a way of getting in contact with them?" She was not going to take no for an answer. One way or another she was going to try to talk sensibly to those men. It was obvious the blackhearts would have more chance getting at least something from Justin if he was left alive than they could possibly gain by killing him.

"Aye. I do, but . . ."

"Then send a message that you want to talk to them. Ask them to meet you somewhere. We have to at least try."

Although Justin continued to refuse to set up a meeting, he finally agreed to at least see they got a letter. Christina spent the rest of the afternoon carefully wording her plea, in hopes of convincing them to take the four hundred now and give them a little more time to come up with the rest.

Reluctantly, Justin left the house with the letter tucked away in his pocket, and when he returned hours later, he claimed the deed had been done. Afraid to confront them in person, he had hired a neighbor boy to carry the letter to one of them. Now all they could do was wait for a reply and hope that they would rather have what little money Christina had than Justin's life.

That night, Christina was last to go to bed, though she

doubted she would be able to sleep. She was too worried about what the men's response would be to her letter. After half an hour of tossing and turning, she lit her bedside lamp and tried reading to occupy her mind. But the situation was far too serious to let her think of anything else.

Though her eyes scanned the words in the book that lay open before her, her thoughts were on how stupid her brother had been to get involved with such men. Then she thought about Todd and how he had used her brother's stupidity to his own advantage. Anger joined her fear and welled up inside her until she thought she would scream.

It angered her even more to know that all she had to do was promise Todd she would marry him, and she could get the money they needed to pay the men off. She almost felt it would serve Todd Aylesbury right for trying to manipulate her and her brother the way he had. But, no, that would be a last resort. There was no real reason to ruin Todd's life, and more important, her own, because of something her brother had done. Not if it could be worked out in any other way.

Growing frustrated with the book's inability to take her mind off her troubles, she closed it and tossed it aside. Still knowing sleep was impossible, she sat forward and stared around her for something else that might help. There was another book on the vanity table across the room, a book of poetry of which she was particularly fond, but she was certain it would no more hold her attention than the other book, and she decided against it.

Then she heard Little Yabber barking in his usual incessant manner, probably at a mouse or an unfortunate frog that had happened into the pup's pen. Shaking her head at the annoyance, she wondered when and if that silly dog ever slept. Quickly, she threw back her covers and slipped out of bed. She was headed to the window to shout out to the animal to be quiet when she heard the pup give out a loud yelp of pain. Something was out there. Something more than a mouse or a frog.

She turned back and reached for her dressing robe draped over the back of her rocking chair. Her heart was already in her throat from fear of what had attacked the little puppy. Her first thought was that a wild dingo had gotten inside the barn. She had to get Justin. As she swung the robe around behind her and slipped her arms into place, she was already headed for the door. Suddenly she heard the crashing of glass and spun around in time to see pieces of her windowpane shower the floor and a large rock bounce off a table and fly across the room.

She was barely aware she had screamed as she dove for the lamp and quickly turned out the flame. Her heart slammed hard against her chest again and again while she waited for whatever would happen next. Then she thought of the boys in their room. Alone.

Stumbling in the dark, she hurried to their door, flung it open, and was relieved to find them both sound asleep in their beds. The moonlight filtering in through the lace curtains cast enough light for her to see inside the room. She moved quickly, and when she neared the window, she crouched down. She eased the curtain back and peered out into the yard below, but saw no movement.

"What was that?" She heard Justin's voice in the darkness and turned to see his black form advancing into the room.

"Someone threw a rock through my window," she responded in a hushed voice so as not to wake the boys. She met him halfway and pulled him back out into the hall, but did not close the door for fear something might happen in the boys' room.

Justin pulled away from her and disappeared into her room. He cursed softly when he stepped on a large piece of glass but did not take the time to pull the shard from his bare foot. When Christina followed she could see him kneeling at her window, peering cautiously out at the yard below. Then he moved back across the room, sidestepped around her, and limped back out into the hall.

"What are you going to do?" she asked, her voice barely a whisper when she followed him.

"Go out there and face them," he said matter-of-factly and stopped long enough to pull the sharp sliver of glass from his foot. "What else can I do?"

"Then you think it is the men you owe the money to?"

"Who else would it be?"

She heard the metallic click of the rifle he held. "Justin, don't."

"It's me they want," was all he said before he turned to go downstairs.

Christina stood motionless, trying to think of what to do, then hurried after her brother. But when she reached the bottom of the stairs, she could not find him and went quickly to the nearest window. She approached it carefully so as not to be spotted from the outside.

There in the yard, she could see Justin standing bravely alone, looking around for the attackers. Though he had his rifle at his side, he did not have it aimed. It dangled, pointed toward the ground.

She listened for movement, wondering when a bullet would bring her brother down, praying fervently that they would decide to spare him. She heard him call them by name. Randolph. Hank. There was no answer. He called out again. Still there was no answer. Then she heard the floor creak slightly behind her, and she screamed.

# Chapter XVII

When Christina spun around to face the darkened room she saw nothing, only the familiar shadows of the walls and furniture. But she knew those shadows could easily be hiding something from her—or someone.

"Who's there?" she called out fearfully, then screamed again when the front door suddenly crashed open and the black, menacing form of a man bounded into the room.

Another scream had filled the room and blended with her own, but she had been unable to determine the direction from which it had come. All fell silent again until she heard a tiny voice call out from the bottom of the stairway.

"Aunt Christina?"

"Alan?" she called out, then realized the danger the boy was in, for he was only a few feet away from the man who had burst through the door. "Alan, go back upstairs! Don't let that man get you!"

"It's okay, Christina. It's me," she heard Justin say, and relief washed over her, leaving her too weak to stand.

She sank against the wall beside the window and watched as her brother's dark form moved toward the stairway. Gently, he gathered his son into his arms.

"Father, what's wrong?"

"Nothing, Alan. We thought we heard something outside, but it turned out to be nothing. Come on, let's get you back in bed."

Christina waited until they disappeared at the top of the stairs, then turned back to the window and watched the soft, moon-defined shadows of the yard, while also keeping an eye on the now half-opened doorway.

She watched for the slightest sign of movement outside as she listened to Justin's quiet footsteps as he carried his youngest son back to bed. Was it over? Had it just been some sort of warning? Or was someone still out there waiting?

When Justin returned, he brought a small lit metal lantern. Christina saw how stricken and deathly pale his face was, making his beard and his eyes appear that much darker by contrast. Though he still had on his nightshirt, he had donned a pair of trousers and had haphazardly tucked the long tails into the waist. He clutched his rifle in his other hand as he headed for the partially opened door and held up the light to see the damage he had done to the door frame.

"I'll have to get some nails and nail this door shut," he said. His tone of voice was far more calm than she would have expected under the circumstances, and his hand was steadier than her own.

Opening the door wide, Justin walked out into the night, and Christina could tell by watching the faint glow of his lantern that he was headed for the barn.

Despite her deep, gut-wrenching fear of who or what

300

might still be out there, she followed Justin out of the house. She kept in the shadows as she glanced behind her in the direction of the house. As she made her way, she scanned the paddocks and the garden, then searched the area in front of the barn, then looked behind her again. Christina cautiously approached the barn door, which Justin had left open. Her heart felt as if it might explode at any moment from fear.

When she neared the door, she could see the dim glow of the lantern, and when she stepped inside, she found Justin raking his hand through the different-sized nails inside a large tin bucket. He jerked his head up and moved his hand to his rifle, which leaned against the wall, when he heard her enter. Once he realized it was she, he resumed his search for the nails.

His expression was hard, his lips pressed together into a fine, determined white line while he continued to pick out the nails he needed. Then suddenly he lifted his head again and looked in the opposite direction, to the back of the barn.

"What is it?" she asked, breathless with fear. "Did you hear something?"

"It's what I don't hear," he said. Although he kept his voice low, he had not actually whispered.

Christina frowned, not fully understanding until he set the nails down, picked his rifle up, and headed for the pen the boys had built for Little Yabber in the furthest corner of the barn. It occurred to Christina the puppy should be yelping wildly, in his usual effort to get their attention. Yet there was silence. All she could hear at that moment was the distinct hammering of her own heart.

Her stomach twisted into a cold knot of apprehension

301

when Justin stopped just a few feet away from the pen and stared down helplessly. His shoulders drooped and his hands held the lantern and the rifle so tightly that white patches formed at his knuckles. For the longest moment, he did not take a breath.

Reluctantly, Christina joined him, and when she looked into the small pen, she felt as though someone had taken a board and slammed it against her stomach. The poor little puppy lay perfectly still, his shaggy head pointed in the wrong direction from his lanky body, his neck broken.

Reaching for Justin, she clutched his nightshirt and sobbed hysterically against his shoulder. She thought of the confusion and pain the poor little dog must have suffered in those last few seconds of his life. He had been so quick to trust anyone who put out a hand to him. Such a loving little animal. Then she thought of having to tell Alan and Edward their beloved puppy was dead. The pain inside of her grew worse. She wanted to double over from the severity of it.

"Go back to the house," Justin ordered her sternly and gently pushed her away. "Go back to the house and stay there. This might not be over yet. They obviously killed the pup to shut him up so we would not know if they were still about or not."

Christina's eyes opened wide as she comprehended what her brother had said. Whoever had done this awful thing to the puppy and whoever had thrown the rock into her window could still be around. Could be in the barn with them at that very moment. She quickly looked around the interior of the barn.

The light from Justin's lantern created long, eerie shadows near the front of the barn, shadows large enough to hide a man. The blood in her veins turned to ice as she realized she could have walked right by one of them and not known it. And now she would have to walk back by those shadows to take the shortest route to the house. Going out the small door at the back would mean entering the darkened paddocks and walking around the barn before reaching the yard. That was even more frightening.

"Go on," Justin prodded her. "It's me they want."

"Do you see them?" she asked as she continued to search the undefined shadows for the dark form of a man.

"No, but then they may not be inside the barn any longer. They could be anywhere by now. Once you get outside, you run as fast as you can to the house and close the door. Then blockade it and hide."

Christina wondered if she would not be safer staying at her brother's side. At least Justin had the rifle. But then she thought of the boys alone in the house and unaware of the trouble.

"Don't take any foolish chances," she pleaded quietly. She pressed a kiss to his bearded cheek before turning away to do exactly as she had been told.

Justin followed her as far as the center of the barn and stood where he could see the house. From the barn, both the back yard and side yard were within view, but the front door was not. He planned to watch her until she had fully disappeared around the front, and he held his rifle ready while she continued alone to the door and then outside.

Cautiously, Christina lifted the soft white material of her cambric nightdress and the pale blue cashmere of her dressing robe and stepped outside. Her heart felt as if it was on fire, burning through her lungs and into her throat. She held her breath and made a wild run for the house.

By the time she had crossed around to the front, scampered up the steps and inside, and closed the door behind her, she felt as if she had run forever. She gasped for air and could not seem to get enough, but she found the strength to move a small mirrored bookcase the five feet necessary to blockade the door.

After that, all she could do was wait. But, because she was clearly aware the men could already be in the house, she chose to do her waiting inside the boys' room. She would do everything within her power to assure their safety.

For the next hour, Christina sat in one of the boy's small chairs near the window and facing the hall door, listening for unfamiliar sounds. The house creaked again and again, as if to taunt her for being so afraid, but not enough to make her believe someone was inside. From the boys' room, she could not see the barn. About all that could be seen from the boys' window was the orchard and part of the garden. She had no way of knowing what was happening to Justin and could only pray for his safety. Finally, an hour and a half after the rock had crashed through her window, though it seemed as though days had passed, she heard heavy footsteps on the back veranda, then heard Justin call out to her to let him in.

She hurried down the stairs, stumbling twice in the darkness, and opened the back door for him. As soon as he was inside, she pushed the door shut and shoved the bolt back into place. She then moved one of her smaller worktables against it. After she had secured the door, she turned to face Justin.

He walked across the room and without warning struck

304

a match. The sound of it seemed to fill the quiet room and it made her jump. Her hand flew to her throat to still her throbbing pulse.

"Did you ever see anyone?" she asked. Her gaze focused on the small yellow flame as he bent to light the lamp nearest to him.

"No, never did. Whoever was here, I think he or they are gone now."

"Then what took you so long?" she asked, exasperated that he had let her suffer over an hour of not knowing anything, and for no reason.

"I had to bury the puppy," he said solemnly. He bit down on his lip, trying to control the emotion that tore at him.

"What do we do now?"

"No real sense going back to bed. It'll be light out soon. I guess maybe you could go ahead and start breakfast."

"Breakfast? How can you possibly be hungry at a time like this?"

"I'm not. It's just something for you to do and I want things to seem as normal as possible around here when the boys wake up. I don't want them to have to know about any of what happened. I don't want to frighten them."

Christina could see the reasoning in that. "I'll go ahead and get dressed. Then I'll start breakfast. Try not to let them find out about the puppy until after they have eaten."

"Maybe we can get them a new puppy," Justin suggested hopefully, but then shook his head, for he knew it would be hard to replace Little Yabber. Glumly, he chose not to talk about it anymore. His next words were simply, "I'll get your fire started."

305

When Christina entered her bedroom, she felt disoriented and stared in confusion at all the glass. It was as if her brain refused to deal with the problem any longer. But she knew she had to be strong. She was concerned about what had happened during the night, and she had to worry about what might happen next.

Before changing out of her robe and nightdress into her regular clothing, she went downstairs for the broom and a wet, soapy rag. Quickly, she swept her bedroom floor clean of all the splintered glass, wiped the splotches of Justin's blood that trailed across the room and out into the hallway, then moved her rocking chair and set it in front of the window.

She positioned the chair so that the back of it hid the jagged hole and the tear in her lace curtain. She hoped the boys would not notice the damage right away and ask too many questions before she was emotionally strong enough to handle them. At that moment, her insides were in too much of a shambles to think up any plausible answers. Her brain felt too numb even to try.

After she swept and started to get dressed she noticed the large rock. It had slid under her bed and had come to rest against the wall. Frowning, she knelt down in just her chemise and underskirt, and retrieved the rock, intending to toss it out the window and into the yard. But when she pulled the rock out and lifted it into her hands, she noticed it had something scraped across it in black. The message was simple: "NO DEAL."


Alan's and Edward's faces when they learned their puppy had died were the most heartbreaking things Christina had ever been forced to witness. Though

306

Edward tried to handle it bravely and did not allow himself any tears when shown where his father had buried the pup, Alan wept bitterly. Justin knelt beside the trembling Alan, crumpled in front of the tiny grave, and gently took the boy into his arms and held him close. Christina did not think her heart could bear it.

Alan plastered himself against his father's chest, burying his tear-streaked face deep into his father's neck, and sobbed long and hard. Edward had to turn away and even then he was able to keep tears from finally filling his eyes. It was such a noble and determined attempt to be grown up that it only made Christina want to cry.

Edward remained behind at the gravesite while Justin carried Alan back into the house and Christina followed. Just before she closed the kitchen door behind her, she looked out toward the puppy's grave and noticed that Edward had dropped to his knees. His head was bent and his shoulders shook violently. She dearly wanted to go to him, take him into her arms and hold him against her heart until his tears finally ceased, but she knew that would only embarrass the child. He had tried so hard to remain strong, and she would not undermine his efforts. With tears in her eyes, she closed the door and went to help Justin console Alan.

Later, having learned about the message on the rock and knowing full well what those men were capable of, Justin showed Christina how to load and unload the rifle. He asked her to keep it near her at all times while he was at work, but out of the boys' sight. His sons had already suffered enough, and he did not want to add fear to their grief. He promised to check back with her several times during the day, but at the same time tried to convince her she was safe on her own. It was he they wanted, not her, and not the boys. Still, he wanted her to take every precaution.

Only minutes after she had watched Justin ride out, Christina returned to the kitchen and heard a horse ride in. She thought it was probably Justin returning, having forgotten to tell her something. Nevertheless, she hid the rifle in the folds of her wide merino skirts and stepped out onto the veranda to see who the rider might be.

To her relief, it was Todd. She let out a deep sigh and stepped back inside to place the rifle just out of sight. When she returned to the veranda, he had already dismounted and was headed toward her with a stern expression on his face and a determined glint in his eyes.

"Good day," she said cautiously, realizing his mood was deadly serious. She wondered if he had somehow learned of the attack on their house and of Little Yabber's death, but then she remembered his words of the day before and knew why he was there. He had said he would come by to get her answer to his marriage proposal, and obviously that was what he was there to do.

"Good day, Christina," he responded slowly, just as cautious as she was. There was none of the usual charm in his voice. No insolent little smile tugging at the corner of his mouth. No playful glimmer in his eye. "I'll not mince words with you. I'll get right to the question I've come to ask. Are you going to marry me or not?"

Christina fell silent while she considered what her answer should be.

"I hope your brother explained everything to you in detail," he added, in an effort to prod her from her silence.

"Aye, he did." As she looked at him, she noticed the dark red marks on his neck and remembered having been the one to put them there. She felt a brief flutter of satisfaction, but it was short-lived, for too many other emotions warred inside her.

"Then you know about his large gambling debt and how he tried to rob my safe to get the money to pay it."

"Aye, I do," she admitted and pulled her lower lip between her teeth and chewed nervously on the edge. She had to make her decision quickly, but was not yet sure what her answer should be.

Should she try again to talk some sense into the men to whom Justin owed so much money? Or should she agree to marry Todd so he would give Justin the money he needed to pay the debt and be done with it? But would it be right to do that knowing she would never be able to give Todd the children he would expect from their marriage? Did Todd really deserve to have the rest of his life ruined because of her brother's foolish blunders?

"So, are you going to send your brother to jail by refusing me, or are you going to quit being so bloody damn stubborn and agree to marry me?" His eyes were cold with anger, his face hardened with resolve.

That hateful little outburst decided it for her. Aye, Todd did indeed deserve to have his life ruined. After all, it would really be more the result of his own evil attempt to manipulate her and her brother then because of Justin's foolish mistakes. Aye, she would marry him, get Justin the money he needed, and then make the rest of this arrogant blackheart's life a living hell.

As she now saw it, he would be getting exactly what he deserved. A marriage based on his inner lusts instead of love would never bear him any true happiness. And he would be getting a wife who would never be able to bear him the sons he wanted.

No, any heirs of Todd Aylesbury would have to come from outside the marriage. Suddenly her anger turned to misery at the thought of Todd with another woman. It was suddenly very apparent that not only was she about to make his life a living hell, but she was doing the same to her own. And all because of this arrogant man's selfish manipulations and her brother's blatant stupidity.

"Well, Christina, I'm waiting. The choice is yours. Do I have Justin arrested or not?"

"Not," she finally said through tightly clenched teeth. Her chest heaved with anger, for he had finally won and she had lost. But then, in all honesty, he had lost, too. He just did not know it yet.

"Then you will marry me?" For the first time since his arrival, his face relaxed and a smile almost appeared, but then he tensed again as he looked at her suspiciously. "When? When will you marry me?"

"Whenever you say."

"The sooner the better."

Those had been Justin's exact words. Justin—who had already proven what a fool he could be.


Though Christina had not felt like facing Penelope, or anyone else for that matter with their news, she had willingly agreed that Todd should send a carriage for her and the boys that afternoon so they could make their announcement. She saw it as a way to get the three of them away from Justin's house until he could send word to the cattle thieves that all the money would be forthcoming.

Penelope had been just as ecstatic as Christina had expected and became even more delighted, although a

310

little put out, to learn the wedding would take place within a matter of weeks. Immediately, she started to make plans to have the ceremony in the main salon, hoping to get the same minister to officiate who had married Todd's parents. She named people she wanted to invite, most of whom Christina had never even heard, many from the Hawksbury District and Sydney. But because she lacked the same enthusiasm as Penelope, Christina decided to leave the planning in Penelope's hands. She felt she would be doing enough by simply being at the wedding and placing the rest of her life into Todd Aylesbury's hands.

"We'd better get the invitations posted as quickly as possible. Father will want to come. I'll need to make arrangements to get him here. Poor Millicent. Probably hasn't recovered from the last trip and now she'll have to turn around and come back. I wonder if I can catch Deen before he leaves Derrick's house. What are we going to do about your wedding gown? We need to go into town first thing in the morning to have you measured. Otherwise it will be Monday before we can do that, and every day counts."

"Slow down, slow down," Todd said with a hardy chuckle as he grasped his frantic grandmother by her slender shoulders. "You are going to make yourself sick if you don't slow down. You'll get it all done. I have faith in you. But you have got to slow down or you'll end up being put to bed because of exhaustion."

"But you said we only have until the thirteenth of March," she reminded him. "That's only twenty-two days. Now I'm not trying to mar your eagerness to be married, but twenty-two days is not a lot of time to get everything done. And some people consider the thir-

311

teenth unlucky. Can't we postpone it just one more week? Can't we make it Saturday the twentieth?"

"I'd rather move it up to the sixth," Todd told her, his eyes twinkling with mirth.

"The sixth!" both Penelope and Christina declared in unison.

"That's impossible," Penelope went on to say. "You have never been a superstitious lad, so the thirteenth should pose no problem for anyone who is not superstitious. What about you, Christina? Are you superstitious?"

Preferring the thirteenth to the sixth, Christina shook her head. "No, I've never been the superstitious sort."

"Good," Todd said with a happy nod. "The thirteenth it will be. I'll leave you two to make your plans. I promised the boys I would let the colts out into the side paddock so they could watch them exercise."

For the rest of the afternoon, Penelope made lists of whom to invite, of what to purchase while they were in town the following day, of everything she wanted the housekeeper to prepare for the guests, of how many would probably stay the night and would need a place to sleep.

Christina had quickly grown tired of all the list making and paced about the room restlessly, trying her best to keep from thinking about the future and at the same time the horrible events of the recent past.

"You certainly are a nervous little bride-to-be," Penelope pointed out as she finally laid her pencil aside. "I hope my grandson's eagerness hasn't made you too apprehensive. We'll get everything done in time. It'll be a lovely wedding. You'll see."

Christina looked at the woman's concerned face and

smiled. Her present predicament was in no way Penelope's fault. "I know. It's just that I really had not planned on everything happening so quickly." She tried not to frown or show the guilt she felt, for although what she had just said was true, she knew it was no way near to being the whole truth. What she should have said was that she had not planned on any of this happening at all.

"I know, but isn't it exciting? Just think, in a few weeks you'll be Mrs. Todd Aylesbury. Doesn't that sound wonderful?"

What it sounded was terrifying. Poor Penelope. There was no doubt in Christina's mind that the woman was already planning her great-grandchildren. Though Christina felt Todd deserved the disappointment that lay ahead, she hated the thought of what it would do to Penelope. Because of Todd's manipulations and her brother's utter foolishness, the woman would have none of the great-grandchildren she so eagerly anticipated.

"Don't be so frightened, Christina. Every bride-to-be suffers doubts at first. But as long as you love my grandson and he loves you, it'll all work out."

Christina thought about that. She did love Todd, even though he was the most irritating and exasperating man she had ever met. And he had openly claimed he loved her. If only that was all it took to make a full and happy marriage, then maybe they would have a real chance at happiness. But as soon as he discovered that she could not bear children, any happiness they might have found would be lost. Todd would come to resent her. Then where would his love be? No longer with her, that was for sure.

For a moment, she considered telling Todd the truth, or at least telling Penelope. But realized that would only

313

result in Todd's refusal to go through with the wedding, and Justin would not get the money he needed to get out of trouble. And the trouble he was in was far more serious than she had at first realized. She knew that now.

No, she had to keep in the forefront of her mind the realization that Todd did not really deserve to know her secret. He was the one who had made the decision to leap into this marriage without considering any of the problems it might create. She must remember this was what he wanted and had demanded, even though he knew she was against it. He had never even cared to ask her *why* she was so against it. He had not considered her feelings in the matter at all. Why should she now be so concerned about his?

# Chapter XVIII

The wedding plans proceeded at a frantic pace. With both Penelope and Rose eager to help, the pattern for Christina's gown was quickly selected and the material chosen from what was already on hand at the dressmaker's.

Invitations went out immediately and responses started to arrive within the week. Almost everyone Penelope had invited wrote back that they planned to attend. And as Rose was to tell Christina the first moment they had alone, her upcoming marriage to Todd Aylesbury had become the talk of the town.

"I couldn't possibly try to guess the number of people who have come into the mercantile hoping to pick up a little gossip about this marriage," Rose told her with a wry smile. "Just as soon as everyone learns that I happen to know you personally, that we are in fact very close friends, she, or sometimes even he, comes into the mercantile in pretense of wanting to shop. But those people are so curious, so full of questions about the wedding, it is obviously their real reason for coming in.

My, but we are doing a brisk business these days."

"And do you give them the gossip they want?" Christina wanted to know, almost afraid of her answer. Knowing Rose's lively nature, she might supply them with more than the truth.

"Depends on who is doing the asking and how they go about it. If they try to be too coy with their questions or if they act like they are hoping to find out that the marriage is the result of some shady doings, I tell them nothing at all. That seems to bother them more than if I try to deny anything. But if they seem genuinely curious and it looks as if they might spend a pretty penny in the process, I tell them a wondrously romantic tale of love at first sight, which seems to satisfy them quite well. And it puts them in a great frame of mind to spend their money."

"You are incorrigible," Christina laughed. "How can you sit there and tell me you are actually using our friendship to make a profit?"

"It's easy enough," Rose said, looking quite innocent. "I just open my mouth about yea wide and I say, Christina, we are making quite a tidy sum by taking such clever advantage of our friendship. I just wish the news could get around a lot faster, or that you could get married more than once. Wouldn't it be grand if you could make it an annual affair?"

"Incorrigible," was all Christina could say to that, but she couldn't help but laugh as she shook her head in disbelief.

Although the news did continue to spread like bushfire, it did not reach the wrong ears until the night before the wedding. Justin had two midnight visitors who expressed their disapproval of the marriage, and wanted Justin to prevent it before it was too late. He was reminded that until he was able to pay back all the money he owed them, he was their pawn and had better do as he was told. If he didn't, the next time they came to visit it would not be a puppy's neck that was twisted, it would be his own.

Knowing how explosively angry the two men could become, Justin did not argue with them. Instead, he openly agreed that the marriage was not exactly a match made in Heaven. He also told them that although he had already warned his sister against the marriage, he would speak with her again.

Justin knew he was lying to them, but at the moment he saw it as the best way to stall for time. He knew that after the wedding, he would get the money he needed to pay the three of them off and would be finished with them once and for all. He innocently believed he would finally be free from their clutches and could resume his life the way it had been before he had foolishly become involved in their crimes.

"Just see to it when you have that talk with your sister that you clearly point out how much Todd Aylesbury is in love with another woman."

"Another woman?" Justin repeated with a frown.

"Aye. Another woman. Whatever your sister did to trap Aylesbury into this marriage won't work because Aylesbury's in love with someone else. Make sure she understands that. And explain how, for her own good, and for the good of the baby she is probably carrying, she'd better see that the marriage never takes place," the taller of the two men told Justin as he turned away to leave. Looking back, he slapped his wide-brimmed felt hat onto the top of his shaggy blond head with a gloved hand, adjusted it at an angle with his bare hand, then stepped off the veranda.

"Randolph, I'll do what I can, but I warn you, my sister rarely listens to me," Justin said as a way of covering for himself in advance for when the marriage did indeed happen.

The man looked back and lowered his eyelids in warning. "You'd better find a way to make her listen to you this time. The boss is dead set against that marriage, and it would do you right to try to stay on the boss's good side. You are just one step away from a bullet hole as it is."

"Yeah," the other man, the older of the two, put in quickly as he, too, stepped off the veranda and adjusted his high-crowned hat. "Besides, the boss said that even if your sister is foolish enough to go ahead and force Todd Aylesbury into marriage, it's not going to last. One way or another, the boss is going to see that Aylesbury is free to marry again."

A cold wave of anticipation ran through Justin as he realized the extent of the man's threat. He believed more than ever now that William Stone had to be the boss they kept referring to. William would definitely be eager for Christina to stop the wedding because of how much his own sister wanted Todd. Vella was probably the "other woman" these two had indicated Todd was in love with, though Justin sincerely doubted Todd had ever cared that much for Vella.

Hoping to get more to go on than just his gut feeling, Justin decided to try and trick the two men into admitting the truth by pretending he already knew the third man's identity.

"Randolph, tell William I'll talk to my sister, but that if she remains determined to marry Todd, there's little

318

that can be done to stop it. She can be an awfully stubborn woman. And if they do go and get themselves married even after I try to talk her out of it, he might as well accept the fact and learn to live with it. Oh, and tell William I hope to have that money by tomorrow night. Tell him to meet me in town. I'll be staying over at the Cassowary Hotel."

"You've been warned," was all Randolph said as he swung himself up onto his saddle and gripped his reins in his gloved hand. Then, after exchanging brief glances, the two men rode off into the darkness. Justin stood alone on the veranda in only a nightshirt and a pair of hastily donned trousers, wondering if he should tell Christina about any of what the two men had said. By the time he turned to go back inside, he had decided against it.

"Christina, I truly don't understand it," Rose said with a shake of her pretty head.

"You don't understand what?" Christina asked, having let her thoughts stray for far too long, until she realized she had absolutely no idea what Rose was talking about.

"If I was about to marry someone who was as handsome as Todd Aylesbury and who was as wealthy as Todd Aylesbury, and knew I was going to get to live the rest of my life in a beautiful house like this with housekeepers and doormen to take care of all the work, I really think I could show a little more enthusiasm than that," Rose said and indicated Christina's solemn expression in the mirror.

Christina attempted a smile for her friend, but it never

quite materialized. "I'm a little nervous."

"That's understandable, but at the same time I'd think you'd show a little excitement, too. Everyone else around here is giddy and gay. What's bothering you that you haven't told me about?" Rose asked as she resumed working with Christina's hair. Then she paused with the hairbrush in midair and her gaze went directly to Christina's stomach. "You're not really . . . I mean . . . there's been gossip, but you're not really . . ."

"Expecting a child?" Christina finished for her. Though her first thought was *hardly,* she answered a simple, "No."

"Then what's bothering you?" Rose insisted. "I can't imagine anyone looking so sad on her wedding day. Don't tell me you are worried about your nephews. They will get along just fine with the new housekeeper Todd got for them."

"I know they will," Christina agreed.

"Those two boys get along with everyone. They are wonderful children. I just hope Justin does not try to get along with her too well." Rose lowered her eyes to convey her meaning. Clearly, she did not like the idea of Justin's new housekeeper being so young. Jeanne looked to be only a few years older than he was, and though rather plain, the woman was not so unappealing that she would be completely unnoticed.

Christina saw no reason to put her problems off on Rose and decided to let the conversation drift onto this new subject. "Don't tell me you are jealous of the woman. You? Why, you have twice the appeal she has."

"Then why hasn't Justin ever come by to call on me?" Rose wanted to know. "Why did he cancel our plans to go out the weekend after the Anniversary Ball? And why hasn't he been in to see me?"

"He's had a lot on his mind lately," Christina stated honestly. "But he has mentioned you on several occasions. And he has asked about your welfare many times. Rest assured, dear friend, he has not forgotten about you."

"I hope not. But even so, I'm not too fond of the whole idea of that woman living right there in the house with him and the boys. You should hear the talk that's already started."

"In this place there's always talk. Maybe you should find a way to convince him to marry you, then you could move in, too, and keep an eye on things," Christina said with a light laugh.

"If I thought I could do that, he'd have no need for a housekeeper at all," Rose said with a thoughtful twist of her mouth. "All he would need is me."

"You mean you'd put poor Jeanne out of a job, just like that?"

"And smile while doing it," Rose said with a pert nod. "After all, he would not have any need of her services at all, not if he had me for his wife."

"Wouldn't you want to have a housekeeper to help you with the daily chores?"

"Not unless she weighed at least three hundred pounds or was well over fifty years old. Neither of which Jeanne is." Rose laughed. "Besides, I think I'd like doing things for Justin myself. At least for a while."

For the next few minutes there was silence. Both women were lost in their own thoughts of marriage. Christina was in utter despair, while Rose was overcome with wistful thoughts of what it would be like to be married to Justin and be mother to his two adorable little boys.

All too soon, the time came for Christina and Todd to be married. The main salon was filled with people Christina did not recognize. She already knew Millicent Aylesbury and Todd's station boss, Coolabah Cecil, and had been introduced to Penelope's father, Oliver Cranston, the day before. Besides Rose, Penelope, and Todd, the only truly familiar faces she noticed were Justin's, who was smiling from ear to ear, eagerly anticipating the money Todd was to give him that very afternoon, and the boys', who seemed far more interested in stretching out their neckties than in their Aunt Christina's getting married.

Justin had awaited her at the hallway door and quickly linked her arm into his.

"Nervous?" he asked, needlessly, because her expression revealed she was indeed very nervous.

"Scared to death is more like it," she muttered. "How did I let you get me into this?"

Justin patted her hand reassuringly and waited until he had the signal from the minister, then proceeded to escort Christina to where Todd stood impatiently waiting. A wide assortment of flowers sat in every corner and on every flat surface of the room, but gave off little fragrance. The room smelled more of pipe tobacco and perfume.

The salon furniture had been pushed against the walls, and some of the tables had been removed entirely. There was more room for the guests to stand and witness the event and still leave an isle wide enough for Christina to walk at her brother's side. When she had entered the salon on Justin's arm, she took a quick glance about her and realized there had to be at least sixty or seventy smiling faces in the room, all anxious to witness their marriage. They obviously considered it to be a blessed and happy event. Some had even started to shed the customary tears.

It was a traditional wedding. Christina wore a gown of white cambric lawn, with a wide double ruffle around a high, curved neckline. The bodice was pleated across the front and the gown gathered at the waist. It flowed softly to the floor, the flounced overskirt edged in delicate white lace set with a fabulous sprinkling of tiny white pearls. Lightly puffed sleeves, adorned with matching lace and pearls, were gathered at the elbow, then ran fitted to the wrists. She held a beribboned bouquet of white and yellow flowers and wore a tiny white bonnet trimmed with white velvet roses and narrow silk ribbons, which had been set at a forward angle on top of her thick array of dark brown curls.

Todd wore a three-buttoned cutaway made of black satinet cassimere, well stitched kip boots, and black trousers that were not quite as snug as those he ordinarily wore. His usually thick, unruly dark brown hair had been brushed away from his face and perfectly parted to the side. He stood with his hands clasped behind his back, watching with open admiration as Christina came gracefully down the aisle to stand at his side.

The vows were quickly spoken, promises made that were to last until death should part them. And before family, friends, and the God that bound them, Christina Lapin and Todd Aylesbury were married.

After the ceremony, while all the guests clamored around the pair wishing them well, Justin's boys disappeared upstairs with lightning speed. When they came down, they were dressed in their usual moleskin trousers and crimean shirts. The other children who had come did likewise, joining Edward and Alan outside for the last few hours of daylight.

Christina watched as they disappeared outside and wished she could go with them. She did not know most of the people who thronged around her and felt uncomfortable accepting their congratulations and warm wishes for a bright and wonderful future. Especially knowing that at some point in that future, Todd was going to find out that she was not the woman he thought she was. That, in fact, she was not a whole woman at all.

Finally the wellwishers began to thin out, venturing at last into the dining room where food was set out on large silver trays and a ruby-red punch filled a huge cut glass bowl. Christina now noticed Vella Stone standing across the room, a dark-haired man who looked vaguely familiar at her side. Vella, dressed in an exceptionally lovely silk dress of emerald-green, which Christina realized was the woman's favorite color, was already staring in her direction. Pointedly.

Christina froze when her eyes met the woman's cold, direct gaze. Her first inclination was to be afraid, and her heart reacted accordingly. But she had no reason to be afraid of Vella, at least not at the moment, for surely she would not try anything in the presence of Todd's guests. As soon as Christina had convinced herself of that, she tried to appear smug and quickly scooted in closer to her new husband's side.

To Vella's dismay and Christina's delight, Todd responded by placing an arm around his new wife's shoulders and pulling her even closer. Though his attention was mostly drawn to what Coolabah and another man Christina did not know were saying about married life, he had sensed her presence and had responded.

Christina tried not to put too much meaning into the casual gesture, but she did hope that Vella had taken notice and had placed plenty of meaning on it. One quick glance in the woman's direction was all it took to let her know that she had indeed seen Todd's gesture and was not at all pleased. Her unusually large gray-green eyes had narrowed and her thin nostrils flared wide with her anger. The message of hate was so clear it sent a tiny shiver up Christina's spine, spreading into her shoulders and along her neck. The sensation grew so intense that Christina finally had to look away.

"Aye, that you are, mate. Lucky indeed," Coolabah said with such enthusiasm that it drew Christina's attention. "If only I could 'ave convinced some pretty little lass to marry me while I was still a worthy catch. I'd be a much 'appier man than I am today. And I'd be lookin' even more forward to 'avin me own place. But then again, could you imagine the world if I were to let loose sons of me own? Little Coolabahs would be runnin' around everywhere, disruptin' things wherever they went."

"What a thought," Todd laughed and slapped his friend on the shoulder. "Maybe it is just as well you never did marry. I can just see the hairy little imps now. Would probably be against nature to bring such ugly children into this world."

Coolabah threw back his head and laughed. "Aye, it might be at that. I just 'ope your children 'ave a mind to take after your wife in acquirin' their looks. Pity the child who 'as to go through life with a gob like yours."

Christina felt the same surge of guilt that had plagued

her since she had known Todd as she listened to their good-natured teasing. Todd would never have to worry about which of them their children took their looks from, because there would be no children. Fighting the empty ache that swelled deep inside her, she tried not to listen to the rest of their conversation and turned her attention to her hands, which were folded before her.

"How many children do you hope to be having?" the other man asked as he raised a glass of something amber to his mouth and took another big swallow.

"As many as we have room for," Todd laughed and absently hugged her closer to him.

"Todd." Christina finally broke into their conversation. She truly did not want to hear any more. "I am feeling a little tired. I think I'll go upstairs and rest for a little while."

Todd's jovial mood turned suddenly serious. "You aren't ill, are you?"

"No, it's just that I didn't get very much sleep last night, and if I'm to last out the night, I'd better get my rest."

Although she was referring to the dancing that was scheduled to begin after dark, the two men took it another way and began to hoot and holler and poke each other with their elbows. Embarrassed, she turned to leave, but stopped after taking only a couple of steps. Vella and her escort crossed the room and stood in front of Todd. Suddenly, she was not so eager to depart.

"Todd," Vella said, moving closer to him, "I don't know what she did to convince you to marry her, but I want you to know that if you ever need a concerned friend to talk to, someone with a caring shoulder and a

326

loving heart, I'll be there for you." Her eyes searched his face as she spoke, as if hoping to glean something from his expression that would reveal that he still cared for her.

Christina could not believe Vella had made such a brazen offer in front of Todd's friends and her own escort. Had she no pride? Christina felt her face grow crimson. She did not have the courage to look at Todd to see his reaction, but she noticed the wide-eyed look Coolabah and the other man had exchanged and how all the friendly banter had suddenly stopped.

Silence prevailed, until finally Todd spoke. "I appreciate what I think you are trying to say, and I hope that we can indeed remain friends. But when I find myself needing a concerned friend or a caring shoulder, I'll now have Christina to turn to." He reached out and pulled Christina back into the crook of his arm and held her proudly at his side.

The man at Vella's side shifted his weight from one leg to the other, drawing Christina's attention again. Clearly, he was just as unhappy about what Todd had said as Vella was. Christina could also tell by the way he spoke that he was angry. And the more she studied his solemn face, the more certain she was she had seen him somewhere before, several times, though she was certain they'd never been introduced. Yet still she was unable to place him. It was not until Todd spoke to the man directly that she finally realized who he was and why he seemed so familiar.

"Aye, William, I have indeed made my decision about the station boss's position." Todd spoke in response to what the man had just asked. "I had planned to announce

327

it later on tonight before Christina and I leave for our honeymoon trip, but I don't see why I can't tell you now."

"I hope you haven't let *her* persuade you in any way," Vella put in quickly, indicating Christina with a pert toss of her head. "I do hope you have kept hold of enough of your good sense to know that William is the better choice. He's a hard worker and far more dedicated to this station than Justin will ever be. And he's not as prone to take a drink as I hear Justin is."

"William is a hard worker, that's true, but then so is Justin," Todd replied. "And as long as a man does not do his drinking while on the job, it's none of my concern how much he puts away. And as for loyalty, I don't know which of them has the better loyalty to me, because I have no way of looking into any man's heart. But I have made my decision, and Justin will be the one to replace Coolabah. In fact, Coolabah has told me he plans to leave the day before we get back from Sydney, and Justin will already have taken over by then."

Christina was just as stunned as Vella appeared to be.

"Justin? You've chosen Justin?" Christina asked, confused. Why would Todd choose a man who had tried to rob him? The thought of Justin getting the job delighted her, but at the same time, it did not make sense.

"As if you didn't know," Vella said bitterly and lifted her nose slightly as she looked at her. "Of course, he chose Justin. Anything to keep peace with his new bride. I don't know what you have over him, my dear, but I assure you that whatever it is, it won't hold him true to you forever."

"Vel-la," Todd said in a warning tone in an attempt to interrupt her before she went too far, but she'd have none of it.

"Dear, I know Todd well enough to be able to tell you what his likes and dislikes are, and *you* are far more likely to fulfill his dislikes than his likes." Vella's hands curled into fists as she spoke.

"That's enough," Todd spoke again, only louder, and took a step forward, as if he feared Vella might resort to physical violence at any moment.

"She's only speaking the truth," William said bluntly. His face had grown so hard with anger that it looked as if his cheeks and his narrow jaw had been chiseled from granite. "You picked Justin because of her. It was a foolish thing to do. Damn foolish."

"We'll see," was all Todd said. Then he turned his attention to Christina. "I'm feeling a little tired myself. I'll walk with you to your bedroom. I think we both could use a rest."

The last thing Christina noticed before she turned to leave was Vella's piercing glare at her. She also saw Coolabah and his friend exchange knowing looks, elbowing each other silently as if they did not believe for a minute the two of them were going to Christina's bedroom to "rest."

"I'm sorry that had to happen on our wedding day, but it was only natural that William would be upset to learn I have decided to make Justin my new station boss. It is hard to blame him for his anger. He knew he had a good chance at the job and had set his hopes on it. And I'm afraid Vella was upset that I not only had decided against William for the job, but that I had also chosen to marry you instead of her." Todd's explanation came the moment they were finally alone.

"Why did you choose Justin?" she asked, pausing

outside the closed door that opened into the room she and Rose had used earlier to dress. "Was it really because of me?"

"Partly," he admitted. "I knew it would make you happy. I know how much you care for your brother. Obviously, enough to marry me despite all your earlier misgivings. But that's not the whole of it. I also have had a long talk with Justin. He's really sorry about trying to rob my safe and explained how the men he'd lost the money to had started to make threats against him and his family. His attempt to rob me was the act of a desperate man. The men seemed serious enough in their threats that he felt forced to do something drastic."

"So you've forgiven him?" Christina wanted to know.

"Aye, I have. Besides, once he has the station boss's job, he'll be making more money and will be able to pay back the money I'm lending him that much quicker. So you see I had many reasons for choosing your brother over William. Another is that lately I've started to get an eerie feeling about William. I don't know why, but I sometimes get this unexplainable feeling he's watching me, and that makes me nervous. And I sure don't need a station boss who makes me nervous. It's bad enough having a wife who makes me nervous."

"I do?" she asked. Her eyes widened with disbelief, but she found she had to fight a sudden urge to smile at the prospect.

"Nervous as hell," he admitted with a broad smile, then bent to kiss her lightly on the corner of her mouth.

A tingling wave of warmth spread through her.

"That's silly. I never set out to make you nervous," she said and the slightest hint of a smile forced itself to her lips. It felt good to know she unsettled him even a

330

little, because he certainly made her extremely anxious.

"But I've learned to live with it," he teased and bent to kiss the other side of her mouth. His gaze bored gently into hers. "I'd better leave before I do something to make you angry. You go on and get your rest while I try to find Justin. I'd like to be the one to tell him he got the job, but if I don't do it pretty quick, the news will have already reached him secondhand."

Reluctantly, Christina reached for the door. "I'll be out in a little while."

"Just be sure you are out in time to share the first dance with me," he warned her. "It's customary for the bride and groom to dance the first dance. It just wouldn't look right if we didn't."

Christina felt her insides flutter at the thought of being swept into his arms again, the arms of her new husband, and she smiled. "I'll be out in plenty of time."

They stood staring at each other for a moment, as if trying to assess each other's inner feelings, then finally Todd turned and walked back down the hallway and out of her sight.

When Christina stepped inside the room her thoughts were still on Todd's statement that she made him nervous. But she was soon brought back to her surroundings when she noticed Rose standing in the middle of the room, her eyes as wide as saucers and her face as pale as a sheet. "Rose, what is it? Who did you think I was?"

Rose's gaze darted from Christina to the corner of the room behind Christina, then quickly to the floor.

"Rose, what is the matter with you?" Christina asked, alarmed by her friend's strange behavior. Her heart felt like ice as she slowly turned to see what had captured

Rose's attention in the corner of the room. Her brother stood there, just as wide-eyed, and as pale and nervous as Rose was.

"I-I . . ." Rose started to explain, and by then had turned a lovely shade of red.

Christina's face registered shock, then confusion, then pure delight. "No need to explain anything to me, I only came in here to check my hair. I won't be but a minute."

Then without further comment, she crossed the room to the mirror and pretended to be interested in the curls on top of her head. But her eyes went beyond her reflection and caught the guilty look Rose and her brother exchanged. She also noticed that the back of Rose's hair was mussed and that Justin was not wearing his coat.

She did not know how this rendezvous had happened so quickly, for the ceremony had been only half an hour ago, and before that Rose had complained that Justin paid her no attention. Christina was delighted that the two had again found a reason and a way to be together. She wondered if the ceremony had prodded her brother into doing something about the way he felt about Rose. It had been a moving testimonial of love and commitment.

"There now, that's better," Christina said happily, though she had barely made any changes to her hair at all. As she moved away from the mirror and headed for the door, she turned to smile at them both. "I'll be out of your way now."

Just before she closed the door behind her, she winked so that Rose was able to see it, but Justin was not. It was a message of good luck and a way of letting her friend know she was clearly in support of whatever happened between the two.

The smile stayed on her lips as she made her way back into the salon, all thought of rest gone from her mind. With her room occupied and all the other rooms assigned to guests, she had nowhere to rest, anyway. And after having seen Rose and Justin together, she felt exhilarated. She now wanted to find Todd and explain how Justin would be unavailable to receive any good news for a while, but that when he was again available, she was almost certain he would not have heard anything at all about his having been chosen for the station boss's job.

"Christina, I thought you were resting," Penelope said as she came forward through the crowd to embrace her for the fifth time since the ceremony and for the dozenth time that day.

Realizing Penelope must have spoken to Todd to know she had left their guests for a short rest, she explained, "I found I just couldn't rest. My body realizes it is tired, but my brain just doesn't seem to be getting the same message. Do you happen to know where Todd is?"

"In the kitchen, I believe. After having received a few complaints, he went to see if he could catch Shirley on her next trip by here and have her concoct an additional punch with a little more bite to it. For our men guests, of course. If you hurry you might manage a moment alone with him."

The thought of having another moment alone with her new husband was as intriguing as it was frightening. Christina hurried toward the kitchen, wanting to get there before anyone else did. Secretly she hoped he would place another kiss or two upon her lips. She told herself there could be no harm in a friendly little kiss between husband and wife, especially not one exchanged in the kitchen. But then again, she knew Todd's passionate nature. If they were left totally alone for very long, the kiss might lead to something a little more intimate and far more demanding. The thought of that made her tingle all over.

She was smiling shyly at her own brazen thoughts when she entered the kitchen, eagerly searching for the only man who had ever had the power to stir her heart. But the smile quickly dropped from her face and her heart came to a sudden stop. In the middle of the well-lit room, Todd and Vella stood locked in a passionate embrace.

## Chapter XIX

Christina's first impulse was to confront the two lovers and explode in a tirade of anger, letting everyone in the house know what she had so innocently discovered. But she did not give in to such an emotional outburst. Instead she crossed her arms defiantly, cocked her head at a slight angle, and watched the proceedings closely. Eventually one of them would notice her, and because Todd was the one facing her, she expected it would be he. She was determined to approach the horrible situation with as much dignity and pride as she could muster.

"Vella, don't," she heard Todd say only moments later, and Christina brought her head upright with sudden surprise. When he lifted his hands to grasp Vella by her arms and firmly push her away from him, Christina almost did not believe her own eyes.

"Todd, please don't turn me away. I love you. You know that. And until that little trollop entered your life, you loved me, too. I know you did." Vella's voice held enough of a tremor to let Christina know she was crying.

"Don't call Christina a trollop," Todd warned in a low

voice, continuing to hold her away from him. "I'll have you know . . ."

He stopped and saw Christina watching them from just inside the doorway, wide-eyed and obviously very interested in their conversation.

"Christina! How long have you been standing there?" he wanted to know and jerked his hands away from Vella as if they had just been burned. He then placed them protectively against his chest.

Vella whirled around to face her. Tears glistened along narrow trails down her cheeks, and her eyes were slightly reddened. But in Christina's opinion the tears only served to make Vella more attractive, and she found she resented the woman for that. But she resented her far more for what she was obviously trying to do with Todd.

"I've been here for a few minutes. Why? Am I interrupting something important?"

If looks could injure, Christina knew she would have been severely wounded. Vella's eyes had narrowed and grown so intense with her hate and her resentment that Christina had the urge to take a step back. But she remained where she was, proudly facing the two of them.

"I don't know what you did to get Todd to marry you," Vella said. Her tone was venomous and her gaze dipped to Christina's abdomen. "I can only guess. But I want you to know he doesn't love you. I don't think even he sees that yet, but I know what's in his heart, and he doesn't truly love you."

"Why is it everyone thinks I did something to make Todd marry me?" Christina asked, boiling with rage, but sounding merely annoyed and frowning lightly.

"Because they know how very close he was to asking *me* to marry him," Vella answered quickly. The muscles

336

in her pretty jaw flexed with the hatred that consumed her as she took a step in Christina's direction.

"That's ridiculous," Todd put in and reached out to grab Vella by her arms again to stop her advance.

"It's not at all ridiculous, and you know it," Vella retorted. "Until she came into your life, doing whatever it was she did to lure you into her trap, you were planning to marry me. You never would have done or said all those wonderful things if you were not serious about us."

Todd looked suddenly wounded, and he brought his gaze up to meet Christina's.

"Todd, you can't possibly forget how close we came to making love right here in this very house," Vella went on to remind him. "If Gomer had not come in and interrupted us, we would have. Don't you recall how eager you were for me then?"

"But that was before I met Christina. She has changed the way I feel about everything," Todd said, and he looked at his stunned wife pleadingly, hoping she would understand.

"Todd, don't say that," Vella responded. Tears once again glistened in her large eyes. "Not even to appease a suspicious wife. Don't fill her with lies. Nothing has really changed between us. You still love me, and you still desire me, I've seen it in your face."

When Todd looked at Vella then, there was so much pity evident in his expression that Christina could easily see the truth. He might at one time have cared for Vella, but those feelings, whatever they had been, were now a part of the past. If he felt anything toward her now, it was guilt.

"Vella, I love my wife. I've tried to be patient with you, but I'm not about to let you drive a wedge between us. I want you to leave. Ask William to drive you. I don't think you are in any shape to be handling a carriage."

Vella looked proudly from Todd to Christina, then back to Todd. With her chin thrust high, she agreed, though reluctantly. "All right, I'll leave. I realize now is not the time to discuss this. You would not want any of your guests to overhear anything so scandalous on your wedding day. Go ahead. Act out your part as a loving husband for your little wife there, and for those who have come to see you married at last, but when your desire for me becomes so great that you can no longer stay away, remember that I will be willing to forgive you for your unkind remarks today." Her gaze then went back to Christina. Her eyelids lowered. "Todd, my bed will always be open to you. Always. Whenever you come to your senses, I'll be waiting to take you back."

Todd stared at Vella helplessly for a long moment. Christina sensed his anger, but also knew that he was not about to release that anger against her. When he spoke again, his teeth were firmly clenched, his lips did not move, but he pronounced the words clearly. "Vella. Leave. Now."

Vella hesitated as if she intended to say or do more, but instead she walked toward the door that led to the back veranda. As soon as she was outside, Todd walked over and peered through the window beside the door, then turned to Christina with an apologetic expression. He was unable to think of the right words to say, but his expression spoke for him.

"She doesn't take to losing any better than her brother does," Christina observed whimsically, then smiled despite the anger that still burned inside her. She had never felt such jealousy or known such relief. Suddenly it seemed almost amusing.

The tension that had been building inside Todd from the moment he discovered Christina standing in the room visibly drained from his body as he studied her face. Then he moved forward to put his arms around her and held her gently.

"Aye, she doesn't take well to losing at all," he agreed. Laughter had returned to his eyes when he bent to kiss her. "It seems I'm continuously having to apologize today."

"No, you don't." If anything, she felt she owed him an apology for having believed the worst.

"But I do want you to know how sorry I am that had to happen, especially today. I guess Vella misread my intentions, what there were of them, but I assure you, I never once considered marrying her."

He looked at Christina another thoughtful moment, as if hesitant to speak, but aware that he should. "Maybe I should have told you about how serious things almost got between us that one night. I know it's no excuse, but I'd had a little too much to drink and so had she."

"Why *should* you have told me that? That happened in the past, and whatever happened to you before you met me is really none of my concern. No more than what happened to me before I met you is any of yours."

Todd frowned and looked at her suspiciously. "Do you have secrets you are keeping from me?"

"Aye," she answered honestly, relieved at admitting the truth. Not only was she easing her conscience by being open about her secrets, she recognized a hint of jealousy in Todd's manner, and that delighted her. "And the time to worry about any secrets that I might have had was *before* you asked me to marry you, not after the vows have already been spoken."

His frown drew into a look of pure amusement. "That's a point well taken. By the way, what brought you in here at such an inopportune moment? I thought you planned to rest for a while."

"I was looking for you?"

"Oh? Can't stand being away from me for even a moment?"

"Don't flatter yourself. I just wanted to tell you where Justin was so that you wouldn't spend all your time looking for him. But then, that was before I realized you had already ended your search and had gone on to other things," she said sweetly, her expression coy.

"I have a feeling it will be a while before you let me live down the fact that you caught me in the kitchen fighting off Vella Stone," he commented with a wry twist of his mouth.

"It didn't appear you were putting up much of a fight there at the first," she put in. "I could have done a much better job of fighting off such unwanted advances, if that is what they truly were."

"And you have, my dear. You have." He nodded in full agreement. "I've never come across a more worthy opponent in all my years. You fought valiantly, right from the very start. I almost hate knowing the battle between us is over."

"Is it?" she asked with such open-eyed innocence that it made Todd frown instantly.

"Isn't it?"

"We shall soon see," she said playfully, then pulled gently away from him. "We shall soon see."

\*       \*       \*

Rose reappeared in the main salon where the furniture had also been removed and the musicians were already tuning their instruments, and it was not long before Justin also appeared. Having been told about the scene Christina had witnessed in her bedroom, Todd smiled knowingly at the way the two tried to appear casual and at how both immediately started up conversations with friends on opposite sides of the room.

Christina noticed that meticulous repairs had been made to Rose's hair. If she had not happened upon the two of them, she never would have suspected a thing. How sorely tempted she was to single Rose out, get her away from the crowd, and demand to know if her brother had kissed her and if so how many times. It was Rose's turn to blush for a change.

But the music started before Christina could think any more about taunting Rose, and Christina knew she and Todd were expected to dance the first dance alone. By the time the first dance ended, Justin and Rose had already found their way to each other's side again, and Christina knew she would never get Rose away from him now. The moment the second song began and the dance floor was open to everyone, Justin immediately whirled Rose out into the mainstream of dancers. The two remained together until the first intermission.

Christina finally had the opportunity to tease Rose a little during that first intermission, when Todd took Justin aside and asked that he follow him into his office. Christina and Rose were left alone and Christina quizzed her friend about what had gone on in the bedroom with her brother.

"Tell me, Rose, did he kiss you?" she asked straight out, the way Rose had asked her when she had first suspected there was something between her and Todd. Christina was rewarded with a lovely pink blush on Rose's fair cheeks, but was given no answer to her question. "Come on, now. You once told your aunt that you would gladly tell me if a handsome young man ever kissed you. It was the reason you gave for having such a sticky beak about what was going on between Todd and me."

"All right, all right," Rose said in a hushed voice, placing her finger against her lips to get Christina to be a little more discreet. The crimson color in her cheeks darkened. "Aye, he kissed me."

"What a thing to blush about," Christina teased, using the exact words Rose had used on her. How she enjoyed being able to turn the tables on Rose for a change! She went on to ask, "And did you play coy?"

"Not too," Rose admitted with a huge grin. "I guess it did not occur to me."

"Then tell me, is my brother a good kisser?" she prodded even further and laughed at Rose's look of utter exasperation.

"Your brother is certainly right about you," Rose said after a lengthy pause. "You ask too many questions."

"And you don't seem too eager to answer any of them," Christina laughed, then hugged her friend.

Meanwhile Todd and Justin slipped into his office unnoticed. Todd extracted the money from his safe, counted it out, and handed the proper amount to Justin. While Justin tucked the money away into his coat pocket, Todd finally announced that he had made his choice for the station boss's position.

"I imagine William is very happy about that. You'd think he would have stayed to hear all the congratulations," Justin said in response. Suspecting that William was the leader of the three men he owed the money to, he kept a keen eye on the man and had noticed that William had disappeared shortly after the ceremony. Now he thought that strange. If the announcement had been made about his new job, Justin would have expected the man to stay and bask in the glory.

"No, actually William is still very angry with me," Todd said as he double checked his safe. "He was not at all pleased to learn that I had chosen you."

It took a few seconds for Todd's words to register. When they did, Justin's eyes grew wide and his mouth gaped open with disbelief. "Me? After what I did?"

"Aye, you. And after what you did. It's my way of showing you that I believe you never would have tried to rob me if you had not been in such a desperate situation. I want you to know I still trust you. After all, you are my wife's brother. We are family now."

"And you won't be sorry you put your trust in me, either, Todd. I promise you that. And like I already told you, I intend to pay you back every penny of this money," Justin said and patted the thick wad of bills hidden inside his coat pocket.

"I know you will," Todd said, with no qualms.

"And I also want you to know, I've given up gambling. I haven't been in a single card game since all that happened," Justin told him earnestly. But then, when had he had the time? He had been too busy trying to impress Todd and trying to keep those men off his back to take time out for a casual card game.

"I hope you see now how foolish gambling can be, especially if you don't have the money to lose in the first place," Todd said and watched Justin closely for his reaction. He was pleased to see only remorse on the man's face.

"I was a fool. I don't know why I let myself get into them for so much, but I'm not going to let anything like that happen again."

"See that you don't, because I won't be so willing to pay off a second gambling debt," Todd warned him, then decided they had dwelled on the subject long enough. "So tell me, now that you will have many of your Sundays free, are you planning on spending any of that time courting your sister's friend, Rose Beene?"

Justin's gaze dropped, but slowly lifted to meet Todd's. "Aye, I was thinkin' I might."

"Pretty lass, that one," Todd commented as he moved toward the door. "Who knows? Maybe the next wedding you attend will be your own."

Justin remained behind to think over everything that had just been said. He was overjoyed at the thought of being made the station boss, especially after everything he had done wrong. And he was filled with an intense sense of wonder to discover he was in love again and that Rose claimed to love him in return. With everything going his way at last, maybe he could hope to get back on his feet and eventually ask her to marry him. He wondered what her reaction would be to a marriage proposal, then laughed out loud when he considered she might say yes. He was still grinning when he rejoined the others in the main salon.

Although most of the people in the room attributed his jovial mood to his sister's marriage and his new position as station boss, Justin knew it stemmed mostly from the prospect of asking Rose to marry him. He wondered how long he should court her before proposing.

Though Todd and Christina would arrive in Bathurst after midnight, they waited until almost ten o'clock before bidding everyone a final farewell. Their things had been loaded into the carriage earlier in the day, so when the time came to leave, they changed into their traveling clothes, made their final farewells, and left.

Christina had not rested during the day and had had a sleepless night, so twenty minutes into their ride she nodded sleepily at Todd's side. When they arrived at the Duchess Hotel, she was nestled in the warm curve of Todd's arm, her cheek pressed against his chest, pleased that he had again held her while she slept. Again he had put her comfort before his own. Though she did not move away from him to inspect her appearance, she was aware her hair had come undone, or else Todd had released it from its pins, because it now fell softly about her shoulders.

"Come, Mrs. Aylesbury," Todd whispered into her ear. "Our room awaits."

She was too comfortable to want to move. Instead, she snuggled closer.

"Shall I carry you?" he offered eagerly.

She shook her head and reluctantly pulled away from his warmth. "No, I can walk."

She became aware of the grinning doorman who waited at the side of their carriage.

"I don't mind carrying you," Todd said in earnest.

Though she tried not to look at the grinning doorman, she found it hard not to. She caught her eyes returning to the man again and again as she eased herself to the side of the carriage and allowed him to help her down. She was tempted to ask him what it was he found so amusing, but was too afraid of the answer.

No sooner had her feet touched the ground than Todd was again beside her and the two of them were promptly led into the two-story brick building by the still grinning doorman.

"Mr. Holtermann, the newly-marrieds have finally arrived," he announced to the thin, balding man behind the desk. "Should I show them on to their rooms?"

Christina was relieved to hear the word rooms. There was to be more than one. Evidently Todd had sensed her reluctance and had requested separate accommodations. It was something she truly had not expected, but was very grateful for. She would be afforded privacy this first night.

"Yes, Pete, here's the key. I'll see if I can rouse Jack and have him carry their baggage up," the desk clerk said, holding out a single key for the doorman, who obviously doubled as the courtesy boy at this late hour.

*Key? Only one key?* Christina wondered. Why would one key fit two doors? Suddenly she wondered about the safety of such a place if the same key fit more than one door, and she was glad they would be there for only one night.

Still groggy with sleep, Christina followed the doorman up the stairs and down the short hall to a dark brown wooden door that was wider than the rest. She noticed it had no number on it while she waited sleepily to be let in.

"I'll do that," Todd offered as the man bent to fit the key into the lock. "You go back downstairs and help with the baggage. It's late. The sooner we can get settled in, the better."

"Aye, will do," the man said with a knowing wink, and for lack of a hat, tugged on the front hank of his hair in salute. He left the key in the lock and hurried down the

346

hall, chuckling lightly to himself.

Todd held back a chuckle as he reached for the key, turned it until he felt the lock give, then twisted the knob. Once he had the door open, he stepped aside and allowed Christina to enter first.

"I hope it meets with your approval," he said as she walked into the already lit room.

"It's lovely," she remarked in honest admiration, for the room far surpassed any she had ever stayed in and met with her approval in every way—except for one strange fact. There was no bed in this room, only the stylish rococo parlor suite and an elaborately ornate fireplace. Where was she to sleep, on the sofa? Although it was a large sofa, it hardly looked comfortable enough to sleep on.

"Then you like it?" Todd asked as he followed her inside and closed the door.

What was there not to like? It was a beautiful room. The walls were made of smooth pink stucco, with dark wooden baseboards and doors. The furniture was mahogany, and the tufted fabric a lovely shade of dark rose. The ceramic appointments about the room were accented in different hues of rose and pink, as was the fringed carpet in the center of the room that covered much of the brightly polished wooden floors. Even the curving glass globes on the gaslights had a rose tint to them, making the color scheme complete.

"Aye, Todd, I like the room," she assured him, sitting down on the sofa to see just how comfortable it was. She frowned. Although it was fine for sitting, it left a lot to be desired as a bed. Her next thought concerned her covers. What would she use?

"Aren't you curious to see our bedroom?" Todd asked.

"Our?" She felt a slow, sinking feeling in the pit of her stomach. "Bedroom?"

"Aye," he looked at her curiously. "Where'd you think we were going to sleep? Here on the floor?"

She was not about to admit she had considered the sofa and slowly stood to follow him to a narrow door across the room. "Our bedroom." That meant he intended to share it with her. But then, she had expected as much; after all, they were husband and wife now. And if he planned to demand his husbandly rights, she no longer had any reason to deny him.

She was startled to discover that her heart had taken wing and now flew wildly about inside of her. Although it still scared her that she knew so little about such things, she was not at all appalled by the idea. As a matter of fact, she almost looked forward to it. Almost. At any rate, she clearly did not dread it the way she had expected to.

When Christina reached the bedroom door and looked inside, she wanted *not* to notice the bed, but that was the first thing she saw—even before she realized this smaller room was as blue as the other room was pink. Entering the room, her eyes lingered on the bed. It had to be the largest bed she had ever seen, wider than it was long, with shiny brass arches at either end and a blue netting canopy overhead. She estimated it could easily sleep three to four people and realized that would mean more space between them during the night. But was that what she really wanted? She frowned.

"You are not pleased," Todd said, disappointed. He had seen the frown and misread the reason for it. "The room is not what you expected."

"No, it's a lovely room," she told him quickly.

"Then what?"

"Nothing. I'm just surprised by all this grandeur. I've never stayed in a room so beautiful."

She hoped that would appease him, because she did not want to tell him about everything else she was feeling inside. She did not want him to know that she hoped he would demand his husbandly rights, that she was suddenly eager to finish what they had started so many times in the past. Now that they were husband and wife, there was no longer a reason to be afraid. Or was there? She had never been so confused about what she wanted in all her life.

The knock at the door took Todd's attention away from her temporarily, and he left the room to let the men in with their armloads of baggage. Though they would only be needing one change of clothes, he had decided to have it all brought up to their room. He wanted to be certain he could get his hands on it early the following morning. They were due to board the first coach, which was scheduled to leave at eight o'clock, and could not afford any delays in getting their baggage transferred to the station.

While Todd attended to the baggage and saw to it the men were properly rewarded for their promptness, Christina was drawn to the bed and walked over to stand beside it. Mesmerized more by the thought of what might happen there than by the beautiful velvet cover, she bent forward and stroked the surface lightly. When Todd returned, he found her standing there, staring down at the pale blue cover, her brown eyes wide and the edge of her lower lip drawn between her teeth. Understanding her apprehension, he went to her and put his arms around her.

"Christina, I won't force you to do anything you are

not ready to do," he promised, his voice falling gently against her ear. "I want whatever happens between us to come naturally. If you have doubts, just voice them. Nothing will happen until you are ready."

Christina looked up at him with tears in her eyes. How could a man who was as exasperating and as conniving as Todd say something so sweet, so terribly understanding, and sound as though he meant every word? It was almost as if he were two people. Though she was extremely cautious about that other Todd Aylesbury, the one who had eagerly forced her to marry him even though he knew she was against it, she truly loved *this* Todd Aylesbury—a man of such tenderness, of such candid concern that it made her want to cry.

"Todd, why were you so determined to make me marry you?" she asked, surprised she had asked the question that was uppermost in her mind.

"I've told you. Because I love you," he answered, then bent to kiss her lightly. "And because I fully believe that one day you are going to love me, too."

She wondered if she should tell him that she loved him already, or at least a part of him. She loved the Todd she saw before her now. A man of tenderness. A man who claimed to love her. But even though she knew such words were what he wanted to hear, she decided against it. She would wait until she had grown to love the other Todd Aylesbury, as well, if she ever could.

"I'll bring in your valise now and let you get ready for bed. We have a long trip ahead of us," he finally said. Slowly, he brought his arms away from her, then moved toward the door. "I'll get dressed in there."

When he returned only seconds later, he had her valise. He set it on a small table near the bed. Then, as he had promised, he left the room so she could get undressed in private. Grateful for that, she hurriedly opened her valise to take out her white cotton night dress and was surprised to discover it was not there.

She was even more surprised to find that it had been mysteriously replaced by a shocking garment made of black moire silk, with wide strips of black lace set into the side seams of the garment, which would no doubt allow tiny sprinklings of her bare skin to show through.

Her first thought was to blame Todd for the switch in her night garments, and she was angry with him. But then she knew where the blame should really lie. Todd would have had little opportunity to make such a switch. It had to have been Rose. That was why her friend had been so eager to see that her baggage was loaded early.

As she lifted the night dress out of the valise and studied it more carefully, she found that the lace also crossed the front in several carefully thought-out places, and she had no doubt that a man had designed it. She could feel the blood rising in her cheeks and would very happily have strangled her friend. What was Todd going to think if he was to return and find her in such a garment? Clearly what Rose expected him to think.

Christina considered having Todd bring in the rest of her baggage so that she could dig out one of her other gowns. But she was not too sure that Rose had not replaced them all with such outlandish garments and did not care for the thought of spending most of the night unpacking and then repacking her clothing.

Knowing she would feel ridiculous sleeping in her street clothes or even in her undergarments, she had little choice in the matter. After only a moment more, she finished undressing, then slipped the garment over her head and let it fall softly down around her curves. Though it had silk-covered buttons that ran along the opening in the front, the gown had been cut full enough not to have to use them.

At first she avoided looking down at the way the garment clung to her every curve and parted slightly between the buttons to reveal tiny slivers of her bare skin. But her natural curiosity drew her to the large gilt mirror on the far wall. One peek was all it took to put the blush back into her cheeks and send her hand flying to cover her gaping mouth. That was how Todd found her when he reentered the room.

# Chapter XX

"I-I . . ." It was the only sound Christina's throat could produce when she first noticed Todd had returned. She was too embarrassed by what she had on to realize that he, too, wore black.

"You are beautiful," he said with open admiration. "Absolutely beautiful."

"But I-I . . . I didn't . . ." She gestured helplessly to the shimmering black gown that clung to her every curve, revealing not only the tiny glimpses of ivory skin through the delicate design of the lace and the narrow opening between her breasts, but her glorious shape, as well.

"I know, neither did I," he said, and laughed as he looked down at the silken nightshirt that he wore. "Appears as if someone tampered with our things. Someone who wanted to have a strong hand in helping us pack for this trip. I clearly suspect Grandmum had something to do with this. Maybe I should have locked my valise as soon as I put my things in it."

Christina was relieved to know he had been duped, too,

and laughed with him. "I think Rose can take part of the blame. As I recall, she followed my baggage outside to make certain it was loaded properly and was gone for quite some time."

"Whoever the culprits are, they certainly do seem partial to black, don't they? What shall we do to get back at them?" he wondered aloud. When he looked at Christina again and saw how beautiful she was in that gown, all thought of retaliation left him. Instead, his next thought was what he could do to show his true appreciation.

Seeing that the laughter had suddenly left his eyes, replaced now by that same dark glimmer of passion she had seen there so many times before, Christina knew he would kiss her. Her heart jumped wildly to her throat when he slowly came toward her. It did not jump because of fear, but because of nervous, yet eager anticipation.

While he slowly continued to close the distance between them, she felt her heartbeat grow ever stronger, until her pulses throbbed with an alarming intensity. She knew she could stop him with mere words if she wanted to. He had claimed he would do nothing against her will. Yet she did not speak. She waited with her arms hanging awkwardly at her sides and turned her face upward to meet his.

When his mouth lowered to take that first kiss, her lips parted and her arms slowly lifted to accept him willingly. Overwhelmed by a sudden need to be close to each other, their bodies met in a hungry embrace. Both knew then that this time, neither would try to pull away, because there was no longer any reason to.

When he brought his lips free of hers, he murmured gentle words of love, words that cascaded joyously against Christina's ears and caused her pulses to race harder and her heart to pound even more briskly beneath her breast.

"Sweet, sweet Christina, I love you more than I have ever loved anyone before," he said in a low, golden voice.

Christina was not ready to proclaim her feelings for him and responded by leaning forward and luring his lips to hers once again. It was enchanting to hear such words of love from him, but words were no longer what she wanted most. At that moment all she wanted was to feel his embrace about her, to explore that wondrous magic of his kiss. To find out at last what it was she had so long denied herself.

As in the past, Todd's tongue dipped lightly past her parted lips to tease gently the sensitive inner edges of her mouth, going deeper and deeper, until she could not help but do the same to him. She savored the tantalizing taste she discovered when she allowed her tongue to follow his and enter his mouth.

It was like nothing she had ever experienced—to explore such intimate recesses and feel his lightly shuddering response made her want to discover more about him. She brought her mouth harder against his, dipped her tongue deeper, and pressed her body closer, all the while wishing she could find a way to bring them closer still.

Todd realized the passions in Christina were fully ignited and now raged deep within her. He knew that he could take her then and that she would let him, but he chose to proceed very slowly. He let his lips linger on her sweetly demanding mouth while he eased his hands down the curve of her back and around to her rib cage. He was well aware that her breathing became more labored with

355

each touch, and it delighted him that he created such a response in her. There was a beautiful sense of accomplishment in knowing he was capable of giving her such true and basic pleasure. He held back his own response while he worked to bring her to one new height of arousal after another.

Unhurriedly, he moved his hand upward along the smooth surface of her gown, until at last he was able to feel the soft undercurve of her breast. He cupped his fingers around the precious find, then gently played with the tip through the thin fabric until he felt it grow rigid. He chose to wait before undoing the four buttons that ran between her breasts. Instead, he allowed his hand to continue its hungry prowl on the outside of the silken gown—ever seeking, ever searching, but never quite finding.

Christina became lost in the deep, swirling torrent of emotions that Todd had stirred to life inside her. Liquid fire coursed through her veins as her arousal spiraled ever higher, quickly possessing her entire being.

Every part of her yearned for more. Why did he not try to remove her burdensome gown? Why didn't he attempt to free her breasts so he could touch them in the way he had those times before? Unable to bear the rapacious flames that burned deep to the very core of her, she considered removing the garment herself, but could not seem to find the courage to do it.

Finally, Todd began to work with the buttons. His fingers dipped inside the garment and brushed against the swelling curves of her breasts, which sent even more of the delicious waves of pure ecstasy and eager anticipation through her body.

She closed her eyes and trembled with expectation

when he stepped back just enough to slip the opened garment over her shoulders. He allowed himself a leisurely view of her thrusting breasts as he eased the silken fabric down until at last it fell to the floor in a black, shimmering heap. She was as exquisite as he had remembered, and he stood staring at her quivering beauty a long moment more before he gathered her into his arms.

As he carried her the short distance to the bed, his eyes grew darker with desire. His lips sought hers once more before he gently lowered her onto the soft mattress. Then he stood again and stared at her, watching her breasts heave with each labored breath she took.

Her eyes drifted partially open and she looked at him expectantly. Slowly, he raised his night shirt over his head in one lithe movement, revealing his splendid body to her. When he moved toward the bed again, he was breathtakingly naked, and she felt no desire to look away. She lifted her arms to receive him—her husband.

Lying on the bed just to one side of her, he bent over and claimed her lips once more and gently let his hand slide over her bare skin, eagerly exploring every curve. It took more and more effort for him to put her pleasure before his needs, especially knowing he could take her at any moment and find complete fulfillment.

As if to torment her, Todd's fingertips teased and taunted, coming closer to the sensitive peaks of her breasts in slow, circular motions. Unable to bear the gentle torture, Christina arched her back and thrust her breasts higher, wishing frantically that his hands would hurry and reach their destination.

When he broke off the kiss to gaze down at her writhing form, Christina moaned. How could he bring her to such a state of madness and not fulfill her needs? She moaned again and reached out to bring his mouth back to hers.

Todd obliged her with another long, plundering kiss, but then brought his lips away again, only this time to trail feathery kisses downward until he finally reached one of her heaving breasts. Deftly, his tongue teased the hardened tip with short, tantalizing strokes, nipping and suckling until she cried aloud with pleasure. Then when she thought she could bear no more, he moved to her other breast. Again he brought a cry of ecstasy from her lips.

Christina was not certain how long she could endure the tender torment, and grasped his shoulders to make him stop his delicate torture and bring her the release she so desperately wanted. But his mouth continued its assault and she shuddered from the delectable sensations building inside her, until she was certain she would burst. A delicious ache centered low in her abdomen, and her body craved release from the sensual anguish that burned within her.

"Todd," she called, only vaguely aware she had spoken aloud.

Todd suckled first one breast, then the other, one last time before moving to fulfill her. Carefully, he eased through the barrier that proved he was her first lover, and with smooth, lithe movements, brought their wildest longings, their deepest needs to the ultimate height. When release came for Christina it was so wondrous and so deeply shattering that she gasped aloud with pleasure. Only a moment later, the same shuddering release came for Todd.

Once their passions had been fully spent, the bonds of

marriage made complete, they lay perfectly still, listening to the steady rhythm of each other's heartbeats, bound together in each other's arms. Slowly they sank into the warm depths of satisfaction. Both were in awe of what had happened between them, for it was like no other experience in their lives. There was nothing that even closely compared.

Settling contentedly at his side, Christina marveled that this exquisite man was her husband. Such happiness was to be hers forever. She refused to let any other thoughts enter her mind, refused to worry about what would happen once he learned she could not have children, refused to wonder if he would then accept Vella's offer and thus be given the children he wanted. For the moment, all she wanted was to bask in the warm aftermath of their wondrous lovemaking and enjoy the feel of her husband at her side. For the very first time in Christina's life, she felt blessed, truly blessed, and she did not want to consider that it might not last.

Christina usually awoke groggy, especially when she was unable to get a full night's sleep. But that next morning she woke with such feelings of wonder and exhilaration that she came very close to singing out loud as she quickly dressed. They planned to have breakfast before catching the eight o'clock coach for Lithgow. At Lithgow, they would board a train Todd claimed would take them to Sydney in a fourth of the time the coach took.

It amazed Christina, and frightened her a little, to think they could reach the coast within two days. And when the railway link between Lithgow and Bathurst was finally completed, which would be any month now, they would be able to make a trip into Sydney within a day's time. Traveling at such a rate of speed was enough to make anyone nervous, and Christina was in no hurry to reach Lithgow.

When the time arrived for them to board the huge metal monster that sat vibrating in the brightly painted train station in Lithgow, Christina understood why Coolabah preferred to travel by coach. The roaring noise of the stopped train was deafening. She could imagine what it would be like when the thing started to move. She hoped it would not be so loud that it would burst her ears, or move so quickly that she would ride the entire distance frozen with fear.

Todd did what he could to reassure her. "Christina, traveling by train is just as safe as traveling by coach. Maybe even more so, since the wheels on a train rarely collapse or break from wear, and the engineer does not have to try to pick his way along a rutted and washed-out track."

"But if something went wrong while a train was traveling at its highest speed and it crashed, surely it would mean the death of us all," she insisted, not willing to be lured into a feeling of false security.

Even after she was inside the sturdy metal car, seated alongside Todd on one of the bench seats nearest the center, and the thing had chugged and clanked and lurched and panted until it was well on its way without as much as a single incident, Christina did not relax. She kept her eye on the tiny window at her side and her ear keenly tuned to the constant clatter of the wheels on the metal tracks in order to detect any variation of speed.

Every time the whistle shrieked, she jumped, and if

they hit a particularly rough stretch of track, she reached for Todd's hand and held it tight. She thought of little else than what could go wrong and discovered how truly vivid her imagination was.

An eternity later, they arrived in Sydney safe and sound, as Todd had promised, though Christina was unable to convince her legs that all danger had indeed passed. When she first stepped off the train onto the solid platform, her knees were a little wobbly. And after they had settled into the carriage that was to take them to the hotel, she still felt the vibration of the train beneath her.

Since Todd's announcement about a honeymoon, he had been evasive about the exact place where he planned for them to stay. When the driver of the hired carriage asked where to go, Todd leaned forward and whispered their destination in the man's ear without Christina being able to hear.

"Why do you feel you must keep where we are going a secret?" she asked when he settled in beside her.

"Because I want it to be a surprise," he said, and smiled at the thought of her reaction when she saw the place he had chosen. "Don't you like surprises?"

"I'm not sure," she said with a raised brow, but did not pursue the matter further. She was certain it would be only a short time until she saw the place for herself.

Even if he did tell her the name of the hotel, she knew very little about the city and would not really know what to expect anyway, so she fell silent. She watched the many buildings and parks they passed as they made their way through the busiest part of town, headed in the direction of the bay, toward the docks. She began to wonder if he planned for them to board a ship, and if so, where they would go. He had told Justin they would return within a week, hardly time to go anywhere by ship.

The further they drove toward the docks, the more her suspicions turned in another direction. The shops and hotels they passed were vaguely familiar, then very familiar, until finally they came to a stop in front of the very same hotel she had stayed in on her first night in Australia. His wanting to bring her back to the place they had first met touched her heart, and tears glistened in the corners of her eyes.

"So are you surprised?" he asked as he helped her down by grasping her around her waist and lifting her out of the carriage.

"Aye, I am," she admitted, and smiled warmly when he set her down in front of him. "Very surprised."

"Pleasantly so?"

"Aye, pleasantly so." Her smile grew.

"Wait until you see which room I have asked for," he said, and laughed when her eyes widened. "Aye, the very same room. Only this time I have requested that a lock be placed on the window. You never know what sort of riffraff will come stealing into your hotel room through a window. It's best to take precautions."

She wanted to stamp his foot for teasing her, but instead laughed and went eagerly with him to see if, indeed, they were going to get the same room.

The days in Sydney were joyous. They spent their time getting to know each other and finding out the many things they had in common. They went to the cricket matches one afternoon and sailing on a small schooner the next. They picnicked along the cliffs outside the city and also visited the finest restaurants Sydney had to offer. But no matter what they found to do or how much energy they spent doing it, they never returned to the hotel too exhausted to further explore the pleasures they could bring each other.

Though she tried not to dwell on such thoughts, Christina suffered occasional bouts of guilt and unmeasurable anguish whenever she thought how short-lived their happiness would be after he discovered she could not be a complete wife to him. She wanted to enjoy the time they had together, to enjoy the happiness while it lasted, and refused as best she could to consider the inevitable.

But the feelings of guilt persisted, until she knew that she would have to tell him. Even if it meant ending her happiness and possibly their marriage, he deserved to know the truth. Justin now had the money, and more than enough time had passed for him to have paid it to those men. She really had no other excuse not to tell Todd the truth.

On the last night of their stay in Sydney she finally got the courage to confess her secret. Her guilt had become unbearable, and his little innuendos about the children he hoped they were creating became too hard to bear.

"Todd, I have to tell you something," she said quietly. They had just made love for the second time that night, and he now lay with his head on her breast. She wondered if he could hear her heart breaking beneath his ear.

"What is it?" he said groggily. Sated and utterly content, he had begun to drift off to sleep.

"It is something you are going to hate me for. It is the reason I was so reluctant to marry you."

Todd sat up and looked at her, his expression suddenly fearful. "What is it?"

"You remember Justin telling you how I was in an accident just before I came to Australia?" she began.

"Aye." His expression grew even grimmer. "He said a horse had trampled you and that you were lucky to be alive."

"I don't know if I'm so lucky or not." Her emotions tightened her throat until her voice grew almost too raspy to hear. "I may be about to lose the only real happiness I have ever known."

"Christina, what is it?"

Through the blur of tears, Christina looked at him and admired his masculine form and his handsome face, hoping to commit every little detail about him to her memory, because after tonight she might not have the opportunity to be this close to him again.

"Christina?" he encouraged her once more.

"I know I should have told you when you first mentioned marriage, but you have to realize that I had Justin to consider. He needed that money desperately, and the only way he could get it was if I married you."

Todd's face grew hard and he looked away. "What you are trying to say is that you don't love me enough to stay married. Now that Justin has his money and has had the time to get it to whomever he owed, you feel safe in finally letting me know. But if that's true, why all the farce? Why pretend the way you have these past few days?"

"No, Todd, that's not it at all."

"Then what?" He looked back at her and waited for her answer.

"The accident did a lot of damage inside of me. The doctors said that as a result I would probably never bear children. And even if I should become pregnant, as mangled as my insides are, I would not carry the baby long enough to matter. I can never give you the children you want."

Todd stared at her. The muscles along the side of his jaw flexed as he brought up his hand and covered his mouth, as if hoping to hide the fact that he had been so hurt.

"I'm sorry, Todd. I know I should have told you, but I couldn't. Justin had to have that money."

When Todd refused to speak and his hand tightened over his mouth until his fingers pressed deep into his face, she clutched the covers to her and wept. She had hurt him and she had not wanted to. Seeing his pain now was like driving a knife through her own heart. "I'm sorry. I really am. And I won't fight you if you want to have this marriage annulled or if you seek a divorce, or whatever it is you have to do to be rid of me."

She turned and buried her face into her pillow. Her shoulders shook from the force of the emotions that tore through her.

"Christina, don't," Todd said. His voice was low and gentle when he finally spoke. Slowly, he reached out and pulled her to him. "I don't want to end our marriage. I love you too much. True, I had hoped to have children, but mostly as a way of becoming closer to you. I don't want them so much that I'd be willing to share my life with someone else, someone who might be able to give them to me. Christina, just because you can't have children doesn't mean I am going to love you any less. My love is not based on what you can and cannot give me."

Christina pressed herself against him and cried. He had meant every word he said. He was not going to put her out of his life. She only hoped that in time he did not come to realize all that he was missing by not having children and change his mind.

\*　　　\*　　　\*

365

By the time Todd and Christina returned to Bathurst, Christina was looking forward to settling into Todd's house. Justin had promised that her things would be taken to Todd's house while they were in Sydney. By her own request, everything was supposed to be waiting for her to unpack when she returned, and she could hardly wait.

Originally, Todd had offered her her own bedroom, but to her delight, the offer had been withdrawn on their second day in Sydney. She was to move into Todd's bedroom. It would seem silly for her not to, for they had truly become husband and wife and wanted to share the same bed.

"I wonder how Justin is adapting to his new job," Todd said as the coach rolled to a stop in front of the station. He waited for the dust to settle before reaching for the door.

"We shall see. Since he is supposed to be the one waiting for us with the carriage, we should find out soon enough," Christina remarked as she lifted her handbag from her lap and looped the drawstring securely around her wrist in preparation to disembark.

"Aye, unless, of course, he got sidetracked somehow by a pretty little dark-eyed brunette who happens to work at one of the local mercantiles," he said, his eyes twinkling.

"I suspect they both will be waiting for us," Christina said with a slight laugh. "Rose will be too eager to find out how everything went to be able to stay away."

Todd laughed, too, nodding that he thoroughly agreed, for Rose had the curiosity of a young koala. When they stepped out of the coach into the bright sunlight, they both glanced around, looking as much for Rose as for Justin.

"I wonder where they are?" Christina frowned when she did not see either of them among the small throng of people who had gathered to meet the coach.

Todd reached inside his vest pocket and pulled out his watch. "We are almost a half hour early. It may be a while yet."

As he snapped the watch closed and slipped it back into his pocket, he glanced around again, then frowned when he noticed a man coming out of the office and headed their way. "There's Coolabah. What's he doing here? He's supposed to be on his way to his own station by now."

Christina turned to find the tall, burly man among the others and watched with growing concern as he came closer. The way he walked and his expression made her strongly apprehensive. Something had gone wrong at the station. Her first thought was that the cattle duffers had struck again.

"What is it?" Todd asked as soon as Coolabah was close enough to hear. He had come to the same conclusion as Christina. "What's happened?"

Coolabah's gaze darted to Christina, then rested on Todd. He passed a hand over his bushy beard, then ran his tongue across his lower lip. "I'm afraid I got real bad news for you two."

"Grandmum?" Todd asked fearfully. Coolabah's stern expression was deadly serious.

"No. It's Justin."

"Justin?" Christina and Todd responded.

"Aye. Seems 'e's disappeared."

# Chapter XXI

"Disappeared?"

"Aye. The same night you two left. Justin escorted Christina's friend, Miss Beene, back to town, and then never came back. I already talked to 'er about it. The last she saw of 'im, 'e was 'eaded to the Wattle Bud Tavern for a quick drink before 'eading back 'ome."

Coolabah paused and ran a hand over his bushy beard as if reluctant to go on. "Only 'e may 'ave never made it back 'ome. That next day when 'e did not show for work, your grandmum and me went to check on 'im. We figured 'e just got mixed up and thought because you told 'im 'e was to be the new station boss, 'e figured 'e was to 'ave that Sunday free. But 'e wasn't there at 'is 'ouse, either. We found the bed unmade, as if 'e 'ad slept in it, but we 'ave no way of knowin' if that was from the night before or after the weddin'. But wot really scares us is that we found a window broke out in one of the upstairs bedrooms."

"Where are my nephews?" Christina was almost certain he would tell her they were still at Todd's house, but she needed to be reassured.

"With Todd's grandmum. The way Justin just up and disappeared like that, we didn't dare take them back 'ome," Coolabah explained. "Especially not after findin' that window broke out."

"What about his new housekeeper, Jeanne? She was supposed to come that next morning to start taking care of the boys."

"Todd's grandmum told 'er she could go on back home until Justin returned and sent for 'er. Miz Penelope did not think it wise for the lass to be a-stayin' there, either. It's the broke window that 'as us worried. I've been out askin' questions and tryin' to find out just wot might 'ave 'appened to 'im, but no one seems to 'ave seen Justin since 'e was at the Wattle Bud. And though some of them remember 'avin seen 'im sit in on a card game for a little while, no one I questioned seems to remember seein' 'im actually leave. It's as if 'e vanished right from inside the tavern. And no one 'as any clue as to why. And the broke window is a real mystery."

Christina felt her legs grow rapidly weak. She reached for Todd's arm to steady herself. "Not to me. I know about the window, and I might know other things that could help. Justin was in a lot more trouble than either of you ever knew."

"Trouble?" Coolabah asked, clearly unaware there had been any trouble at all.

"What kind of trouble?" Todd wanted specifics, then seeing that Christina was ready to crumble, he put his arm around her and led her to a bench outside the station office. "Does it have to do with that gambling debt?"

"That's where it began," she told him. The time had come for Todd to know everything, even the part about

370

Justin helping to duff Todd's cattle.

When she finished her long tale by explaining to him about the incident that had resulted in the broken window and Little Yabber's death, Todd's face reflected the mixture of emotions inside him.

"Todd, he was a victim of circumstances. True, he never should have gambled money he did not have, but once he had, he was trapped. He had to help them steal and sell your cattle or face their vengeance. They are ruthless men. Then after he had foolishly gambled away the money he got from the sale of the cattle, they threatened to kill him on the spot." She covered her mouth with a trembling hand. They might have killed Justin because he had taken so long in finally getting the money to them.

"Did he tell you who the men were?"

"No, he was afraid to," she admitted, but frantically tried to remember if there had been any useful clues to the men's identities. "Wait, I think I might know the first names of two of them. That night they attacked the house, Justin called out the names of the two men he knew. Randolph and Hank. Or at least, I think it was Hank." She frowned, doubting her own memory.

"Randolph?" Coolabah repeated with a thoughtful frown as he studied Todd's face. "I know of about a dozen Randolphs off'and. And at least five men called 'ank. Wot about you?"

"At least that many," Todd said, and exhaled sharply as he realized the magnitude of the trouble Justin had gotten himself into. "But at least it's a place to start. Maybe someone around here will know of a particular Randolph and Hank who have been seen together. Or who may have been seen with Justin."

"Good place to start is the Wattle Bud," Coolabah put in. "It seems to be one of Justin's regular stoppin' places." He pushed his wide-brimmed hat to the back of his head and glanced off in the direction of the tavern. "You want me to get over there and start askin' around?"

"No, I'd rather do it myself. Why don't you go with Christina to the house? I imagine those boys would be very happy to see her about now."

"I know they would," Coolabah nodded. "All right. I'll see 'er 'ome, then come back to 'elp you see wot you can find out about Justin."

"Bring my horse when you come," Todd said as he stood and offered Christina his hand. Once he had helped her to her feet and was certain her legs would hold her, he turned back to Coolabah. "I'll check in with Rose every few hours. She should be able to tell you where to find me when you get back. She may even have an idea about who Randolph and Hank are."

"You goin' to stop by and report this to the police?" Coolabah questioned.

"I'd rather keep them out of it if I can. I'm not sure just how deep Justin is involved in the cattle duffing. And until I do know more, I don't want to get the police involved. I imagine I'll have to go to them with this eventually. Just not yet."

"Wotever you think," Coolabah said agreeably.

Christina was grateful that Todd was not going to the police with what he already knew, and that he would investigate himself what had happened to Justin. If there was a chance her brother was still alive, she did not want him in any more trouble than he was already. Bringing in the police might make the men he had been forced to work with even angrier.

So worried that her stomach had knotted into a painful twist, she wanted to stay and help, wanted to play an active part in the search for her brother, but at the same time she knew Todd was right. The boys would be terrified that their father was missing and would need her emotional support, or what she could offer of it, for right now her emotions seemed to be in shambles.

"Be strong," Todd said, reading her thoughts. "For the lads' sakes, be strong."

"I will." She tried to sound confident. "You be careful."

"I'll see you in a little while," he promised. When he bent forward to kiss her, she closed her eyes to keep from crying. Todd was putting himself in danger. Justin was already gone, possibly killed or so badly hurt he could not get help. She knew Todd could be next. It was all she could think about during the long ride to the house.

Christina unpacked her things only moments after she had arrived, exactly as she had planned to do before she had learned of Justin's disappearance. She hoped the boys believed she was not nearly as concerned about Justin as she was.

Working busily, she combined many of Todd's things to make more room in the drawers and cabinets for hers. To take the boys' minds off their worries, she encouraged them to help her hurry to get her things put away, promising in return to help Edward make teacakes. And for a while, the boys did not mention the fact that their father was still gone.

"Edward and Alan certainly have cheered up since you arrived," Penelope told Christina as soon as the lads had abandoned the huge mound of teacakes to go outside and attend to their twin colts. "I can't imagine what has happened to Justin. He's always been such a good father. It's just not like him to run off and leave the boys like this."

Rather than worry Penelope with the true danger of the situation, Christina kept her response simple. "No, that's not like him at all."

"At first I thought he was just taking advantage of having the boys here for the night and was off having a good time in town. I did not really fault him for that. After all, it can't be easy for him to be strapped with a family to care for and no wife to help him. But when we found that broken window, and he did not show up by the day he was supposed to take over for Coolabah, I started to really get very worried. And after Coolabah asked all those questions in town and heard some people say he was probably off drunk somewhere, while others claimed something bad had happened to him, I didn't know what to think."

Penelope shook her head. "I do hope nothing bad has happened to him, but if it turns out he was off on a lark of some sort, I do think I'll take him over my knee and lash him good."

"And if that's what it turns out to be, I'll help you hold him there," Christina said with a firm shake of her head, though she was almost certain that was not how it would turn out.

As always in Australia, darkness descended quickly after the sun had settled behind the distant gum trees. And with the coming of darkness, Christina's worries multiplied. She had hoped Todd and Coolabah would be back by now. It had been six hours, plenty of time to ask their questions, get the answers, and be home. She was having a harder and harder time trying not to show how deeply worried she was.

With summer gone, the evenings were very cool, causing Christina to shiver from more than her mounting fear. When she went outside to wait for Todd and Coolabah, it was cool enough to warrant a shawl. Silently, she sat on the veranda watching the main track, clutching a white woolen shawl tightly around her shoulders. Soon Penelope joined her.

"As Todd's mother, Jessica, used to say, 'waiting is the hardest thing a woman has to do,'" Penelope offered, as a way of starting a conversation. "And we certainly seem to do more than our fair share of it."

Christina smiled. Penelope was trying to take her mind off whatever worried her, and she appreciated the effort. "Aye. I had thought Todd would be back by now."

"Coolabah warned you they might be late. He even asked that we not hold supper for them," Penelope reminded her, and placed a reassuring hand on Christina's shoulder. "He'll be home soon enough, and when he gets here, you will be so delighted to see him that you will forget all the frustration of having had to wait for him."

Penelope was unaware of the seriousness of the situation, unaware of the trouble Justin had gotten himself into. Christina understood why Penelope thought she was merely frustrated at being kept waiting. And she *was* frustrated, but she was more afraid. Afraid of who or what was keeping Todd from coming home. Afraid he might not be coming home at all.

It was well after nine o'clock before Todd finally did return. Though it was past the boys' bedtime, they were still awake, and they appeared the moment they heard the horses enter the yard, making it impossible for Christina to question her husband about what had happened.

"Did you find out where our father is?" Edward wanted to know as he ran barefoot across the yard to meet Todd. "Did you find out when he's coming back?"

Todd's face sagged. He could either lie to them and let them hold on to their hopes or he could tell them the dismal truth, that no one knew anything about Justin's disappearance and that he was starting to fear the worst. He finally decided on a mixture of both. "No, Edward, I didn't find out where your father has gone, but I don't think he'll be away much longer. How could he? He has you two boys to take care of. He should be back just as soon as he's through with whatever business he went to see about."

"Think so?" Edward asked. Though he frowned, his voice still held hope.

"I know so. How could any man in his right mind run off and leave boys like you behind? He'll be back just as soon as he can." His teeth gritted against the half lie he had felt forced to tell. In truth, he had no way of knowing if Justin would ever be coming back. He had started to have his doubts that Justin was even still alive. But until he knew for certain, he would not have the boys' hopes dashed. "Say, isn't it a little late for you two lads to be up and about?"

Edward and Alan looked at each other, then grinned guiltily.

"I think if you two don't get back to bed right now, I'll have to do what I know your father would do and redden your little backsides."

The boys took off like fire rockets, squealing with

delight when they realized Todd was chasing them into the house.

Christina stayed behind and waited for either Coolabah to come out of the barn or for Todd to return from the house. She knew that nothing concerning Justin should be discussed in the presence of the boys. Though still unaware of the magnitude of the trouble, Penelope sensed something terrible was bothering Christina and stayed with her.

Todd and Coolabah emerged at almost the same moment, as if on cue. Since he was the closer, Todd arrived at their sides first, but waited until Coolabah could join him before starting to explain.

"So, what did you find out?" Christina asked, impatient to know.

"Not much," Todd answered with an apologetic shrug. His gaze cut back to the house to make sure the boys had not followed him outside. "But it doesn't look good. After a lot of questioning, I did discover that Justin registered at the Cassowary Hotel but never checked out. The manager found Justin's good felt hat and his necktie still in the room when we asked him to go up and take a look around. Strange thing is that the bed had been sat on, or maybe even lain on, but the covers had never been pulled back. Justin had never actually slept there."

"He never even used the wash basin," Coolabah put in.

"The desk clerk on duty that night said he thinks he remembers Justin stumbling in drunk during the early hours of the morning and going on up to his room," Todd added. "But he doesn't remember ever seeing him come back down."

"Nobody remembers ever seein' 'im come back

down," Coolabah explained further. "We talked to the man who worked the desk that next morning, and 'e said 'e never remembered seein' Justin at all."

"Because the barkeeper at the tavern also remembered that Justin had drunk a little too much that night, we can only assume he decided that he would never be able to sit his horse that drunk and decided to stay over. But then we found out he checked into the hotel just after midnight, probably before he ever went to the Wattle Bud. I think he intended ahead of time to get good and drunk. Maybe in celebration of having the money to pay those men off."

Penelope's brow rose in question, but she remained silent, listening carefully to the rest of what they had to say.

"That is *if* Justin ever got the chance to pay those men off at all. There's no way to know if 'e did or not." Coolabah wanted Christina to understand how little they really knew.

"Did you speak with Rose?"

"Aye," Todd responded. "And she is just as confused as the rest of us over what could have happened. She told me he left her about ten minutes before midnight, claiming he was going to have one drink at the Wattle Bud, then would be heading on home."

"Well, 'e 'ad that one drink. And then some. Then 'e played some cards, though we 'aven't been able to talk with anyone else who was actually in the game to find out if 'e might 'ave said somethin' then that could 'elp."

"Nor do we know if he lost any money during the game," Todd put in pointedly.

Christina's stomach coiled into a tight knot. "You don't suppose he might have lost some of that money and

378

then did not have enough to pay those men off after all?"

"I don't know what to think." Todd shook his head glumly. "I just don't know. And if that is what happened, if he did lose some or all of the money, I don't know if Justin then left on his own accord to save his skin, or whether he was harmed in some way by whomever it was he owed the money to. Or it could be someone else, possibly even someone in that card game, saw the amount of money he was carrying in his pocket and decided he wanted it for himself and paid Justin a little visit in his hotel room later that night."

"Did you find out anything that might let you know who those men are?"

"Who? The ones in the card game or the ones he fell in with and owed the money to?"

"Randolph and Hank," she stated specifically.

"No, not a thing. No one seems to be able to pair up a Randolph and a Hank in any way. But we are going back tomorrow to see if we can't locate some of those men who were in on that card game and hopefully talk to some more of the hotel's employees. Most of the ones who would have been working last Saturday night had this Saturday night free. Seems they aren't all needed and they start to alternate Saturday nights once the summer is over."

"But on Sunday? Would they be there on Sunday if they had Saturday night free? Would the card players be back on Sunday if they weren't there for a Saturday night game?" Christina wanted to know.

"No way of knowing, but we have to try to find out something more. Right now, we don't have enough to go on to even know if Justin is in real danger."

Coolabah ran a hand over his bushy beard thoughtfully and added, "Or even if he's still alive."

Christina gasped and felt Penelope's hand on her arm. Todd reached out to trail a reassuring finger along the curve of her cheek.

"Christina, I'll do everything I can to find out what has happened to Justin. That I can promise you," Todd said and hoped that whatever he did find out would be what she wanted to hear.

"I know you will," she said with a slight tremor in her voice, and walked into his arms, needing to be held.

"And I intend to stay on and 'elp until we find out somethin' definite," Coolabah added. There was so much concern in his hazel eyes that it touched Christina's heart.

Todd shivered and looked up into the moonlit sky as he held Christina close. "It's getting cold out here. We should be inside." Then, in an effort to change the subject to something far less painful, he asked, "Did you get your things put away?"

"All settled in," she assured him and pulled her cheek away from his shoulder to smile up at him.

"Good. I'm tired. Let's all go on to bed."

"See you first thing in the mornin'," Coolabah said to Todd just before he turned to leave.

Todd, Christina, and Penelope walked in the direction of the house, while Coolabah went on toward his own quarters. Though sleep did not come for hours, Christina felt better lying in Todd's arms, held close to his reassuring heartbeat. She tried not to think about Justin at all. There was nothing they could do until the following morning, anyway. Yet she was able to think of little else.

Eventually, exhaustion overcame her and she drifted

off into a fitful sleep. At one point during the early hours of the morning, she threw back the covers and started to leave the room. When Todd called her and she did not respond, he realized she was sleepwalking and gently guided her back to bed. She awoke just as he was trying to get her to lie down.

"What is it?" she asked, her brain fogged with sleep, unaware she had been out of the bed at all.

"You were sleepwalking," he told her simply, with a slight smile. It had reminded him of that earlier incident in which she had walked in her sleep and ended up in his room. How she had stirred his blood to life right from the very first.

"That's nice," she murmured as he tucked her under the covers.

When she awoke the next morning, she discovered Todd already gone from their bed. Hurriedly she dressed and went in search of him, but Penelope told her that he and Coolabah had left for Bathurst before sunup.

"I had hoped to go with them," she said, letting her shoulders droop with disappointment.

"You are needed here," Penelope reminded her. "The boys feel more secure knowing that at least you are still close by. It helps them feel less abandoned."

Christina knew that was true, but still she hated waiting all day, without knowing what Todd and Coolabah had found out or if they had gotten themselves into trouble by asking so many questions.

As she had expected, the day dragged along at a snail's pace. She tried to keep busy by spending much of her time with the boys. Though the sun had crested and begun its slow decent in the west, it seemed to Christina that it had somehow become suspended over the distant treetops. Something she could not see was holding it back, making time stand still.

"It'll be dark soon," Penelope said, standing beside Christina in the yard and looking up into the same azure sky Christina seemed so mesmerized by.

"Are you sure? I don't think that sun has moved at all in the past hour," she commented glumly, then looked back down to face Penelope. "I'm so afraid that they might have found themselves in serious danger because of all those questions they are asking about Justin. If someone has killed my brother," she paused to try to ease the sudden constriction in her throat before continuing, "if someone has indeed killed Justin, they are not going to like the way Todd and Coolabah are probing into the incident."

"Todd knows how to take care of himself," Penelope said with so much confidence that it made Christina smile at last.

"Aye, he does. And I know I'm probably worrying needlessly for him, but I can't seem to stop myself."

"I know. That's just the nature of love," Penelope said with a gentle smile, and she patted Christina on the shoulder. "When my husband, Aaron, was so determined to go off to the goldfields and provide medical services for those thousands of men, I was terrified, especially when he chose Ballarat for his medical tent. Almost every day I would read terrible accounts of some violent act that had caused another man's death or about some strange new disease that had been brought into the country by those goldseekers who came here from other nations. I so worried that my Aaron would either come across some man intent on robbing him for his medications or would help someone with one of those dreaded diseases and contract it himself. I was barely able to keep my sanity, much less keep my mind on my work."

"What happened to your husband?" Christina asked, feeling they were close enough as friends for her to ask.

"He and Todd's mother were killed in an Aboriginal attack when Todd was still a young boy. Jessica had gone to deliver a baby at a station that was at that time part of the backblocks. Aaron went with her because there had been several uprisings in the area by Aborigines who were tired of being pushed back farther and farther into the outback. He realized the danger, and he was right. They were both killed on the track before they ever reached their destination."

"How horrible," Christina responded with a shudder.

"Aye. I miss them both dreadfully, as I also miss Eric, Todd's father," Penelope said. "That may be one reason I've become so attached to my grandson. My son, Eric, was killed while he was serving his final two years in the detective force, and then Jessica and Aaron so soon after that. Todd was all I had left of them."

Christina smiled sadly, and as a way of offering her sympathy, she hugged Penelope, but broke away when she heard the sound of horses' hooves on the main track. Glancing in the direction of the sounds, she pressed her hand against her hammering heart and prayed that it would be Todd and Coolabah returning early with good news. But there was too much dust being stirred for her to tell who it was.

Penelope also turned to face the riders, but was distracted when Alan came racing out of the barn, followed by a very angry Edward. He was screaming and flailing his arms as he tried his best to catch his little brother. Only seconds later, Sam, an older man who was the only groomsman working that Sunday, rushed out after the both of them. He stopped and threw up his arms when he realized he was never going to catch them and that there was little use in trying.

"Hey, you two. Stop that. That's no way for brothers to behave," Penelope called out harshly, but then she remembered how Aaron and his stepbrother, Mark, had behaved as children and even as adults. She had to smile when she went toward the boys to see what had started this argument and what could be done to resolve it.

When the riders turned their horses into the drive, Christina saw there were two of them, but she instinctively knew that neither was Todd as she moved toward the front of the yard to greet them. Her heart continued to hammer violently in her chest as she hoped that whoever the riders were, they would have news of Todd or Justin for her. Good news.

"May I help you?" she called to them as they came closer.

Because patches of grass grew in areas along the narrow drive that joined the main track to the dooryard, the dust had thinned out enough to let her see more of the two riders. Her heart skipped a beat and her brow drew into a sudden frown when she realized the men had dark neckerchiefs pulled up around their faces. She hoped the neckerchiefs were because of the dust, but she had a sinking feeling in the pit of her stomach that the dust had nothing to do with the men's decision to wear masks. She was almost certain now that these men had news of Justin or Todd, but she guessed it would not be news she wanted to hear. She braced herself for what was to come.

"Aye, I think you can help us, all right," one of the two

men said as he lifted his hat in greeting, revealing a thick head of shaggy blond hair. He looked over at his companion, and Christina could tell he was amused at what he had just said. "Aye, I think you can help us real good."

"In what way?" Her stomach twisted tighter as she waited for the answer.

Penelope had stopped and turned back to stare at the riders, but was too far away to say anything and be heard. The boys, too, had stopped running to listen to what the men had to say. Although Sam had gone back into the barn, he stood in the doorway to see if he could tell who the men might be.

"You can come with us," the blond man said and suddenly produced a pistol from behind him.

"What?" she gasped as she looked back at Penelope, but she quickly returned her gaze to the man with the gun. When she noticed one bare hand resting on his thigh and a tight black leather glove on the other hand, the hand that held the pistol, she realized who he was. He was the same man who had called Justin outside at the Anniversary Ball.

Suddenly Alan took off running toward the men, rage in his eyes, and screamed in a pitch almost too high to hear, "You are not taking my aunt nowhere. She's staying here with us."

Before Christina could grab the boy, he had passed her and come to a sharp halt beside the tall horse. Instantly, Alan pummeled the man's leg with both his fists.

"Get out of here right now, mister. Leave my aunt alone."

The man's eyes narrowed, and he lifted his booted foot out of the stirrup and kicked the boy sharply in the forehead. The blow sent Alan sprawling backwards into the dirt.

"Don't," Christina screamed and ran to Alan's side. "Don't hurt him. He's just a boy."

When she reached Alan, a large blotch of blood had formed along a jagged cut just above his left eye. Though stunned by the blow just long enough for Christina to dab away a little of the blood with the hem of her sleeve, Alan was ready to resume his fight. Before Christina got a firm hold on him, he was again on his feet, flailing his fists in an attempt to get even.

"If you don't want either of the lads hurt, and if you don't want the old lady hurt," the man said, indicating Penelope with a sharp jerk of his head, "then climb up here and don't give us no trouble." While he spoke he moved the barrel of his pistol, pointing it directly at Alan's head. There were only a few feet of distance between. "But if you don't get up here right now, I'm going to shoot both these brats and the old lady, then I'll force you to go with me!"

Christina yanked Alan away and pushed him in Penelope's direction. "Get away from him, Alan."

"Don't go with him," he pleaded as he stumbled and fell.

"Do as I say," Christina stated firmly.

Penelope had come forward and gathered Alan to her, pressing the child deep into her skirts as if hoping to hide the boy from the man's view.

"Randolph! Look out," the other man said, and Christina looked over in time to see that he, too, had produced a large pistol and had it raised level with his eye. The weapon discharged just as she glanced back to see where he was pointing it. She saw Sam, with a rifle in his hands, jerk backwards, hitting the edge of the barn door, then crumpling forward to the ground. The rifle clattered in the dirt at his side.

The name Randolph had not escaped Christina's notice, and when she turned back to face him, she used it. "Please, Randolph, leave these people alone. I'll go with you."

"Christina, don't," Penelope pleaded.

"I have to," she responded flatly and glanced back to where Sam lay in a folded heap outside the barn door, blood spreading across his chest. "They don't offer idle threats. They will shoot all of us if I don't go with them."

"What do you want with her?" Penelope asked.

"You will find out soon enough," the blond man who had turned out to be Randolph told her as he scooted back in his saddle to make room for Christina. He held out his hand to her. "Hurry up."

Christina was angry that her hand trembled when she reached for his hand, letting him yank her off the ground and onto the saddle. Once positioned in front of him, facing Penelope and the boys, she tried to smile reassuringly. "I'll be all right. As soon as I find out what these two want, I'll be back."

"Don't be too sure about that," the blond man chuckled loudly, causing his mask to flutter in front of his face. "Just don't you let yourself feel too bloody sure about anything."

Then they were off, leaving behind them a thick cloud of dust and a severely wounded groomsman.

# Chapter XXII

"We might as well get ourselves on back to the station," Coolabah said, with a deep sigh of disappointment. "We aren't makin' any progress around 'ere, and I'm sure your family is worried that we 'aven't come 'ome before now. We can always come back tomorrow and start all over again. Maybe by then someone who actually knows somethin' about Justin will 'ave come into town."

"That's true," Todd said as he reached up to rub his throbbing right temple. "It's just that I had hoped to have something new to tell Christina and the boys. Something to give them hope."

"But we can't find out anything else about 'im if we can't find no one new who knows anything. Unless, of course, you want to ride back out to Voncille Pyle's house and see if 'e 'as come 'ome yet."

Todd let out a long, heavy sigh and looked around the smoke-filled tavern for anyone they might not have spoken with yet. When he saw only familiar faces, he shook his head from disappointment and finally agreed with Coolabah's first suggestion. "No, his wife said she didn't expect him home until Tuesday. We will just have to try back here again tomorrow. Maybe one of those other three who were in on that card game will show up then. Let's go on home."

It was already dark outside when they stepped out onto the boarded walkway and untied their horses. As Todd mounted, he glanced up at the moon to see if there was plenty of light for traveling. He decided they could travel safely if they kept their horses at a walk.

"What time *is* it?" he asked Coolabah as he pulled back on his horse's reins and the animal took several steps backward. Then he nudged the horse with his knee and the animal started forward.

"I'm not sure, but I'd say it's probably been dark at least an hour." Coolabah had been the last to mount, but he had already brought his horse alongside Todd's.

"Christina is going to be frantic," Todd said with a frown, wishing he had been considerate and called a halt to their search sooner. He flicked the reins and sent his horse into a trot, knowing he took a slight risk in moving along that quickly in the dark.

"Aye, you are probably in for a real tongue lashin' when you get 'ome," Coolabah agreed as he urged his horse into a pace that matched Todd's.

Though they passed several riders and one carriage on their way out of Bathurst, Todd hardly noticed them more than to offer a friendly wave in passing. But his attention was keenly drawn to the sound of rapidly approaching horses' hooves on the track ahead as they reached the thickly wooded area less than a mile outside of Bathurst.

"What fool would drive his horse at such a rate with it

as dark as it is?" he asked aloud and squinted into the darkness to see if he could make out the horse and rider on the track ahead.

"Someone very late for supper and has an angry wife waiting on him, I suppose," Coolabah said with a light chuckle.

Todd chuckled, too, and as the rider rapidly approached them, he raised his hand to wave as he passed.

"Todd? Coolabah?" the rider called out, pulling his horse to an abrupt halt only a few feet after he had passed them.

"Aye, Hawley, it's us," Todd called back to him, also stopping his horse. "What are you doing out this late on a Sunday night and driving your horse like a madman?"

"There's been trouble at the station," Hawley, who was one of Todd's newest and youngest stockmen, rushed on to say as he quickly maneuvered his horse to join them.

"What kind of trouble?" Todd could feel the panic start to rise in his chest. His first thought was of Christina, then of his grandmum and finally, the boys. What kind of trouble, and were any of them involved?

"I wasn't there when it happened, but two riders rode in while your grandmum and your wife were outside and demanded that Mrs. Aylesbury—your wife—leave with them. They drew pistols and threatened to kill your grandmum and Justin's boys if your wife didn't do exactly what they said. In fact, they shot Sam in the chest when he tried to stop them."

"They wot?" Coolabah growled in anger, his eyes narrowed as he looked at Hawley's flushed face.

Todd did not wait to hear more. He kicked the sides of

his horse sharply and sent the animal racing into the night.

When Todd turned off the main track and headed the short distance to the yard, he could see Edward pacing back and forth across the lantern-lit veranda with something held tightly in his right hand. The boy turned to face out into the darkness when he heard Todd's horse and held up the object in readiness. Todd could tell, once he got closer, that it was a large blacksmith's hammer.

"It's all right," Todd called out, aware of how frightened the child must be. "It's me."

Edward let the hand that gripped the hammer drop to his side, but did not let go of his weapon. "Did Hawley find you?"

Todd was already off his horse and headed toward the boy as Coolabah and Hawley approached on the main track. "Aye, he did. He said two men rode in here and took your Aunt Christina."

"Aye, sir, they did," Edward told him, and turned his concerned face up to look at Todd after he had come to stand beside him.

Todd saw that the boy had been crying and had cried hard, but he was not crying now and was determined not to. "Did you know the two men?"

"I don't think so. They wore their neckerchiefs up over their faces like masks. But they were both about your size, maybe a little skinnier, and one had yellow hair and one had brown hair," Edward told him as he thought back on what he could remember.

"Did they happen to call each other by name?" Todd asked. He knelt on one knee so Edward did not have to strain to look up at him.

"Not that I recall. I wasn't standing too close and I didn't get to hear what all they said." Edward looked at the planked floor of the veranda as if he had failed Todd by not being able to report everything said.

"You didn't hear one of them call the other Randolph or Hank?" Todd probed.

Edward's eyes widened. "Aye, I did. Just before they shot Mister Sam, I heard the one with brown hair call the one with yellow hair Randolph. I did. I really did. I just forgot."

Todd glanced beyond the boy and thought over the new information. Of all the Randolphs, he knew only two who had blond hair, and only one of them was thin. Randolph Schiller. He frowned in doubt, because it seemed too out of character for Schiller to go to so much trouble to do anything. The young man was well known for doing as little as he could possibly get by with and still have enough to eat.

Schiller had taken over his grandfather's place just a few miles south of there, and in a few short years had managed to turn it from a halfway productive vineyard and wheat farm into a huge patch of useless weeds and bush. If it wasn't for the eggs his chooks laid, which Randolph did manage to find the energy to gather up and sell every now and then, the man would have had no income. But then, wealth and success had never seemed to concern Schiller very much, which was probably why he had not moved to Victoria with the rest of his family, who, Todd understood, were doing very well in the wine industry.

"Thanks, mate, you may have given me a good clue about who one of those men might be," Todd said, and he patted Edward soundly on the shoulder before standing to go inside the house. He left Edward standing guard over the front door with his hammer.

Inside, Todd called out for his grandmum, and following the direction of her voice, he found her bent over Alan and Sam, who had been brought in and put in the same bed. She had a damp towel in her hand, and a basin of cool water sat beside the bed.

Setting the towel aside as soon as she had bathed Sam's brow with the cool water, she came forward to meet Todd halfway, worry firmly implanted on her face. "They've got Christina."

"I know. Hawley and Edward told me about it. And after talking with Edward, I think I know who one of them might be."

"Who? Who could do such a thing?"

"Randolph Schiller."

Penelope's eyes widened and her mouth dropped open. "Of course. That's why the young blond man seemed so familiar to me, though I was sure I had never met him. He's Regie's boy. You are right. That is who the blond man was."

Todd frowned. He had forgotten the link Randolph had with his family. He had forgotten that Randolph's true grandfather was not Karl Schiller, as everyone had been led to believe. Randolph's father was the bastard son of Mark Aylesbury, his own grandfather's half-brother. Neither Randolph nor his father, Reginald, were truly Schillers, but they were part Aylesbury. And Todd also remembered having been told what an uncanny resemblance Randolph had to his father, Reginald. Penelope had known him during his adolescence, because Reginald had at one time tried to court Todd's mother, Jessica. If

Randolph did look so much like his father, of course he would seem familiar to Penelope. Penelope, who had at one time been tricked into marrying Mark, but had never loved him. The only man she had ever loved had been Aaron, Todd's grandfather, whom she had married after Mark's death.

"But what would Randolph want with Christina? She's never done him any harm, and neither have you," Penelope said, trying to figure out a reason for what had happened. "Or have you?"

"Indirectly, I may have," Todd admitted. "If he is one of the three who has been stealing the cattle around here and duped Justin into helping them, it's likely I've been causing them quite a lot of concern with all the questions Coolabah and I have been asking around."

"Is that what Justin did? He helped them steal cattle?"

"Aye, against his will, as I understand it. And he was hoping to finally get out of their clutches by using the money he borrowed from me to pay off a debt he owed them. I believe if we could read into their black hearts, we would find out what became of Justin. I suspect they have taken Christina as a way of getting back at me for interfering in the matter."

"Maybe it is just a warning," Penelope inserted hopefully. "Maybe it is their way of telling you to stay out of it, and as soon as they are sure you have taken their message to heart, they will release Christina and let her come home."

Todd ran his hand through his hair while he considered Penelope's reasoning. His gaze moved restlessly about the room until it lighted on Alan's swollen forehead, then on the bloodstained bandage around Sam's chest. "Are they going to be all right?"

"Aye, as far as I can tell. I've given them both pain powders that have made them very sleepy. It was the only way I could keep Alan in that bed."

"Have you sent for a doctor?"

"Not yet. The bullet went all the way through Sam, leaving a clean wound. I was able to get the bleeding to stop almost immediately, so I agreed not to send for a doctor right away. You know how stubborn Sam can be about doctors. Aaron used to have to get someone to help hold him down just to administer anything stronger than cough syrup, and that had to be so strongly laced with whiskey that he could not taste the medicine."

Todd smiled briefly. He was worried about what had happened to Christina and he had to figure out what he should do about it. He turned to face Coolabah when he heard him enter the room.

"How's Sam?" Coolabah wanted to know. Coolabah and Sam were longtime friends. They had worked together as secret detectives for Todd's great-uncle, James Cranston, who had been a captain for several years under the direct command of another friend, Stuart Mays.

"I think he is going to be just fine," Penelope told him. "He's sleeping right now."

Coolabah stretched his neck to get a better look at his friend sleeping across the room. As soon as he was satisfied his friend was indeed in good hands, he turned his attention to Todd. "What do we do now?"

"Good question. Maybe we can try to track them."

"I doubt it," Penelope said. "They used the main track, and on Sunday there'd be too many fresh horse-tracks to know which were theirs."

Todd ran his hand impatiently over his face and down

his throat where he paused, resting it lightly at his collarbone. "The only other thing I can think of is for the two of us to ride over to Randolph's house and see if they might have taken her there."

"Randolph who?" Coolabah questioned, unaware that at least that mystery had more than likely been solved.

"Schiller."

"How do you know it is Randolph Schiller?"

Todd explained as they walked out of the room and back outside.

Coolabah also thought it a little out of character for Randolph Schiller to do anything that took so much effort, but agreed it was something for them to do and mounted his horse just seconds after Todd had mounted his. Several of the men had come in from the paddocks and had already been told what had happened by Hawley and Gomer. They were all eager to ride with Todd and help in whatever way they could, but Todd chose to leave them behind to protect the rest of his family. When he rode out, only Coolabah was at his side.

To their disappointment, though they had expected it, when they arrived at the Schiller house less than an hour later, the house was dark and there were no signs of movement. Even the chooks that could usually be seen strutting about the yard had gone off to roost.

Todd dismounted and went to the door. Without bothering to knock or announce his arrival, he kicked the door open and marched inside. When he lit a candle he had located near the door, he found the house was in too much of a shambles to tell if a struggle had gone on there. Papers, dirty dishes, empty food jars, broken furniture, and dirty clothing were strewn everywhere. There were chicken pilings and dribblings of candle wax on the floor.

Ashes overflowed the fireplace, obviously from the winter before. But there was some semblance of order, and Todd decided that they had not brought Christina there.

Vaguely relieved that Christina had not been brought here and made to stay in such filth, but at the same time disappointed that he had not found any clue to her whereabouts, Todd walked outside. Coolabah had climbed down from his horse and had left the animal tethered to a broken plow that lay in the yard. Todd then noticed a faint light in the open doorway of the barn and realized Coolabah was searching the dilapidated old building for clues.

"Find anything?" Todd asked when he entered the doorway of the barn and found Coolabah tossing things around inside. He had already stirred up a cloud of dust so thick that it made them both cough.

"Nothin' worth anything. How can anyone live like this?" Coolabah asked, his expression twisted with disgust as he glanced around at all the rusted tools and broken implements lying in heaps, crusted with dust. He wrinkled his nose and fanned the air in front of his face. "I don't think 'e ever cleans out 'is 'orse's stall. Poor animal."

Todd nodded as the smell of horse manure reached him.

When they both went back outside and took several deep breaths of fresh air Coolabah spoke again. "Now what?"

There were no other buildings to search on the Schiller place. They had all been destroyed years ago after a wind storm. And Todd knew Randolph would never bother to rebuild anything that was not absolutely necessary to his comfort. Shrugging his shoulders in answer to Coolabah's question, he looked at his friend helplessly.

"I know it won't be easy, but it looks like we're goin' to 'ave to go on back to the 'ouse and wait until somethin' else 'appens," Coolabah said with a reluctant shake of his head.

"I can't just wait around for something to happen. I've got to keep looking for her."

"But where?"

"I don't know. But I'm going back and get all my men to saddle up and help me look. We'll search every house and every building we can think of until we find her."

"I'm with you all the way, mate," Coolabah said, and he followed Todd back to the horses.

When they arrived at the house, all the workmen except for the night riders were bunched together outside on the veranda. Most of them either had handguns strapped to their thighs or held their loaded rifles in their hands. All were ready to help in any way they could. But before Todd got them fully organized into pairs, they heard a rider approach, and everyone turned their attention to the drive. When the rider reached the outer glow of the lanterns, they were surprised to see it was a young boy, about ten years in age. In his hand he clutched a letter he'd been paid to deliver to Todd.

"Who paid you to give this to me?" Todd demanded. He left the veranda and walked to where the boy had brought his horse to a halt, not realizing that his harsh tone would scare a boy that young into total silence.

"I asked who paid you to give this to me?" Todd shouted again. Though his hands worked to unfold the letter, his eyes continued to bore angrily into the terrified young boy's face. "Who?"

The boy glanced around at the serious expressions on the faces of the men who had gathered quickly around him, and he gulped hard. "A man. I don't know who he was. I was on my way home from my cousin's house. He stopped me on the track. Offered to pay me if I'd bring you this letter," the boy said with one huge burst of breath. His grip on his reins tightened as he waited for a response.

"Did he have blond hair? Can you at least tell me that?"

"It was too dark. I didn't notice." Then, before Todd could question him again, he prodded his horse into a gallop, nearly causing the animal to trample one of the men, and left as quickly as his animal could carry him.

Todd stared after the youth for only a moment, then carried the letter to the veranda where there was more light to read it. The men followed.

"What's in it?" Coolabah asked, watching Todd closely.

Todd finished reading. He became pale as he reached the end of the letter, then looked up at Coolabah, then around at the other concerned faces that surrounded him. The rest of the men did not know anything about what Justin had done, so he answered simply, "They want money."

He then signaled for Coolabah to follow him inside.

Even after they were well away from the others, Todd motioned for Coolabah to stand close to him, and he spoke in hushed tones. "Justin never gave them that money. That is why they have kidnapped Christina."

"Christina in exchange for the money Justin owes them?"

"Only now they want more money. Seems they feel I have also betrayed them in some way. Probably because we have been asking so many questions around here about them. They now want the money Justin owes them, plus six thousand more from me. That's fourteen thousand in all. And the strange part is that they want Justin to be the one to deliver it to them."

"Justin? Then they haven't killed him?"

"Looks like he must have taken off on his own," Todd said, reaching up to rub the side of his face. "They want Justin to deliver the money tomorrow night, by midnight, or they will harm Christina."

"And it has to be Justin?" Coolabah asked, immediately seeing the problem in that.

"Aye, they specifically state it has to be Justin who brings the money. If anyone else tries to deliver it or if the police are told anything about any of this, they will kill Christina immediately and be gone."

Tears of frustration and anger burned Todd's eyes at the thought of what Christina must be going through in the hands of such men, especially someone like Schiller. He could easily imagine what sort of person that Hank was, as well as the third person, whom Justin had never even been allowed to meet. Helplessly, he threw up his arms and asked, "What am I going to do now? We still have no idea where Justin might be."

"We've got twenty-four hours to try and find out," Coolabah told him. "Either that or go ahead and send the men out to search for 'er like you were about to do before you got that letter."

"No, I can't. Not now. I'd rather pay off the ransom. I don't want to put Christina's life in any more danger than it is already. What we've got to do is find Justin like you said. I want everyone out there, except Gomer, Frank, and William, trying to find out where the hell he has gone. I want him back here by the time it gets dark tomorrow."

"William is not out there," Coolabah pointed out and frowned as he turned to stare at the door to the outside, where the rest of the men sat huddled together.

"He should have been back from his sister's by now," Todd said, and he too frowned.

"To tell you the truth, 'e 'as not been around very much all this week. William just may 'ave finally decided to quit. He 'as been threatening to ever since you chose Justin over 'im for my job," Coolabah said.

"Well, then, have Lloyd stay back with Gomer and Frank. There should be at least three men here to protect the house. I want everyone else out looking for Justin. Send someone in to check with Rose. He may try to contact her yet. Tell the men as little as you have to, but leave no stone unturned."

"It's done," Coolabah said simply and went outside to organize the search for Justin.


After having to return from Bathurst with only the eight thousand dollars he was able to raise from the local banks on such short notice, Todd waited impatiently for one of the men to return with news of Justin's whereabouts. To fulfill the ransom demand, Todd gathered up as much jewelry as he could find and added it to the amount, hoping Randolph would agree to accept the jewelry in place of the remaining cash.

All the men, except for the three who had stayed behind to help guard the house, had ridden off in pairs just before midnight, to search for Justin. No one seemed to know where Justin was. Not even Rose, whom he had checked with twice before leaving Bathurst. Justin had successfully vanished from sight.

By the time Todd had added the jewelry to the money and had bound it securely with leather straps, ready to take to Christina's captors, it was after five o'clock. Time was rapidly running out.

As the sun slowly sank toward the western horizon, Todd paced the veranda like a caged animal. He opened the letter he kept in his shirt pocket and read it for the dozenth time, even though he had already committed every word of it to memory.

When none of the men had returned by dark, Todd realized Justin was not going to be found in time. Without telling anyone where he was going or exactly what he was up to, he carefully placed the ransom into a leather swag, attached it to his saddle, then mounted the horse that had been made ready early that afternoon, and rode swiftly away. Penelope came outside just in time to watch his horse turn onto the track and take the direction that eventually led to Bathurst.

By the time Coolabah and three of the men did return, it was almost nine o'clock and Todd had been gone for well over an hour. Penelope was waiting outside, frantic with worry.

"I think he is going to try to deliver that money himself," she told Coolabah, meeting him in the yard.

"It's what I'd probably do given the same situation." Coolabah nodded in agreement, but his jaw worked furiously beneath his beard as he thought about the

403

danger his friend was in. "I wished I 'ad gotten 'ere in time to go with 'im."

"Do you happen to know where those men wanted Justin to take the money?" Penelope asked hopefully and clasped her hands together in front of her, as if in prayer.

"No, 'e never did let me take a look at that letter," Coolabah answered with a scowl that let Penelope know just how frustrated he was.

"Then there's no way for us to help him now, is there?" Penelope pulled her hands apart, unlocking her fingers, then pressing her damp palms against her cheeks. She closed her eyes and spoke in a trembling voice. "He's on his own out there, isn't he?"

"Aye," Coolabah said, letting his gaze scan the darkness hopelessly. "He's on his own. All we can do for him now is offer a prayer for his safe return."

Todd had tried both the doors of Justin's house and found them locked, precautions his grandmum had taken, no doubt. He frowned and ran his hand through his hair in a display of frustration. But knowing he had to get inside, he stepped back and was just about to kick the back door in with his boot when he remembered the broken window.

One brief inspection showed him that he only needed a ladder or a stout rope to get inside. Still, he debated kicking the door in simply because it would be quicker, but chose instead to search the barn for something he could use to get up to that window. Although he was not sure why, he felt the less evidence he left behind that proved he had been there, the better.

Inside the front door of the barn, he found not just

one, but two sturdy wooden ladders of different heights. He reached for the shorter one, knowing it would be easier to handle, and carried it around to the side of the house. To his relief it was high enough for him to reach the broken window.

Once inside, he hurried through the darkness to the stairway, then went down and around to the room he knew Justin used as a bedroom and quickly dressed in some of Justin's work clothes. He put on a pair of Justin's boots, though they proved a snug fit, and pulled on one of Justin's battered cabbage tree hats. He then wadded his own clothing into a ball and tossed it under Justin's bed.

Having noticed Justin's horse in the barn, Todd headed back for it, taking the ladder with him. As he thought more about it, he realized Justin must have used the boys' horse the night he took Rose home, probably because the boys had the better pulling horse of the two. Even so, he had been surprised to find an animal there at all, and wondered why Coolabah had not taken the horse to their barn to care for it while Justin was gone. Surely they had noticed the animal when they came looking for Justin. He just hoped the animal had survived the neglect.

When Todd returned to the barn and replaced the ladder, he was relieved to find that they must have noticed the animal, because it had been provided ample feed and water. It would not be weak from hunger, after all.

Quickly, he saddled the horse with Justin's own saddle, then transferred his swag and attached it securely. Because the letter had been adamant that Justin not be armed when he delivered the money, Todd did not transfer his rifle. Before riding out, he unsaddled his own horse and led the animal into the now vacant stall. He put his saddle and his rifle in the tack room where he had found Justin's saddle.

Knowing the place he was to deliver the money had to be at least an hour's ride away, Todd hurried the horse, first along the main track, then onto a narrow trail that led through the bush. He tried to remember the instructions as best he could in his panicky state of mind. His heart raced frantically, beating more quickly the closer he got to his destination.

In case he came across any lookouts who might recognize him, Todd made certain his hat brim was low as he rode along. He wondered what he should expect once he reached the clearing. Though Justin had told Christina he thought there were only three men involved, Todd had no way of knowing for sure. He had no way of knowing anything, except that they had Christina and he wanted to rescue her.

Finally, Todd found the small clearing with the three large gray rocks. Beside them was the freshly fallen tree. Following the instructions closely, he dismounted and moved away from Justin's horse.

"I'm here and I have the money you want," he called out gruffly. It was the only time he intended to speak, afraid they would be able to tell his was not Justin's voice.

When no one appeared, he untied his swag and carried it over to the fallen tree and hid it in among the branches that still held on to their gray-green foliage. He waited near the tree for a moment, staring around at the dark shadows that surrounded him. The letter had not stated what would happen after that, but he had a pretty good idea that they did not intend for him to ride away. Their grudge against Justin was too strong for them not to try something.

But when nothing happened during the next few minutes, he decided they must be planning to catch him on the way out and he finally headed in the direction of Justin's horse. Before he reached the animal the first shot rang out.

# Chapter XXIII

The bullet bit deep into the ground and sent a spray of ochre-colored dust flying just inches away from Todd's left boot. Another shot rang out within a second and took a plug out of a tree several feet beyond.

Todd jumped back and held up his hands to show that he was unarmed and harmless. His breath held and burned deep in his chest. He realized those shots had been fired as a way of playing with him, a way of catching his full attention. They wanted him to be aware of the danger. They wanted him to be afraid. And he was. Only a fool would not be afraid when dealing with madmen. He continued to stand perfectly still. All he could do was wait to see if another bullet would follow, one that was meant for his heart.

"Go get that money bag and bring it over here," he heard someone say. The voice had come from a different direction than the bullets, which let him know there were at least two of them.

Todd turned without a word and walked to where he had hidden the money. Moving very slowly so as not to threaten them in any way, he pulled the swag out from beneath the branches and headed back in the direction from where the voice had come. As he did, a man sitting astride a tall, roan horse appeared from a thick patch of wattle and pea vines with his pistol already drawn and aimed directly at Todd's head. Todd thought he heard noises behind him, metallic noises, but did not turn to look. He assumed the noises came from whoever had fired those shots. Todd kept his gaze planted on the man who had decided to let himself be seen.

"Ya aren't hiding a pistol or a knife from us are ya, mate?" the man asked, putting sarcastic emphasis on the word mate and narrowing his eyes as he studied the man who approached him.

Todd shook his head as he looked up from beneath the low brim of his hat. He tried to keep a shadow over his face so the man could not see him clearly. There was easily enough silvery moonlight streaming into the small clearing that, should it happen to fall across his face, the man would see that someone other than Justin stood before him. On the other hand, the light was enough to let Todd know for certain that he had never seen this man before in his life. The man was definitely not Randolph Schiller. He was much older than Schiller, and not quite as handsome, and he had the makings of a four-day-old beard that was anything but blond. Todd wondered if he might be the man Justin had referred to as Hank.

"Speak up, mate. I didn't hear ya reply," the man said in a singsong voice. Clearly he enjoyed having the better of the man he thought was Justin. "What's a matter? Cat got yar tongue?"

Todd could tell by the man's slurred speech that he had been drinking. He hoped that would be to his advantage.

Lowering his voice to a gruff and hopefully unrecognizable level, he answered with a quick, "I'm unarmed."

"Just to be sure, pull yar pockets out so that I can see ya don't have nothing tucked away."

Todd shifted the swag to his left hand and used his right hand to do as he had been told, willing to show them what was in his belt, but hoping they would not ask him to remove his boots. The only weapon he had brought was the small knife he had strapped to the side of his leg, down near his ankle. It was not something he could easily get to, but it was all he had dared bring.

"Now, mate, turn around so I can be sure ya don't have nothing tucked into the back of yar belt."

Again, Todd did as he was told.

"Good. Now unbutton yar shirt so I can see ya don't have nothing there."

After Todd had unbuttoned the shirt and pulled it up out of his trousers, the man smiled broadly, then shouted out, "He's unarmed."

The crackling of leaves and sticks brought Todd's attention to another thick patch of wattle behind his left shoulder where another man, also on a horse, appeared in the clearing. Todd lowered his face more, because he had immediately recognized this one. It was Randolph Schiller. His next thought was that if both Randolph and his friend were here to get the money, then Justin had to be right about there being a third man. Either that or they had left Christina all alone tied up somewhere—or else . . . no, he refused to believe she was already dead.

"Bet you hoped never to have to lay sight on us again, eh-what, Justin?" Randolph did not seem very upset when Todd did not answer. "I hear you went and lost our money again. That was a damn foolish thing to do, because you have already been given more chances than a worthless bludger like you deserves. I warn you now, the boss is furious with you. I guess you'd better get on your horse and follow old Hank there without giving us any trouble. But before you do, why don't you just hand that money bag on over here."

Todd stepped over and raised the swag high so that Randolph could get it without Todd's having to look up and chance being recognized. Though he knew the hat created a wide shadow across his face, he did not want to take any unnecessary chances. If there was enough moonlight for him to recognize Randolph, then there was enough light for Randolph to see who was really standing before him.

The moment he felt the weight of the swag being lifted out of his hands, Todd released the bag and turned away. He headed immediately for Justin's horse.

"Come on, get between us," Randolph said as soon as Todd was on the horse and had the reins in his hands. "We are going to pay the boss and your sister a little visit. I'm sure we'll find Christina eager to see you. We've already told her how you gambled our money away, then hid out so we couldn't find you. Didn't take too kindly to that news. I'm sure she'll have plenty to say to you on the subject." Randolph then laughed.

A wave of relief swept over Todd. Christina was indeed still alive. Or had been, the last Randolph had seen of her. Desperately, he held on to the hope that not only was she alive but also unharmed. He maneuvered Justin's horse to stand directly behind Hank's horse. When they started through the thickest part of the bush, Hank held the lower branches of the gum and satinwood trees a little longer than was necessary, then let go of them so that they snapped back to snatch at Todd's face and clothing.

While he fought to duck the brush Hank continued to fling at him, Todd heard Randolph's horse only a few feet behind him, though he never glanced back to see how far behind he really was. When they arrived in a less dense area of bush, Hank quit his pranks and returned his attention to a flat, curved flask that had been tucked away in his hip pocket. He did not return the flask to his pocket until he had drunk the contents dry.

After twenty minutes of following an almost undetectable trail, Hank finally veered off into the underbrush where there was no path at all. Low-hanging branches again took menacing swipes at their faces and clothing, but Hank no longer seemed as intent on flinging limbs back at Todd. He was happy just keeping them from taking hold of his own clothing.

Todd wondered if the liquor had mellowed the man or if he had just grown tired of the game playing. Either way, it was to his advantage, and he wished Hank had had more to drink in his flask. Now that Hank had given up his game with the limbs, Todd followed as closely behind him as he could, trying to assess how drunk Hank was.

While they continued through the dense brush, he heard Randolph still somewhere behind him, though he had dropped back far enough that Todd detected a difference in distance.

"We're just about there," Hank called back to his prisoner, no doubt hoping to encourage his fear.

Todd peered through the darkness for sight of something—anything—besides all the surrounding wall of trees, vines, and brush. Finally, he noticed a faint light in the distance. When they cleared the thicket and entered into a small, unfenced yard, he saw a poorly constructed cob hut with a narrow wattle lean-to built onto the side, no doubt meant to provide shelter for horses.

There was no barn and no other buildings. Only the hut, with two windows and one door in the front. It seemed hardly big enough to have more than one room. If it did, then the rooms were very small. Even so, he figured there could be no more than three, and he wondered if each room had a window.

Still concentrating on the hut and his surroundings, Todd pulled Justin's horse to a halt behind Hank's horse and waited to be told what to do. When he heard Randolph drop from his horse and approach him from behind, he glanced back to see if he was still armed. Randolph held a rifle in his right hand, but Todd also noticed that he held a half-empty whiskey bottle in the other. He then listened to see if he could detect any slurred speech from Randolph.

"Here we are, mate. End of the line for you," Randolph said with a delighted laugh.

Though his speech had not seemed slurred, the way he laughed a little too loudly offered Todd hope that he too had drunk enough to slow down his reflexes. He wondered how hard it would be to wrestle that rifle away from him, and whether he could do it quickly enough before Hank could draw his pistol and fire. He then wondered if the third man was armed and how alert he was.

"Better get on in there and greet your dear sister," Randolph ordered. "You'll be glad to see that we took real good care of her." Again Randolph laughed a little too loudly. "In fact, last I saw her, she was sleeping like a little baby."

Todd frowned. Why would Christina be sleeping when surrounded by such danger? What had they done to her? Drugged her? He hoped not. Once he made his move, he needed her to act under her own power. He might not be able to hold these men off and carry her out at the same time. He felt his gut tightening as he followed Hank to the front door. As he watched, the man knocked twice, paused, then swung the door open wide. Todd wondered if it was the only door to the outside. He reasoned that for a hut as small as this one, it probably was the only means of escape.

"Inside, Jus'in. Ya sis-thur awaits," Hank said as he stepped back to let Todd enter first. Because of the light streaming from the room, dim though it was, Todd looked down as he passed the man, but he saw how loosely Hank now gripped his pistol. He was obviously far more drunk than Randolph. Todd knew then that he would not bother with Randolph's rifle. He would try to snatch the pistol away from Hank quickly and face Randolph before he could raise that rifle and hopefully before the other man could respond at all. But first he had to see Christina. He had to know more about the situation inside.

When he entered the small room, he was disappointed. It was empty, except for a roughly built table and five wooden chairs. On the table lay a large lantern and another rifle, but it was open at the breech and was unloaded. He thought that it might make a useful club if he needed one.

"Where's Christina?" he dared to ask, but continued to make his voice low and gruff. He kept his hat pulled low and his face down.

"She's in the other room. Boss is taking good care of

her," Randolph supplied for him happily.

Todd heard the sound of splashing liquid. Randolph had just taken another swig from his bottle. Todd hoped that it had been a large one.

"You eager to see your sister, are you? So am I. Very pretty lass, your sister. I can almost understand why Todd Aylesbury chose her over the rest."

Todd did not like the way Randolph had said that, and it took all of his self-restraint not to tear into him. He looked away.

"Guess I should warn you. The boss sure was angry about that wedding ever taking place. Blames you for not stopping it like you were supposed to," Randolph said.

"But we warned ya. Didn't we, Randolph? We told him he'd better make sure his sis-shur called the weddin' off," Hank quickly added with a noticeable slur, then belched quietly.

"Aye, we did. We warned him to talk his sister out of it," Randolph agreed, then turned his attention back to the man he still thought was Justin. "We warned you the boss would be angry as hell if you didn't find a way to talk her out of it. Oh, and then when Todd went and chose you for the station boss's job on top of that, whoo-ee!" He paused for effect before going on with his little speech, "Justin, you are going to regret ever having stolen that station boss's job from William. But I don't imagine you will have to regret it for very long." Again Randolph considered what he had said clever and laughed loud and long.

Todd's insides grew rigid. Though it had crossed his mind that William Stone was the third man, having something against him as he did, and having the opportunity, Todd had never believed it. But now he felt certain of it, and the facts seemed to back up his theory completely.

William had not been around when they'd organized the search for Justin. Coolabah had said he had not been around at all since the announcement after the wedding that Justin was the new station boss, nor had he been there when Todd's cattle were duffed.

As for the brash decision to take Christina, no doubt William thought Todd had made the wrong decision about both his station boss and his wife. Evidently William had hoped Todd's choice would be his sister, Vella. Todd's stomach coiled as he wondered just how deeply William's anger ran and exactly how far the man would go in his efforts for revenge.

"Sit down here and I'll go see if your sister is awake yet," Randolph commanded and pushed one of the wooden chairs in Todd's direction.

Todd placed the chair so that he faced the inner door where Christina was being held and at the same time kept the light of the only lantern in the room from falling directly across his face.

"Hank, keep your pistol on him while I see what the boss wants us to do next," Randolph said, then took one more swig from his bottle before setting it down in the corner of the room nearest to the door. He obviously did not want the boss to see him with the bottle in his hands. He opened the door of roughly hewn planks and slipped quietly inside, the swag draped over his shoulder and his rifle in his hand.

"I've got him taken care of," Hank said in a delayed response, clearly unaware Randolph was already gone. Moments later, he walked over and picked up the bottle that had been left behind. Then, as if still talking to

Randolph, he added, "He isn't goin' nowhere."

That was a true enough statement. Todd was not going anywhere without Christina. Carefully he listened to the muffled voices coming from the room and kept his eye trained on the door. Though the voices were too low and the walls surprisingly too thick for him to hear much, he was almost certain one of the voices was female. That meant Christina was lucid enough to speak. He hoped she would be alert enough to make a run for it.

Behind him he heard liquid pouring and realized Hank was refilling his flask. He hoped the man planned to drink the contents dry again. Hank was well on his way to a stupor.

When Todd heard the door open again only moments later, he felt his tension mount and raised a hand to partially cover his face. He had no way of knowing if it would be Randolph, William, or Christina coming through the door first. If it was Christina, he hoped she would not recognize him right away because she might say or do something that would reveal his identity. And if William came through first, Todd hoped he would prove no more observant than his two friends. He had no way of knowing how the three would react when they finally realized they had been duped and had the wrong man.

Keeping his face low and his hand raised in pretense of scratching his jaw, he watched the lower portion of the door from beneath the brim of his hat and waited. He was surprised to see a pair of emerald slippers at the door. Christina did not have emerald slippers. Nor did she have a dress made of such shiny emerald satin. He looked up to see who had entered the room. He had never been more surprised than when his gaze came to rest on the boss. Vella was clearly angry as she held her skirts raised several inches to avoid sweeping across the dirt floor.

"Not only did you get shorted on the money, that's not even Justin," Vella cried out in exasperation. Her expression had already been tense, but it grew angrier when she realized they had brought Todd to her instead of Justin. But she quickly adjusted to the new circumstances and her expression relaxed. By the time she moved toward him, she seemed almost pleased.

Randolph hurried into the room. "What do you mean it's not Justin?"

Todd was relieved to see that instead of his rifle, Randolph's hands were full of money. No doubt he had started to count the money to see how much was there. For the first time, Todd appreciated the man's greed. Now, if only he knew for certain there was no one else in there with Christina, no one with a gun pointed at her head even now—if only he was sure, he would make his move for Hank's pistol. But he realized there was still a good chance that William was a part of all this and that he might be in there with Christina.

"Todd?" Randolph exclaimed, in total confusion.

Todd smiled at the strangled expression on Randolph's face. "Aye, Randolph, your dear distant cousin, Todd Aylesbury."

Randolph's eyes twitched with anger.

"What do ya mean it isn't Jus'in?" Hank said, keeping one step behind in the conversation. "Sure it's Jus'in. And he brought us the money."

Vella walked over to him and snatched the bottle out of his grimy hand and flung it against the wall as hard as she could. Then she snatched his metal flask and slung it across the room, where it clattered to the floor beside the broken bottle. "Hell no, he's not Justin. He just told you himself that he's Todd Aylesbury. And if you weren't so damn drunk you would have already realized that."

Hank flinched at her show of anger, then stared lamely at the wet blotch that had splattered across the wall. Slowly, his red-rimmed eyes trailed downward to where the amber liquid had puddled around the broken glass and the dented flask that lay on the floor. A pout curved his lips downward as he muttered to himself. "He sure looked like Jus'in to me."

"And he is *supposed* to be Justin," Randolph cried out in a wild rage. Looking over at Todd again, he shouted, "We told you to send Justin!" He then came forward and grabbed Todd by his shirt and tried to shake him. "Where the hell is Justin?"

"That's what I'd like to know, where'z Jus'in," Hank asked and stuck his chest out defiantly, as if hoping such a gesture would help put fear into Todd Aylesbury, but his action only succeeded in making him belch again, more loudly this time.

Todd looked first at Hank, who no longer posed a real threat, then at Randolph, who did, and who still held him by his collar. "I don't know where Justin is. I tried to find him but couldn't. And I realized I had no other way of getting the money to you than to bring it myself."

"Then why didn't you bring all the money?" Randolph was so angry now, his hands shook.

"Let go of him," Vella said to Randolph, having turned her attention away from Hank after one final look of disdain that had caused the man to hang his head in shame. "And get back in there with the money. I told you to count it. I can handle Todd."

Reluctantly, Randolph did what his boss told him. He gave Todd one last curious look, as if he still could not believe he had been tricked so easily, before he disappeared into the next room.

"Where's Christina?" Todd demanded.

"She's in there with Randolph," Vella told him. She frowned that Todd was concerned about his new wife.

"May I see her?"

Vella looked at him a long moment before she replied. "Certainly. Why not? You can see your precious little Christina if that's what you really want. Go. Take a look. There. In that room."

Todd rose quickly and went to the door. First he noticed Randolph seated at the table where he had dumped out the money and jewelry, then he noticed Christina lying on a small, ragged bed on the far side of the room. Rage tore through him when he saw she had been beaten very badly.

"What the hell have you done to her?" he demanded angrily, hurrying to the side of the small bed where she lay unconscious, one arm hanging limply over the edge.

"She lacked the respect we thought she should show us," Vella answered simply. She had followed Todd into the room and now stood just inside the doorway. There was a slight smile on her lips when she looked down at Christina's bloodied and swollen features. "She was really quite stubborn about it."

Seeing how terribly disfigured Christina's face was, Todd realized the severity of the blows they had dealt her. His fury overwhelmed him. Every muscle in his body tightened in preparation to attack. When his anger finally burst, it surfaced as a low, throaty growl. Then he made a wild lunge for Vella, but before his hands reached her satin-covered shoulders, he felt a sharp blow between his shoulder blades.

Randolph had come immediately to the rescue and had slammed the butt of his rifle into Todd's back, just inches below his neck. It stunned him temporarily, and before Todd was able to move again, Randolph had spun the rifle around and had the barrel pointed directly at Todd's head.

"Better not," was all he said as he cocked the hammer back.

Todd stared at him helplessly, his breath ragged, his anger still so much a part of him he could feel it pulsating through every fiber of his being. He knew he had to wait until he had an advantage or chance their both losing their lives.

"Don't be so foolish," Vella said with a lively shake of her head as she brought a small derringer from a pocket hidden within the folds of her voluminous skirt and waved it around, letting him know she was also armed.

When she was sure he had gotten the message, she went on. "Besides, it's not as bad as it looks. She hasn't been beaten unconscious. She proved too damn stubborn for that. But because she is so foolishly stubborn, and because I was afraid we would eventually have to beat her to death when I knew we might still need her alive, we finally chose to drug her."

Todd looked down at Christina and hoped that what Vella had said was true. He hoped she had not been beaten unconscious.

"And I might add that she doesn't take her medicine very well. We had a delightful time forcing her to swallow it," Vella chortled, casually aiming her derringer at Christina and closing one eye as if taking aim. Then she lowered the small pistol and held it at her side. "And she's been sleeping like a little babe ever since."

Todd tried not to reveal the terror that had seized him when Vella had raised her derringer and pointed it at Christina. He kept a calm expression and hoped that Vella's action was not an indication of what was on her mind. But the thought of Vellas anger reaching that point made it seem that much more important to get Christina out of there.

Glancing down to study Christina's face, he wondered how long she had been drugged. How long until she would come awake and be able to make a run for it. Though there was now noticeable movement beneath her eyelids, she was still out cold. Even with all the noise they made, Christina continued to sleep. Did he dare wait, or should he try to get the upper hand over all three of them, possibly tie them up, and then carry Christina out of there?

He was aware that she needed a doctor's attention right away, because most of her injuries were severe. He knew then he would use the first opportunity they gave him and take one of their weapons. His eyes were then drawn to the shiny little derringer in Vella's hands.

"Does this make you nervous? Do you actually think I want to shoot you?" Vella asked with an easy smile as she waved the derringer in front of her. Then suddenly her smile faded and anger drew her lips into a thin line as she glanced briefly at Christina. "It's *her* I'd like to shoot. And I do plan to shoot her. I have no reason to let her live."

Todd's blood ran cold as he watched Vella's anger mount with each word she spoke.

"You look stunned. You didn't think I actually planned to let her return to you, did you? Not when it hurts me so deeply to think of the two of you together."

As quickly as it had appeared, the anger left her face and was replaced by something else, something less volatile. "Todd, I love you so much. Why can't you see that? Because I love you as much as I do, I cannot bear the thought of another woman in your bed. Don't you see? I should be the woman in your bed."

Todd did not respond for fear of making her angrier. Instead, he watched her carefully, listened to more than what she said, and waited.

"Do you want to know how much I love you? I'll tell you. When William and I first came here, we came with plans to get you to make me your wife and then have you killed."

Todd's expression hardened with that bit of information, but still he remained quiet, listening, waiting.

"Don't you see? When we made those plans, I had not counted on falling in love with you. All I cared about was getting repossession of our land. Falling in love with you changed everything. I still wanted revenge for what your father did to my grandfather, but not so much that I was willing to have you killed. Not when I had come to love you so much."

"What did my father ever do to your grandfather?" Todd was trying to make sense of what she was saying, but found it impossible. He did not even know who her grandfather was.

"Your father had my grandfather sent to prison and had his land stripped away from him," she responded, and a glimmer of her anger returned.

"When?"

"Can't you figure out who I really am?" she asked with a disbelieving shake of her head. "Can't you figure it out that my last name is not really Stone?"

424

"Then what is it?"

"Livingston. Vella Livingston."

Todd felt the realization slam against him. Vella and William were Livingstons. Probably the children of Gordon Livingston. And the grandfather she had mentioned, was Judge Rodney Livingston.

Todd knew the story only too well. His own father had pretended to be a bushranger to gain the trust of the other bushrangers and learn more about those among them who had definite government connections. Connections that had eventually led to Judge Livingston. It was the information his father and a few of the others in the secret detective force had gathered that had brought about the judge's conviction and directly resulted in his land being stripped from him. Because of his brave accomplishments, Todd's father had been given a large amount of the land as a reward. The rest had been put up for resale, and Todd's grandfather, Aaron, had bought much of that.

"I see you now realize who my grandfather was," she said proudly. "The man your father falsely accused and had jailed just so he could get his hands on more land. I hope you also remember how my grandfather died in that bloody jail."

Todd's eyes widened and he came to a quick defense of his father. "Now, wait a minute. It wasn't my father who used his powers as a magistrate to lure criminals into doing his evil deeds. It was not my father who offered to cover up evidence against each one and bring about a certain verdict of not guilty in exchange for their undying loyalties."

"Neither did my grandfather. Your father was the one who made up that story and then manufactured enough

425

false evidence to make the courts believe him, but that doesn't make it true. Actually, your father wanted my grandfather dead right from the beginning. My father told me how my poor grandfather was manipulated into a situation that was meant to bring about his death but merely resulted in his capture. And it was *your* father who set the whole thing up. They were out to get him from the beginning, especially your father. They just wanted to get their hands on his prime land. And they did."

"Your father lied to you. I imagine because he was involved in many of your grandfather's illegal activities. There may never have been quite enough proof against your father to have him convicted, too, but he was guilty just the same."

"How do you know?" Vella demanded. "You weren't even born yet. How do you know what happened?"

Todd thought about that. Other than what he had been told as a child by Coolabah, Sam, his Uncle James, his cousin Ben, and his grandmum, he did not know. "How do you know that what *you* have said is true? You certainly had not been born yet, either."

"It is true! William and I both know it is. And that's why we devised our plan to get our grandfather's land back. It was our father's dying wish that William and I see that you Aylesburys paid for what you did to his father and get back what rightfully belonged to the Livingstons. That's the whole reason we came here."

"To get me to marry you so that when you had me killed you would be the one to get my land," Todd concluded. "But what about my grandmum? Did you not consider that she still has rights to the land?"

"She is old. She does not have many years left,

anyway. A few less would not have mattered."

"You two were willing to kill her, too?"

"Aye, to relcaim not only the land that was stolen from our family, but everything that had ever belonged to Eric Aylesbury," she said with a sharp nod. Her anger brought her short gasps for air as she stared at Todd's astonished expression. "But don't you see? We made those plans before I had ever met you and found out that you are not at all like your father. And as soon as I realized I had fallen in love with you, reclaiming the land came to mean less to me and I saw to it that our plans were immediately changed."

"How changed?"

"I realized I would be happier to live my life at your side, as your wife. We figured since William was to become your station boss anyway, he would be able to steal from you whenever he wanted. I would reclaim my grandfather's land as your wife, and any future generations of my family would, too, through my marriage to you. I even planned to see to it that William's children, should he ever have any, would get part of the land.

"William was satisfied with the new plan and agreed to do it my way and let you live. It was all going to work out beautifully. But then Christina had to come along and ruin everything! The bitch!" Vella's eyes glazed with anger and she again lifted her derringer and pointed it directly at Christina's head. Her lips tightened against her teeth as she cocked the weapon and then slipped her finger over the trigger.

## Chapter XXIV

Christina moaned quietly and moved her head to one side, unaware of the danger. The movement caught Vella's attention and caused her to hesitate long enough to give Todd a chance to try to distract her.

"Vella, I never realized you loved me that much," he said in a loud voice, so that she heard him, even through her anger. He then held his breath while he waited to see if she was going to respond by letting her attention be drawn to his voice or follow through with her obvious intention to shoot Christina.

Although Vella continued to aim the small pistol in Christina's direction, she turned her head to look questioningly at Todd.

Todd hurried to speak again in order to keep her distracted. "To think, you loved me enough to see that my life was spared when it would have better suited your needs for me to be killed." For Christina's sake, he forced admiration into his voice. "I feel ashamed now to realize I treated you as badly as I did. How could I have been so blind? Why did I not realize until this very moment how deeply you loved me? I must have been out of my mind to have turned a woman like you away."

Vella remained quiet, but she had given her full attention to what he had to say. Her eyes studied his every movement.

Todd shook his head and looked sincerely regretful. "What a fool I was to have chosen someone like Christina over someone like you." The words tasted bitter coming across his tongue, but he was more than willing to say them if it meant saving Christina.

His heart slammed hard against his chest and he held his breath. Vella's hand had started to tremble, the derringer still pointed at Christina, her finger still across the trigger. But then the short barrel slowly started to drop, until the small pistol was no longer aimed at Christina. It now pointed to an area of the dirt floor beneath the bed.

"Do you mean that?" Vella asked, hesitant to believe he had had such a complete change of heart in so short a time.

"I'd be a fool not to," Todd told her and he took a small step toward her. "Not many men are lucky enough to find a woman who loves them as much as you obviously love me."

Leery of his action, Vella swung her arm around and pointed the derringer at him. She narrowed her gray-green eyes with cautious disbelief. Even so, Todd knew she wanted to believe him.

"Look at you. You are such a courageous woman. Standing up for what you believe in. I don't know why I never saw that before now," he continued, carefully moving closer to her.

"Stay away from her," he heard Randolph warn him

and then heard the metallic click of the rifle's hammer being cocked.

Todd did not turn to look at Randolph or his weapon. "You don't have to worry. I have no intention of harming her. It's just that I have a sudden need to touch her, to hold her close," he said as convincingly as he could. His eyes never strayed from Vella's while he spoke, and he held her gaze with his.

His fear for Christina's life gave him remarkable acting abilities. He knew he had to get Vella away from Christina before she was again overcome by her irrational hatred and remembered how she had intended to kill her before he had drawn her attention away. And once he had put distance between Vella and Christina, he had to get his hands on that derringer. "I'm not even armed, Schiller. I just want to hold her a moment."

Vella's lips trembled and tears formed in her eyes. Slowly, she lowered the derringer and spoke to Randolph in a raspy voice. "He won't harm me."

Todd went to Vella then and enveloped her in his arms. He was relieved to find no resistance from her. Pressing her quivering form close, he pulled her firmly against him and held her for a long moment. Though everything in him rebelled, he put a fingertip beneath her chin, lifted her face to his, and gently kissed her. When he pulled away, he fought a coiling pain in his stomach as he stared adoringly into her tear-filled eyes.

Well aware that Randolph still held his rifle ready, Todd whispered quietly, so that only Vella heard his words, "Please, can't we be alone? Just for a little while? Maybe in the next room?"

Vella stared longingly at him for a moment before she nodded and blinked back her tears. With his arms around her, Todd quickly maneuvered her away from Christina's bedside and toward the door.

When Randolph moved to follow, Vella insisted he stay to count the money.

"I don't trust him," Randolph stated adamantly.

"I don't care if you trust him or not. I do," she responded quickly, and her adoring gaze returned to meet Todd's.

"What if he tries to get away?" Randolph asked, wanting her to see past her emotions.

"I still have my derringer," she pointed out and frowned, not fond of even so short a delay. She was very eager to be alone with Todd, to let him say and do the things she had longed for.

"All right, I'll stay in here and count the money," Randolph finally agreed and exhaled sharply to let her know how displeased he was by her decision. He then shouted out so that he could be heard in the next room. "Hank, they are coming in there. You be sure and keep an eye on him. Don't let him make a break for it."

"I assure you, I'm not going anywhere," Todd said in a husky voice, drowning out whatever response Hank had given. By making his voice almost a growl, he hoped he sounded as if he were so overcome by his desire that he could hardly speak.

The moment they stepped into the other room, Todd swept Vella into another passionate embrace, forcing his lips to meet hers again. He let his hands roam over her body as if eager to explore more of her, which he knew she expected of him. This time when he pulled his lips free, he took deep, ragged breaths, as if her kiss had left him breathless. He then glanced over at Hank, who sat watching them with obvious displeasure. Todd frowned, showing his own discontent, then bent close to her ear again and muttered, "Can't you get rid of him? I really don't think we need an audience at the moment."

"Hank, go in there and keep an eye on Randolph. Make sure he doesn't put any of that money into his pockets," Vella said quickly. Her own breathing was labored as she waited for Hank to do as he was told.

Never one to dispute Vella, Hank rose quickly, frowning at the idea that Randolph might cheat them, and left the room, closing the door behind him.

A smile slowly spread across Todd's face, and he hoped none of his apprehension showed when he spoke again. "Alone at last."

"What the hell?" they heard Randolph shout from inside the next room just as Todd was about to kiss Vella again.

Todd paused with his lips still inches from hers and listened.

"Hank, if you are in here with me, who's to keep that son-of-a-bitch from shoving Vella to the floor and getting clean away?" Suddenly Randolph appeared at the door, his rifle in hand, with Hank right behind him.

"Randolph get back in there," Vella demanded angrily and turned her head to confront him with her wrath.

"Not on your life," he told her and came on into the room.

Todd felt his heart ramming violently against his chest. His frustration overwhelmed him. He had come so close.

"Randolph, you had better remember who is in charge here. I said get back in there," Vella repeated, carefully pronouncing each syllable of each word so that he understood she was deadly serious.

"And I said no! I'm not letting him get away. He knows too much. We have to keep him here until we can get that money divided and be on our way. Besides, I thought you said there were to be no witnesses."

"That was before you bungled up in getting Justin here. I'm not about to let Todd be killed."

"Why not? He's got two strong legs. He can go running to the police just as easily as anyone else could," Randolph pointed out.

"Because I said so. Todd is not to be killed. I will stay here with him until you and Hank have had plenty of time to get well away. He's not going to try to go anywhere."

"That's easy to say, but I want to make sure he stays. I want to be absolutely sure we keep him here until we've had time to get that ransom divided and then get far away from here." Randolph still had made no move to return to the other room.

"Then get outside and guard the door if you are so sure he plans to make a run for it. Both of you. Get outside!" Vella's anger had been quick to return, this time to be vented against Randolph and not Christina. Her hand gripped the derringer more tightly.

Randolph stared at her, then at Todd. Todd sensed his distrust and tried his best to look trustworthy.

"All right, Vella. We'll go outside and guard the door. But if I see as much as one hair of his head try to come through that doorway, I'll shoot to kill."

"Fine, shoot," Todd said agreeably. "Just give us a little privacy for now." It was better if they were on the outside and not in the same room with Christina.

Randolph eyed him suspiciously, but did as he had

been told. When he went outside, Hank was right behind him.

The moment the door closed, Vella turned her face to Todd again, tilted her head back, and parted her lips. Todd obliged her with a long, lingering kiss, while he paid careful attention to her responses. When her body started to relax, he knew that her hold on the derringer had to have relaxed, too. He had just decided the time was right to grab the derringer when she suddenly pulled away and looked up at him. Her eyes were dark with desire, her lips full from having been so thoroughly kissed, but her distrust had edged its way back into her heart.

"Todd, it is just so hard for me to believe that your feelings for me could change so completely and so quickly," she said and her forehead drew into a tiny frown.

Afraid she really doubted his ardor and would ruin his chances of getting that derringer, he gently cupped her chin with his hand and stated as convincingly as he could, his eyes roving hungrily over her face as he spoke, "I don't think my feelings have changed. I don't think I ever truly stopped loving you. You were right all along. I never should have married Christina. I could never love her the way I can love you." His need to convince Vella kept him from choking on his words.

A loving smile quickly replaced her doubtful expression. "Didn't I tell you?"

"Aye, as I recall, you did. You also promised that when I finally did come to realize my true feelings you would willingly take me back," he said, relieved she had decided he was telling the truth, after all. "Does that promise still hold true? Will you take me back?"

"You know I will." Vella's smile deepened and Todd knew she believed him, but then she suddenly tensed again. Her gaze darted away from his face and rested on something behind him. When Todd spun around to see what had her attention, he was horrified. Christina had entered the room.

Vella reacted swiftly, backing away from Todd as she brought the derringer up and aimed it at Christina's heart. "Get back in there. There's nothing you can do about this. I told you all along that he loves me."

Christina did not respond. Instead she continued heading for Vella, her face devoid of all emotion, her arms dangling at her sides. Her disheveled appearance and the dried blood and bruises across her face gave her a menacing appearance.

"Get back in there or I'll shoot," Vella threatened, taking a few more steps back.

"Christina, please, get back in there," Todd pleaded, his voice desperate for her to obey.

As Christina continued to move slowly toward Vella, her face emotionless, Todd suddenly realized she was sleepwalking. Christina was completely unaware of the danger she was in. Instinctively, he dove for the gun in Vella's hands before she could fulfill her threat and shoot Christina. With both hands, he held the small pistol firmly in his grip as he spun sharply around, prying it free of her hands. Then in the same motion, he brought the weapon around and placed it at her throat.

Christina was close enough to the two of them to be knocked aside and slammed hard against the heavy wooden table. She fell back and over the top, striking her head on the far corner of the table's rough surface. She cried out in pain, but it was not quite loud enough to

436

cover the sound of the dull thud of her skull on the wood. Rolling on off the table, she crumpled to the dirt floor, never awakening.

"Todd, what are you doing?" Vella cried out.

"Taking over," Todd told her. He wanted to go to Christina and see how badly she had been hurt. But he held the short barrel of the derringer firmly against Vella's neck.

The noise had brought Randolph and Hank hurrying into the room with their guns raised and ready. When they saw the predicament Vella was in, they did not shoot. Hank stood dumbfounded, staring at where the derringer pressed into Vella's tender skin, while Randolph's eyes quickly darted about the room.

Aware the derringer had only one shot, Todd knew his only hope was that the two of them were so devoted to Vella that they would not want her harmed. He tightened his hold on her, having wrapped his left arm around her shoulders, and pressed the barrel of the derringer harder against her throat, forcing a cough from her. "Put down your guns. Both of you. Or I'll shoot. And at this range, there's not much chance I'll miss."

Hank's handgun hit the floor with a resounding thud, but Randolph's response was not so immediate.

"You won't kill her," he said, though there was little conviction in his voice. He pointed his rifle in Todd's direction while he tried to consider his options.

"Won't I? If it comes down to either her or me, just who do you *think* I'll choose?"

"Randolph, put your rifle down," Vella cried out in a strangled plea. Her eyes were cut in Todd's direction even though he stood behind her. Her expression revealed her terrible fear.

Randolph looked at her with a frown, then down at the rifle he held aimed at the two of them.

"Damnit, Vella, didn't I warn you about him?"

"Toss it over here," Todd said calmly. "Toss it over here and no one gets hurt."

"Toss it over there," Hank said and nudged his companion with his elbow.

"Nice and easy," Todd added.

Randolph's expression remained tense as he lowered the rifle and studied the situation. Finally, he did as he was told and slung the rifle across the floor so that it came to a clattering stop against Todd's boots.

Todd was relieved to have the rifle at his feet, but he did not pull the derringer away from Vella's throat. "Now, kick Hank's pistol on over here."

When Hank quickly did as he was told, Randolph's hands curled into fists and his lips pressed into a tight white line. Clearly he had hoped to make use of that pistol.

"What are you going to do now?" Randolph demanded.

Todd did not like the way Randolph's gaze kept darting to the floor where the two weapons lay. He knew that although Hank was ready to do whatever he was told, Randolph had not given up hope of regaining control. Rather than take the derringer away from Vella's throat while he bent to pick up the weapons, he pulled her down to the floor with him, which proved to be a mistake.

Despite the derringer at her throat, Vella made a grab for Hank's pistol. While Todd fought to get it away from her, he dropped the derringer, and Randolph made a move toward them both. Luckily, Todd managed to get the pistol in his grasp. He pointed it at Randolph before

438

he had completely crossed the room and before he had gotten any of the weapons. Seeing Hank's pistol pointed now in his direction, Randolph suddenly became docile and quickly backed away, his hands raised in surrender.

Vella made one last attempt to get a weapon and tried for the derringer that lay on the floor near her ankle. But Todd kicked the derringer and the rifle out of her reach and grabbed her by her hair so that she could not go after them.

With the pistol pointed at Randolph, and Vella successfully captured by her hair, screaming loudly in painful protest each time he moved away from her, Todd stood and kicked the weapons across the room. He wanted to get them as far away from the others as he could. He dragged Vella along at his side until he sent both guns clattering through the door and into the other room, out of everyone's sight.

"Now, I want you two to back up into that corner over there," he stated matter-of-factly and nodded to indicate which corner he had meant, then waited until they had done so.

As soon as they were in the opposite corner of the room from where he and Vella stood, Todd gave a sharp jerk on Vella's hair, forcing her to go with him to Christina's side.

"You're hurting me," Vella complained again as she moved across the room with him, her head bent to accommodate the painful hold he had on her hair.

"After what you did to Christina, you are lucky I don't beat the living hell out of you," Todd ground out and gave her mane another sharp tug, causing her to drop to her knees. Keeping his hold on her, he examined Christina. He discovered a gaping wound at the back of her head and saw that blood had already soaked her hair and pooled onto the floor, forming an ugly dark patch in the dirt.

He knew then that he needed to get her to a doctor immediately. He could not worry about getting these three to the police. He no longer had any time for that.

"Take off your clothes," he said as he let go of Vella's hair and shoved her roughly to the floor. When she simply lay there staring up at him with disbelief, he repeated his command. "I said, take off your clothes."

"Why?"

"Don't ask questions. Just do as you are told. Take off your clothes."

Vella gasped with indignation, but when she realized he was serious, she moved her hand to the buttons along the back of her dress and undid the ones she could reach.

"You too," he said to Randolph and Hank. "Off with your clothes. And your boots."

Randolph said nothing as he unbuttoned his shirt and then the waist of his trousers. Hank simpered a complaint, but he eventually turned his back to the room and began to undress.

Todd kept his eye on the three of them. When Vella had trouble reaching some of the buttons at the middle of her back, he gave the garment a hard yank, which sent the remaining buttons scattering across the floor.

Hank spun around to see what had happened. When he saw that Vella was down to her flimsy undergarments, he stopped what he was doing to gawk.

"Keep going," Todd said and nodded in Hank's direction, but when Vella reached for the strap of her camisole with the intention of removing even that, he quickly told her, "Not you. That's far enough for you.

Hand me your dress."

Slowly she wadded the shimmering green garment into a large ball and held it out to him. Her nostrils flared with anger and she stood proudly with her breasts thrust out and her shoulders erect when he took it from her.

"Now get over there and gather up their clothes," he told her, clearly not interested in what lay beneath the thin material of her underclothes. He waved at her with the pistol.

Her expression hardened further, but she did not argue with him. She went to where Randolph's clothing was strewn and knelt down to pick it up.

"And the boots," Todd added.

Next she moved to where Hank's clothing and his boots had been laid in a single heap and she knelt down to gather those things, too. When she looked up at him, Hank awkwardly placed his hands down to cover the crotch of his underwear.

"Now what?" she asked as she stood and turned back around to face Todd, her arms full of rumpled clothing.

"Bring it all over here and put it on the floor, then get back over there with them."

Todd waited until she was beside Randolph and Hank before he bent over to remove the suspenders from the trousers. Then he had Vella and Hank come to him one at a time so he could secure their hands behind them with the wide straps. For Randolph, he took off his own leather belt. He made sure he had his cousin's wrists securely bound behind him, too, before he tore some of the clothing into strips and tied the three of them together, back to back.

Finally, he had them sit on the floor and used more of the torn clothing to bind their feet. He then took what clothing was left, doused it with the whiskey that had remained inside Hank's metal flask, and set fire to it.

"I'll see you burn in hell," Vella threw at him as she watched the yellow and blue flames slowly eat through the clothing and then realized that he intended to leave the three of them there in just their underclothing. "You will regret this day. I will see to that."

Todd did not have time to argue with her and ignored her viperous remarks. He went into the next room to take care of the rifle and the derringer. He knew better than to leave any weapons available. After he smashed Randolph's rifle against the wall, he slipped the derringer and the money and jewelry that had been left out on the table into his pockets. He then returned to smash the rifle that had clattered to the floor when Christina had fallen across it.

Having taken care of all the weapons he knew about, he quickly gathered Christina up and stood, shifting her weight so she lay balanced in his arms.

"What about the fire?" Hank asked when he realized Todd was about to leave with the clothes still burning on the floor.

Todd hesitated. "What about it?"

"You can't run off and leave it burning. The whole hut will burn down. Us too."

"I don't think there's much chance of that. It's a dirt floor," Todd muttered. "And this is a cob hut. About all that will burn in the whole structure is the wood in the frame. So I guess you are just going to have to take your chances."

"What about the smoke?" Hank asked worriedly.

"I'll leave the door open." Then, while he moved with Christina to the door, he added with a half smile,

"Besides, I'll be coming right back."

"But we won't be here," Randolph shouted defiantly just before Todd disappeared from his sight. "As soon as you leave, we'll be out of here. By the time you get back, we will be long gone; off somewhere getting our hands on the guns we will need to kill you. And you'd better believe we will see you dead for this. You and her both."

Todd ran the other horses off into the night before turning Justin's horse toward Bathurst. He could not let Randolph's threats worry him. He had to get Christina to a doctor.

Todd stayed with the doctor and his wife, who was assisting him, long enough to be assured that Christina was being properly cared for before he headed straight for the police. The doctor told him that Christina's head wounds were very serious, and Todd was more eager than ever to have Randolph, Hank, and Vella brought to justice—and also William, for the part he had played in Vella's evil scheme.

Within minutes after he had told the captain in charge what had happened, nine troopers were called out of their beds and assembled. Weapons were quickly checked and instructions given. When they rode out only a few minutes later with their captain in the lead, Todd rode with them.

The man who rode in front beside the captain held a large lantern, but the small glow of light was little help at the rate they traveled. Horses stumbled and riders were jostled. The troop did not slacken its speed until they reached the densest areas of the bush, at which point Todd had a difficult time finding his own tracks, and they slowed down.

As Todd had feared, by the time they finally arrived at the small hut, the three had worked their way out of their bonds and had escaped. When he and the captain entered the hut, all they found besides furniture and the dark stains of Christina's blood were the remnants of the clothing Todd had used to bind them and a pile of ashes. Only a part of a boot heel remained recognizable in the smoldering heap.

"How long has it been since you left them?" the captain asked as they left the hut.

"Several hours," Todd admitted. He scanned the area around them. If the three had had weapons hidden that he had not known about, they could all be the victims of an ambush at any moment.

"Well, I doubt they got very far in the dark with no horses and no shoes," the captain said, then stepped out into the yard and shouted to his men. "They have to be around here somewhere. Spread out and look for them."

Within minutes, one of the troopers shouted that he had found their footprints, and with the coming of daylight, they followed them with little difficulty. The sun was not yet above the treetops when they heard shuffling noises in the bush. The troopers drew their weapons from their scabbards and moved toward the source of the noise.

Randolph and Hank immediately recognized the hopelessness of the situation and gave up without a fight. The troopers found the two of them standing in the middle of the bush in nothing but their underwear with their hands held high. Within minutes, they were both handcuffed and in custody.

"Now all we have to do is catch up with the woman,"

the captain said, pleased that the two men had given up so easily, and he motioned for two of the troopers to remain behind with the new prisoners. "The rest of you remount. Proceed with the search."

Suddenly, before anyone had had a chance to react to the captain's command, Vella appeared from behind a huge gray rock. Dressed in only her camisole and bloomers, she made a wild lunge at one of the horses and came away with a loaded rifle in her hands.

"Damn you, Todd," she cried out, so overcome by her anger that tears streamed down her face as she pointed the rifle at Todd's heart. Her dark hair fell down around her face and shoulders in wild disarray and her chest heaved from the fury that consumed her.

"Put that rifle down or we'll shoot," the captain commanded in a stern voice. Two of the troopers who had kept their rifles at their sides slowly raised them, ready to fire.

"Damn you all. Damn you all to hell," Vella cried, and she closed her eyes and pulled sharply on the trigger, screaming when the rifle bucked back against her shoulder and roared.

Barely a split second after she had squeezed off her shot, the two other rifles roared and Vella fell back onto the ground.

"Oh, my Gawd," Hank cried out his anguish. His voice sounded oddly quiet after the loud report of the guns.

Todd's blood splattered across his face when the bullet bit high into his shoulder, and he reached to cover his injury with his hand. The warm, sticky liquid oozed from the wound, but he did not stop to examine the damage. He was certain the wound was not too serious. But as he looked at Vella's crumpled form and at her blood-soaked undergarments, he realized her wounds were fatal.

"Todd," she sobbed, and tried to raise her head. Too weak, her head fell back and she gazed up at the trooper who had hurried to her side to examine her. She asked fearfully, "Did I kill him?"

"No, you didn't kill me," Todd said quietly as he walked over to where she lay dying. The hatred and anger had gone from him, and all that was left was pity.

She tried to smile for him but couldn't. She whispered, "I'm sorry. I'm so sorry. All I ever wanted was for you to love me."

A sharp wave of compassion struck him as he knelt at her side. He glanced questioningly at the trooper who had quickly examined her wounds and saw him shake his head sadly, then move away.

"Todd? Are you still there?" She lifted her blood-stained hand from where it lay across her waist, only to let it drop again. Tears had filled her eyes so that she was unable to see him and she feared he was the one who had gone away. When she tried to speak again, she coughed and the gurgling sound let Todd know one of the bullets had pierced her lung.

"Aye, I'm still here," he said and choked back the powerful ripple of pity he felt rise in his throat as he took her bloodied hand in his.

"I'm so sorry. C-Can you forgive me?" she asked, hope still strong in her voice. "All I-I ever wanted was for you to love me."

Sadly, Todd stared down at her. His chest grew tight as he considered how very misguided her love had been.

"I know," he responded quietly. "I know."

"Can you? Forgive me?" she asked one last time, and then her eyes glazed as if she was suddenly seeing into another world. Her body relaxed.

"Aye, I can forgive you," Todd said with a sullen shake of his head, though he knew she could no longer hear him. "Now if you can only convince God to do the same." With tears of deep compassion burning the outer corners of his eyes, he stood and walked slowly away. Behind him he heard Hank crying, and he realized the poor man had been in love with her all along.

## Chapter XV

Todd spent most of the afternoon and all of that night at Christina's bedside, despite the doctor's staunchest protests. While he waited there, watching her, he tried not to let his thoughts wander back to the horrible events that had led to Christina's severe injuries and Vella Livingston's death. He also tried not to worry about William and Vella's hatred for his family. They had plotted so cleverly and so completely against him that they had been willing to kill him to regain the land they had been led to believe was rightfully theirs. Though Vella was clearly no longer a threat to him or his family, William still could be.

Knowing that, Todd had gone with the troopers to his station that same morning, only hours after Vella had been killed. They had hoped to find William there and to arrest him while he was at work. But they made the trip for nothing. They learned that William had never returned there. Though the police enacted an immediate area-wide search for him, Todd had little hope William would be found anytime soon.

Being privy to inside information, William might have suspected trouble was finally upon them and run away. That would explain why he had not been with his sister the night before. Or maybe William had given up the scheme after all their plans had suddenly begun to fall through. If that was so, the kidnapping idea might have been Vella's and William might have wanted no part of it. At any rate, William was nowhere to be found and had not been seen in well over two days by anyone the police had questioned. And neither had Justin.

But Todd did not want to think about Justin or William at the moment, or of the harm William could possibly do if he was still somewhere close by when news of Vella's death got out. The police were aware of the problem and had promised to handle it. He also did not want to concern himself with the angry threats Randolph Schiller had shouted as the troopers yanked him off his horse and took him into the jail. There was little chance Schiller would ever be free again to fulfill any of his threats. And most of all, Todd tried not to let the memory of Vella's violently bloody death haunt his thoughts.

Instead, while he sat doggedly at his wife's side, he tried to keep his mind focused on the future, their future, his and Christina's, and how he hoped to make everything up to Christina somehow. He prayed again and again that God would at least grant him the opportunity to try.

The doctor's warning to Todd and his grandmum shortly after he had examined Christina had pierced the very core of Todd's heart, and the fear of what the man had told them lodged painfully inside of him. There was only a slight chance that Christina would live. There had been swelling in her brain and internal bleeding. If she did not come out of her coma within the next few days, her chances of survival were few, and if infection should set in, her chances were nil.

Though the doctor kept a close watch over her and administered medication to her wounds and applied cold compresses almost hourly, he explained that her fate was no longer in his hands. Only God had the power to save her now, and only time would decide Christina's fate.

Todd had never felt such overpowering helplessness, nor been tormented by such overwhelming guilt. If Christina died, it would be because he had selfishly forced her to marry him. None of what happened to her would ever have occurred if he had not been so adamant that she be his wife. Without even being aware there were risks, he had brought her into a dangerous situation.

Though his misery was too deep to be touched, Penelope did what she could to comfort her grandson. Rose had also tried to comfort him in some way when she had visited earlier. But it was Penelope who brought him food and forced him to eat, and made sure the doctor tended to his shoulder regularly so infection would not set in. And it was Penelope who finally convinced him to leave Christina's side, if just to take a walk.

Todd had agreed to a short walk mainly to keep from arguing any further with his grandmum who, he knew, was only trying to help. He also saw it as an opportunity to find out if anything new had been discovered concerning William's or Justin's whereabouts.

Before he left the room, he glanced back at Christina once more and studied her motionless face. His grandmum had already taken his chair and she sat watching Christina carefully. He knew his wife could not be in better hands.

When he went out into the brisk early-morning air it was still dark and he was momentarily dumbfounded. He had been so lost in his concern for Christina that the time of day had come to mean very little to him. He realized that neither he nor his grandmum had slept for the past two nights. He headed down the street toward police headquarters, his heart gladdened by his grandmum's deep concern for Christina's welfare.

Since the building was on the same street, only several blocks to the west, Todd was there within a matter of minutes. He inquired of the night captain, who had ridden with him to arrest Vella, Hank, and Randolph, if there had been any news of William or Justin.

"Nothing on Justin, but on William, we have gotten conflicting reports," the captain told him with a tired yawn, leaning away from the papers across his desk and stretching his muscles by using the back of his chair to arch against. "A man from Cobb and Company swears he sold William Stone a coach ticket last Saturday for passage to Lithgow, which could be true. But a man with our detective force says he's heard that William is still in town, being hidden by friends until they can arrange safe transportation for him out of Bathurst. Our man also heard that William has indeed learned of his sister's death and has made the expected threats of personal retribution against your family, though we have no indication yet just how he plans to go about it."

Todd felt apprehension crawl beneath his skin. "I need to have someone ride out and warn Coolabah."

"That's already been done," the captain assured him. "Plus I have assigned two of our men to help watch over the place until William's exact location is discovered.

And as you may have noticed, I have dispatched another of my own troopers to guard your wife's door so that William can't do her any harm, either."

"I didn't see any guard," Todd said as he tried to recall having glimpsed anyone in the corridor outside his wife's door or even anywhere outside the building. He could barely recall having passed through the corridor to the outside at all and felt he should admit that before the captain came to believe his trooper had been negligent in his duty. "But then my mind was preoccupied with other things. I may have simply missed noticing him."

"Well, he's supposed to be there," the captain told him. "And he's supposed to stay there until he either gets word from me or Captain Hicks to return or is relieved by another man."

"Good. I appreciate the added protection for my family," Todd said earnestly. "I just hope you can find William before someone figures out a way to get him out of town. And the sooner you find him, the better."

"I agree. And I can assure you, we are working on it," the captain said, and for the first time since Todd had entered his office the man smiled. Slowly, he pushed himself out of his chair and stretched again with a loud groan, then escorted Todd to his office door. "You have enough to worry about right now. You just leave William to us. We may not have a photograph to go on, but we have your clear description. I'm sure we'll find him, because right now he's got our highest priority and will have until we have him in our custody."

Todd was glad to hear it. As soon as he had left police headquarters, he headed back to Christina's side, feeling somewhat reassured. He also wanted to warn his grandmum of the potential danger William still posed. He felt she should be cautioned to be extra careful in her comings and goings for the next few days. The way she was constantly in and out, she was a prime target for the man, especially if he realized she had no protection.

The more he thought about it, the more he considered asking the guard to see her safely to her hotel room each time she left, so he could at least be assured she had reached the place safely. And maybe he could plan a way for the guard to be with her on her return trip to the doctor's, as well.

As he approached the building, Todd glanced around the lamplit area for the guard before he entered the portion of the doctor's house that was used as a private hospital. But Todd saw no one. Even after he had entered the building, he did not find anyone in uniform. In fact, there was no one in the corridor at all. But he did notice a narrow wooden chair down the hallway, facing his wife's door. It had probably been placed there by the guard, who had obviously gone to take care of private matters in the privy at the back of the house.

Satisfied that a guard was indeed about and also planning to speak with the man about his grandmum's safety, Todd went into Christina's room. His gaze went immediately to his wife as he quietly eased the door open and stood in the doorway. His heartbeat was so strong with the hope he would find her finally awake that he could feel his blood pulsating. But what he discovered only disappointed him more. She had not moved. She was exactly as she had been when he'd left. No improvement at all.

When he then looked at his grandmum, he thought it strange that she *had* moved. She had repositioned her chair so that she now sat with her back to Christina and her face to the door. He noticed how unusually wide her eyes were. How very tense her expression. His first thought was that Christina had slipped away while he was gone and he felt suddenly weak. But in the same moment, he realized that his grandmum would have been overcome with her grief if that were true. There would be tears. Her eyes held no tears.

He gazed at her curiously for a long moment before he slowly started to close the door. Then he realized she was staring purposely at the area behind the door and he knew immediately who he would find there if he was to turn and look. He paused with the door half closed and considered what he should do. He wondered if William was armed, and if he was, did he have a gun, a club, or a knife?

"Close the door, Todd," William said quietly, and when Todd's reaction to his words registered no surprise, no immediate alarm, he quickly added, "Do as I say or the first bullet goes through your grandmum."

So William had a gun. Although Todd wondered if it was a pistol or a rifle, he did not turn around to find out. He did not want to make any move William might consider aggressive. He had no idea of the man's state of mind.

Needing time, Todd did exactly as he was told. He moved very slowly and deliberately when he pushed the door behind him, until he felt it close and heard a metal click.

"Now what? I'll do whatever you say," Todd told him agreeably, facing away from the man.

"I heard all about what happened to my sister," William began. His anger was evident in the grating tone of his voice. "It wasn't enough that you Aylesburys murdered my grandfather. You had to bring financial ruin to my father, which in an indirect way brought on his early death, and now you have murdered my sister, too."

"I didn't kill her," Todd said.

"It may not have been your bullet that brought her down, but it was you who brought the toopers. And it was you who caused her to try anything so risky in the first place. I tried to warn her there were too many faults to her plan, but she was beyond listening to me. If you hadn't used her the way you did and then tossed her aside like so much garbage, and if Justin had not tried to cheat her out of so much money, she never would have done anything as drastic as kidnapping your wife. It was your betrayal that brought on her death. Yours and Justin Lapin's. And before I leave Bathurst, I'll see you both dead."

"How are you going to kill Justin when no one knows where he is?" Todd asked, hoping to get William thinking logically.

"When he hears about Christina's death, he'll come," William said with so much conviction that Todd's initial reaction was to turn then and try to take him. But he controlled his anger.

"Christina is not going to die," Todd responded adamantly and finally turned to face William. He thought it strange that William was dressed in a policeman's uniform.

"Aye, but she *is* going to die," William said with a confirming nod. "Very shortly after you die, as a matter of fact."

Penelope gasped aloud, then covered her mouth with both her hands when William responded to the noise

456

with a glowering scowl. He pointed the pistol he gripped in his hand directly at her face.

"Why the uniform?" Todd asked, wanting to get the man's attention away from his grandmum.

"It was a way of getting in here," William said with an easy shrug. "Most of the men on the night patrol don't even know the men on the day patrol because they have little occasion to see each other. So I pretended to be on the day patrol and told the guard outside I was sent early to be his replacement. He was tired of sitting and eager to go home. He didn't even question my being there at all, much less so early."

"Very clever. You do look authentic. How'd you ever get your hands on an entire uniform like that?"

"I have my ways," William said with a chuckle. To Todd's relief, William lowered his pistol as he glanced down at his attire. "Perfect fit, don't you think?"

"Aye. You would have fooled me," Todd said, trying to ease some of William's anger by bragging about his cleverness. "You look just like you belong in it."

"I thought about being a trooper once," William started to say, but then, as if he suddenly wondered why he was telling Todd any of that, he changed the conversation. "But then I found out what a trooper makes and decided against it. Besides, being a trooper would not have allowed me to weasel my way into your employ."

"Aye, Vella told me all about the plans you two had made before coming here. She also mentioned to me all the things your father had told you both about what happened to your grandfather. I tried to explain to her that none of what your father had told you was true, but she did not want to believe it."

457

"Why should she believe you? You are an Aylesbury same as the rest. Lies are bred into you." The muscles in William's jaw tightened and a trickle of sweat rolled from his short-cropped brown hair down the side of his face. "You were born to lie. Just like your father. Just like your grandfather."

Todd saw Penelope bristle at William's last remarks and he looked at her pleadingly to persuade her to keep quiet. She never looked at Todd. She sat leaning forward in her chair, both hands gripping the sides with such pure fury that her knuckles were white and the veins in her hands protruded like little ropes. He had never seen her so angry. His blood turned cold as he thought about what she might do if William said anything more against the Aylesbury name.

"So what do you plan to do now?" Todd asked quickly.

"Shoot me some Aylesburys," William said with an amused laugh. "Just think. I'll be able to get me three at once. And when Justin shows to pay his last respects to his sister, I'll pick him off, too, then I'll be gone from here. I may not be able to get my hands on the land that was stolen from my grandfather like Vella and I had hoped, but then, neither will it stay in the hands of the Aylesburys."

"Are you forgetting my great-grandmother?" Todd asked calmly. He had to make William see how faulty his plan was. "She is an Aylesbury. And once you have killed me and Grandmum, the land will go to her."

"Then maybe I'll have to make a trip to Hawksbury and pay her a little visit," William mused aloud and waved the gun as if to confirm the purpose of the trip.

It must have been the malicious smile on his face that

finally triggered Penelope into action. At that precise moment she flung herself out of the chair toward where William stood facing Todd. Todd made a dive for the gun, as much to draw the man's attention away from his grandmum as to get possession of the weapon.

A three-way struggle ensued and all three got their hands on the weapon at the same time. They tried pulling it free, and at different times the barrel pointed at each of them. Then Penelope quit struggling against the two stronger men and sank her teeth into William's arm instead. William's grip loosened and Todd got full possession of the gun.

William immediately grabbed ahold of Penelope and brought her firmly against him. If Todd took a shot, he would shoot his grandmother. William held his human shield in place with a viselike grasp at the base of her throat.

"What if you should miss?" William asked, more as a suggestion than a question, as he stared nervously down the barrel of his own gun.

"Let go of her," Todd stated calmly.

"Hell, no," William said, and looked at him as if he might not have all of his machinery in good working order. "If I let go of her then what defense would I have against you? Hell, no. I'm getting out of here and she's going with me." He dragged Penelope along with him across the room and toward the door.

Todd watched helplessly, knowing the man was right. There was too much of a risk involved to try to shoot him now. Though William was considerably larger than Penelope and much of him was unprotected, there was the possibility he might miss and end up killing his own grandmum. But there was nothing really preventing him from stepping forward and simply beating the living hell out of the man. Though William might strike his grandmum or shove her to the floor, the man had no weapon to injure anyone fatally.

"You are not going anywhere," Todd said and moved to stand between William and the door. He stood staring at the man with pure determination.

"That's true, you are not going anywhere," Penelope put in, and as she spoke her next words, she brought her booted heel against the front of his leg, below his knee. "At least not with me."

As William let out a loud yelp of pain, Penelope broke free from his grasp and ran across the room, far away from the man's reach.

"Looks like we have you," Todd said and slowly let out the breath he had been holding as he continued to aim the pistol at William.

William looked at him, his eyes wide with fear, then over to where Penelope stood gently rubbing the reddened area at the base of her throat.

"Grandmum? Would you step outside and see if you can locate a policeman? Tell him we have someone in here whom his captain would be very interested in," Todd said calmly, though his insides were still in a knotted mass and his heart pounded so hard he could feel his pulse in the tips of his fingers that now clutched the pistol aimed at William.

Though he had spoken to Penelope, his eyes never left William's angry scowl. He watched for even the slightest movement, the slightest indication that he intended to try something. Todd knew he would shoot the man if he had to. But evidently William had come to the same conclusion about Todd's willingness to kill him, because he made no attempt to escape while Penelope was gone. When she returned with two policemen and the captain, William surrendered quietly.

He made no open threats to either Todd or Penelope when he was led to the door, but he paused in the doorway to give Todd one last glaring look before being shoved on out into the hall. There was enough hatred in his expression to make up for his silence, and Todd shuddered to think what the man was capable of doing to them. And would yet, if he ever managed to get free again.

"I think I'll go with them to make sure they get him safely locked away," Todd said to Penelope after they heard the door to the outside close. "Stay and keep an eye on Christina. I'll be right back."

He paused to look at his wife and shook his head dismally when he realized that all the commotion had not disturbed her in the least. He felt his heart breaking as he walked out the door.

Leaving the building, he passed the doctor, who was on his way into the hall from his private living quarters, dressed in nothing more than his nightshirt.

"What's going on here?" the doctor asked as he smoothed his tousled hair with his hand. "What's all the commotion? Was that the police I saw leaving here?"

"Aye, we had a little riff," Todd said calmly. "But it's been taken care of now. The man who caused the trouble has been arrested and is on his way to jail. I'm going along to see that he is securely put away where he can do no further harm. I'd appreciate it if you would check on Christina once more before you go back to bed."

"Why, was she harmed?" the doctor asked, clearly concerned, and turned to do as he had been asked.

Todd waited until the doctor had gone into the room and closed the door, then hurried on to the police headquarters. He would not breathe easy again until he personally saw William inside the jail, securely locked behind an iron door.

# Chapter XVI

Todd returned to Christina's side as soon as he was certain William could cause them no further harm. Again he was disappointed to see no change in his wife's condition. There was no indication that she had made even the slightest movement while he was gone. Nothing that might offer him the tiniest ray of hope.

Penelope stayed with him for a little while after he had returned. But shortly after daybreak, she finally left him to go back to the hotel. She had taken a room the day before so that she could have a place to rest, but had yet to stay in it to sleep. Both she and Todd had been two nights now without any sleep. Although Todd was adamant that he did not need any sleep, she felt she just could not go on any longer unless she got at least a few hours rest.

Before she walked out of the room, Penelope made one final request that Todd try to get a little sleep too. Again Todd refused even to consider it, claiming there would be plenty of time for rest after he was sure Christina was going to be all right.

It was midmorning before exhaustion finally got the better of Todd, and he dozed still sitting in his chair. He was unaware he had drifted off at all until he was suddenly startled awake by the opening of the door. His first thought was that William had returned, because in his dream the man had escaped. But to his relief, and to his utter surprise, Justin entered the room.

"Justin," was all he could say when Christina's brother came across the room, hat in hand, to gaze remorsefully down at his sister's motionless face.

Though Todd's brain cried out for him to make Justin tell him exactly where he had gone and demand to know how he could have deserted them knowing the problems he would create, all Todd could do when he spoke again was repeat the man's name. "Justin."

Tears filled Justin's green eyes as he knelt at his sister's bedside. He placed his battered hat on the floor beside his knee. He trembled as he gently ran his fingers down the outer curves of her cheeks. "Oh, Christina. I'm so sorry. Don't die. I didn't mean for you to be harmed in any way. I never should have left you to face their anger. It's just that I was so scared. I didn't know what else to do. I lost part of the money I owed them, more than half of it, and I was too afraid to face them."

Justin's face twisted with the deep pain he felt. "I was afraid they would kill me for sure this time. I know now it was the wrong thing for me to do."

Todd could not have agreed more, but still he said nothing. Quietly, he leaned forward in his chair and watched the agony Justin's face displayed and listened to what he had to say to Christina.

"I should have stayed and faced them myself." Justin's voice became strained as he lifted her hand from the bed and pressed it against the tear-dampened beard on his cheek. His face drew into a tight, pain-filled grimace and his shoulders began to quake. "I never should have run."

Todd gave his brother-in-law a moment to control his emotions before he finally spoke to him. "What brought you back?"

"I couldn't stay away," Justin said, turning to face Todd while gingerly holding Christina's hand between his own. "Everything I hold dear to my heart is here, in Bathurst. My sons. Christina. Rose. When I finally realized that, when I finally realized life was not worth living without the ones I love, I knew I had to come back and face whatever it was I had to face. When I went by the police headquarters to tell them everything, like I should have done in the first place, that's when I heard about what happened. They let me come right over."

Todd glanced across the room and noticed that Captain Hicks stood in the doorway waiting to take Justin back to jail. Then he looked back at Justin's stricken face.

The anger Todd had harbored for Justin and that had festered inside him these past few days left him easily when he realized how sincerely sorry the man was. Slowly he smiled. Todd felt so proud of Justin at that moment. Justin had returned to face whatever danger awaited him. He had gone directly to police headquarters to tell them everything in order to get their help, even though it had meant admitting his own guilt.

"When they told me she might die, I had to come see her one more time." Justin's voice cracked from the painful emotions that gripped him, and for a moment he did not speak. When he did, his voice was only a little better under control. "I had to come tell her how very much I love her, and how sorry I am for what I did. A-and to ask her not to die. I could not live with myself if she was to die."

Then Justin turned his attention back to Christina. Pressing her hand to his cheek again, then to his lips, he began to weep openly and bitterly. "Please, Christina. Please don't die. I need someone I can trust to see that my boys are taken care of for me. Please, don't die. I'll make it all up to you somehow. I promise. Give me that chance."

When Christina did not respond, he wept harder. "I did this to her."

"It's hard to say who is to blame," Todd said compassionately. After all, if Vella had not been out to seek revenge on the Aylesbury family, she might never have come to the Bathurst District, and none of what had happened that night would ever have occurred. He felt Justin was almost as much a victim as Christina was. Gently, he gave Justin a reassuring pat on his shoulder. "I think it was a combination of many things."

The captain then came forward, cleared his throat, and spoke quietly but firmly. "It's time to go. You are only supposed to have five minutes. I've given you ten."

Justin looked back at him. A new rush of tears fell and he pressed Christina's hand to his cheek one last time. "Take good care of her, Todd. Don't let her die. My boys are going to need her while I'm in jail. I don't want them living with a total stranger while I'm gone. They are going to need her."

"I intend to see that everything is done for her that can be done," Todd promised, fighting back his own rush of emotion.

Gently, Justin put Christina's hand back at her side

where he had found it, then rose to his feet. "I know you will. And I want to thank you."

"For what?" Todd asked as he stood.

"For saving her from those bludgers. I know them. They would have killed her. I can't bear to think about what all else they might have done before they actually did end her life." He looked down at her one last time, at the horrible bruises and cuts across her face and neck. "It's bad enough what they *did* do to her."

Todd could no longer speak. Instead he patted Justin's shoulder again, nodding that he understood.

"I want you to know how sorry I am for having caused all this. I never wanted any harm to come to Christina. Never. Will you tell her that when she wakes up? And will you go to Rose and tell her how sorry I am for what I did? I know she will probably never forgive me, any more than Christina will, but I want Rose to know how truly sorry I am. I want them both to know. Will you tell them?"

Todd nodded. Then, as he looked on, Captain Hicks placed a set of handcuffs on Justin's wrists and quietly escorted him out of the room. Todd stood staring at the vacant doorway for several minutes before walking over and quietly closing the door. Emotionally drained, he leaned heavily against the hard surface and pressed his burning cheek against its coolness.

"What will they do to him?"

Todd's eyes widened, but at first he did not move. Finally, certain that he had indeed heard Christina's voice, he turned to look, his blue eyes glimmering with hope.

"What do you think they will do to him?" she wanted to know. Her voice was barely above a whisper.

Slowly his mouth opened with wonder, and he stared at her in disbelief. The tears Justin had caused still clung to his eyelashes and the rims were slightly red, making his smile seem ludicrous. He rushed to her side to gather her into his arms, but quickly decided against it and held her gently by her shoulders instead.

"You are awake," he stated needlessly. She had only one eye open, and it only halfway, but she was clearly awake. "How do you feel?"

"Proud," she said, and attempted to smile, but the expression quickly turned into a grimace when the movement of her face resulted in a sharp pain through the right side of her head. After a moment, she again opened the one eye and tears quickly filled it. "Proud of my brother and proud of my husband. I'm quite a lucky woman. If I was to die right now, I'd die happy."

Todd's face registered the horror of her words. "Don't say that. Don't even think it. You are going to be just fine. All you need is a little more bedrest and doctor's care. You'll see. We will be going home in just a few days."

"Home." She said the word longingly, then attempted to smile again. This time the pain was too much for her and she slipped gratefully back into the painless state of unconsciousness.

Days went by and Christina did not again regain consciousness. The swelling in her head had gone down and her smaller wounds had started to heal, but she did not come out of her comatose state. The doctor tried to get Todd to go home or at least to his grandmother's hotel room and get some much needed rest, but he refused to leave his wife's side. Even Penelope and Rose were unable to convince him to leave, though both promised to stay with Christina and to come tell him the moment there was any change.

Finally the dreaded morning came when the doctor, with no hope in his eyes, suggested that Todd get the family together so he could prepare them for the inevitable. Christina's heartbeat was becoming weaker and she was not getting enough liquid, though he and Todd dribbled spoonfuls of water in her mouth regularly and massaged her throat with light pressure to make her swallow. She was dehydrated and rapidly losing what strength she had. He felt she had only a matter of days left.

Todd did not know what to do. Edward and Alan had come to see Christina once, but had been so overcome with the fear that she might die that Penelope had thought it best to keep them away after that. But now the decision had to be made whether to let them see their aunt one last time before she died or to keep them away.

"What should we do?" Todd asked Penelope after he had pulled her aside into the corner farthest away from where Christina lay. He did not want to discuss any of what he had to say anywhere near Christina, who might overhear him. Even though the doctor was adamant that she could not hear anything, Todd did not want to take any chances. He worried that she might be aware of what went on around her and did not want her to know they were discussing the possibility of her dying.

"Do we dare allow them to see her one last time, knowing how it is going to upset them?" His voice broke at the finality of what he had just said. *One last time.* His heart crumbled at the thought of never seeing her again, holding her, laughing with her.

"I don't know," Penelope responded sadly as she put

her arms around her grandson to console him. Having seen the death of loved ones before, she knew she could be strong through this. For Todd's sake, she would have to be. Still, the tears filled her eyes. "Who's to say which is better. Do we keep them away and let their memories be of the happier days they spent with her, but in the process cheat them out of the opportunity of saying goodbye? Or do we let them come and see her like that." She turned to stare at Christina's pale, motionless form. "Knowing the memory of it will be with them forever."

Todd's darkest emotions swelled in his chest, squeezing and twisting his heart, until he could not bear it any longer. Pulling away from his grandmother, he went to Christina's side and sagged to the floor, a broken man. On his knees beside her, he bent over the bed and gently pulled her into his embrace. "Please, Christina. Please, don't die. Please."

His tears flowed unceasingly down his cheeks. "Show that doctor he's wrong. Show him that you want to live. Please."

He held her in his arms for several minutes, breathing deeply of her scent, and quietly purged himself of his tears. Then, gently, he eased her back onto the pillow and stared at her longingly, lifting a finger to the hair that no longer held the luster it once had, and stroked it lightly.

"She's beautiful," he said to Penelope, but his gaze never left Christina's face. Through his tears, he saw her the way she had been that first night. Her eyes so alive with fire, her face so full of anger and indignation, yet her young heart so ready to respond. What a struggle she had put up. His little tigress. A tear dropped from his cheek and landed on her wrist. He reached to brush it away with his thumb.

Penelope stood at his side, resting her hand on his shoulder. There was nothing she could say to ease his grief.

Suddenly his heart stopped. "Did you see that?"

"What?"

"Her eyelid moved. I saw it move!" He held his breath and waited for another movement. When it came, it was so slight, he almost did not see it.

"Aye, I saw it," Penelope said, her voice filled with sudden hope.

"Go get the doctor," he told her, though he was not sure what the doctor could do other than be told there was eye movement. But hadn't the doctor himself said how important eye movement was?

Penelope hurried out of the room and up the stairs to the doctor's living quarters, while Todd watched Christina's eyes carefully. When there was movement again, he called out, "Christina? Can you hear me?"

She did not answer him, but her eye moved again beneath the lid, this time more noticeably.

"Christina? Can you hear me?" He touched her cheek. Her eye twitched in response.

"What is it?" Dr. Edison asked as he burst into the room.

"She's starting to respond," Todd said in a hushed voice, too afraid to hope, yet at the same time too afraid not to.

The doctor studied her face for a moment, then leaned over and pulled her eyelid back. He smiled when he was met with resistance. "Aye, she is starting to respond all right. That was the first response she's shown to light in days." He released the eyelid and stood. Quickly, he dipped a clean cloth into the cool water that sat on a table next to the bed, wrung it out, and bathed her face. Her eyes fluttered. "Looks good. Looks very good."

Again he bathed her face with the cool water, and at the same time Todd called her name. Her eyes fluttered again, only this time they opened and she focused on Todd's hope-filled expression. Everyone held their breath as they waited for what might happen next.

She looked at him for a long moment, frowned first, then slowly smiled. "Todd, you need a shave."

Laughter filled the room. Deep, joyous laughter. Hysterical, boisterous laughter. Christina looked at them all as if she doubted their sanity, but soon joined them in their laughter. This time no pain resulted from her movement, and she laughed with them until finally Todd pulled her into his embrace and held her close.

Weakly, she raised her arms and encircled his neck, but when he pulled back to look at her again, she loosened her grasp, expecting to be let back down.

"No, don't let go," he said as his laughter turned to quiet tears of joy. Pressing her back to him, he closed his eyes tight against the powerful surge of emotions that ran through him, possessing him fully, and said quietly, reverently, "Christina, don't ever let go."

# Chapter XXVII

*February, 1878*

"Grandmum Penelope, Aunt Christina is out of bed again," Edward and Alan chimed together when they saw Christina entering the kitchen, knowing Penelope would flutter about like an old mother hen in her efforts to send their aunt right back to her room.

"Christina Aylesbury, you get yourself back in that bed," Penelope admonished, just like everyone had expected her to, even Christina.

"I'm bored to tears in that bed," Christina complained with a childish pout, hoping to arouse at least some sympathy for her pitiful situation. Actually, she loved all the attention she had been getting ever since she had learned she was pregnant. "Besides, I feel fine, and I'm not at that stage in my pregnancy where the baby is in any danger." Which was the truth. The doctor had told her she would not have to worry about taking it easy until the fourth month, and she was barely into her third. For the next few weeks she was to do anything she wanted—

within reason. But there was no reasoning with Penelope.

"I don't care. I'm not taking any chances with my very first great-granddaughter," Penelope told her, waving the ladle she had in her hand for emphasis. Penelope had decided from the very beginning that the baby was going to be a girl. "Either go back to bed on your own, or I'll call Todd in here and have him carry you back."

"But if I start my bedrest this early, I'll end up having to be in that bed for six months. I'll lose my mind out of sheer boredom."

"You had better enjoy that boredom while you have it, because once that little girl is born, you will have more than enough to keep you busy. Now get back to that bed. The doctor told you that as long as you stayed in your bed like you were supposed to and ate all the right things, that you have every chance of carrying that baby to full term."

"But he also said I didn't really have to worry about staying in bed until the baby was large enough to put stress on those damaged muscles," she tried to argue again, and indicated her flat stomach with a gentle pat.

"I don't care," Penelope said stubbornly and walked to the back door. "If you don't get back in that bed right now, I'm going to call Todd in here like I told you I would."

"Call him, then," Christina said defiantly, because if Penelope knew the truth, that was one of the main reasons she had gotten out of bed. In fact, she thought, it could become a daily ritual until the baby really did grow too large for her to risk it. She enjoyed having him barge into the room, gently sweep her into his arms, then carry her back to bed, where he would first lecture her, then

474

shower her with greatly appreciated kisses, which sometimes developed into something more. Her toes tingled at the mere thought of it. How she dreaded the latter months of her pregnancy when they would have to be satisfied with merely touching and kissing. Those would be four very difficult months for them.

"All right, I will call him," Penelope said, and she stepped onto the veranda and called Todd's name at the top of her voice. When he did not respond, she reached over and rang the emergency bell that Todd had put up.

To Christina's complete satisfaction, Todd came running out of the barn toward the house.

"She's out of bed again," Penelope told him and pointed her ladle accusingly in Christina's direction when he came up onto the veranda and could see inside.

Todd looked at his beautiful wife of nearly two years with an amused smile and then rushed to gather her into his arms. "Shame on you," he admonished, mostly for his grandmother's benefit. "Keep this up, young lady, and I'll have to find some way to punish you. I know. I'll deny you visitors."

"You can't do that, Rose is coming today," she said with a defiant frown, though she knew he was not serious in his threat and really only carried her back to bed to humor his grandmother.

"And if you plan to visit with her, you'd better stay in that bed like you've been told," he said sternly, but playfully. His dimples deepened as he tried to restrain his laughter. "Come now, I plan to personally see you back under those covers."

"As if I had a choice," she muttered in happy defeat. "All right. Put me to bed and I'll be good."

Todd's blue eyes glimmered with his private thoughts

but he waited until they were out of the boys' earshot before muttering, "Putting you to bed and finding you were so good, my dear wife, is exactly what got you in this condition in the first place."

She laughed out loud and shook her head, as if to say he was a hopeless case. "But what a fine condition to be in," she pointed out with a loving smile and gently rubbed the abdomen that would soon grow round with a lively, wiggling burden of joy.

"Aye, a fine condition indeed," he agreed, giving her a lingering kiss. They entered their bedroom and he gently lowered her to their bed.

"But it really is not necessary for me to be in this bed quite so soon, and you know it," she pointed out as he busied himself with fluffing the pillows behind her back and then carefully tucking the covers in around her.

"Maybe not as far as the doctor is concerned, but it is necessary as long as Grandmum is here and in charge of things," he told her with a rueful smile. "And she intends to stay until that grandchild of hers is born and you have completely recovered from having it."

Christina sighed, for she knew it was the truth. Penelope had been adamant that Christina do everything the doctor had told her to do, right from that very first day she had arrived, which had been three very long weeks ago. Christina twisted her mouth into another playful pout. "I wish now we had waited at least a month more before writing to her about the good news."

"Wouldn't have done you much good. Rose was with you when you found out, and if Grandmum hadn't come right away to help take care of you, Rose herself would be out here every day, behaving exactly the same way Grandmum is."

That was true enough. As it was, Rose came out at least twice a week to visit with the boys, and she had sided with Penelope about something each and every time she had visited over the past three weeks—ever since Penelope's early arrival. In fact, Rose was so agreeable to what Penelope had to say that Penelope had enlisted Rose and Rose's Aunt Jane, who sometimes came with her, as her personal reinforcements. With the lot of them against her, Christina had no choice but to obey their commands. And she really did not mind. It was nice to know they cared so much about her.

"You'd think Rose was already my sister-in-law, the way she carries on so, ordering me around, almost as if she had somehow been elected my mother when I wasn't paying close enough attention," Christina muttered, then grinned. "But then, when Justin gets out of jail at the end of next month, she really will become my sister-in-law. Just think how badly she'll start bossing me around then. Maybe you should have pressed charges against Justin, after all."

"Or maybe you shouldn't have pleaded his case to Rose quite so eloquently right after he had turned himself in. It was your teary-eyed testimonial that convinced her to go to the jail to see him in the first place. If she had never made that visit to see him, they might not be getting married at all."

"Don't put this off on me. She would eventually have gone anyway. Those two were destined to be married one day. No, I think maybe *you* should never have gone to testify in Justin's behalf at his trial. Then he might have been sentenced to more than two years and that would have put off the inevitable at least a little while longer." Christina shook her head at the mere thought of what

Rose would be like once she was finally made a member of the family.

"Shame on you," Todd laughed, and shushed her with a slight wag of his finger. "Besides, I think once Justin is out and they are finally married, she'll have her hands too full to find time to come here and boss you about anything. She'll get more than enough bossing done being a mother to those two boys."

"Aye, but who will be doing the bossing? Rose or the boys?" Christina laughed at the thought, because both lads had a way of getting whatever it was they wanted out of their future stepmother. "It will be interesting to see."

Christina thought more about what it would be like to suddenly be Justin's wife and an instant mother to those two boys. "If I was Rose, I think I'd demand a l-o-ong courtship first."

"Oh, you like the thought of being courted?" Todd asked as he bent forward and braced himself over her, placing an arm on either side of her waist. "Do you regret the fact that we had such a short courtship?"

Christina nodded that she did, but she grinned again when she admitted the truth. "What our courtship lost in length was compensated for well enough by its depth and intensity."

Then she raised herself up from her pillows to meet his cocky smile with a tender kiss, but was pulled immediately against him. The kiss between them became more demanding when he rolled over to lie beside her, his hand, as usual, having already started to roam.